THE CORPORIAN DILEMMA

C. R. BRACHER

Disclaimer:
This is a work of fiction. All characters, locations, and businesses are purely products of the author's imagination and are entirely fictitious. Any resemblance to actual people, living or dead, or to businesses, places, or events is completely coincidental.

GELU OCEANUS
RIVER BRUN
TURICUM
ERYX MOUNTAINS
COPORIA
RIVER STOUR
HERCYNIAN FOREST
HOBART GAP
CALOR RIVER
REGILLIUM
PERGAMON
VINDIUS MOUNTAINS
BERT
BOAR'S TUSK
THE ACADEMY
EMON
HOG'S END
FINCHES FIELD
RIVER GILPIN
BATH
CAVERNS OF CARCEREM
TYRUS
BELUM
SINUM OCEANUS
GUARACI

THE CARAVAN

The creaking pine tree swayed in the wind under Eldred as he gripped the trunk, hidden among the topmost branches, watching the long line of wagons winding over a hill between two dense clumps of forest. Some wagons carried passengers, but most were loaded with crates and sacks, prospective citizens and supplies for the city the Corporian invaders had built on the Night Mother's land. They looked quite a muddle with their varied hair color: brown and blonde and red and black. The only attributes their distracted stone bearer had been able to keep uniform was their copper-colored skin and green eyes.

The caravan had teeth—a hundred fifty armored warriors on horseback milled about, looking alert and ready to fight. They were big men too, not quite so large as Mercians, but much larger than Deirans. Some of the folk on the wagons had arms as well; perhaps another hundred men were ready to raise swords. And there were archers too, both men and women, though mostly women. All in all, a formidable force if they were not facing bonded warriors, the greatest creation of Regula, the greatest of stone bearers.

But that is who they faced. Twelve pods of the Mother's own, totaling sixty men, had made their way into the forest across the clearing earlier that morning. With his far sight, Eldred could make out a few of the Deirans lurking behind the trees atop their mounts. After seeing the variety of the Corporians, the Deirans almost looked identical with their uniform pale skin, brown eyes and dark hair—the same as Eldred himself, save for his larger size, the size of a Mercian.

At the front of the Corporian column, a woman bedecked in armor gestured excitedly at her companion, an unusually large Corporian warrior who kept nodding at everything she said. Eldred sighed. If only the man paid as much attention to his surroundings as to her, he might have noticed the danger.

The action started once the last of the caravan guards crossed over the crest of the hill and went on fifty yards. Seven pods, the better part of the Deiran forces, came out of the woods to stand behind the Corporians in a straggly line across the hill. They just sat there on their horses as if they were out for a morning ride, chatting with each other and smiling down at the mass of Corporians below them.

A cry went up from the civilians in the rear wagon. At the front, the woman in armor made a series of hand gestures, and the greater part of the cavalry turned to join the twenty guardsmen at the back. Meanwhile, the wagons started lining up eight abreast, assuming a more compact, defensive position. Archers and swordsmen dashed out to the outer wagons while children and the aged huddled on the wagon in the center of the formation.

The thirty-five Deiran warriors surveyed the situation from atop the hill. Below them, around one hundred twenty Corporian horsemen formed a line twenty yards from the hastily assembled wagon fortress. The armored woman rode to the side of the caravan for a better view of the Deirans but stayed back, keeping her distance. Some thirty men clumped around her, including the large man with whom she had been conversing earlier.

And so everyone stayed, locked in place for five full minutes, enough time for Eldred to rock back and forth on the breeze fifteen times on the gently swaying tree. He watched as the Corporians below moved from initial expressions of wariness, if not outright fear, to irritation and indignation as the Deirans waited nonchalantly on their horses.

Finally, the armored woman raised her fist and called out a command that set the line of horsemen in motion. They crossed half the distance to the Deiran line before the bonded warriors wheeled around and disappeared over the hill. The Corporian cavalry followed without hesitation.

Eldred shook his head as he looked out over the people huddled on the wagons. He could see Deirans lurking in the adjacent woods, but the Corporians kept their eyes trained on the hill.

A minute later, the Deirans came charging out, five pods of bonded warriors—most likely the strongest of them, Eldred grudgingly allowed. The thirty Corporian horse soldiers clustered by the wagons had no time to turn before the first two Deirans pods reached them and started cutting them down. The other three pods of warriors leapt from their horses onto the wagons and started hacking their way through the defenders.

In the shock of the initial onslaught, the Deirans killed five horsemen and dozens of footmen. The children and the more sprightly elders started leaping from the wagons and fleeing into the trees. Amidst the milling horses, the armored woman took the measure of her situation and retreated, accompanied by the large man and eight companions, leaving fifteen riders to slow the onslaught.

A single Deiran pod broke off in pursuit and quickly gained ground. The Deiran riders were lighter, lacking the heavy armor donned by the Corporians. The Deiran horses were likely higher quality too, fashioned as they were by the Mother over centuries. The first verutum thrown caught one of the fleeing Corporians in the back. The second hobbled a horse that went down hard, tumbling its hapless rider onto the turf, where he sat dazed for a moment before a Deiran sword found his neck.

The fleeing Corporians veered headlong into the forest, nearly passing under the tree where Eldred perched a hundred feet above their heads. They charged down a game trail that disappeared into a wall of low branches, pushing through as far as they could, but their horses proved too tall. After a moment's hesitation, accompanied by considerable cursing, they abandoned their mounts and ducked under the branches, continuing on foot. Eldred frowned. Not a good choice, but perhaps the Corporians didn't have any sound choices left.

Eldred turned back towards the caravan. The pursuing pod of Deirans had stopped at the treeline, taking a moment to tie their horses and check the action back by the wagons. Everything was going strongly in their favor. The last two Corporian riders had fled, followed by a pair of Deirans on horseback. Three injured bonded warriors withdrew from the fray while the other fifteen stormed the caravan, putting everyone to the sword and chasing after the Corporians who had escaped into the far woods. There was no sign of the men who had charged over the hill.

Nearby, the leader of the Deiran pursuit, the leader of the entire Deiran force, barked a harsh laugh. A broad smile showed across his pockmarked face, marred by a misshapen scar on his cheek. Then he and his podmen resumed their hunt, sprinting past the tree where Eldred perched.

Eldred took a breath. It would take some time for the bonded warriors to mop the civilians. Some of the quicker children might even escape. The Deiran warriors below would be on their own for a while. Eldred considered:

a pod of Deiran warriors against eight Corporians. Even allowing that they were elite Corporian fighters, nothing their forces had demonstrated so far suggested they would put up much resistance.

Eldred crinkled up his face and tapped the tree trunk with his knuckles as he considered the odds. "By the Mother," he muttered. He gave a deep sigh and started a rapid descent of the tree. A moment later, he too was chasing after the others into the forest.

He found them in a glade. The Corporians had squeezed into a tight line between two thick pines, shields raised and weapons in hand. The large one stood in the center while the woman crouched behind him brandishing a sword. The Deirans formed a loose line, having arrived an instant before Eldred. They looked ready to act.

"Hold!" bellowed Eldred. "Hold up, Wulsin."

There was a pause as everyone turned to look at Eldred, both Deirans and Corporians. By their faces, they were unimpressed. It didn't help that he was dressed in a rough wool tunic that was too tight in the shoulders and old, worn breeches decorated with patches. It wasn't clear whether they noticed the sword on his belt which was of good quality, the only valuable thing he possessed. He'd snatched it three nights earlier when one of Wuslin's men had gone for a late night swim.

After a moment, the Deiran leader, Wulsin, eyed Eldred with surprise. "Ah, it's you, Eldred. What in the Mother's name are you doing here? Last I heard, you were murdering your relatives in Maldavia."

Eldred drew his sword. "I'm here for you. I'm here to settle matters regarding Dreven."

Wulsin frowned. "Who's that?"

Eldred's face hardened. The bastard didn't even know Dreven's name. "The young man you hanged by the neck on the Northern Highway almost eight months ago, right after the battle with the Corporians. He was my friend."

"Oh, him. I didn't hang him." Wulsin beamed, stretching the scar on his cheek. "Lord Ferris did. I just brought down his horse."

"For that, then," said Eldred, raising his weapon.

Wulsin gave a light laugh as he cast a glance over at the Corporians. "He was fair game, Eldred, not just some stupid steward. He'd assaulted Lord Ferris the week before."

"I know. You're fair game as well," said Eldred.

Wulsin gestured towards the line of Corporians, still gripping their swords. "Fine. We can go a round with you as soon as we finish with them. It'll just take a minute."

Eldred sought the eye of the armored woman. "No. You can fight us both."

She looked on without expression.

Wulsin shrugged. "You're right about that. I'll show you the proof." With that, Wulsin and the man beside him dashed at Eldred while the other three began their attack on the Corporians.

Eldred gave ground and withdrew into the trees, keeping both men in front of him as they advanced, each one seeking to hit his sword arm. They were fast, wickedly fast, and this was no game. If they disarmed him or wounded him, they would kill him. It would take a while, but they could do it.

So Eldred backed away, watching their dancing blades that moved so nimbly, parrying their blows and keeping them back with occasional feints. He took a grazing cut to the arm on one of Wulsin's attacks, and their eyes grew brighter with anticipation.

On their next attack, Eldred showed his speed, darting forward and extending to find the throat of Wulsin's companion, his thrust impervious to their parries, for his was the strength of a shard bearer. Wulsin paid Eldred back with a slash across the shoulder of his sword arm, but it was difficult to incapacitate a shard bearer, a lesson Eldred knew from his own experience. Eldred had stabbed the previous shard bearer more than a hundred times before he'd dug the shard out of his forehead.

Eldred smiled grimly. "One down. The magic fades a trifle, doesn't it?"

Wulsin said nothing and came again, pressing hard, moving fast. He didn't seem much slowed. He drove Eldred back thirty paces with his furious onslaught, but then Eldred's chance came. After a ringing parry that almost knocked Wulsin's sword from his grasp, Eldred drove his sword into Wulsin's chest. Wulsin's eyes grew large as he dropped to his knees, but he took one last bite, impaling Eldred's left shin.

Eldred crouched and cupped his hand over the gushing wound. "Was it truly a lucky throw, Wulsin? I heard Lord Ferris praise you. I was there, hiding in the wine merchant's wagon. Was it lucky? Do you still think so?"

Wulsin had no words, no breath. His convulsing face showed no comprehension as he keeled over. After a moment, he lay still. He was dead.

Eldred straightened up and released his shin, which still leaked a trickle of blood. He had killed Wulsin, but he felt no better for it. If anything, he felt angrier. This worthless coward had tormented Dreven as part of Lord Ferris's treachery. The image of Dreven hanging from the tree filled Eldred's mind, and the pain and hate came flooding back. Eldred had been helpless then, unable to even stand on his feet, but he was not helpless now. These worthless bastards would pay a price. He strode back to the glade.

Four Corporians remained on their feet, fighting the three surviving warriors from Wulsin's pod. On the left, the large Corporian was holding his own against a bonded warrior while the Corporian leader slumped against a tree behind him, clutching her gut. On the right, two Deirans pressed three overmatched Corporians. Three other Corporians already lay dead or dying.

For a moment, Eldred stood, watching, wishing them all a miserable end. Then, when one of the three struggling Corporians was stabbed through the eye, he was reluctantly moved to action; facing three bonded warriors might be more than he could manage. He hurled his sword from thirty feet and impaled the rightmost Deiran in the back—a death blow. The two nearest Corporians were startled and paid the price for it as the bonded warrior facing them, a thin-faced man, sliced the neck of one before piercing the ribs of the other.

The thin-faced warrior turned—blade in one hand, knife in the other— and glowered at Eldred, who calmly drew his dagger. It was different now with only two bonded warriors. Eldred took a relaxed breath. The two remaining Deirans were dangerous, no doubt, but Eldred bore the Shard of the Mother, the prized gift of power she had created for Bonitus, the Son, the greatest of all her children. The warrior charged, but the Bond with two was weaker than the Bond with five. Now Eldred was the quicker; he batted the warrior's sword arm aside and drove his dagger into the blackguard's heart.

With that, there was no longer a pod at all, only one sorry Deiran warrior left to face the oversized Corporian, who stood as tall as Eldred. Eldred watched them duel as he retrieved his sword. It would be the Corporian, he realized as he watched them fight; it would only take another minute or two. Meanwhile, the Corporian leader had fainted away, sliding down the tree trunk on her back. Nearby, the Corporian who had been stabbed in the ribs was still breathing, but his eyes were shut.

As Eldred waited, arms crossed, he used his foot to nudge the knife free from the hand of the dead warrior who had charged him. It was well crafted and looked to have a sharp edge, a modest improvement on Eldred's own dagger. Eldred bent over and picked it up. The balance was good, and the grip suited Eldred's hand. As Eldred tucked the knife away, the battle reached its end. The Corporian had finally bled the Deiran enough to weaken him and ran him through. As the victor faced Eldred, his green eyes were wild, distrustful; his thick beard and long blond hair stuck out from under his helmet. He stood panting, covered in sweat, bleeding from a dozen cuts and nicks.

"Why are you coming here?" asked the man in a deep brusque voice.

Eldred drew himself up. "Revenge."

"Yes." The man nodded. "They knew you. They spoke your name."

Eldred tensed. That was inconvenient. Finally, a Corporian demonstrated a modicum of skill, and it had to be one who knew his name.

The man cast an anguished look over to his superior—she looked to still be breathing—and then glared challengingly at Eldred. "What is happening next?"

Eldred held out his hands. "Nothing from me, but they'll come. The Deirans were already mopping up when you fled into the woods. They'll come and torture and kill any of you as are left." Eldred gestured at the woman and the Corporian who had been stabbed. "You would be doing them a favor to end it. These Deirans are the worst sort, and they won't be pleased to find their leader slain."

The man shook his sword. "You stay back." He hurried over to the woman and kneeled by her side.

Eldred followed the Corporian over, stopping ten feet away as the man set down his blade and made a hurried examination of the injured woman. As the Corporian started pulling her armor free, Eldred shook his head. "You don't have the time. They'll be here shortly."

The man didn't look up as he went about his work. She looked smaller once she was out of her armor. Her thin, copper-colored face was heavy with pain. The man lifted her blood soaked tunic away from her stomach, which was considerably paler than her face, pausing to glower at Eldred as he angled to get a better look. Only one wound, but deep, too deep.

Eldred stepped back. "That looks fatal. Even if they weren't about to come and kill her, she's dead."

The man scowled. "Am I asking you for your thoughts?"

"You had best leave," continued Eldred. "You're only moments away from your own demise."

"Why are you caring?" asked the man, pressing lightly on her wound. "If you are done drinking your revenge, it is you who should be leaving."

Eldred cursed under his breath.

"What?" barked the man. "Your name—'Eldred'. Is that worrying you? Are you fearful I will be sharing it?"

Eldred frowned. "I'm certain they could persuade you or one of your companions—if they last long enough."

The man wet his lips. "Then be bringing me our horses. We could be leaving on them."

Eldred shook his head. "Nobody your size will be outdistancing Deirans on horseback. The only way we escape is on foot, deeper into the woods."

The man slumped slightly. "We have other men. The battle could be turning."

"No. You showed the right understanding when you fled. This battle is done. Now, you had best free them and get to running."

The man hesitated a moment before buckling his shield over his shoulder and sheathing his sword. Then carefully, like he was gathering up a child, he slid one arm under the woman and lifted her up, pressing one hand over the puncture wound.

Eldred made a face and pointed at the injured Corporian still on the ground. "What about him?"

"You will be carrying him," said the man.

"No," said Eldred. "He's dying. I'm not going to haul him around."

The man's lips twisted on his face.

"Well?" demanded Eldred.

"I only have two hands," said the man with a sigh. "You will be following your practice. All of you are such fine killers."

Eldred gave him a sharp look before walking over to the injured soldier and cutting his throat. There was a momentary gurgling, and the man was gone. One problem cleared away.

"You know the way?" asked the man.

"Yes, I do. Away from here as fast as we can," said Eldred, and he led the man deeper into the trees.

A BURDEN

Once he shed his armor, the man proved quicker than Eldred expected. Even carrying the woman, he was able to scramble up gullies and step over fallen logs at a good pace. But as the day grew warmer, the man started to falter. After three hours, his legs were shaky and he paused before every upward climb. You couldn't have told by his face, which remained as determined as ever, but Eldred felt the man would soon fall to his knees.

As the man puffed his way up a short incline, his face more red than bronze, Eldred turned back to address him. "At least drop your shield. It must weigh twenty pounds."

The man gave a wheezing laugh. "Yes, Captain. I will be parting with my shield as soon as you hurl away your sword."

Eldred furrowed his brow. "If they catch you, it won't make a whit of difference. A pod of warriors won't even be slowed a second in cutting you down."

"Yet I am having choices left to make. If I am fighting, then I will be choosing to keep my shield."

Eldred glanced at the limp figure in the man's arms. "What about her? When she dies, can you leave her or must you bury her?"

The man said nothing, favoring Eldred with a molten stare.

"Is she your mistress or wife?" asked Eldred.

The man's eyes darkened. "You will never be speaking of her again, or I will be killing you."

Eldred blew out his breath and continued up the trail. If only the Deiran had finished this one off, things would be much simpler. The man was vexing.

What was an accidental ally due? Death didn't seem fair. But the man knew Eldred's name, and it was too early for that to be flying about—too many friends who could be harmed, too many enemies with power. What would Cousin Harold, the Deiran King, say if he learned Eldred was killing his warriors? How many people would Lord Ferris poison against him with the news?

When they crossed a creek half an hour later, the man laid the woman down on a patch of shaded grass and rinsed out the bloody rags he had tied across her belly. Eldred watched the red streaks flow down with the current; there was much blood. She would die soon. The man seemed to know as well. He had an air of defeat about him.

Eldred had his own markings from the battle, one on the shoulder, the other on his shin. He walked down the sandy bank into the water and washed away the crusted blood to reveal unbroken skin, perhaps a trifle pink but otherwise unblemished. The man looked up as Eldred stepped out of the water, but he made no comment. He sat by the woman, his shield and sword on the ground by his side.

As Eldred approached them, the man shifted his hand closer to his weapon but did not pick it up.

"Are you done resting?" inquired Eldred.

The man shook his head. "No. It is time that we should be parting. We will be remaining here."

Eldred stood, listening to the stream. It was a pretty spot with patches of grass and openings for the sunlight through the trees. In the distance, Eldred could hear a woodpecker busy at work. A light breeze blew past, rustling the man's long blonde hair which was freed from his helmet.

Eldred gestured towards the woman. "Would she want you to die?"

The man frowned. "I told you not to be speaking of her."

Eldred nodded. "Yes, you did."

The man looked away, back towards the way they had come.

Eldred took a glance as well, but nobody was there yet. "You were very quick. I expect that you may even have a few hours, but I have no doubt they'll follow our trail. They hate to be off their horses; they hate to walk, but they'll want revenge more."

"Like you," said the man.

Eldred smiled. "Yes. And like me, they'll have it unless you get back on your feet."

"Not moving," said the man softly. "This is a good place for her. You are saying we may have hours? I am thinking that will be time enough."

Eldred glanced at the woman. Her freshened bandages were already turning red. "You bade me not to ask, but is she your sister?"

The man looked up. "I am serving her, nothing more."

"Hmm," said Eldred. "Then you're an honorable man, after your fashion."

The man gave a slight nod. His gaze turned back across the creek whence his killers would come.

Eldred clasped his hands. It was time to move on, time to go. The man would say Eldred's name, or he would not. It felt as if he wouldn't. He would most likely hoist his bulky shield and get run through standing over the dying woman—another small tragedy on a day full of blood. Doomed people drifting to their end, which was ever so close at hand. Eldred had been the same once, trapped in a cell waiting for his executioner, watching time tick down as the sun crossed the sky.

He was just about to step away when a thought crossed his mind. "I think I may be able to help her."

The man narrowed his eyes. "No. You will be keeping your blade away from her."

"I won't kill her; I'll heal her. I can try to heal her."

The man bit off his words. "What are you speaking of? Nothing is healing her. Look at her."

Eldred sighed. Her face was very pale. "I have a powerful medicine, a powder, blessed by the Night Mother." He paused. "It would work for my people. I don't know what it'll do for her."

A look of distrust crossed the man's face. "Huh, you are mad."

"Look," said Eldred. He pointed at his shin, now cleared of injury, and tapped his shoulder, which was likewise unmarked. "My injuries are gone. Not by the powder—by another means—but it's healing. I can heal."

The man looked tired, like he had nothing left inside. He sat for a moment staring at Eldred's shin. "You are right; that was bleeding. This medicine, does it bring pain?"

Eldred fished out a transparent bag out of his trouser pocket. Inside was a small woven packet, nearly spent, the last of the Balour powder from the Sun People. It could heal almost anything—valuable, irreplaceable—but he had the shard now.

"No," he said with newly found confidence. "It will not." Eldred waved his hand at her bandages. "Can you clear those away? I need to sprinkle this powder on her wounds."

The man examined Eldred's face, then carefully undid the bandages. The puncture was deep, the flesh around it red and angry. Eldred knelt close and sprinkled what was left of the powder an inch above her skin. The white powder disappeared into the seeping blood.

"There," said Eldred. "You can put the bandages back."

The man did so hurriedly, resetting the bandages and pulling her sodden tunic down to cover the wound. The man sought Eldred's eye. "You will be staying? If it is a small company, we would not be without some hope."

"No," said Eldred. "Even a single pod would kill us, and they'll send at least that."

"But you could be enjoying more revenge."

Eldred shook his head. "Wulsin was the one I sought. I'm not certain about the others. You'll have to carry her, but I can take your shield."

The man was loud. "Do you mock me? She is nearly gone!"

"My wounds are gone. This is different, but the same. We'll wait five minutes and go. I expect she'll live. This is a medicine without equal."

The man made a face. "I will be carrying my own shield."

Eldred raised an eyebrow. "I'll hand it back to you if it comes time for you to die."

The man considered. "Do you swear upon your stone bearer?"

Eldred drew himself up. "By the Night Mother, I swear to return your shield to you."

The man rose to his feet. "I will be washing. This chase goes on longer than I was expecting."

AWAKENING

They had been walking for an hour on a winding trail up a barren ridge when the woman opened her eyes and stared up into the man's sweaty face. "Stop. Put me down," she commanded weakly.

The man paused and set her down gently in a sitting position on a rock next to the trail. She was shaky, but she was able to sit unassisted. She looked down the hillside at the vast panorama before them, slowly turning her head to take in the scene as the wind stirred her long red hair. She froze when she caught sight of Eldred, standing and watching her from slightly up the trail. "Gundlach, why is this man not being restrained?"

Gundlach, for that appeared to be his name, stood at attention. "He is assisting us, my lady."

She shot a sharp glance to Gundlach before returning to her examination of Eldred. "I see he is holding your shield."

Gundlach stiffened. "He swore to return it."

Her eyes flashed with anger. "Did he?" She leaned forward on her arms. "Be retrieving your shield. Then you will be giving me a full report. I must be deciding our course of action."

Eldred stepped forward and held out Gundlach's shield. "There's nothing to decide. We're fleeing from the Deirans. We must press on. And Gundlach will be able to carry you more swiftly if he is not burdened with his shield."

The lady creased her brow and stared straight ahead, out at the hills stretching away in front of her. "I was not addressing you. I do not wish to be addressing you."

Gundlach stepped forward and took his shield with a quick bob of his head.

"Uhh, well, then, perhaps it has come time to part ways," observed Eldred.

"Yes," said the woman.

"Very well," said Eldred, making a small bow.

Gundlach cleared his throat. "Wait. We are finding some use from each other. We are possessing a common enemy not far behind us on the trail."

"Yes, but though he is one of the other ones, he still serves Regula and is equally our foe," said the woman.

"He killed four of the Deirans. If he had been wishing us dead, I could not have repulsed him," said Gundlach.

The woman narrowed her eyes. "Since when have you been fearing an opponent, Gundlach?" She looked down and brushed her hand over her blood stained tunic. "What is this?" She patted the tunic, feeling the bandages underneath.

"You have taken injury, my lady," said Gundlach.

She furrowed her brow and reached under her tunic, pulling out a mess of bandages, still damp with her blood. She gave them a puzzled look as she felt under her tunic with her other hand. She bristled as she noticed the two men watching. "Avert your eyes!"

Eldred and Gundlach turned away.

After a moment, she spoke. "What is this madness? I have taken no injuries. Why have you been sticking these bloody rags to me?"

Still facing away, Gundlach answered. "You have taken serious injury, my lady—a deep sword thrust that I was fearing had ended you. That is why you were facing unconsciousness. But this man has demonstrated a surprising means of healing you."

"Were you letting him touch me?" hissed the woman.

"No, my lady," said Gundlach, taken aback. "He was never laying a hand upon you; I am swearing it. But again, I am reporting, he brings great usefulness. Given the importance of our mission and his value to us, we should be making a contract."

"Turn around, both of you." The woman looked Eldred over once again. "What is this miraculous quality you are finding in him, Gundlach?"

Gundlach approached her and whispered in her ear. As he spoke, her pale green eyes changed. They were no less hard but held more interest as she examined Eldred.

As Gundlach stepped to the side, she offered Eldred a humorless smile. "By the reporting of my assistant, you have proven helpful, Mercian, but you bear the look of poverty. You have, without doubt, already considered killing us and robbing us. But you are having the sense to see we have little on our persons. If you are getting us to our city, we will be granting rewards to you such as suit a man of your utility."

Gundlach smiled. "You will be receiving great rewards, Eldred."

Eldred considered for a moment. "Just to your gates?"

"No," she said. "You will be accompanying me to the Eighth ring of our city. I will be requiring you to stay for a short period of time, not more than a few days."

"To what end?" asked Eldred.

"I am wishing to show my people a man who killed four Deirans," she said.

Eldred nodded slowly. "I see. I suppose I would be free to leave at the end of my visit."

"You should not be doubting that we will be wishing to see you go," she said. "State your price."

"Uhh, I don't know," said Eldred.

A flash of impatience showed in her eyes. "We must be fixing a price to create a contract. Will you be requiring a gold coin? Are you desiring a small gem? You could pick one from a variety of colors."

Eldred shrugged. "I do not need such things."

"What are you needing?" asked Gundlach.

"Not much," said Eldred.

"You are lacking a horse. I am seeing no saddle. Why not be replacing rags with fine armor?" asked Gundlach.

"I do not need those items," said Eldred.

"Then what are you asking for?" asked Gundlach.

Eldred tilted his head. "Well, let's just say that if I should see something during my visit—and it would not be large, it would be something I could carry—I may ask for it."

The woman uttered a sharp laugh. "From what my assistant has been telling me, you are possessing strength enough to hoist a golden statue bedecked with jewels. You would be leaving me destitute, as much a wrecker of my fortune as those filthy Deirans."

"Then let it be something that I request of you as well as something that you're content to grant me. And if there's no such thing, I'll accompany you to your city and stay for a few days without any pay at all," said Eldred.

"And you will be fighting for me?" asked the lady.

"If needed," said Eldred.

She smiled. "Then I swear upon my name, Lady Yslana of Wismar, the true Wismar, that you shall have this reward you have named: a small thing that you may ask for, but that which you may only take with my consent. Now, for your part of the contract, you are swearing your service to me by the name of your stone bearer."

Eldred paused. "I have already sworn on the Night Mother once today. I should not wish to abuse her name. Let me instead swear on the Son. Do you know of him?"

Lady Yslana frowned slightly. "I have some knowledge of that person. He served as Regula's warlord against the Sun People. Though we do not care for him, I know he means much to you. You may swear upon him."

"Then I swear upon he who bears the shard of the Night Mother that I shall accompany you, fighting as is needed and visiting you in your city unless he, himself, the shard bearer, should give me leave to break this vow," said Eldred.

The two Corporians exchanged a look, then Lady Yslana nodded. "The contract is set."

Eldred gestured at the narrow trail ahead of him. "We should hurry on. The Deirans will be making their way without the burden of negotiation."

She reached out her hand to Gundlach and rose stiffly to her feet, taking two short steps, holding onto his arm.

"Perhaps Gundlach should resume carrying you, my lady?" suggested Eldred.

The woman narrowed her eyes. "I will decide the manner of my own passage. And you should not address me in that manner."

"How should I call you, then?" asked Eldred.

The woman frowned. "You may be addressing me by my title."

Eldred bowed his head. "Very well, Lady Yslana. I suggest that once you have stretched your legs, I reclaim Gundlach's shield and he should carry you a ways. We must make the greatest speed possible. The men in pursuit are driven by a powerful thirst for revenge."

"I will be giving it thought," allowed Lady Yslana.

After a few minutes, she was moving well on her own, though not as fast as Gundlach might have carried her. She hung back with Gundlach, the two struggling to keep up with Eldred as they whispered back and forth.

CAMP

Hours later, as dusk fell, Lady Yslana called for Eldred to halt. She and Gundlach slumped on a large gray rock, exhaustion showing on their faces.

Eldred perched on a small white stone across from them and pulled his waterskin from his belt, holding it up in offer to them. It had been hours since they had passed the last rivulet. Lady Yslana shook her head, and Gundlach looked away.

Eldred took a swig of water. "You'll be needing something to drink if we're going to make much progress tonight."

"We will be staying here," said Lady Yslana.

Eldred set his waterskin on the rock beside him. "They may well reach us here."

"You have been setting an impossible pace," said Lady Yslana. "Should they be reaching us here, which I doubt, we will simply escape them."

Eldred rubbed his hand together. "I'm not certain we all could do that successfully."

Lady Yslana frowned. "They will be seeing only two pairs of footprints leading from the battle. Are they such cowards that they will be sending more than one grouping after us?"

"They'll likely send a single pod, five warriors," agreed Eldred.

"If they are exhausted, the numbers may be proving close enough to work for us—three against five," said Lady Yslana.

Eldred made a face. "I don't agree. You must have observed the damage they inflicted earlier today. The numbers that opposed them did not appear to matter."

"But you killed four," said Lady Yslana. "And now you are under contract to me."

"I killed the first two while your company occupied the others. I'm not confident that we could repeat that feat," said Eldred.

"I have decided. We will be stopping," said Lady Yslana.

Eldred shrugged. "Fair enough." He dug back into his pockets and produced four small radishes and a collection of wilted greens. "I have some miner's lettuce and radishes. This will have to do until we get back below the treeline."

Lady Yslana and Gundlach said nothing.

"Well, aren't you hungry?" asked Eldred.

"We are having hunger," said Gundlach. "I could be eating the brain of a full-sized sheep, but these weeds of yours are making no appetite in me."

Eldred stuffed most of the produce back in his pocket, leaving only a couple of radishes and lettuce leafs in his hand. "Let me know if you change your mind." He crunched down on one of the radishes, ignoring its bitter taste.

Lady Yslana fixed him with a stare. "How many are you?"

Eldred swallowed. "Just me."

"No, I am meaning your people. How many are your people?"

"If you mean how many Mercians, many thousands."

"Your army is many thousands?" asked Lady Yslana.

Eldred nodded. "Yes, if they gathered all the warriors, there would be some thousands."

"This is more than the Deiran army, is it not?" she continued.

"Yes, but not more powerful," said Eldred.

"But you are more than a match for a Deiran. I have witnessed the proof of that," said Gundlach.

Eldred raised his index finger. "One against one, perhaps. A Mercian warrior, your common Mercian warrior, can defeat a single Deiran and probably would. But that changes with numbers. Perhaps two Mercians could battle two Deirans, but when it gets to five, a pod, well, then the Deirans will prevail. They'll always win. It's the Bond, the greatest gift of the Mother."

"What if the Mercians were fighting our soldiers?" asked Lady Yslana.

"It would depend," said Eldred.

Lady Yslana pursed her lips. "On what?"

Eldred frowned. "If there were some trick—if all the Mercians fell down."

"Ah, yes," she said with a thin smile. "That would be making for an easy victory."

Eldred looked down. "A cheap victory."

They sat in silence for a few minutes before Eldred straightened up. "If we're staying here, I'll take first watch."

Lady Yslana pressed her lips together. "Perhaps Gundlach is taking first watch."

Eldred raised his eyebrow. "We've a contract. Don't you trust me?"

"I do," she said. "Very well; be waking Gundlach when the night is halfway turned."

"I will," said Eldred.

The Corporians settled down for the night. Lady Yslana lay upon the rock, which looked fairly smooth. Gundlach leaned his back against the base of the stone, his shield to the left and his sword to the right. They were soon asleep, with Gundlach's snores occasionally calling out his presence.

Eldred settled against the trunk of a small pine tree some fifty feet from the Corporians, a spot where he could look back down the ridge trail while keeping them in sight. Only a sliver of a moon rose that night, but he could see with perfect clarity thanks to his dark vision, one of his Maldavian gifts. Gundlach looked just under the edge of sleep, as if he could wake and seize his arms to join battle without hesitation. Perhaps he could; the man appeared well trained.

Lady Yslana appeared softer in her slumber. Her face lost its hard lines, though Eldred did not doubt they would snap back the moment she woke.

He gave a wry smile. They had thought him Mercian, and why wouldn't they? He looked the part—six feet tall and broad, much taller and heavier than your usual Maldavian or Deiran. But he was Deiran, though only by half his blood. His father, Alfred, King of the Deirans, had died trying to take the gates of the Corporian city. He'd fallen due to a twisted Corporian spell.

Eldred had fallen too, only to rise lame and weak. In the aftermath, there had been much loss. Eldred's beloved horse, Hobbie, run through in a scrimmage with Lord Ferris. Dreven, his dear friend, hung by the neck. Others too, killed and injured: Mateline, Oudin, Henreit, to name a few. It had all started with that vile Corporian trickery.

Now, it was time for some Deiran trickery. His companions thought him useful, which of course, he had been—Wulsin would have slain them. They entertained the thought of showing him off in their city to build the courage of their troops, the Mercian that killed four Deirans—missing the point of which four he had killed: four awful ones. An unexpected opportunity, not for a gold coin or a gem, but for something sweeter, something Eldred had found the taste for—revenge. Somewhere in the city was the Corporian stone bearer. She had taken so much from Eldred. It was time she paid her dues.

THE CHASE

Shortly before midday, Eldred spotted movement up on the ridge that they had just spent the morning descending. He caught a glance of a few warriors flitting on foot between two lines of trees.

He turned to the Corporians, some twenty yards behind him. Gundlach moved slower than he had the previous day, but it was Lady Yslana who held them up. It seemed that the powder had provided her with a burst of speed that was no longer in evidence.

"They're coming!" called Eldred in an even tone.

Lady Yslana slogged on, expressionless. Gundlach walked by her side, glancing back up at the ridgeline.

"I only saw a single pod, but it's more than enough," said Eldred.

Lady Yslana glanced up at Eldred. "Then we will be making for a fight."

Eldred's shoulders tightened. "Or we could avoid it."

A flicker of amusement crossed her eyes. "You would be reasoning with them?"

"No," said Eldred. "There'll be no diplomacy. But we're only a day's walk from your city. If we keep a fast enough pace, we can outrun them."

Lady Yslana frowned. "I am doing what I can."

"No, you're not," said Eldred. "If you would allow yourself to be carried, we could avoid this fight, a fight I expect will mean the end of you."

"We are having a contract," she replied with a frosty tone.

Gundlach sighed. "And in further thinking, I cannot carry her with much greater speed."

"But I can," said Eldred.

Lady Yslana stopped and fixed Eldred with a piercing stare. "No. This is not an option I will be entertaining. We have a contract. You will be finding the courage to fight."

Eldred narrowed his eyes. "This could cost you your lives."

Lady Yslana spared him a contemptuous glance and continued up the trail.

Gundlach stopped alongside Eldred, watching Lady Yslana walking on ahead. "You must stop saying these things. You will never be carrying her. Even I should never have been carrying her but for the circumstances."

"We face the same circumstances today, or do you think we are going to defeat a pod of bonded warriors?" asked Eldred.

"We must be taking the honorable course," said Gundlach.

"So you chose honor over your life?" asked Eldred.

"Such must be the choice of any person of dignity," said Gundlach.

"If you say so," said Eldred, looking back up at the ridge. He could not see the Deirans, but they were surely drawing closer. "An ambush, then— that might be our only hope. I'll go ahead and find the likeliest spot."

A sharp glint showed in Gundlach's eye. "Should we not be staying together?"

"No," said Eldred. "I'm going to need a huge pile of rocks and the perfect vantage point, some place where they're all boxed in. Just follow the trail."

"We are having a contract," protested Gundlach.

"I'm well aware," said Eldred. "I'll see you up the trail."

Eldred turned and bounded up the path. As he passed Lady Yslana, she shot him a sour look.

"Just ask Gundlach," said Eldred.

Eldred ranged ahead, checking wide to either side of the dirt track. As he searched, it became clear that what he needed wasn't there. He needed a wide open space with an abundance of good throwing stones, but it could not be so wide open that they would spot him as they approached. Without surprise, they might dodge everything he threw. Regardless, there were few useful stones. While many enormous flat stones, dozens of feet long, poked up through the dirt, all the loose ones were thin, light rocks that anyone could snap with their fingers.

When he came to a break in the trees, he spotted the Deirans. They had reached the bottom of the valley and were starting up in pursuit, only an hour behind the Corporians and gaining. Though he strained his eyes, even he could barely make out their faces. He thought he could picture the men sitting on their horses next to Wulsin and Lord Ferris as they clamored for

Ceolwin's wine, but he wasn't sure. It might have only been his imagination.

Eldred looked for his companions. He had a good sense of where they would be, but a hillock hid that portion of the trail. They were certainly honorable according to their standards, much too honorable to be carried even at the cost of their lives. Eldred muttered a curse. In that moment, he almost uttered the words that would terminate his odd contract with the Corporians for he had sworn upon his own self; he was the shard bearer. He stopped though. What would be the point if they didn't even know it had ended?

So he pressed on, searching ever farther to either side of the trail in his hunt for an ambush site that he was not even sure he wanted. That's when he found it.

THE CAVE

Gundlach grabbed for the hilt of his sword as Eldred burst from the trees but released it when he saw who it was.

Sweat ran freely down Lady Yslana's forehead as she trudged up the slope. She was slower than earlier in the morning but moving well for someone who had nearly died the previous day.

"You returned," she said, a note of surprise in her voice.

"Our contract," said Eldred. "Come this way. They're only minutes behind you."

Lady Yslana took a deep breath and pushed on at a faster pace.

Eldred scoured the lower slopes for signs of the Deirans and motioned for the Corporians to hurry. "Give everything you have. Fifty feet could make the difference."

As the pair were entering the stand of trees where Eldred had retreated, he spotted the Deirans two hundred yards downslope. "Run!" he called, but it was too late. The Deirans were shouting and pointing; the hunters had marked their quarry.

Lady Yslana trembled with exhaustion as she crossed the rocky ground and loose dirt, waving off any assistance that Gundlach offered as he jogged at her side. Eldred kept his eyes locked on their pursuers. The Deirans were closing the distance but didn't seem hurried. Where was there to run, after all?

When they reached it, the Corporians paused, staring blankly at the narrow cave entrance.

"In there?" asked Gundlach, his voice full of doubt.

"Yes, or die out here," said Eldred.

Lady Yslana turned to face the Deirans, her eyes defiant even as she panted for breath. They were fifty yards away and starting to accelerate.

Eldred grabbed her hand. "Follow me."

At first she pulled back, but then she relented and stepped into the darkness with Gundlach close behind. Eldred blinked, and the cave revealed itself to his dark vision. A wet cave with cold breath, the cavern extended through a maze of rooms, the largest more than forty feet across, joined by narrow passages barely wide enough to squeeze through. Sharp-tipped stalactites crowded the ceilings of the chambers, sending occasional drops of water to the floor below.

Eldred led the Corporians down to the deepest room of the cave, where he settled Lady Yslana on a rock. As he released her hand, she tightened her grip and jerked her head around, looking blindly in the dark. He gently peeled her hand free and placed it in Gundlach's palm, moving him next to her.

"Is there some other way out?" whispered Lady Yslana.

"No," said Eldred.

"Then why?" she asked.

"If they insist, I'll fight them," said Eldred.

Gundlach grimaced. "It is freezing in here. We cannot last. They need only be keeping the entrance to finish us."

"Yes, that could be true," said Eldred. "Perhaps reasonable men would do that, but they've come for revenge. They're not likely to sit and wait. And they don't know we're trapped."

"We should have been fighting them outside with honor," said Gundlach as he twisted about, seeking some sign of light.

"Short lived honor," said Eldred. He stepped away from the Corporians, straightening as much as he could in the confined space. Their faces were set with dread. It seemed to Eldred that they feared the cold darkness more than the steel of the bonded warriors.

"We made a contract. You swore," said Lady Yslana.

"I have not forgotten," said Eldred. "I apologize for your discomfort. It won't be for long. Gundlach, if I call for you, you must come quickly. Follow my voice."

Gundlach shifted, his lips curled in a disagreeable expression.

Eldred frowned. "Come when I call you, Gundlach. If you hesitate and there's even two left, they'll be the death of you both."

"I should not be leaving Lady Yslana," said Gundlach.

"Yet, you must if you want her to survive," said Eldred.

"He will be seeking you as best he can, but you made this predicament. You must be getting us free," said Lady Yslana.

"I intend to," said Eldred.

Eldred stepped away and retraced his steps unhurriedly, pausing at the entrance of each room to pile a collection of fist-sized rocks, which were as plentiful here as they were rare above ground. Finally, he neared the entrance and peered around the curve in the wall at two warriors standing alertly outside, swords in one hand, bucklers in the other. They were older men in their late twenties whom Eldred didn't recognize. As he lingered, a third warrior, a bit more gaunt than the other two, passed behind them, carrying a few thick branches. Eldred sniffed and caught the faint scent of smoke. It would be torches then. They would have built the fire right at the mouth of the cave if they were trying to choke the Corporians out.

Eldred sighed. It had been too much to hope that they would have charged right in after them, but he felt certain the warriors must have considered it. Torchlight would even the situation; just how much would depend on how strong the Bond was in them. Back on the expedition, Lord Vance and Lord Kenelm had been deadly against the wolves in the depths of night. These men, craven followers of Lord Ferris, lacked such greatness, or so Eldred hoped. It was time to find out.

"Hello!" shouted Eldred.

The guards scanned the cave entrance, trying to spot him, but made no reply. A short man walked up behind them, carrying a burning torch.

Eldred called out again. "Hello!"

The short man stood next to the two guards. He had an air of confidence, likely the pod leader. "Who's there? Come out and show yourself."

"No, thank you. I'll stay here," said Eldred.

The man grunted. "If you come out, I'll make this quick. No reason to be nasty about it, but you and the other two must die."

Eldred frowned. Menacing as it was, the man's words sounded more courteous than something one of Lord Ferris's men would say. "What's your name? What do they call you?"

The man narrowed his eyes. "Who're you? One of you looked different."

"Do you serve Lord Ferris?" called Eldred.

"No," answered the man. "How do you know that name?"

Eldred took a breath. "But did you ride with Lord Ferris? Allowing that you don't serve him, did you ride with him?"

The short man exchanged a glance with his podmen. "Look, I don't care who you're friends with. You might be Lord Ferris's favorite little Corporian pet; it doesn't matter. The outcome will be the same. We're going to kill you."

Eldred grimaced; he still didn't know if these were Lord Ferris's men. "If you come in here, I'll have to kill you."

The man studied the cave entrance with amused eyes. "Why not come out here and fight if you're so confident. Better than getting butchered in the dark."

Two more men approached from behind the man with swords and torches in hand. The pod was ready.

"Last chance!" called their leader, but Eldred was already retreating into the cave.

Eldred hurried, racing through the narrow passage that led to the first room. Tight as the passage was, it would be a good place to make a stand, but the pod was too dangerous. Deirans, the most favored of the Mother's children, were crafted with the most extraordinary ability: five warriors, one pod, acting as one, thinking as one. Even lined up in single file, they could turn the situation against him quickly. If they did, it would be a long, miserable death, since the bearer of the Mother's shard would never pass quickly. For all of his predecessor's threats of a painful end for Eldred, it had been Magner's own torturous demise—ripped and cut a hundred different ways by Eldred and the golden eagle—that had reached new limits.

Still, powerful as they were, bonded warriors had their weaknesses. Given enough confusion and distraction, you might hit one with a brick. Eldred had seen the proof of it in earlier days when his father had built his golden pod. Eldred raced across the first chamber and snatched up the rocks he had stockpiled. The Deirans were just entering the chamber as the first stalactites showered down from the ceiling, dislodged by his missiles. They hung back in the passage, lined up, unharmed, but they were looking upwards.

As a cloud of debris rained down, Eldred changed his target and crushed the ankle of the Deiran in front, whose foot twisted to an unnatural angle. It was a sickening sight that made Eldred flinch. But he barely hesitated before hurling more rocks into the passage. A cry called out the success of one of his ricocheting stones just as two Deirans sprinted into the room through the dust, bucklers ready. Eldred did not try them and ran deeper into the cave.

He crossed the second chamber, the largest one, and grabbed the rocks he had placed there. Three Deirans were already entering the room, Eldred had time to make two throws—one went wide and one was blocked—before he scurried down the passage just ahead of them.

The smaller Deirans were quicker through the narrow confines. He was just short of the entrance to the third room when he had to turn and fight.

"Gundlach! Gundlach!" shouted Eldred.

The first two Deirans had swords and bucklers, the third—the pod leader—carried a sword and torch. It was a battle of stabbing, since that was all the confines of the tunnel allowed. With reach and strength, Eldred pushed them back, but they extracted a price for each step gained.

The first Deiran acted purely in defense, parrying with his sword and blocking with his buckler. Eldred could not land a blow. Meanwhile, the second Deiran was striking out and landing small, painful cuts on Eldred's arms and legs. Nothing that would kill the shard bearer of the Mother, but enough to slow him.

If the Bond could pass through rock, they might have finished him on the spot, but the two injured warriors were far up the winding passage and the pod was only at half strength. Eldred caught the buckler of the forward Deiran and ran him through, even as the second Deiran drove his sword into Eldred's ribs.

Eldred pulled away, blood running down his side, walking backward down the passage with his hand pressed to his wound. The Deirans hesitated and held their ground. Eldred paused twenty feet away and watched as their leader knelt beside the fallen warrior.

Willing the pain away, Eldred took one deep breath and then another. The wound was sealing; it hadn't been deep. After a few more breaths, it closed. He dropped his bloodied hand to his side, holding his sword low. Behind, in the depths of the cave, he heard cursing. Gundlach was trying to find his way to the fight.

The Deiran leader held up the torch and studied Eldred from where he knelt. "We've cut you. We've stabbed you. But it's as if we've done nothing. What manner of man are you?"

"I warned you before. I told you not to come in here," said Eldred. He could hear Gundlach's footsteps now.

The man wet his lips. "You asked my name earlier. I'll give it to you now. I am Aistan, born of Boar's Tusk. May I ask your name?"

Eldred crinkled up his face.

"Well," said Aistan. "I've given you mine, for what it's worth."

Eldred cursed under his breath.

Down the passage, behind Eldred, Gundlach blurted out. "Light! I am seeing light!"

Eldred took a breath and hurled his sword. The unnamed warrior deflected it with his buckler, but then Eldred was upon him, throwing him down on top of Aistan, who lost hold of his blade. Eldred fell upon the men, slapping the nameless man hard on the jaw, stunning him.

Aistan held up his arm to defend his face. The pod was gone. He was just one man, sprawled over his dead companion. Eldred pushed Aistan's arm aside and slapped him hard. It took three strikes before Aistan lay still.

Gundlach ran up behind Eldred, shield and sword at ready.

Eldred held up his hand. "Stay back."

Gundlach paused, staring fixedly at the torch.

Eldred got to his feet.

"Where are the others?" asked Gundlach.

Eldred gestured vaguely up the tunnel. "Up there." He stepped over the Deirans and picked up the torch, which he handed to Gundlach. "Go, get your lady. I'll clear them out of the way."

Gundlach lowered the torch close to Aistan. "This one is living."

"I'll take care of it. Go get Lady Yslana."

Gundlach stared at Eldred, sword and torch in hand. "We must be taking no chances."

"I'm well aware," said Eldred. "Now, get going."

Gundlach stayed put.

Eldred sighed. "She is alone in the dark. Do you mean to make her wait?"

Gundlach glared at the still warriors. "I will be returning with Lady Yslana. Be certain the way is clear." With that, he turned and hurried back down the passage.

Eldred retrieved his sword and grabbed the two stunned Deirans by the back of their tunics, just below the neck. He carried them up the passage to the second room and hid them in a nook off the side. He didn't return for the dead warrior, heading instead for the first room, which still swirled with dust but was otherwise empty.

In the narrow passage beyond, which led to the exit, lay one bonded warrior on his back with his chest caved in. The stone Eldred had thrown was still lodged in the man, two inches below his heart. Eldred paused, surprised. He had thrown low, or had intended to anyway. He had only meant to injure his targets, but the rock had decided otherwise.

Eldred found the last warrior as the man was crawling out of the entrance. His left foot and ankle were a bloody mess that made Eldred cringe. The man pulled himself forward with evident pain, crying out as his twisted foot dragged across the ground.

After a moment of squeamish indecision, Eldred snatched up the man as he had the men before, ignoring the man's threats. As Eldred ran down the slope, away from the cave, the man went for a dagger in his belt. Eldred struck it from the man's hand. The man continued to struggle weakly in Eldred's grip until Eldred set him down in a stand of trees and ducked away.

Gundlach and Lady Yslana were coming out of the cave when Eldred returned. To Eldred's inspection, the Corporian's blade was clean. He hadn't found the stunned Deirans.

Gundlach dropped the torch and sheathed his blade, wearing a wide smile on his face. "You have been making magic, Eldred. I was thinking we were at our end."

Lady Yslana shivered, not yet warmed by the sun that still hung high in the sky. "Where have you been hiding?"

Eldred pointed down the slope. "I caught the last warrior. He's down in those trees."

"Excellent. Excellent," proclaimed Gundlach. "If they are all that is coming, we will make it. A brief rest and we shall be getting on our way."

"No," said Eldred. "Best you two press on. Let's take nothing for granted. Besides, walking will warm you up. Lady Yslana looks chilled."

"You are staying? What of our contract?" asked Lady Yslana.

"I have not forgotten our agreement," said Eldred. "But these warriors have valuable gear. Or do you two lay a claim?"

Lady Yslana made a face. "We are wanting nothing from these men. If you must be plundering their arms, so be it. Do not be taking long."

Eldred nodded. "I won't. I'll find you on the trail."

Gundlach gave a small bow. "Truly excellent, Eldred. Truly amazing."

Eldred gave a small smile and watched them head up the trail. Once they were out of sight, he took a deep breath and entered the cave. The warrior with the crushed chest had been rolled on his side, perhaps to spare Lady Yslana the indignity of stepping over him, but Aistan and his companion were lying where Eldred had left them, still breathing. Eldred carried out Aistan's companion before returning for Aistan, the servant before his lord.

Eldred found a patch of dirt in the shade of a tall bush for the two warriors. They were starting to shift and groan, perhaps only moments from coming awake. It seemed they would be fine, certainly in better shape than the man down the hill who might never walk again. A hard fate, that, being a cripple, as Eldred well knew.

As Eldred lingered by the cave entrance, considering whether he should retrieve the corpses from the tunnels, Aistan sat up and looked at Eldred through the shifting leaves of the bush. Eldred met his gaze for a moment before turning away and heading on up the trail after the Corporians. Aistan could clean up the mess. Eldred had warned him not to enter the cave.

New Wismar

They reached the plateau that held the Corporian city as dusk deepened into night. Lady Yslana pushed on through her exhaustion, walking under the dim light of the crescent moon.

As they cleared the woods, Eldred spotted the city scarcely a mile away. A patchy line of torches marked the top of the red walls. Only a few guards were in evidence. "Almost there."

His companions trudged on in silence.

"What is the name of your city?" asked Eldred.

Lady Yslana wet her lips and answered. "New Wismar."

Eldred smiled. "So you're from here?"

"No," said Lady Yslana with a sour tone. "I am from Wismar, the proper capital of my people. This is New Wismar; there can be no comparison between the two."

"If you say so," said Eldred, looking around. "I don't see any patrols outside."

"No, not at night. We must be getting to the gate," said Gundlach.

Eldred nodded and followed after them, scouring the ground for some trace of the great battle, now more than eight months in the past. But there was nothing, only grass, neatly cropped by some absent herd.

As they entered the wall's moon shadow, Lady Yslana heaved a great sigh.

"Is something wrong?" asked Eldred.

Lady Yslana glanced back, her lips pressed tight. "This is not how I should be arriving here. Those barbarian degenerates were butchering my soldiers as well as the others in the caravan. Beyond the loss of loyal men, it will be making my mission nearly impossible."

"Not necessarily," said Gundlach. "We are having some luck—with Eldred."

Lady Yslana sniffed. "We will be seeing if your suggestion bears fruit. For now, I suggest you restrain your enthusiasm, Gundlach."

Gundlach dropped his eyes. "I am regretful, my lady."

Eldred raised his eyebrows at the mention of his name. "I'm only staying a few days. That's what we agreed."

Lady Yslana waved her arm tiredly. "Yes, we have been making a contract. You can count on us to be meeting our obligations. You will be having your pick of treasure, within reason. You need not fuss."

"I wasn't," muttered Eldred.

Neither of his companions answered.

As they neared the gate, they passed through a smattering of red stones, the ones Pounder had been so concerned about before the battle fought nearly a year before. Eldred picked one up and examined it as they walked. A dim red glow came from the rock, and just holding it made him feel uncomfortable, almost queasy.

He was staring at it when Lady Yslana turned and snapped at him. "Drop it!"

Eldred made a face, not really wanting to keep hold of it, but not wanting to drop it at her command either. "What is this?"

"A rock," said Lady Yslana, coming to a stop. "One which must be resting here. You will be releasing it."

Eldred shrugged and dropped it by his feet. "Very well, but why are they here?"

Lady Yslana continued on. "Our contract is not granting you the right to interrogate me. Please remember that. Once in the city, Gundlach will be finding you accommodations. Let that be your focus."

Eldred nodded stiffly. "As you wish."

There was already movement on the walls by the time Lady Yslana presented herself at the entrance. She stood in silence as the massive gate, ten feet high and twenty feet wide, swung slowly inward, revealing a squad of fifty soldiers standing in formation.

A fit-looking middle-aged man with brown hair and an amused countenance walked out. He flashed Lady Yslana a toothy smile and bowed his head. "Lady Yslana, how good to be seeing you—alive. But I am confused. We had reports that you were bringing a considerable reserve of cavalry and swordsmen." The man gave Eldred a questioning look. "Are these all your men? Just these two?"

Lady Yslana fixed the man with a stare. "Keeper Enolf, what a pleasure to be finding you manning the gates, making yourself useful." She paused before continuing. "As you are so keenly observing, my forces are depleted; the caravan we were accompanying was completely destroyed. This can be happening when you have the courage to go beyond the walls. Still, I am thanking you for your kind welcome. But now I will be going with Baron Wortwin to my residence."

At her nod, another man strode forward and bowed low. He was older, with pale green eyes and a bald crown for his head ringed by graying hair. "You are doing us great honor, dear lady. Please come inside. I have been making everything ready for you."

As she stepped forward, Keeper Enolf pointed at Eldred. "What about this one? I can see what he is. Why are we not killing him?"

Lady Yslana gave an exasperated sigh. "He is bound by contract to me. I am granting him protection."

Keeper Enolf gave a small smile. "I am glad to be learning that. But with contract or without, he remains our enemy. I should be failing in my duty to let this one pass."

Gundlach took a step closer to Eldred. "I will be staying with him in the outer ring. I will be monitoring his activities."

"Still, I am feeling he should be executed," said Keeper Enolf.

Eldred narrowed his eyes. "And I feel—"

"That is enough!" interjected Lady Yslana. "My assistant has been accurately conveying my wishes. The Mercian will be staying in the outer ring in Gundlach's charge. Are you suffering any further confusion, Keeper Enolf?"

Keeper Enolf scowled. "I will be raising this issue with the other Keepers. This man is our foe. I am finding it questionable that we would allow him within the walls. If you are insisting, Lady Yslana, you will be bearing the full responsibility for his actions. I will be sending a detachment of soldiers. I will be having this man watched."

Lady Yslana shrugged. "Watch him all you want. Watching is what you do best." With that, she strode through the gate, and Baron Wortwin fell in beside her.

As the gate started to slowly swing shut, Gundlach gestured to Eldred, and they entered the city.

While Keeper Enolf sorted out who would accompany them, Eldred glanced over the surroundings. A faint red haze hung in the air, separate from the red color of the walls. A stink too, a smell that choked him slightly.

Gundlach gestured grandly. "Welcome to the Eighth Circle of New Wismar."

Eldred made a face. The place was a dung pit. Row after row of animal pens stretched into the distance, filling the wide space between the high outer wall and a slightly shorter inner wall. A huge mass of goats, pigs, chickens and cattle had contributed their excrement, but the haze, the smell, that sickened him felt like it was something different.

A few low stone buildings devoid of decoration squatted against the outer wall. The inner wall harbored no structures, though it marked the boundary of many pens. Eldred glanced up at the dozens of archers who patrolled that wall, watching him with bows at ready. There would be no cover against their arrows.

"Ah, he is finally done picking his men," said Gundlach. "Come, it is not far. We will be staying at the inn."

Gundlach set out through the winding fences with Eldred and the detachment trailing after him, while atop the wall a band of archers shadowed them. The pens were laid out in haphazard fashion, a small pen of ducks and geese set next to a larger enclosure of cattle positioned next to a mud pit for hogs. It repeated endlessly, each collection of animals tended by a motley crew of young Corporians of both sexes. Only their peculiar green eyes were the same. The shape of their faces, the shade of their dark skin, the color of their hair all looked to have been fashioned by different shard bearers, not the single shard bearer they all served.

They walked half a mile through the muck before they came to a two-story wooden building with a large chimney at each end belching smoke. A sign bearing the image of an iron gate hung down over the door.

"A prison?" asked Eldred.

"No. It is the iron gate, the best inn here in the Eighth if the reports I was hearing are correct. The only option we are having," said Gundlach.

The men followed them up onto the porch but did not go inside, electing instead to sit on a line of rough benches. Across the yard, on the inner wall three hundred feet away, the archers rested their elbows on the parapet, watching the proceedings with bored expressions.

Inside the building, the air seemed cleaner, despite the smoky fire. Gundlach collapsed on a chair at the first table. Eldred joined him.

A wiry man who was missing an arm came out from behind the counter, watching Eldred from the corner of his eye. He addressed Gundlach. "What business are you having?"

Gundlach rubbed his forehead tiredly. "I am needing rooms. One for him, one for me. And bring the best beer you are keeping. I know it is the Eighth Circle, but I almost died and I am wanting something good."

The man nodded. "I have a fruity amber. You will not be confusing it with ale from the Sixth, but it is fine to drink. Will you be wanting something to eat? I have fresh pork. We killed the pig this morning."

Gundlach looked ready to fall over asleep. "That is good."

"Just water for me," said Eldred. "I'll try some pork, but I'm not feeling well."

The man half glanced at Eldred and left without saying a word.

Eldred raised an eyebrow. "Did he hear me?"

"Yes, but there is no love for your kind here. He was probably losing his arm to your friends. They killed hundreds." Gundlach stifled a yawn.

Eldred raised an eyebrow. It had been more than a thousand; he'd seen them fall.

Momentarily, the one-armed man returned, clutching two mugs in his hand. Gundlach grabbed his beer and drained it as Eldred studied the pale red liquid in his cup, the water.

"Oh, that was good. I have been lusting for beer for a week. Another, please," said Gundlach.

Gundlach was finishing his dinner and his third beer when Baron Wortwin arrived.

Gundlach raised his glass. "Now that you have been arriving, I can be going. I am so tired."

Baron Wortwin smiled, though the emotion did not appear to reach his cold green eyes. "Yes, be taking your rest. You have done well. I will be taking charge of this one."

Gundlach pushed himself slowly to his feet. "I may be sleeping all day."

"Whatever you are needing," said Baron Wortwin.

After Gundlach trundled off to his room, Baron Wortwin ordered a beer and sat, studying Eldred. "I see you did not care for your food. Very sensible. It is Eighth Circle refuse. I have always known it was terrible, but I am just now learning it is not even fit for a Mercian."

Eldred looked down at his untouched pork. Like the water, it radiated a pale reddish glow. Not as strong as the rocks outside, but noticeable now that Eldred was looking for it. "I prefer lighter fare."

"Well, let me know what you are wanting. I could get you something from the lower circles. You were making a great contribution by helping my patron."

"Thank you," said Eldred. "I'll let you know. I'm here for a few days. I take it that Lady Yslana wishes to present me to some people from your city."

Baron Wortwin set down his cup. "It is, uhh, more than a presentation. We are wishing that you might be demonstrating your considerable abilities."

Eldred spread his hands. "What do you mean?"

"I have been arranging a boxing match—just fisticuffs. Will this be worrying you?"

Eldred crinkled up his face. "I'm not worried, but I'm not sure I see the point. Of course, I can outbox your man, whoever he is. What does that have to do with anything?"

Baron Wortwin gave a stiff smile. "Your friends, the Deirans, are well known to us. Even the most doubt-filled citizen would be acknowledging their prowess. But your people, the Mercians, are not well known or respected. I am suggesting that nobody gives your kind a second thought. Certainly, there are no citizens who are thinking that you could kill nine of those bastards when so few of us can kill any."

Eldred uttered a short laugh. "Very well; I'll box. Whatever else is true, Mercians are the champions of boxing. I've seen the truth of that."

"It will be very good if you are proving that," said Baron Wortwin with a curt nod.

"Why?" asked Eldred.

Baron Wortwin paused and took a sip of beer before continuing. "Let us be saying that our leaders here are not all possessing the insight, the understanding, of Lady Yslana. She is aware of your abilities. If others are learning of it, they may be persuaded to adopt a more sensible course of action."

"So if Enolf sees me box, he'll become more reasonable?" asked Eldred.

"Not him, no. He will not be persuaded," said Baron Wortwin.

"Persuaded to do what?" asked Eldred.

Baron Wortwin frowned. "You have many questions, but I am not here to be providing you with answers. You should be focusing on your contract. Though I understand Lady Yslana could limit your compensation to nothing, you may be trusting in her measured generosity. Fight and you can be having these rewards. Am I being clear with you?"

Eldred gave a slight smile. "You're clear enough. I'll fight."

"Good," said Baron Wortwin. "One more matter—Lady Yslana's protection only holds if you are remaining here with Gundlach or myself. Should you find yourself wandering the city, you can be certain Keeper Enolf's men will kill you."

"Are all the men his?"

"He keeps the Eighth Circle, such as it is," said Baron Wortwin.

"Who keeps the other circles? Does Lady Yslana rule one?" asked Eldred.

Baron Wortwin's eyes sharpened. "These are not matters for you to be worrying about. You need only be using your fists."

Eldred nodded. "Very well. I'll take my rest."

Eldred's room was small and windowless, with a single cot barely wide enough for him to lie on. The door opened outward, precluding the option of blocking it shut. As Eldred leaned his sword against the bed, he reflected that it was odd he was still in possession of it. But perhaps it made sense. If the 'Mercian' went berserk and killed a few Corporians, that might make more trouble for Lady Yslana than if he only beat them with his fists. And some, at least Keeper Enolf, seemed at odds with her.

He lay in the dark with half-opened eyes. He felt the small sample of water he had taken moving through him. He could have traced its passage with his finger if he had wanted to. As it moved, he sensed the red glow growing dimmer and dimmer until it gradually faded away. It was the same for the befouled air that he breathed in. He was in the lair of the Corporian stone bearer, but he could survive its sickening nature, at least at the current levels of contamination.

BRAWLING

The Iron Gate stirred to life early the next morning. When Eldred came out to the common room, he found Baron Wortwin sitting alone at a small wooden table next to a half-dozen of Enolf's guards, who were devouring a meal of bacon and eggs. The food smelled appetizing but possessed an unpleasant red glow to Eldred's eyes.

Baron Wortwin gestured towards the seat across from himself. "What will you be having?"

Eldred took a seat and eyed the food on the guards' plates. The bread appeared to be less corrupted than the meat or the eggs. "Just toast and a cup of water."

"That is all? Surely, you will be needing your strength for the fight," said Baron Wortwin.

"I never box on a full stomach," said Eldred.

Baron Wortwin passed Eldred's request on to the one-armed innkeeper, who continued to ignore Eldred.

As Eldred waited for his food, he studied Baron Wortwin's face. There was a very slight ruddy glow to his dark features as well, easy to miss if you were not looking for it.

Baron Wortwin noticed Eldred's stare. "Is something in doubt?"

"No, not at all," said Eldred. "I'm just curious who I'll be fighting."

"Ah, yes. Two matches. One man from the Eighth and one from the Seventh."

"It is Grimo you will be boxing from the Eighth," piped up one of Enolf's men from the other table, his dark features narrowed in disdain. "He will be beating the crap from you."

The man's companions chuckled and nodded their agreement.

Eldred shrugged and turned to the tray the one-armed man was setting in front of him. "The fight will be the fight," he said airily. "So, I face Grimo here in the Eighth Circle. Will the other match take place in the Seventh Circle?"

Baron Wortwin gave a small shake of his head. "No. Their man will be coming here. I believe his name is Ditwin. Gundlach knows him, or so they were saying."

"Are these the great champions of the Corporians, then?" asked Eldred after taking a hesitant sip of reddish water. "The warriors you all admire?"

Baron Wortwin cast a quick glance at Keeper Enolf's men. "They are both good men, worthy combatants."

Eldred nodded and picked up a piece of dim-glowing toast, eyeing it warily before taking a small bite. It tasted normal. One cautious bite followed another until the toast was gone.

As he was reaching for another piece, one of Enolf's men addressed him, this one with tightly cropped blond hair. "Have you been testing Gundlach?"

"Testing him?" asked Eldred.

"Were you two fighting?" continued the man.

"No. We fought together, in aid of each other," said Eldred.

"We all know his name," said the man.

"Do you?" asked Eldred. "So, Gundlach—he would be considered a champion of the Corporians?"

"Have you not seen him guarding the princess?" asked the man.

"She called him an assistant," said Eldred.

"All who are serving her are her assistants, even me," said Baron Wortwin.

"I see," said Eldred, starting on the toast.

Gundlach did not rise until the eleventh hour. He took a plate piled high with bacon and sausage in the common room, which was empty except for Baron Wortwin and Eldred, the guards having elected to return to the benches on the porch.

"Grimo is the tougher of the two," observed Gundlach between mouthfuls.

Eldred nodded distractedly. "I see."

"Following our customs, you will be fighting in a ring fifteen paces wide. If you are seen exiting the ring or are even touching the line, you will be forfeiting. And as you might be expecting, you lose if you are pummeled senseless or cry out in surrender. Watch for Grimo to be grabbing at your arm and spinning you over the boundary. He has great cunning," said Gundlach.

"I'll watch for that," said Eldred.

"Ditwin is more straightforward. He is always thinking he can exchange blows with anyone. He will be stepping right into you with angry fists," said Gundlach.

"You know them both?" asked Eldred.

Gundlach nodded. "I have spent time sparring with them in past days, back in Wismar." He paused and scratched his beard. "You, uh, I doubt you will be finding them a challenge. I just mean to be telling you what they would do."

"Thanks. So, I just have to shove them out of the ring?" asked Eldred.

"Yes. That is all," confirmed Gundlach.

Baron Wortwin leaned forward. "We are seeking a definitive victory. That is what the contract is requiring. Throw them out and be done with it."

"Right. And I'll get my reward," said Eldred.

Gundlach grinned and turned to Baron Wortwin. "Are you carrying what I asked you for?"

Baron Wortwin gave a slight nod.

"Something for you to be considering, Eldred, once you are done winning the match," said Gundlach.

Eldred smiled. "I look forward to it."

Not much later, Keeper Enolf bustled into the common room accompanied by a shorter, slighter man, though one still large and burly compared to Maldavians or Deirans. He addressed Baron Wortwin. "Has the Mercian been made ready?"

Baron Wortwin bowed his head to each of the men in turn. "Keeper Enolf, Keeper Renz, he is ready."

As they came out of the inn, Eldred saw a thirty-foot wide ring marked out in the dirt between the animal pens. One contingent of men stood on the left, another on the right. A single man stood in front of each group, the contestants, to judge from their large stature and angry faces. Both men looked to weigh as much as Eldred, though they were both more squat. Across the way, on the inner wall, no less than fifty archers stood at attention—about a third of them women. Dozens of children tending the animals in the surrounding area were also glancing over as they performed their chores.

Eldred tapped Gundlach. "Where is Lady Yslana?"

Gundlach laughed and shook his head. "We are standing in the excrement of the Eighth Circle, Eldred. She cannot be coming here."

"Oh, I thought this was her plan," said Eldred.

"We will be sending a runner with the news once we have finished," said Gundlach.

Keeper Renz, his face frozen in a frown, gestured at the man to the left. "My man, Ditwin, should be going first."

Keeper Enolf smiled pleasantly. "Of course, all due honor to the Seventh. If the Mercian can still be standing afterwards, my man, Grimo, will be sitting him down."

Baron Wortwin gave a small bow. "Then let us be starting with Ditwin and the Mercian in the ring."

Eldred glanced at Gundlach for confirmation and stepped forward.

Ditwin had already entered the far side of the ring and was directing a baleful stare at Eldred from his dull-looking face. The men behind him were calling out encouragement.

"We will be starting the match on my call," said Baron Wortwin. "Begin!"

Ditwin raised his fists and charged at Eldred. As he closed, Eldred reached out and grabbed him under the shoulder and hurled him ten feet through the air. Ditwin hit the ground and rolled out of the ring, where he sprang to his feet, his face twisted in surprise. The match had only taken three seconds.

Keeper Renz sputtered furiously. "By the Goddess, what was that?"

"The match," said Keeper Enolf with a poorly suppressed smirk. "But do not be concerned, Keeper Renz. Where the Seventh has been suffering misfortune, the Eighth stands ready to meet the challenge. Grimo, are you prepared?"

Grimo strode forward bearing a stern face atop his thick neck. He made fists and tensed his muscular arms and wide chest. "I am."

"Then start the fighting," called Baron Wortwin.

Unlike Ditwin, Grimo stood where he was, watching Eldred warily.

Eldred waited a moment to see if Grimo would approach, then darted forward. He shot out his right arm and shoved Grimo hard, lifting him off the ground. Grimo sailed backwards through the air until he landed awkwardly and staggered backwards out of the ring.

"Your man did no better," noted Keeper Renz.

Keeper Enolf studied Eldred with narrowed eyes. "You are right. This Mercian is a brute."

Eldred shrugged. "Your men are weak."

"You had best be watching your tone!" snapped Keeper Enolf.

Baron Wortwin gave a small, tight smile. "But Keeper Enolf, that is the point of this demonstration. That is why we were obtaining the Mercian, that you could be observing his strength. This is all to inform you of what Lady Yslana is already knowing. To this Mercian, your strongest man is standing as weak as a child. He has slaughtered nine Deirans. This was witnessed by Lady Yslana and Gundlach. The whole rest of her forces did not kill as many. Just one Mercian was making such damage—and there is an army of them, thousands."

Keeper Enolf glared at Eldred. "Let us see him fighting two."

"No," said Gundlach. "Put in ten men, your ten best men, your strongest men. Then they might be having a chance."

Baron Wortwin turned to Gundlach with narrowed brows. "Gundlach, we did not discuss—"

"No, it is well, Baron." Gundlach gestured at Eldred. "Is it not fine, Eldred? Can you not be managing ten of our paltry men?"

Eldred spread his hands. "I can. I will if that is what you wish."

Gundlach grunted. "Yes. Let us be speeding this process. We do not have time to humor the fine Keeper of the Eighth. I was just coming from Wismar. I can be attesting that time grows short."

Baron Wortwin clasped his hands and took a breath. "Well, then. Why not? What of it, Keeper Enolf? Do you have ten men you can be placing in the ring with the Mercian?"

"Are you being serious?" exclaimed Keeper Enolf. "I have ten men right here. When they finish beating your Mercian dog to the ground, perhaps then you and Lady Yslana will be ceasing these doltish games." Enolf started calling his men's names while Keeper Renz looked on sullenly.

Shortly, ten of Keeper Enolf's men crowded into the left side of the ring along with Ditwin, who had volunteered himself.

"That is eleven," observed Baron Wortwin.

"It will be making no difference. Or are you concerned, Eldred?" asked Gundlach.

Eldred shook his head. "No." It would just be one more face to strike.

Baron Wortwin raised his arm. "Begin."

The men were standing in tight formation across from Eldred, Grimo and Ditwin at the front. Eldred stepped forward and punched Grimo in the chin with his right fist, dropping him. Ditwin struck Eldred on the side, but Eldred absorbed the blow and floored him with a left. Then Eldred grabbed the man who had been standing next to Ditwin and shoved him into the men trying to get around the two fallen combatants.

Four men were knocked to the ground, including two in the back who touched the edge of the ring and were out. Eldred grabbed the man he had pushed and tossed him out of the ring. He snatched up the other two fallen men and did the same with them. Only three foes remained.

One ran forward and kicked Eldred in the shin; Eldred swung him around and sent him tottering out of the ring. The two remaining men hung back, uncertain. Eldred stepped forward and shoved them out of the ring, one after the other. Only Eldred and his two unconscious opponents— Grimo and Ditwin—remained in the ring. The contest was over. It had taken less than a minute.

Eldred stepped back to his side of the ring and crossed his arms. Keeper Renz's eyes went wide with surprise. Keeper Enolf gaped silently.

Baron Wortwin gave a small sigh. "So, now you are seeing what Lady Yslana has been knowing. Your eyes have informed you. Are your thoughts reaching an understanding?"

Keeper Enolf looked over Eldred, his lips curled in disgust. "This was a trick—an obfuscation that you and Gundlach have sprung upon us. This demonstration lacks bearing upon our true circumstance. We will not be facing these barbarians without weapons. We will not be packing ourselves into tight quarters to grapple with these savages."

"Of course," agreed Baron Wortwin. "Though if the Mercian had been using his sword, your men would be as dead as the nine Deirans he left on the battlefield. Let us now be sharing with our factions what we have been observing. Eleven men, your finest, lost in the ring against one Mercian. And upon him, I am not seeing a mark. We must all be sharing this same information."

Keeper Renz nodded stiffly.

Keeper Enolf let out an exasperated sigh. "Your facts are correct, Baron Wortwin. I will not be disputing your facts, and I will be sharing them. But I will not be agreeing with your speculative conclusions."

Baron Wortwin gave a half bow, and the two Keepers walked away through the muck while the soldiers carried away their fallen comrades.

Gundlach approached Eldred once the other combatants were cleared away, bearing a small brown pouch. "Here, you should be looking at this." He turned the pouch over and shook out five gold coins into his hand. "A fine reward for you, Eldred. These coins are pure gold, finer than anything your people possess. This is for earlier, when you saved Lady Yslana. Today was fine as well, though if you can be killing nine Deirans, then, of course, you can beat the men of the Eighth."

Eldred eyed the coins which appeared to be well-crafted. They bore the effigy of a regal woman above the legend, "By the Spirit of the Goddess." They possessed a faint red glow, contaminated by the spirit of the Corporians. As he looked them over, he thought of the Deiran blood he had spilled, also red. Wulsin and his pod, that was rightly done. But the last two, that was a mess—not exactly an accident, but not desired either. All in all, he didn't want payment for those deeds, especially not with tainted coins that would upset his stomach. "A worthy offering, very generous. I thank you for it but decline."

Gundlach frowned. "Are you wanting even more gold than this? This is three years' wages. Three years, and you have only been working a few days."

Eldred held up his palm. "No, I just don't need gold. These are fine coins. They appear well-minted, as you said. But they're not for me."

Gundlach grunted and placed the coins back in the pouch. "You are lacking sense, Eldred. This is the finest payment you can be hoping for."

Eldred shrugged. "If I take anything, it'll just be something small."

Gundlach held out the pouch. "Something you could be buying with these coins, then."

Eldred gave a short laugh. "Probably."

Baron Wortwin approached them. The three were standing alone; the remaining guards were back on the benches on the porch. A number of archers across the way ambled off on patrol, though a dozen still leaned their bows against the wall.

"We should not be making last minute changes in our plans," complained the Baron. "What if they had won? What then, Gundlach?"

Gundlach gave a small shake of his head. "It was not possible. You have seen it now, Baron. Do you think twenty of Enolf's men could be toppling Eldred?"

Baron Wortwin eyed Eldred. "He is a strong man, but all men have their limits. And this matter is too important to be leaving to chance."

"What matter? What are you trying to persuade Enolf to do?" asked Eldred.

"It is not your concern," said the Baron.

"Then you may consider my cooperation at an end. I'll take my leave," said Eldred.

The Baron scowled. "You have a contract."

"Consider it fulfilled. Lady Yslana safely delivered to New Wismar. Eleven men pushed out of a dirt circle. What more could you want?" asked Eldred.

"But you have not even taken payment!" exclaimed Gundlach.

"And we are just beginning negotiations with the factions. We may be requiring another demonstration," protested Baron Wortwin.

"Then let us sit inside and discuss what you need and why you need it. If I agree, you'll have my help, most likely without any fee whatsoever," said Eldred.

Baron Wortwin sighed. "First, I must be consulting with Lady Yslana. Stay with Gundlach; do not be going anywhere. Do not be hasty. I will be returning as soon as I can."

QUESTIONS

They waited in a dark corner of the inn. Gundlach drank his ale, and Eldred sipped his water.

"The Baron is taking a while," said Eldred.

Gundlach shrugged. "It takes time to traverse the city. Crossing each gate comes with its own review."

"Is she in the First Circle?"

"I am doubting that," said Gundlach.

"Then she stays in the Second? Is that where she has her residence?" persisted Eldred.

Gundlach shifted his mug and frowned. "She is keeping facilities in each circle of the city. Even here in the Eighth, some of these pens are housing her beasts."

Eldred gave a small smile. "You mean me?"

"No, of course not. You are being noble in your fashion, even if you are foolish."

"Foolish how?"

"A contract—we are always making and following contracts. It is simple. Even children know how to do it." Gundlach's eyes glinted. "But I am finding you erratic. You make no sense. You are not taking your rewards. You have a contract with the most noble woman in this city, and all you are doing is making trouble."

"I fought Enolf's men," said Eldred.

"Yes, and you saved her when I could not." Gundlach's shoulders slumped. "You saved her three times: on the battlefield, beside the stream and in the cave. Those were miracles, not some chance. You should be staying. I am finding this so clear, and now you may be wandering off with nothing, for no reason."

Eldred sipped his water. "Well, it's done. She's here—safe in your city."

Gundlach shook his head. "Nobody is safe. The walls of New Wismar will be holding this day, but these are troubling times. I have seen where strong walls are not enough. You could be making a difference. Such a contract you could be having if you could stop with your questions. You shoved around some men from the Eighth. Well done. But there is so much more for you here if you can be showing patience."

Eldred raised his eyebrows. "You want me to be one of her guards?"

"I am serving as Lady Yslana's guard. I would give my life to save hers. I am having a purpose, a contract. If you are leaving and go wandering the lands, what will you find? What will you have? You do not appear to have much. Here, I can be getting you whatever you wish: a sword hammered from the purest steel, armor light enough that you can run in it, gems and gold and beer. Nobody is saving someone's life three times by accident."

"Well, we'll see," said Eldred. "If she feels as you do, she might share her plan."

"It is my plan," said Gundlach quietly.

"Your plan?" asked Eldred.

Gundlach nodded. "I whispered it to Lady Yslana when she was waking from her injuries."

"Why don't you share it with me?" asked Eldred.

Gundlach frowned and shifted his mug. "I cannot be doing that. But I can be saying it is not opposing the interests of your people, such as they are."

"What do you mean?" asked Eldred.

"I am saying that if your people show good reason, then the work of this plan goes for them, just as it does for us. On this matter, there is perhaps not a sharing of a common cause, but there is no evident conflict."

"And I should just trust you?" asked Eldred.

"Always," said Gundlach.

Eldred laughed. "But can you trust me?"

"I already do," said Gundlach.

THREE GATES

Eldred had eaten several pieces of bread topped with slices of Nieheimer cheese by the time the Baron returned. The cheese glowed eerily but had an enticing flavor, both sharp and spicy. He had the hang of eating now and could feel the red glow extinguishing as the food slipped down to his gullet. If he focused, he could even wipe the food clean in his mouth, with a pulse of his own energy. A morsel of cheese was no match for he who carried the Shard of the Mother.

Baron Wortwin gestured for them to get to their feet.

"What happened?" asked Gundlach. "Is she allowing us to share the plan?"

"No, but she will be meeting with him," answered the Baron.

Gundlach's eyes grew wide. "She is meeting with us? Where?"

"In the Fifth. I have papers. We must be hurrying. We cannot be making her wait," said the Baron.

Eldred stood and stuck the dagger he'd been using to slice cheese in his belt.

"No, not that," said the Baron. "Nor your sword either."

"What?" asked Eldred.

"The papers are granting you passage, but not your weapons. You will have to be leaving them here. You should be thankful you get to keep them in the Eighth," said the Baron.

Eldred hesitated.

"All will be well, Eldred. You can be counting on our protection," said Gundlach.

Eldred scowled. "My contract with Lady Yslana didn't mention anything about me being disarmed."

"Nor did it stipulate that she would be sharing her plans," said the Baron. "Are you coming or staying? If we are going, we are already late."

Reluctantly, Eldred laid out his four daggers and his battered sword on the table.

Baron Wortwin exchanged a glance with the one-armed man and shook his head. "He does not want those here. Put them in your room."

"So much for Corporian hospitality," said Eldred, taking up his gear.

Outside the inn, twelve soldiers in bright red uniforms sat atop their horses with three spare horses in tow. Enolf's men were on their feet, standing off to the side bearing sullen expressions.

"Can you be riding, Mercian?" asked Baron Wortwin.

"Yes, though I prefer to walk," answered Eldred.

"No time for that now," said the Baron.

Eldred gestured at Enolf's men. "Aren't they coming with us?"

"No. As I was telling you, I have papers," answered the Baron.

They mounted up and rode against the swarm of cattle and sheep that were being herded back to their pens.

"This is not much faster than walking," said Eldred as they paused for the tenth time for a line of cattle to pass.

"Better than stamping our way through the muck," said the Baron.

They came to the source of the herds at the outer gate, which stood open to receive an endless stream of cattle that maneuvered around the formations of spearmen on guard.

"You graze them outside every day?" asked Eldred.

The Baron nodded. "Most days."

"You're not afraid of attack?" asked Eldred.

"Not here," said the Baron. "Sometimes we are seeing a few of their scouts in the distance, but they do not trouble us."

The gate to the inner wall was another fifteen minutes ride, slightly hastened by going with the flow of livestock. To Eldred's eyes, the gate was the twin of the one that was set in the outer wall—ten feet high and twenty feet wide. As they approached, it stood open. Behind it, several formations of spearmen stood at attention. The walls above the gate bristled with archers.

Baron Wortwin, who rode at the front with Eldred and Gundlach just behind, handed down a wad of papers to one of the guards on duty.

The guard scanned them and looked up at the Baron. "On your oath, the Mercian is bearing no arms?"

The Baron reached down to take back the papers. "Yes, that is so."

The guard turned to Eldred. "Ditwin has yet to wake."

"Oh," said Eldred. He had just tapped the man.

"Such are the risks you are taking when you enter a ring," said the Baron.

"Ditwin is a tough one. He will be rising," said Gundlach.

The guard gave Eldred a hard stare. "We all are hoping so." Then he turned and signaled his men, who made room for the party to pass.

As they started into the Seventh Circle, Gundlach turned to Eldred. "Perhaps I should be asking after Grimo. I believe you struck him harder."

Eldred shrugged. "If you wish. I didn't mean to harm either man."

"I am thinking the same. If you had been seeking to injure them, I expect you could have broken their necks," said Gundlach.

Eldred nodded and glanced around at the low stone buildings that stretched in all directions. They were not fashioned any better than the dwellings in the Eighth, but there were no pens overflowing with animals, which was an improvement. The reddish haze in the air remained, though. "Who lives here?"

"These are the barracks. Only soldiers can be living in the Seventh, and most soldiers do," said Gundlach.

"So, this is where you will make your home?" asked Eldred.

"No. My home is in Wismar," said Gundlach forcefully. "And while I am residing here, I will be guarding Lady Yslana if I am not watching you in the Eighth."

Eldred sniffed the air, which was definitely fresher regarding dung but still had the haze. "It seems some Corporians mean to live here. You built a city."

"Yes, you are correct," said Gundlach curtly. "Some would be lingering here."

The Baron pressed on. It was perhaps a hundred yards to the inner wall to the Sixth Circle. The inner wall was slightly shorter than the wall between the Seventh and Eighth, perhaps fifty feet high, but like the previous wall, it was devoid of any structures. The archers walking the wall could take unimpeded aim at any enemy that approached.

It was a ten-minute ride along the inner wall to reach the gate that led to the Sixth Circle, which, like the last one, stood open with a formation of guards at ready.

"Did anyone consider lining up the gates when you built the city?" asked Eldred.

Gundlach smiled. "As I was saying, I am from Wismar."

Once again, the Baron produced his papers, which he shared with the commander of the guards. The commander took a quick glance at Eldred and waved them through.

"He seemed more easily persuaded," commented Eldred as they rode into the Sixth.

"Lady Sihild, the Keeper of the Sixth, is on good terms with Lady Yslana. It was her people in the caravan we were escorting. She will never be making trouble for us," said Gundlach.

Eldred looked around. The buildings were much larger than in the Seventh, though not any more graceful. It could have just been their size, but the walls of the structures glowed red with more intensity than in the outer circles. "Are these noble houses?"

Gunlach gave a short laugh. "No, these are warehouses—not palaces for the nobles, just the stores the city is keeping for its defenses. They are much needed. Your friends surround us and would be starving us out if they could."

"Well, you did invade our lands," said Eldred.

"Not truly," said Gundlach.

"How so?" asked Eldred.

Gundlach waved his hand. "Yes, I guess it might be looking so, but I cannot be saying anything. Anyway, these are the stores. We will not be starving."

Baron Wortwin rode through the buildings to the base of the wall of the Fifth Circle, which matched the height of the wall to the Sixth at fifty feet. They turned to the right and rode on for twenty minutes until they reached the gate.

Only a few dozen spearmen were on guard; the archers on the wall were likewise fewer in number.

Gundlach noted Eldred's interest. "They do not believe any enemy will be advancing so deep into the city."

Eldred smiled, since one had just done so. "Time will tell."

The guards took little time reviewing the Baron's note before letting them through. Thus, they entered the Fifth Circle. The wall to the Fourth Circle was visible down the street ahead of them, but the Baron led them to the left down a street bordered by tall buildings, three stories high. They were not elegant by the standards of Turicum or even Boar's Tusk, but they appeared more finely crafted than the low buildings that Eldred had seen in the outer circles.

"So these are the noble houses?" asked Eldred.

"No, here you will be finding merchants and crafters," answered Gundlach.

"Then why are we meeting Lady Yslana here?" asked Eldred.

"This is as low as she can be descending. Even this is quite shocking, but it would be even worse if she were venturing to the Sixth. The Eighth—that is completely impossible."

Eldred gauged the reddish glow of the buildings they were passing—about the same as the Sixth, stronger than the Seventh and Eighth. "But she has a house here?"

"She is the patron of several merchant families. I am expecting that we will be meeting with her at the home of Mertein, the merchant who manages her stores of grain," said Gundlach. He raised his voice. "Is that not correct, Baron? Are we heading to Mertein's compound?"

"You are correct," said the Baron. "She is making a brief visit there. We will not be having much of her time."

Within a few minutes, they came to a place where the street was crowded with spearmen. Perhaps two hundred men stood in formation outside an open gate that led to a courtyard. As the men parted to let them through, many called out Gundlach's name and saluted him.

"You are popular," said Eldred.

"These are my men," said Gundlach softly. "As were the men I lost at the caravan."

"Well, nobody could have done any better with that situation. At least you got Lady Yslana out alive," said Eldred.

"You did that," said Gundlach.

As they dismounted, a stream of men came forward to greet Gundlach.

The Baron spread his hands. "Do not be taking too long with your reunion, Gundlach. She will be wanting you present for her discussion with the Mercian."

Gundlach nodded as he clasped hands with one of the men. "I will be coming shortly."

The Baron gestured at Eldred. "This way."

✦

AN AUDIENCE

Eldred followed Baron Wortwin through a wide door into a large hall, perhaps a hundred feet on each side. In the center of the hall stood a long wooden table crafted from dark wood. At the head of the table sat Lady Yslana.

She looked different now, immaculately groomed. Her long red hair was done up in curls. She wore a gown of red material that glittered as it caught the light. On her head rested a silver tiara set with gems of many colors. The tiara itself glowed deeper red than anything Eldred had yet seen. As she turned to rest her eyes upon Eldred, she looked the perfect picture of reserved aristocracy—no more impressed with him than if she would be by her most lowly servant, which is probably how she thought of him.

Baron Wortwin bowed low. "I have brought the Mercian."

Lady Yslana gestured with her right hand at the seat to her left. "Be seated."

Eldred took his seat as the Baron took the seat on her right.

Lady Yslana looked Eldred up and down. "You have done well. You defeated Lord Enolf's men in the circle."

"I did," said Eldred, meeting her gaze.

"But now, I hear you are wishing to leave. Why is that?" asked Lady Yslana.

"The contract has been fulfilled. You are safely delivered, and I have demonstrated what anyone with sense would already have known, that a Mercian can out-box your soldiers."

Lady Yslana inclined her head slightly. "You have been accomplishing many goals, but there is still much that is remaining to be done. We already have word from Keeper Enolf requesting another demonstration. Other keepers are echoing his request."

Eldred shrugged. "Well, how many more of your soldiers can be squeezed into a ring?"

The Baron raised his eyebrows. "They are wanting a test with steel."

Lady Yslana fixed Eldred with a stare. "Our contract was clear. You swore by the Son—your minor deity—to be in my service, fighting as is necessary."

Eldred smiled. "The fighting which was necessary is complete, or have you forgotten the incident in the cave? You survived. You made it here to New Wismar, where you are surrounded by your soldiers. Are not Gundlach and your many men at arms enough to guarantee your safety?"

Lady Yslana pressed her lips tight and paused. "Are you needing a richer reward? Or have we finally found a challenge that frightens you?"

Eldred crinkled up his face. "I do not fear Corporian soldiers holding steel. And I am not asking for any reward at all. If you wish me to enter a ring and cut down your soldiers, you might begin by explaining why you see it as necessary."

"Lady Yslana will not be needing to explain herself to you, Mercian!" snapped Baron Wortwin.

"That's true," allowed Eldred. "But if you wish me to duel someone, you must give the reason—the true reason."

As Lady Yslana pondered, Gundlach entered the room and sat next to Eldred. Her gaze flicked over to him.

She took a long breath. "Do you trust the Mercian, Gundlach?"

Gundlach gave a small nod. "I do."

She pursed her lips and stared Eldred in the face. Her pale green eyes looked cold. "I think I understand."

Eldred gave a small shrug. "I did save your life. Three times, by Gundlach's count."

"Three times—such a happening is no accident," said Gundlach.

Lady Yslana smiled. As with the Baron, no warmth reached her eyes. "Then we will all be trusting him. It is you who crafted the plan, Gundlach. You may be explaining it."

Gundlach grinned. "It is very simple. Anyone who was seeing you in battle would be thinking the same thoughts. When I saw you killing those Deirans, even though I was fighting my own battle, it was clear to me how dangerous you could be. You killed two on your own, then came back for two more. The eight of us, and we were all hardy men, had killed none to that point. But you killed four. An impossible feat for any of our soldiers, or so I am declaring."

"You killed your opponent," said Eldred.

Gundlach sighed. "Yes, but not before he was stabbing my lady. But as anyone could see, you were very dangerous."

Eldred tilted his head. "As I told you, I had cause. I did not kill them on a whim."

"No. I was seeing that by the words you exchanged with them. I could also see that your dangerous nature could be solving our predicament. You see, we fear the Deirans, but we are also not fearing them. You seem to be knowing something about this," said Gundlach.

"I heard they all fell down outside your gate," said Eldred.

Gundlach nodded. "Yes, they were falling down. So we do not fear them. Not when we are encountering them in the proper circumstances. And so, as you have been seeing, there are many who would live here without fear, who would be settling here."

"I see," said Eldred.

"But what if there were Mercians such as you—a man who can beat ten of us, a man who has killed nine Deirans? If they are considering such a foe, the comfort of these settlers will be fading. The desire of these weak men for this dismal city will be passing. They will be remembering the true Wismar, the Wismar set deep in Corporia."

"Hmm," said Eldred. "So they won't be expecting the Mercians to fall down as well?"

Gundlach paused and looked at Lady Yslana.

"They will not," she said. "Hence, they will be having the fear Gundlach was so aptly describing."

"So your people will become fearful and leave?" asked Eldred. "Won't they have to brave the same roads you tried with your caravan? Won't that be a more pressing danger?"

Lady Yslana's lips twisted. "In the proper circumstances, we will not be needing to fear those marauding killers."

"The proper circumstance," said Eldred. "Your stone bearer—you call her the Goddess—she provides these circumstances?"

"That is beside the point," said Lady Yslana. "You were asking for our reasoning; we have been explaining every part of it. You must see that our plan is benefiting your people, the Mercians, as much as anyone. We will be leaving. We will be returning to Corporia. And so, many of your people will be finding themselves alive who would otherwise be falling to our swords, to our spears, to our arrows."

Eldred raised his palms. "I can fight a few men if you wish. But the men here won a battle protecting New Wismar against a powerful host of Deirans. Unless they're cowards, I don't think they would abandon the site of such a victory at the sight of me winning a few duels."

"You should be leaving the thinking to us. We are the ones understanding our fellow citizens," said the Baron.

"How many can you be battling at the same time if they are having swords?" asked Lady Yslana.

Eldred leaned back in his chair. "If the ring is the same size, perhaps ten men again. Or eleven, if there is an extra volunteer such as Ditwin."

"Ten is more than we need. If you defeat five strong warriors, the keepers would be finding the result most unsettling," said Gundlach.

"Is not ten more unsettling than five?" asked Lady Yslana.

"He must be winning decisively," said Gundlach.

"He must be winning to begin with," noted the Baron.

Lady Yslana stiffened. "Five, then. Go, Baron, and be making this offer to Keeper Enolf and his doltish friends. As time is short, I am wanting this duel first thing in the morning."

Baron Wortwin rose to his feet. "I will be depositing the Mercian back in the Eighth and settling the matter with Keeper Enolf in short order."

Eldred got to his feet and grinned. "Wish me luck, Lady Yslana."

Lady Yslana gave him a hard look. "You are not supposed to be needing luck."

✹

DEEPER THOUGHTS

Eldred sighed with relief as he came out of the gate back into the disordered maze of pens in the Eighth. The smell of the animals was unpleasant, but the red glow in the air and buildings was weaker, less pressing. It was like stepping out of a hot oven into the cool air.

The group split up at the gate. Gundlach and Eldred turned their horses to the right, headed back to the Iron Gate. The Baron headed left, looking to pay a visit to Keeper Enolf. The rest of their mounted companions turned back, headed to their barracks in the Seventh.

After a moment of enjoying the pleasure of his surroundings, Eldred noticed Gundlach's downcast expression. "Surely someone else can guard me if you would rather not be stuck out here."

Gundlach gave a weak smile. "Here is where I would be choosing to stay."

Eldred waved his hand at a muddy pen filled with squealing hogs. "Here? In the Eighth? Wouldn't you prefer to be with your men in the Seventh? They seemed happy to see you."

"They are good men, the finest soldiers." He looked Eldred in the eye. "They are not blaming me for the slaughter, not like they should."

"You mean at the caravan?" asked Eldred.

Gundlach nodded his head slowly. "Yes, Lady Sihild's caravan. We deserted them. Men, women, children—we left them to a grisly fate. I gave the order that we should be fleeing."

"Well, nobody else would do any better. It was an unwinnable engagement."

Gundlach glanced at Eldred from the corner of his eye. "Lady Yslana would have died if you had not appeared. Our mission would have been ending in failure. You did the impossible."

Eldred shrugged. "You know why I was there—for revenge. We were both lucky to escape."

"I am not believing you required good fortune. Tell me that you could not have been running to safety with the greatest of ease if you had deserted us."

"Perhaps," said Eldred.

They rode on, past a pen of squabbling geese.

"The battle tomorrow is very important," observed Gundlach.

Eldred chuckled. "How can it be, though, really? So, tomorrow I duel five of your soldiers, disarm them and knock them to the ground. You mean to tell me that a whole city will pack up and leave in fear of a Mercian army that they have never even seen? And there is a stone bearer here—your Goddess. I don't believe she is going to run off in terror."

Gundlach nodded. "Yes, as you are seeing it, the plan would smell like the dog, a stink. Nevertheless, the men you will be facing tomorrow, I am having a good sense of who they will be. You will be fighting strong men, each one, each most accomplished. For those citizens here, seeing their defeat will take its toll. And as for the stone bearer, well, you would not be understanding, but her strength is not all that it might appear."

"Is she ill?" asked Eldred.

"No, I should not be saying. I cannot be saying. She is not with illness the way we mortals can be. But she is diminished. Everyone here, in some corner of their mind, knows this."

"Well, I'll do my best," said Eldred.

"I am not doubting you. The man who has killed nine Deirans will not be losing to our soldiers, however decorated."

THE DUEL

Eldred allowed himself to actually sleep that night, resting behind the small bed he had turned on its side, trusting that the Corporians would not turn on him, or that he would be too quick for them if they did. After a good night's rest, he rose to find Gundlach waiting in the common room with a large sword in its sheath lying on the table in front of him.

"You are finally waking," said Gundlach with a smile. He pointed at the sword. "Now you can be seeing this."

Eldred gave the sword a quizzical glance as he joined Gundlach. After a pause, Gundlach pulled the blade free and set it before Eldred.

"Is it not a beautiful blade?" asked Gundlach.

Eldred nodded, though he could not conceal a slight frown. The flawless blade appeared razor sharp. A fine blade but for the nauseating red glow that almost pulsed within it. "A worthy weapon."

Gundlach gestured. "Pick it up. Try taking the feel of it, though please do not be severing the timbers of the roof."

Eldred tentatively lifted the sword. The red essence gnawed at him worse than even the red stone outside the city had, roiling his stomach. "A treasure, though not one for me. I have my own sword."

Gundlach stared at the battered blade that hung by Eldred's side. "You cannot be saying that. This divine creation is having a hundred times the worth of your blade. You must be understanding this."

Eldred gave a half smile and set the sword back on the table. "You are doubtlessly correct, but I will stick with the one I have. I would never switch swords on the eve of a duel."

"Huh," said Gundlach in disbelief. "Well, as you wish. And it is bread, I am guessing. Bread and water for your meal again?"

"Yes, please," said Eldred.

As Gundlach placed Eldred's order with the one-armed inn keeper, Eldred spied one of Enolf guards peering in the door, giving him an appraising look.

"I take it the match is on," said Eldred.

"Yes, and such fine men you will be facing. Men from the Seventh and Eighth."

"Wouldn't the greatest warriors come from the First or Second Circles?" asked Eldred.

Gundlach grinned. "You would only be finding the softest people there. Well, excepting Lady Yslana."

"Will Grimo or Ditwin be among them?" asked Eldred.

Gundlach paused as the innkeeper set down a plate of burnt toast in front of Eldred and returned a moment later with a flagon of water. He continued in a low voice once the innkeeper was out of earshot. "Grimo might be holding his blade in the ring. But Ditwin has succumbed to his injuries. He died in the morning. Enolf's men were telling me."

"Dead?" asked Eldred, putting down the toast. "I barely hit him."

"Yes, well, however you are describing your degree of exertion, we are seeing the effect. Mind you, you were striking him during the contest. Nobody can rightly be complaining."

Eldred took a breath; he almost felt bad for killing the man. "They'll be angry."

Gundlach shrugged. "Angry or not, they will be dueling this morning. We are not having the time to worry about people's feelings."

Eldred took a bite of toast. "Very well, but today's injuries might be a bit worse for them than they might have been otherwise."

"So much for the better. Our goal is to frighten the nobles. A death or two may be opening their eyes."

Baron Wortwin entered the common room bearing a genuine smile for once. "Good morning, Gundlach. Good morning, Mercian. I am trusting that you are standing ready for action."

"I am," said Eldred.

"Very good," said the Baron, with an exaggerated nod. "This morning, you will be dueling in the Third Circle. You may be bringing your sword, but only that."

Gundlach looked up. "The Third Circle?"

"Yes, the Third. Lady Yslana and all of the keepers will be attending along with representatives from the most noble houses. And the acolytes will be there as well, including the Second."

"The Second Circle?" asked Eldred.

"No. She who is the Second—second only to the Goddess herself," said the Baron.

"But not the Goddess?" asked Eldred.

The Baron waved the suggestion away. "No. She is sending the Second. There is no need for her to be coming. Now, let us make haste. Lady Yslana's triumph is at hand."

The Third Circle

Baron Wortwin led the procession as they rode through the city, followed by Eldred, Gundlach and a band of forty horsemen dressed in red finery.

As they were passing through the Sixth Circle, with its drab storage facilities, Gundlach pointed ahead, towards the center of the city. "From what they say, the lawns of the Third Circle are very fine. Of course, they cannot be anything compared to the gardens of Wismar, but—for New Wismar—they might be the finest thing we are seeing."

Eldred grimaced, considering just how grating the red glow might be that close to the center. "I'm sure they'll be nice."

"They should be civilized," commented Gundlach. "I have been hearing there are places to eat in the gardens, and drinking too. You have not been sampling the beer in the Eighth, which I am understanding. But there, in the Third, you must reconsider. The beer there will have been shipped from Corporia. It should not be any of the swill they are brewing in this dungheap."

Eldred smiled. "Perhaps, if I'm still alive."

Gundlach laughed. "You will be breathing. That is the plan, my plan. It is you who must be doing the killing. When they are lining up, I will tell you whom you must choose. As I was telling you, this is bigger than you are understanding. When you are finishing this duel, it will set people in motion. Our mission will be succeeding more expeditiously than we were ever hoping."

"My contract will be completed," said Eldred, looking ahead at the gate to the Fifth Circle, which had just come into view.

"Then you should be making a new contract, a bigger contract. You are a man of talent, of worth. Here, in New Wismar, you are not seeing anything you are valuing. But New Wismar is but the weakest shadow of Wismar itself. When we return—and we will be returning as heroes—everything will be returning to normal. Whatever you are wishing for is there in that most glorious of capitals. Bread and water, it will not do. You will have to be lifting yourself to new levels of enjoyment."

Eldred nodded slightly. "Well, you do make it sound pleasant."

"Not pleasant—glorious, beautiful beyond words. And beyond that"—Gundlach hesitated—"it is where my family is waiting for me. You will be meeting them. We will be working closely together. It will be appropriate."

"I should truly enjoy that," said Eldred, bowing his head deeply. He'd never pictured Gundlach as a family man. Did all of his children walk around carrying small shields? "It would be an honor."

"For them as well. Your actions today will be proving that true."

Once in the Fifth, they pressed straight ahead into the heart of the city instead of turning left as they did previously to visit Mertein's compound. As they passed the establishment of a vegetable monger, the man threw a cabbage at Eldred, which Eldred caught in his right hand.

Eldred laughed, but the Baron took umbrage and drew his sword, advancing on the proprietor and shouting curses. A few horsemen in the escort followed up behind the Baron with their hands on their hilts.

Eldred raised his eyebrow and dropped the cabbage by the curb. "It's just a head of cabbage."

The Baron took no notice and continued his torrent of abuse at the man who stood before him, head bowed.

Gundlach lowered his voice. "You are contracting for Lady Yslana. This action—this abuse—was disrespecting her."

Eldred eyed the man sympathetically. "Will he hurt him?"

Gundlach shook his head. "No. I am thinking this is almost over. The Baron, as always, is following the precise limits that etiquette demands."

Gundlach's comment proved correct. After another minute of the Baron's tirade, his escort turned over several tables of the man's wares and they were back on their way.

They barely slowed as they entered the Fourth Circle. The Baron exchanged a salute with the men on duty and continued onward.

Eldred hesitantly followed after him. The glow seemed to pulse in the air. Each breath pulled contamination into his lungs, though it dissipated after a moment.

"Are you well?" asked Gundlach.

Eldred gave him a distracted look. "Yes. Just getting used to these surroundings."

Gundlach nodded. "You are seeing the administrative buildings. The leaders here would be governing the empire if they were not limited to this outpost." He curled his lip. "Why they are needing so many offices, I cannot be explaining. The king in Wismar has his own officials and magistrates. Oh, and he is Lady Yslana's brother, you should know. She is the most high-born here, though the Keepers do not fully credit her."

"More high-born than the Second or the Goddess herself?" asked Eldred.

"Yes. The acolytes are not being born into their station. Each earns it. Even my own brother is wearing white vestments in Wismer, and we are only boasting a lineage of modest importance."

"How is your Goddess chosen?"

"A test is applied to all who are coming forward when the previous Goddess is passing. She who is strongest with the weaves, the most adept at the mysteries, will be passed the Roter Kristall," said Gundlach.

"I thought the Second is the successor," said Eldred.

"Oh, High Adept Ennlin, the current Second, she is the one who would be endowed. But first they would be testing, all lining up and examining. Not that any would be having a chance against her, such is the light that shines through her."

Eldred raised his eyebrow. "It's all strange to me. The Mother was immortal and never had a successor. She was perfect."

"Well, as the current Goddess is showing, ours are far from perfect."

"Because she's ill?" asked Eldred.

Gundlach waved his hand slowly. "No. I was telling you already. She is not sick. But she is not the right bearer for these times. Now, if the Roter Kristall was passing to the Second, that would be something, an improvement, a cause for celebration."

"Is the Goddess an old woman?" asked Eldred.

"No, I would not be saying that," said Gundlach.

The gate to the Third Circle was only manned by four guards. And the wall was low, barely twenty feet high, with no archers on display as Eldred took note. Beyond the wall, a reddish haze floated above hedge lined paths bordering neatly trimmed green lawns.

Gundlach glanced from side to side as the party started down the widest path that led towards the wall of the Second Circle in the distance. "Not as fine as I was expecting. You would be finding lusher grass in any park in Wismar. Still, I am seeing many plants from our lands." He pointed at a delicate red-leafed tree off the side of the path. "That is one I am recognizing. You will be finding those trees all over Wismar."

Eldred frowned as he examined the alien tree that almost disappeared into the background glow. "How nice."

Presently, they approached a long line of pavilions with flags waving in the slight breeze. Inside each one lounged a collection of Corporians in ornate costumes spun of many hues. Eldred was struck by the spectacle. The Sun People of Turicum had worn bright colors, but the diversity of the Corporians went beyond their garments. As he had seen around the city, they had different colored hair: many shades of black, brown, yellow and red. And their faces were all different shades as well, more colorful than the pale offspring of the Mother.

"One hut for each of the noble families, along with one for the acolytes. The yellow harp on the blue pennant is for Lady Yslana," said Gundlach.

Eldred nodded distractedly as he stared at a woman in one of the tents. She wore the same white costume as the women around her, but she stood out from the others. She had a distinctive appearance, blond hair flashing against her dark features. She was bedecked with jewelry, with silver bracelets, sparkling ruby earrings and a golden tiara set with emeralds as green as her eyes. But what made her stand out from the women around her, indeed from everyone in sight, was the strength of the corruption radiating from her person. Others bore a tinge of the red energy; she reverberated with it.

She turned and favored him with a smile, a rare gesture from a Corporian, but Eldred frowned in return. That day, the day of the battle, she was the one who had stood above the gate and called down destruction on the golden pod, on his father. She shattered the Bond in the other forces, sending Harold and Dederick to flight. And Eldred had fallen only to rise as a weak cripple; so much misery had come from that: Dreven, Hobbie, Henreit all dead, along with many others. She was still beautiful in her Corporian way, but now he saw the danger.

"Who is that?" asked Eldred.

"Oh, that is High Adept Ennlin, the Second. The one I was telling you about," said Gundlach. "But come, Lady Yslana is waiting for us."

Eldred glanced towards Lady Yslana's pavilion before looking back at the Second. "Very well."

The men in the escort took the horses as the Baron, Eldred and

Gundlach approached Lady Yslana, who wore a stern expression as she sat on a couch, surrounded by a bevy of fashionably dressed men and women.

The Baron gave a stiff bow. "I have brought the Mercian."

Gundlach also bowed.

Lady Yslana looked Eldred over with a haughty expression, seemingly disdainful of his patched clothes. "Are you feeling ready?"

Eldred nodded. The red glow was oppressive, but he had grown used to it during the brief ride from the gate. And besides, he would only be fighting Corporians.

"Good," said Lady Yslana. "Baron, check if Keeper Enolf has finally picked his champions. Gundlach, take Eldred to the circle. I am wanting everyone to see that we are having no hesitation in this matter. Eldred, be fierce. You must be winning decisively. We must be setting a tone."

The Baron bowed low. "As you command."

Gundlach flashed her a crisp salute. "I will be doing this, my lady. Come, Eldred."

Gundlach led Eldred through her pavilion out to the other side where a ring of stones about thirty feet wide was marked out in the grass. They walked to the far left side, where Gundlach motioned Eldred into the ring. "This is having the greatest importance, Eldred."

Eldred shrugged and glanced at the Second, who had gone back to socializing with the women around her. "Perhaps it does. You all keep saying that."

Gundlach lowered his voice. "I know you will be winning, but you must not just be winning. You must terrify these people." He gestured at the lines of pavilions. "The five men today, they are nothing. These, in the huts, these are the ones you must be persuading."

"I'll win decisively. I can guarantee you that."

"It is not enough. You need to be killing at least one of them." Gundlach nodded towards one of the nearby pavilions, which sported a red flag with a hawk. "There," he whispered. "The man in golden armor. You must be killing him."

Eldred narrowed his eyes and glanced at the man, who was standing near Keeper Enolf. "Why him?"

"That is Esico. He was owning a past overflowing with glorious deeds even before the founding of this unfortunate city. To see him fall will shake the confidence of even the most ardent of the opposition."

Eldred shrugged. "Why not just embarrass him? I could knock him on his ass, or I could throw him around like a doll. If he's your people's hero, why are you so set on getting him killed?"

"You are not understanding. If you are being rude to him, that will be making them hate you, not fear you. If they are seeing his blood, his entrails, that will be making them frightened, for they cannot imagine such an outcome."

Eldred grimaced. "Let's see what happens. If they press me—and these are your champions—I might have to end up killing someone."

"You killed Ditwin."

Eldred sighed. "By accident. I lightly knocked him. I did not intend him any real harm."

"But you killed him. Why not be lightly cutting Esico's throat?"

Eldred's eyes grew hard. "Do you want this so dearly? Do you hate this man?"

"No, I admire him. We all do. But I am serving Wismar. I would be protecting my city, my family, my wife, my son. If we were having more time, I would be searching for another way—any other way. But time has escaped us, and you must be killing him."

"Very well. Let's see what the battle dictates."

The crowd was beginning to line up along the edges of the pavilions. Baron Wortwin walked towards the ring from Lady Yslana's hut. Gundlach gave Eldred a sharp nod and stepped away from the boundary. The Baron stopped at the stones nearest the huts and swept his eyes across the gathering.

"What is a Mercian?" called the Baron, raising his voice. "Only a few of you are starting to know. Here is one, one from among thousands." He raised his hand towards Eldred. "A common Mercian, even a poor one, to be judging by his belongings. And yet, this simple man has already been defeating eleven of Keeper Enolf's men, throwing them from the ring as if they were children. Today, we will be seeing him with his blade. Lady Yslana herself has seen this man kill nine Deirans, nine of those devilish warriors, a rare feat. You are all understanding what that means. Today, he will be fighting our finest warriors, our strongest men. This will be proving instructive to any who are using their powers of reason, to any who are delving into the consequences. For the thoughtless, I will be making it clear. The time has come to be leaving New Wismar. The time has come to be returning to Wismar, where we all belong."

The crowd stood silently as Baron Wortwin walked stiffly back to Lady Yslana's pavilion. From the pavilion flying the hawk banner came Keeper Enolf, followed by five men, including Esico in his golden armor. Keeper

Enolf stopped before the ring in the same spot where the Baron had stood while the others continued to the right side of the ring and turned to face Eldred. Their passion burned in their eyes.

Keeper Enolf himself gave Eldred a dismissive glance. "Behold the Mercian, a frightening figure to some, especially to those who are unseasoned. I am feeling certain that with the best of intentions these fine people have been working themselves up into a state of alarm, fearing a non-existent army of dullards, for at least that much is known. Are any of you not remembering the childhood tales of these simpleminded brutes? Still, if we are entertaining the question: what if these thick-skulled fools were forming an idea—it might be taking all of them to do it—to be coming here, to be attacking us? What would be the sensible response? Would the reasonable citizen set to running, abandoning their home?"

"No!" Enolf shook his head. "We would be killing such men, such barbarians. But how, you are asking? Did not this frightening man kill nine Deirans?" He pointed to Eldred. "Why, even Lady Yslana witnessed the deed herself. It happened right after the Deirans were slaughtering all of the people in her care, under her responsibility. So how can we be matching up against a foe that can kill so many Deirans?"

He smirked. "Perhaps we have killed even more Deirans. Gentlemen." He raised his hand to his champions.

One by one, the champions pulled forth leather necklaces adorned with rings from their tunics. Esico's necklace bore more than a dozen rings. The others had around seven or eight, except for one man, a short stout man, who only displayed three rings, including a black ring of darkest onyx. Eldred stared at him in shock. He knew that ring; it had belonged to his father.

"Let the fighting begin!" shouted Keeper Enolf.

The Corporians drew their blades and stepped into the circle.

Eldred took a shallow breath and drew his sword. "Father's ring," he muttered. A dark rage built within him as he imagined how those rings were won—pilfered from the defenseless, prizes taken without honor. It would be different now; they faced a man who was still standing.

He shot at the men like an arrow flies from the bow. The short man was on the far left, Eldred batted the other blades away and skewered the man's heart, putting an end to his pitiful existence. As the men tried to reform a line, Eldred stepped in and took the sword arm off the nearest man, just below the shoulder. The man screamed in agony.

Esico charged and swung at Eldred, but his attack was laughably slow.

Such a man would never have touched a Bonded warrior, not one who stood awake on his feet. Eldred grabbed his sword hand and sent him tumbling, though Esico remained within the ring.

Ignoring the screaming man who had fallen to his knees, Eldred turned on the other two warriors. They stood together with their swords raised, wearing uncertain faces. Eldred knocked their blades aside before he took the head of one and then the other. Their headless bodies keeled over, and their precious rings scattered on the ground.

Eldred turned. The one-armed man still screamed, though he looked faint. Esico was up on his knees. Eldred waited while Esico clambered to his feet and took in the state of his allies.

"I don't need to kill you," said Eldred. "You only have to die if you're a dullard." He gestured at the fallen men. "What's left to prove? But first, before I allow you to leave the ring, take off your ill-gotten trophies. For no man as slow and clumsy as you ever killed that many children of the Mother, not in anything resembling an honorable fight."

Esico scowled. "I will be killing you, Mercian."

Eldred lowered his sword. "I'm standing here, Esico. Take off your necklace and leave, or come to me and die."

Esico raised his blade and approached, watching Eldred's sword intently. Eldred stood fully relaxed, his blade by his side, a twisted smile on his face. Esico carefully edged into range, and still Eldred's blade remained idle.

With a cry, Esico began a mighty swing. Eldred let Esico's sword come halfway to his neck before spinning away and striking off Esico's head. Esico's headless body continued the swing as his head tumbled to the ground and rolled away.

The nobles lining the pavilions watched in stunned silence as Eldred knelt down and cleaned his sword on the padding of Esico's armor. He then sheathed his blade and strolled past the man whose arm he had taken—the man finally lay still—to the body of his first victim, the short man. He reached down and yanked free the necklace with three rings and held it over his head.

"A prize fairly taken!" yelled Eldred.

For a moment, nobody said a word. Then an alarmed murmuring spread through the huts. Nobles and guardsmen started to draw their swords while others sought safety behind them.

Baron Wortwin burst out of Lady Yslana's pavilion waving his hands. "Calm yourselves! Everyone should be making themselves calm. Put away your weapons! Nothing has been happening but that which I already promised."

Keeper Enolf stepped towards the Baron. "He murdered them!"

"No," said the Baron. "You did, when you sent them in to fight him. The Mercian only did what we said he would."

Keeper Enolf raised his fist. "I am wanting him put down."

Baron Wortwin raised his palms. "It was a fair fight we were all witnessing. Are you having some objections? Are you wishing to be fighting again? Perhaps you are ready to be loosening your own blade."

From the side, Gundlach beckoned Eldred to come over while the Baron and Keeper Enolf continued their toothless debate. Eldred waved him off and went to each body in turn, collecting the rings. He fit some in his pockets, and cupped the rest in his dripping hands. He was soaked in blood, most of it from the man who had lost his arm, and it stank.

As he was collecting the last ring from under Esico's corpse, Gundlach appeared beside him. "You must be coming now," he hissed.

Eldred straightened up and found himself staring into the eyes of the Second. She wore a slight smile, which surprised him. But as he looked more closely, he saw it was an expression of challenge, not of friendliness. She was not cowed.

"Must I be dragging you away?" asked Gundlach.

"No. That was the last one," said Eldred, pocketing the ring.

Gundlach took him by the arm and led him to Lady Yslana's hut. Lady Yslana motioned them past, and they walked around to the other side where their escort waited.

The noise of people shouting and arguing filled the air as they reached the horses. As Eldred mounted his horse and looked back, he saw the Second was still studying him.

"Well done," said Gundlach. "You were very convincing. Even I was seeing you as a bloodthirsty savage. I thank you for all whom you may have saved."

Eldred glanced down at the leather necklace with the onyx ring. "You should thank Keeper Enolf. If they hadn't shown me their trophies, I don't think I would have done that."

Gundlach gave a pensive smile. "By whatever means, so long as it was done."

EXAMINATION

Upon returning to the Iron Gate, Eldred immediately set to washing his tunic and leggings, leveraging a short stack of crates to preserve his privacy. It took ten minutes to squeeze the last trace of blood from his clothes as he worked under the watchful gaze of a dozen soldiers on the porch and almost a hundred archers perched across on the inner wall. Once his clothes were clean, he used the buckets to rinse himself. Finally, he donned his still wet clothes and went inside to join Gundlach, who was already on his third mug of beer.

Eldred sat, dripping water on the floor, as he held his father's ring under the table, out of Gundlach's sight. It was strange to think of someone taking the ring from King Alfred, almost an impossibility. But that is what had happened. Eldred turned the ring in his fingers, its facets catching the dim light. That short, stout Corporian must have pushed through the crowd to get to Father first. Had he killed Father before claiming his ring? How did he do it— a stab through the back, or did he slit Father's throat? And his character, what sort of man would prey on the helpless?

Gundlach took a sip of his beer. "I am sorry we were not drinking in the Third Circle. You were certainly earning it. I would be enjoying that; we both would."

Eldred blew out his breath. "I don't think I would be welcome."

"No," said Gundlach. "Of that I am certain. Still, you only did as I was asking you, and by doing so, you may have been saving them all."

"So you said," commented Eldred absently. "Do you think they are up there planning the evacuation of the city?"

Gundlach grunted. "No, that will be taking a few days. But the Baron, he has what he needs. He and Lady Yslana can be quite persuasive, and nobody here is clamoring to die, especially at the hands of some terrifying Mercian."

"It should have frightened them," said Eldred quietly.

They were still sitting there in silence a few minutes later when the Second—still marked by her red glow—appeared at the door with one of her acolytes. The one-armed innkeeper took a wide-eyed look at the two priestesses and almost ran out of the common room into the kitchen. Gundlach was also affected, sitting stock still and holding his mug halfway to his lips as if he were made of stone.

"May we be joining you?" asked the Second.

As Gundlach remained frozen, Eldred gestured to the empty stools. "Please do."

She smiled and took a seat at the table as did the woman accompanying her. "This is Adept Agnise. She is here assisting me."

Gundlach set his beer down and bowed his head stiffly.

"Nice to meet you," said Eldred.

"Ah, you are being very courteous," replied Agnise. She was older and heavier than the Second. Her face was surrounded with a bundle of thick brown curls.

"In the ring, that was not my usual…" Eldred trailed off. "Well, would either of you like something to drink?"

Gundlach shot Eldred an exasperated look.

"I would be having a cup of water perhaps," said the Second.

"I might also be drinking the same," added Agnise.

Eldred paused for a moment to see if Gundlach would get the refreshments, but he rose to walk to the bar when Gundlach appeared unwilling to move. He fetched a pitcher of water and two chipped cups for the priestesses, the best cups he could find on the counter.

The women nodded pleasantly when he poured the water but neither made a motion to drink.

"I suppose you don't come here often," commented Eldred.

The Second grinned. "You are correct. If we are coming to the Eighth, it is only for going out through the gate. I have never been visiting an inn such as this." She glanced over the walls with a curious eye. "What of you? Are you finding comfort in this place?"

"No, not really. I find it oppressive. Everything here is a bit off. But unlike you, or so I gather, I find my discomfort growing the deeper I go into your city."

"Interesting. How is this feeling, this oppression you described?" asked the Second.

"Like a hot wind that bakes your skin and dries your throat. I found the Third Circle most unpleasant."

"I wonder how you will be finding the First Circle," said Adept Agnise.

The Second cast a glance at Agnise, who promptly went silent. "I have come down to the Eighth to make a small request of you, Mercian, one that is easily accomplished."

Eldred raised his eyebrows. "Really. What sort or request?"

The Second reached into her purse and pulled forth a small rectangular bar of silverish metal, four inches long and two inches wide, one that pulsed with a red glow even brighter than her own. "I will only be needing a moment of your time. I am wishing you to hold this in your palm." She held out the bar, offering it to Eldred.

Eldred gripped his cup.

The Second smiled broadly. "It would not be hurting you. Here, let me demonstrate." She laid it across her palm and nodded encouragingly.

Eldred studied the swirling patterns of red light that moved across the surface of the bar, wondering if she knew he could see them. It appeared to be a device of great power, but what would it do? He looked up again at her face. She still wore a bright smile, but her deep green eyes possessed an intensity that did not match her otherwise playful disposition.

Eldred gave a light cough. "I don't know. Your artifact seems innocent enough, but I'm somehow uncomfortable with the idea of holding it. As I mentioned, what is pleasant for you can be most discomforting for me."

The Second exchanged a look with Agnise. "Surely a man with your ferocity in the ring can be facing a task of such small measure."

"No. I must decline," said Eldred.

The Second blinked in surprise, and Gundlach's face turned a shade red.

After a moment of silence, Adept Agnise set her hand lightly on the table. "Are you refusing to accommodate the Second?"

"I am under contract to Lady Yslana, not to any other person in New Wismar. As my contract does not call for any holding of metal bars, either large or small, I respectfully decline," said Eldred.

Adept Agnise looked flabbergasted. A grimace broke out across Gundlach's face.

The Second's face relaxed into a more natural smile, and her eyes twinkled with amusement. "You are demonstrating a sound understanding of our ways, our contracts. I am supposing you would be unwilling to enter into a contract with me on this matter. Is that correct?"

Eldred nodded. "I'm a warrior, not a holder of trinkets."

"Then you will no doubt be taking satisfaction in the changes Lady Yslana is negotiating in your contract," said the Second.

"What changes?" asked Eldred.

"When Adept Agnise and I were taking our leave of Lady Yslana, she was negotiating yet another battle for you," said the Second. "One I was requesting. I asked Baron Wortwin if you could be facing one more adversary."

Eldred raised his cup. "Another duel? I only just finished washing the blood of your champions out of my tunic. I suppose I can wash it again if needed."

The Second smirked. "Your opponent's blood will not be a problem." She turned her head; the Baron stood in the doorway, looking at her with his mouth hanging open. "The Baron, the agent of your patron, can be explaining what is needed." She and Agnise rose to their feet. "But I will be saying this, Mercian: if you are having the courage to take the next challenge, you should be asking for much more from Lady Yslana."

Once the priestesses took their leave, Baron Wortwin joined them at the table. The innkeeper reappeared and brought the Baron a cup of ale.

Gundlach, restored to his normal state, addressed the Baron. "Who is there left to fight? Are you truly needing Eldred to kill someone else?"

The Baron sipped his drink and considered Eldred for a moment. "The Second proposed a most intriguing match. Keeper Enolf took up negotiations with me on her behalf. We settled on one more exhibition, a duel in the First Circle against one of the Goddess's guardians."

A smile played on Eldred's lips. "The First Circle—that sounds promising."

Gundlach stared at the Baron. "Are you mad? Who could be winning such a fight?"

The Baron pointed at Eldred. "Perhaps he could. The Second was showing great generosity, great openness of thought. She was emphasizing how much victory by the Mercian could be influencing the Goddess. What demonstration could be better for showing the risks we face by staying here?"

"He has already been doing enough!" snapped Gundlach. "He has been saving Lady Yslana countless times. He has been wrestling Keeper Enolf's men. Today, it was the blades he was facing. He has taken nothing from us so far. Now you have him doing the impossible."

"What we are finding impossible may not be so for him," said the Baron. "That is the basis by which we are engaging everyone. We are not asking everyone to leave the city because we are facing a foe as hardy as you, Gundlach. But you are not who is answering. Mercian, what say you? Will you be facing the Goddess's assistant? Will you be committing to this fight?"

Eldred nodded. "I'll do it."

"There, that is the answer," said the Baron. "Gundlach, it is time to be swallowing your doubts and have the Mercian ready for tomorrow. It will be a day we are not soon forgetting."

Gundlach sighed. "Yes, you may be telling Lady Yslana to have no concerns. I will be seeing it done."

The Baron stood up. "I will be heading back to the lower circles then. It is not just the priestesses who are finding the Eighth unendurable."

Gundlach glared after the Baron as he made his way out.

"Are you angry?" asked Eldred.

Gundlach rubbed his temples. "I am not understanding you. You are taking outrageous risks without a moment's consideration. And for what? You are getting nothing in return."

Eldred smiled. "I'm always ready for a fight. In any case, who is this guardian that worries you so? I tell you, I fear nothing. I feel I could kill anyone, anything."

"We are half agreeing—I know you could be killing just about anyone," said Gundlach. "Tomorrow, we will be seeing if you can kill anything."

※

THE GUARDIAN

They set out the next morning from the Eighth Circle accompanied by the same escort as the previous day: forty mounted soldiers and Baron Wortwin, who took the lead. Eldred and Gundlach followed behind the Baron, riding side by side in silence.

As they passed through the Sixth Circle, with its rows of massive store houses, Gundlach wagged his index finger. "In some cases, a warrior can be earning a great victory just by walking away."

Eldred raised an eyebrow. "I've not seen that myself."

"Well, today you might be seeing it," said Gundlach. "Nobody, excepting yourself, is expecting anything other than a victory by the guardian. They are all expecting it to grab you and crush you to death."

"Is that what you expect?" asked Eldred.

"Perhaps, if you are showing foolishness. If you are staying too long in the ring with it, that unfortunate outcome will come about." Gundlach spread his hands. "The wiser course of action is to be using your speed. I cannot be certain, but I am thinking you are quicker of foot. If you were to stay in the ring for just a moment or two, striking it a few times with your sword, I am expecting everyone would be well content when you withdrew."

"I wouldn't be," said Eldred.

"Perhaps not, but everyone has their limits, just as the Baron said before. And why should it be mattering to you if you step away? You have defeated all the men Keeper Enolf lined up for wrestling. You have killed our greatest champions of the sword as was necessary. Should you be stepping away now, who could be mocking you? It is what we would all be doing in your circumstances."

Eldred smiled. "I'll bear your advice in mind."

In the Third Circle, they rode past the ring that had been set up for the previous day's duel. The adjacent pavilions had been stripped of their banners and tables and stood empty.

"That setting worked well enough. Why not have today's duel there?" asked Eldred.

"A guardian will never be appearing far from the Goddess. Today, if it happens so, will be the first time I am seeing one who is not standing by her side. This is an exceptional proceeding," said Gundlach.

"I take it you have never seen one defeated," said Eldred.

"I have never even seen one fighting," said Gundlach.

"Then why are you so confident that it can defeat me?"

"You will know once you see it," said Gundlach. "Such a thing cannot lose."

The boundary to the Second Circle was a wall of red stones waist high— stones similar enough to those scattered outside the outer gate that it seemed to be the source of the same. Unlike the previous walls, it was set with small passages twenty yards or so apart. Though it appeared to be an insignificant barrier and it was unguarded, it glowed with an unrelenting light.

Eldred tensed up as he rode past, feeling the corruption pressing about him, clouding the air.

Gundlach looked over and noted his discomfort. "Oh, is this what you were describing to the Second?"

Eldred shuddered. "This is far worse than the Third Circle."

"Can you still be fighting? Perhaps we can be putting it off."

"No. I'll be fine. It'll just take me a moment to adjust."

Gundlach eyed Eldred. "Why be staining so? Why not simply be turning back? We can explain the discomfort."

"I will see the First Circle. I will examine this guardian. Only after I have done both will I consider turning back," stated Eldred.

They rode on through clusters of fine buildings, each with its own grounds.

"We have finally been reaching the homes of our nobles," said Gundlach. He gestured off to the left. "I believe Lady Yslana has an estate off in that direction."

Eldred looked where he indicated, taking shallow breaths to limit the corruption in his lungs. "How does she have so much here if you and she just arrived?"

"It is the Baron. He has been living here for a year. Lady Yslana and her house have not always been opposing the settlement of New Wismar. It is recent developments that are changing her mind."

Eldred nodded. It took effort, but it was getting easier to breathe. The air felt dry and scratchy on his skin, but it was bearable.

They rode another ten minutes through the reddish haze, which hid everything from sight beyond a few hundred yards.

"We are entering the First Circle," announced Gundlach.

Eldred looked around. "Where is the boundary? I don't see anything to mark it."

"They have not been placing any barriers, but all these buildings moving forward house the acolytes. You can see if you look."

Examining one of the nearest buildings, Eldred noted a few white robed men tending to a garden. The building behind them looked as fine as any in the Second Circle. "Your acolytes stand above the nobles?"

Gundlach frowned. "Only on matters of the Goddess. On matters of trade or the kingdom, the nobles are always getting their way. Well, unless the Goddess is having a strong opinion. But usually she is not caring about such things."

"She cares about this city, though. Doesn't she?"

"Yes," said Gundlach.

Continuing onward, they came to an enormous red dome set in a paved square clear of buildings.

"The home of the Goddess," said Gundlach.

They paused at the edge of the flagstones and dismounted. Only the Baron, Gundlach and Eldred continued on.

The first step on the stones created a twisting sensation in Eldred's stomach. They had much greater strength than the scattered stones outside the outer gate. In a state of discomfort, Eldred followed the other two men across the square to where a large body of people stood facing the dome in a long line.

As they came closer, the people became clearer through the haze. Eldred spotted Lady Yslana, Keeper Enolf and Keeper Renz in the line. None of them spared a look at Eldred or the Baron; they all had their eyes trained on the dome.

When they reached Lady Yslana, standing just behind her, she turned and gave Eldred a brief look over. "Is he ready?" she asked quietly.

"Yes, my lady," replied the Baron in a hushed voice.

She nodded and returned her gaze to the dome.

Everyone in the line stood silently with their attention focused on the dome, their faces expressionless. Eldred examined the Baron and found he glowed a trifle redder than before. It was not anything like the hot glow of the Second, but it seemed as if he was glowing more than he had back in the Eighth Circle.

No such glow issued from Gundlach, who had only recently come to the city. But Keeper Enolf had a shine to him, appearing a shade brighter than the Baron now that Eldred studied the two standing together.

Lady Yslana outshone Gundlach, even though she too had just arrived in New Wismar. Eldred frowned in surprise. He hadn't noticed anything from her the previous day that he could remember. She also looked off, like there was a different air about her. He couldn't say what. She shone almost as bright as Enolf.

Eldred was still studying her when a gate opened in the dome a hundred feet in front of them. Eldred strained to see through the red haze. The Second was there, glowing more brightly than ever. A dozen acolytes followed after her carrying red cubes, each six inches on a side. Stomping along after them came a creature.

At first, Eldred only saw its eyes, which looked like two small spheres of liquid fire. As it walked stiffly forward, its smooth squat shape took form in the haze. It stood as tall as Eldred but was much broader and thicker. It wasn't wearing any clothes, but there was no sign of its manhood, just a smooth patch between its legs. As it approached, following the women, Eldred could see it lacked a mouth and ears. It truly was not a man; perhaps, it was not even alive.

The Second stopped ten feet in front of Lady Yslana, and her acolytes formed a line behind her. The guardian—for that must be what it was—came to rest behind the women, staring ahead blankly, no expression possible on its featureless face.

The Second smiled almost sympathetically. "We are now coming to the real matter, the true test of the Mercian. Are you certain you wish to be continuing? The chances are appearing high that your servant will be grievously injured."

Lady Yslana stood straight as a rod. "A risk I am prepared to take. What of the Goddess? Is she prepared to be returning to her proper station in Wismar should the Mercian be victorious?"

"The Goddess will be doing whatever she wishes to do," said the Second softly. "But we are all interested to see just how long the Mercian can elude the guardian's grasp. Should he put up a good fight, the Goddess will be taking note. She has been asking about this man and his activities."

Lady Yslana cast a quick look back at Eldred, who was studying the guardian. "If you are scuttling away from this fight, it is your people who will be paying the price," she whispered.

Eldred raised his eyebrows. "When have you seen me scuttle away from any fight?"

The Second clapped her hands together. "Place the blocks."

The acolytes spread apart, forming a circle thirty feet wide with the guardian in the center. Each set her block down on the ground and took two steps back, extending their arms towards their nearest partners, forming a circle outside the circle.

"The ring is formed, Mercian. Are you accepting this contest? Again, I am warning you. I am only seeing an outcome where you are dead or crippled," said the Second.

Everyone standing in the line turned their heads to watch Eldred. As Eldred cast his eyes across the crowd, he caught a slight shake of the head from Gundlach. Nonetheless, he stepped forward, passing through the line of spectators and stepping around the nearest acolytes to enter the ring. There was no motion from the guardian, which continued to look straight ahead.

"He has no weapon," said Eldred.

"He is a weapon," said the Second.

A smattering of muted laughter came from the crowd. Eldred turned to see Keeper Enolf and Keeper Renz grinning. Gundlach bore a somber expression. Lady Yslana retained her imperious poise.

Eldred shrugged. "Very well. I'm ready."

The Second nodded. "You can be starting whenever you wish."

Eldred narrowed his eyes and glanced back at the motionless creature. "Now?"

"As you like," said the Second.

Eldred drew his sword, but still the creature did not move; it just stood there, unblinking. Eldred took five strides forward and brought his sword down in a powerful blow on the creature's head. There was a terrible clang and his sword snapped off a few inches past the hilt. Reflexively, Eldred jumped back from the golem, still holding the hilt of his sword. The blade sailed through the air before clattering on the flagstones.

The creature remained motionless. There was another burst of laughter from the crowd.

"Go on, Mercian. Your blade is shattered, but can you not be wrestling? You were so proud of winning only two days ago!" called Keeper Enolf.

Eldred huffed. The thing had a hard shell, but perhaps he could twist its arm off. He dropped the broken sword and advanced slowly on the guardian, which showed no interest in his approach. Finally, Eldred darted forward and grabbed its left arm above the wrist, taking the smooth stone-like arm in his hands. With effort, Eldred began to pull its arm up, twisting it outward. As he did, the creature's head swiveled around and its beady red eyes stared dispassionately at Eldred's face.

It stiffened its arm, resisting Eldred's twisting motion and reached out with its right hand and dragged it across Eldred's shoulder, leaving a trail of blood. Eldred recoiled in pain. While its arms and chest were smooth, its palms were ragged and sharp, like a handful of razors.

As Eldred stepped away, the creature whirred into motion, bounding after him, reaching out with its bloody hand for Eldred's face. He ducked away and started backpedaling, but almost immediately closed on one of the acolytes standing behind her block. Eldred turned direction, barely staying in the ring.

"Your turn to be dying, Mercian!" shouted someone.

It sounded like Keeper Enolf, but Eldred had no time to check. He was now running backwards around the outer edge of the ring while the creature charged after him. At first, it took his full attention to not step out of the ring, but after a few moments, Eldred got the hang of it. It helped that he was much faster than the creature, though the narrow confines of the ring limited this advantage.

It was a strange engagement. Eldred knew he would not tire for hours, but he soon got the sense that the same was true for the creature. As he buzzed around the ring with his foe in close pursuit, Eldred glanced over the bemused crowd, who appeared mesmerized by the scene. Gundlach made a small motion with his hand, unseen by the other spectators who followed the whirling combatants on every step of their revolution.

To quit, to step out—that was the meaning of Gundlach's motion, Eldred was sure. As he ran in reverse, he could see the sense of it. The golem almost seemed to gain energy as it dashed forward through the clinging red haze, the same haze that Eldred felt might eventually drain him.

He could step out, though he doubted that would stop this creature that seemed to do what it wanted. He could run past the laughing crowd as the simulacrum chased him from the First Circle, but he didn't want to.

Instead, Eldred stepped away from the edge and ducked under the creature's outstretched arm. He planted his feet and gave the creature a powerful shove just above its waist. The creature should have flown right out of the ring, but suddenly, its feet held fast on the paving stones. It bent over the edge of the ring, like a tree bending before a strong wind, before rising up to standing again. Eldred caught a glance of an intense red glow from where its feet were glued to the corrupted ground. Unfair!

The creature started towards Eldred, who kicked it hard in the chest towards the edge of the ring. Once again, the creature bent over backwards, but its feet held fast, locked down by the power of the infernal Goddess.

As Eldred paused, caught on this thought, the creature strode forward and grabbed him. Eldred grabbed it back. Its cruel hands ripped at Eldred's back as he went to lift it. He could feel it rising up in his arms, but then, like a cord stretched to the limits of its length, he could lift it no more. Once again, its feet were stuck to the ground, locked by that Motherless power.

Eldred went to squeeze it, but he may as well have tried to squeeze a rock. And the pain was growing as it tried to dig into Eldred's back with its knife-like fingers. With a scream, Eldred pushed up on its armpits, driving himself down to the ground and rolling away, out of its deadly grip.

The creature came after him, but Eldred shot up on his feet and the circling resumed. The blood was running down his back, dripping down on the flagstones and making them slick. It was a worry for him as he ran backwards around the small circle, shutting out the cries for his blood. He doubted the wet flagstones would trip up the creature.

As he ran, he could feel the cuts and tears sealing up. He'd lost some blood, but he still had enough left; all he needed. He could step out of the ring and walk away, but he didn't want to. And then he saw it on the ground, ten feet inside the ring—the discarded hilt of his sword with a short stub of steel still extending from it.

On the next pass, he dove in reverse towards the hilt, throwing his feet out behind him and following after with his chest. As he passed over the hilt, he snatched it up in his hand and planted his feet, barreling back into his pursuer. The creature thrust out its blood-drenched hands for Eldred's throat, but Eldred dodged its attack and drove his short steel into the creature's left eye, shattering it, before ducking to the side.

The creature tripped and fell flat on the erstwhile friendly pavestones, where it slid a short distance. It lay there for a moment, as if considering what to do, then climbed back to its feet. It turned and faced Eldred, but only its right eye glowed in its featureless face, one eye left to smash.

Eldred dashed forward before the creature could even lift its arms and stabbed the remaining eye, stabbing one, two, three times before the lens cracked and fell away. The creature did get its hand up to rip at Eldred's chest, drawing some blood, but Eldred backed out of reach before taking serious damage.

The creature came on, waving its hands in wild motions in the apparent hope that Eldred might choose to stand close. Eldred did not. He stayed well back from the rudderless creature, gripping his broken sword.

The creature moved even faster than it had previously, but it could plainly no longer see, for it was bounding away from Eldred, headed alarmingly for one of the young acolytes who stood at the edge of the ring. The crowd was yelling, but before anyone could take a step, the golem had swiped its hand and landed a blow on the poor girl. She was thrown off her feet and fell, rolling across the ground.

It left the ring, heading right into the crowd. Eldred clutched the hilt in his hand and stared after the charging simulacrum. He'd taken its eyes; he didn't see what else he could do. The crowd scattered in all directions, but three spectators were struck by its frantic blows. They stayed where they fell, a mess of crushed bones and ripped flesh.

As the creature ran into the distance, a few people rushed to help the fallen victims. The Second kneeled by the side of her acolyte—who had the Mother's own luck and was still breathing—while Lady Yslana and the Baron hovered behind her. The other acolytes left their red blocks and ran to the side of the injured spectators, tearing strips of cloth from their own white robes to bind their wounds. These others appeared much worse off than the acolyte. It likely came down to which side of the guardian's hand hit you; the back was smooth as polished stone; the front would slice you a dozen ways, as Eldred's back bore witness.

Eldred was standing in the ring, clutching his broken sword, when he noticed Gundlach give him a small wave. Eldred started towards him but stopped when Gundlach shook his head.

Gundlach approached Baron Wortwin and whispered something to him. The Baron looked up from the Second, who was kneeling next to the fallen acolyte, and gave Eldred an uncertain look. Gundlach whispered something again, and the Baron gave a loud sigh. With apparent reluctance, the Baron reached into his pocket and pulled out a wad of folded papers.

Gundlach gave the Baron a curt nod and plucked the papers from his hand and walked quickly towards Eldred. He continued walking right past, giving a quick motion to Eldred to follow. "Come with me. They will not be wanting you here for this."

Looking past the concerned face of Keeper Enolf, Eldred could see the guardian still lumbering off into the distance. He turned to walk beside Gundlach, still holding the broken hilt in his hand. "What about the guardian?"

"Him? Oh, the Goddess will deal with that. Nobody else can be helping. Are you well? You are looking strong."

Eldred nodded. "I lost some blood, and I need a bath. How is the acolyte?"

"Battered but breathing. The Second will be seeing to her recovery." A furtive smile crossed Gundlach's face and he lowered his voice. "By the way, most amazing, most incredible. That fighting, that wrestling, you will have been winning them all over now. Even Keeper Enolf is losing his words. When he is being silent, you know the argument is won."

"Good," said Eldred. He wiped away a drop of blood that was running down his arm. His back—he could feel the sodden tatters of his tunic sticking to his flesh. Eldred blinked at the red glow of the Goddess's dome, which lay in front of them. "Are we going in there?"

"Oh, yes. For I am finally having the solution, and I am having the means to see it done." Gundlach waved the papers in the air.

"You are?"

Gundlach beamed. "I am."

DESCENT

Each step closer to the dome was a step into the thicker and heavier red haze. For once, Eldred had to hurry to keep up, such was the speed that Gundlach was pacing towards the open gate.

Three young male acolytes in white robes stood by the gate, watching Eldred and Gundlach approach with unhappy expressions.

Gundlach practically ran ahead to hand the nearest one his papers. "Check these with your master. He will be approving our entry."

The man looked them over with an air of disdain. "You will be waiting here." Then he retreated back through the gate.

Gundlach gave Eldred a half suppressed grin. "It will only be taking a minute."

Eldred nodded and looked out from the dome. He couldn't see the guardian anymore. The injured acolyte was on her feet, standing shakily and holding onto the Baron for support. The Second had moved on to the more seriously injured spectators; perhaps she possessed healing arts. Keeper Enolf appeared to have found his tongue and was arguing with Lady Yslana while the others looked on.

After a moment, a few dozen acolytes, both male and female, came running past Eldred carrying gurneys—more help for the wounded. Maybe they would live.

Eldred was still staring after the jogging acolytes when an elderly man in ornate white vestments marked with three dark red stripes on his sleeve appeared, accompanying the acolyte with whom Gundlach had spoken. The man held the papers limply in his hand as he looked out towards the scene of the disaster with a concerned expression, but as he turned back to Gundlach, his green eyes took on a playful glint from within their wrinkled sockets.

"Gundlach, what can you be meaning with these papers?" asked the man.

Gundlach gave a broad smile. "Adept Burgold, you old coot, my brother sends you his greetings."

Burgold's face softened slightly. "I am taking it that Adept Meginard is well, then."

"So I am hoping," said Gundlach. "Such things are no longer certain now, not even for the favored servants of the tower."

"I am seeing a lesson there," said Burgold.

"As am I, though I am finding a different one, I expect," said Gundlach.

Burgold shook the paper in his hand. "So, what am I making of this?"

"You should be reading it clearly, a pass with the blessings of Lady Yslana. Would you be so kind as to be showing us the way?" asked Gundlach.

Burgold furrowed his brow and looked Eldred in the eye. "You are wanting these things, are you?"

Eldred frowned. "What things?"

Gundlach laughed. "He is not yet knowing." Gundlach tapped the side of his head. "I have been figuring it out—a means of closing a difficult contract. Not another word, please, Burgold. This is a surprise."

"If you are saying so, Gundlach. I know we will not be missing this junk," said Burgold. He beckoned to Gundlach and walked back through the gate into a cloud of red corruption.

The arc of the dome rose in front of them up to a height of two hundred feet and crossed a span of half a mile. Eldred could see the sun glowing dimly through the dome to the south; it was some kind of reddish glass awash with streams of energy even brighter than the corruption in Lady Yslana's tiara.

Five equally spaced towers sat in a circle within the dome, each starting wide and squat before narrowing down to a slender tip that pushed up through the roof. These were set near the outer part of the dome which was lower, but still rose to a regal height of more than a hundred feet. Past the towers, the ground sloped downward towards a circular depression directly under the highest part of the dome,

Hundreds of acolytes were visible throughout the space, some walking on the paved paths that connected the towers, others sitting on benches engaged in conversation with their peers.

"Are you not impressed, Gundlach?" asked Burgold.

Like Eldred, Gundlach was looking back and forth, taking in the view.

"The Red Tower in Wismar is standing taller than all of these buildings stacked on top of each other. It is also wider."

Burgold nodded. "It will be taking some time to match the greatest monuments of Wismar, but I am feeling that we have made a decent start. The Goddess herself fashioned the dome, which is a new creation, perhaps unique in all the world. The workmen piled up the materials around the perimeter, and she willed it into place. The towers, though, were built using the old ways, each identical to the others and modeled on the king's fortress in Wismar."

"But standing with reduced stature," said Gundlach.

Burgold extended his hand towards the center of the dome. "There is more to a building than its height. Fortunately for us, we need not be climbing the precipitous stairways of the towers. Unfortunately for us, your rubbish is lying in even more remote depths."

"In a garbage pit?" asked Eldred.

Burgold smiled. "No. Except for our destination, the most holy places are lying below. Well, let us be getting to it. You have a pass from Lady Yslana, even if you are lacking the sense to appreciate the works of the Goddess."

They started down the path towards the center, walking past clumps of white-clothed acolytes of all ages, an equal mix of men and women. The acolytes studied Eldred with friendly interest as he passed; many smiled and a few waved at him.

Eldred drew close to Gundlach and whispered. "Do they know I defeated the guardian?"

"I am feeling certain they do," answered Gundlach.

"They don't seem to fear me," said Eldred.

Gundlach nodded. "They are fearing nothing. They are nestling in the bosom of the Goddess; there is nothing more they could be wanting. It is the nobles in whom we must be instilling fear. If they are fleeing, then the Goddess and all of her acolytes must be following."

"Very well," muttered Eldred as he gave a strained half-smile to one of the waving Corporian women.

After they passed the buildings, the crowds dissipated and the path came to a series of circular terraces, each ten to twenty feet wide, that fell away steeply into a depression ten stories deep. At the bottom stood a single five-sided building set in the middle of a circular patch of reddish grass a hundred yards wide. It was a simple stone building with only one floor, not large, no more than forty feet across. Paths extended from each side of the building, running up the terraces with hundreds of stairs.

As Eldred stood at the top, looking down, he had the sense that if he tripped, he would roll down the stairs to the bottom, tumbling into the soldiers who lounged on benches set out on the lawn. These were the first soldiers that he had seen since entering the dome. They didn't look particularly alert.

Burgold grinned and gestured at the scene. "The stairs I was promising you. More challenging than those in the buildings, at least for my old legs. But the view is always engaging." He looked at Gundlach. "No garden in Wismar can be matching this. The gardeners have been planting each terrace with its own theme, realized through a beautiful rendering of our plants, trees and shrubberies. And artists too have been contributing. If you have sharp eyes, you can make out unique sculptures on each level. Many acolytes spend their rest days sitting on a bench in front of their favorite statue. The practice deepens their minds."

Eldred raised his eyebrow. There were many sculptures strewn across the terraces, and a few had white-clad acolytes sprawled on the grass next to them or sitting on a nearby bench. Most were simple shapes such as a stone pyramid, of which there were many examples across the levels. Other popular subjects included pentagons, cylinders and cubes. They looked well fashioned and carved from handsome stones but hardly had the look of anything that would improve anyone's thinking if they stared at it.

And the supposed themes of the gardens were just a mixing of alien red-leafed plants and trees with beds of red flowers that had just a smattering of yellow blooms. It looked unnatural to Eldred under that unholy dome. Humming with red energy, it looked like the maw of a creature dug into the Mother's sweet earth.

Gundlach, though, seemed lost for words. Finally, he muttered a response about the beauty of the gardens under the Red Tower that were favored by a passing river. Burgold rolled his eyes and started down the steps.

Eldred worried for the old man and was ready to dash forward and grab him if he slipped. Such worry proved unnecessary. Burgold was slow and took several breaks during which he pointed out features of the gardens, but he never seemed close to tripping.

Each level down increased Eldred's sense of disquiet. All the surroundings disappeared behind the upper edges of the pit, making the world seemingly consist of only the alien terraces and the dome that loomed over it. The strength of the corruption increased with each step down.

Halfway to the bottom, after a lengthy exposition by Burgold about a work of art—a ten-foot high arch with the favored pyramid balanced on top—that was close to the stairs, Eldred turned to Gundlach. "Are you certain that I want something down here?"

Gundlach smiled. "I am feeling certain you will like it more than you care for our sculptures. Are your people not having art?"

"No, we have that stuff, but it's people with their bodies and faces, things of that sort. Mostly of dead people, to remember them by. Don't your artists make anything like that?" asked Eldred.

Burgold clasped his hands in front of his waist. "The Goddess sculpts us. Would you have us imitating her work?"

Eldred started down the steps. "I'm just saying that it's an arch with a pyramid on top of it. It's a bit different from a pyramid by itself or a pyramid set on a column, but not enough to hold my interest."

"Perhaps you are missing the concept," said Burgold.

"How could I?" asked Eldred.

After another stop, this for an upside down pyramid, they neared the bottom. The soldiers had seen them approaching, and a contingent waited for them by the stairs. A few looked strangely familiar to Eldred, but he had seen hundreds of Corporians over the last few days.

As Burgold stepped off the last stair, one of the men stepped forward. He was a rough-looking man with shifty eyes, one of the soldiers whom Eldred felt he recognized.

"What are you bringing these men here for, Adept Burgold?"

Burgold pulled the papers from his pocket and handed them over. "They have a pass authorized by Lady Yslana, Captain Kunz. I am taking them down to one of the storage rooms."

Kunz gave Eldred a hard look as he reached for the papers. "He is looking terrible after his beating. What business is he having here?"

"He won," said Gundlach. "He defeated the guardian. I am bringing him here to close out a contract for Lady Yslana. It is not something you will want to be interfering with."

Kunz frowned and studied the papers. After a moment, he abruptly handed them back to Burgold. "These look in order." However, he and his men remained blocking their path.

"Are you seeing some problem?" asked Burgold in a genial tone.

"This man is a danger," said Kunz. "I saw him cut down five good men yesterday. I cannot be letting him down here with his sword."

"This broken thing?" asked Eldred, pulling the hilt out of his belt. He found himself taking a strong dislike to the captain. He felt a powerful urge to punch the man in the throat.

Kunz motioned to the man standing next to him in line. "Take it from him."

This man, a slightly pudgy man with red hair whom Eldred also felt he recognized, stepped forward and stuck out his hand.

Without a thought, Eldred found himself bringing his arm back to slash at the man's face. He stopped himself, surprised at what he was doing, and instead handed over the broken sword after taking a ragged breath.

Kunz glanced over the broken blade. "He was defeating the guardian with that?"

Gundlach nodded. "Eldred injured the guardian, which then went running out of the ring. It struck a young acolyte and several people in the crowd. The Second was there, though. I am feeling confident that she will be taking good care of them."

"Good," said Kunz. He paused for a moment. "This is a day of strange happenings, and not the least strange part of it is this odd business. I am not meaning to take any chances. I will be accompanying you below."

Burgold nodded. "As you are wishing, Captain."

Kunz signaled to his men and started back towards the building.

Gundlach leaned close to Eldred as they followed after. "Are you feeling well? You were seeming a bit strange there for a moment, the way you were staring at the guards."

Eldred grimaced. "I'm well. I just had to catch my breath after the stairs."

"Oh," said Gundlach, who looked Eldred over with concern.

The building had open arches on each of its five sides. Kunz and ten of his men went ahead and started down a circular staircase that descended into the floor.

Eldred paused at the top step, contemplating the corruption which practically radiated from the steps. "How far down does this go?"

Burgold stepped down past him. "You will be having the good fortune of finding out for yourself."

Eldred hung back, taking one last breath before descending into the haze. As he looked up, he noticed a circular plate of metal on the roof over the stairs that shone bright with the corruption, seemingly as bright as the dome. He was in the depths of it now and sinking deeper into the corruption that plagued this stretch of the Mother's land. He wiped his brow and stepped down after Burgold. Gundlach brought up the rear.

Square metal plates radiated a dim red light for the Corporians to see by. Of course, Eldred had no need for them. They shuffled down around two hundred steps by Eldred's count before they came out in a room with tall ceilings that matched the floor layout of the room above.

Five wide passageways led out of the room. One stood out. It was just as tall and wide as the others, but a small gathering of people sat on benches to either side of it: four acolytes and two soldiers.

Eldred drew himself up as he caught sight of one of the acolytes. The man was slight in build, but of the usual Corporian height, about two inches shorter than Eldred. The man had cruel green eyes. Eldred felt an overwhelming desire to break the man's neck. He took a step towards the man before he stopped and clasped his hands, wondering what had come over him. The corruption was so strong here, was this what it was doing? It was almost reaching his lungs before he could clear it.

Eldred stood, staring at the floor and focusing his thoughts as the men conversed and looked over the papers. Kunz's grating voice kept rising boorish and loud while Eldred kept his hands in a tight grip and made an effort to relax his shoulders. He flinched when someone tapped him. When he looked up, he saw Gundlach grinning.

"Almost there," said Gundlach.

Burgold slowly led the group off down one of the corridors across from the one where the men had been sitting. Gundlach and Eldred followed in the middle of the pack of soldiers. Kunz was in the back. Eldred kept his eyes forward, avoiding the sight of that disgusting man and wondering why he felt so strongly about him. The man had come to the previous day's duel; what of it? Why did he want to pummel Kunz's face to a bloody pulp?

They passed several apparent openings off the side corridor, each blocked and filled in with some kind of red metal. Eldred could see the energy flowing through the substance, but there were no door handles or locks that he could discern. After going two hundred feet down the passage, Burgold stopped and touched one of the openings. Kunz's men in front of Eldred stepped to the other side of Burgold so that Eldred was standing right next to the adept when an inner door, only slightly smaller than the opening, took shape. It formed as if someone was engraving it into the metal.

Once its lines came clearly into shape, Burgold gave the door a slight push, and it swung open, revealing a huge room full of tables stacked with items.

"You said you might be seeing something small," blurted Gundlach in a merry tone. "Lady Yslana has been giving permission that you might be taking something from this room. We can finally be fulfilling the contract."

As Eldred turned towards Gundlach, he caught sight of Kunz's glowering face and felt a surge of rage. He gave a sharp nod and stepped into the room to get away from the captain before he lost control. He was standing there for a moment before he realized what was there. The table nearest to him was covered with pieces of armor, Deiran armor.

"Why all of that would be too confining; it is far too small," said Burgold.

Gundlach laughed. "The armor, yes. But their weapons, that is what will be interesting him. Is that not right, Eldred. You were desiring the weapons of the Deirans you slew. This is what we have been taking from all the Deirans we have killed."

"Oh," said Eldred with a distracted air. He moved over to the table. As Burgold had noted, the armor was crafted for Deirans, not someone with Eldred's large frame. He shifted the armor around, checking it. There were flecks of dried blood everywhere, but whether they came from Deirans or Corporians, he could not tell.

He walked to the next table, which was covered with open boxes filled with knives, and continued on. He was not looking for a dagger. But as he passed the next table, which also stored a collection of knives, a strange glow from one of the boxes caught his eye. It was not the corruption, the foul red light that permeated everything in the underground lair, but a pale purple light that drew Eldred closer. He started digging through the daggers, careful of their sharp edges. Towards the bottom of the box, he found a glimmering knife.

Eldred took the blade carefully in his hand, holding it up to study its construction. Just as the hateful red currents flowed through the dome somewhere above them, a stream of purple energy flowed out from the hilt along the edge of the blade until it reached the tip, where it reversed itself and returned to the hilt, which seemingly contained a pool of energy.

It was the most amazing work of craftsmanship that Eldred had ever beheld. He stared at it, mesmerized, following the flow of energy around and around and around. It brought him comfort in that terrible place. He had been staring at it for some time when he heard a faint shout that broke its hold over him.

He turned to see Burgold and Gundlach standing in the doorway, with Kunz's ugly face looking on from behind them. From their expressions, it was clear the sound had not come from them. As Eldred stared at Kunz, he found himself hating Kunz's mouth. Kunz wasn't smiling, but somehow Eldred knew he had a nasty smile. If Kunz had shown it at that moment, Eldred wouldn't have been able to help himself.

"Is that knife what you are taking, Eldred? We should not be staying too long down here," said Burgold.

"Ahh, no. I mean, yes, but I'm looking for something else," said Eldred.

"What would that be?" asked Burgold.

"I am seeking a sword," said Eldred.

"That is right," said Gundlach. "The guardian was costing him his blade. He is due a replacement."

Burgold smiled. "Very well. I am seeing many you could choose from. If you pick one, we can be going."

Kunz groaned. "Just be taking one. And do not be staring at it for ten minutes."

Eldred took no notice of Kunz and started his search. It would be somewhere in the room, he was certain; he could almost feel its presence, but where? There were more than forty tables piled with armor, swords and daggers. He paced through the room, opening every chest, shifting the armor and digging through weapons.

Between two tables, he found a potent sword lying flat on the floor. Its purple light washed around the blade, a named sword without doubt. He was about to grab it when he saw the hilt was wrong. No. That was not it. He passed it by, paying the grumbling of the waiting men no mind.

He could ignore the whining men easily enough, but other sounds seemed to flit around the chamber. Halting cries, weak groans and feeble screams came so soft that he was not sure if he was really hearing them. Each time he paused and looked for the source. Sometimes it seemed to be right next to him. Other times it came from the edges of the room or from outside the chamber. He never saw a thing. He tried to put the sounds from his mind and sped up his search. Was it here? Or had some greedy Corporian taken the sword as an ill-gained trophy?

Eldred was losing hope—he had searched almost all of the room—when he found it standing in the corner leaning against the wall. The scabbard hid most of the light, but a deep purple hue glowed around the hilt. This was the blade, the king's sword, the sword of his father.

As he drew Capito from the scabbard, the light poured out from the blade. The power felt extraordinary, sweeping up his arm and into his heart, flowing into him and flowing back out. He could see his own heartbeat in the pulsing of the sword. He took a breath and smiled. He had never seen Capito glow, nor had he ever heard anyone say it had. Was it only he who could see it? In the past, Regula, who had blessed it, must have seen it just so.

"Are you finally picking one?" came Kunz's abrasive voice.

Eldred ignored him and studied the blade. He was still staring at the blade when he heard one of the voices, thick with pain, seeming to whisper in his ear.

"Help me."

Eldred jerked around. Nobody was there. The Corporians had not crossed the threshold.

"Who's there?" called Eldred, lowering Capito.

No answer came.

In the doorway, Gundlach and Burgold exchanged a look.

"What is that, Eldred?" asked Gundlach.

"I heard a voice. It asked for help," said Eldred.

"I was not hearing anything," said Kunz.

"My ears are old, but I also was not hearing any such voice," said Burgold.

Gundlach looked over the room nervously. "That blade is looking fine. We should be going."

"Yes," said Burgold. "It is time we started making our way back. We will be climbing many hundreds of stairs, a long hike."

Eldred stared back at them, his eyes reflecting the red light cast from the wall plates. "Very well, but something is wrong down here. I heard more than one voice."

Burgold gave a warm smile. "I am assuring you that no place is more right than here. We are standing in the cradle of the Goddess, though it may not be suiting your kind. Let us be departing."

Eldred attached Capito to his belt, joining the unnamed knife he had stuck in a loose leather scabbard. He crossed the room and stood by Burgold in the hall.

Burgold made a motion with his hand, and the door slowly swung shut. He then pressed his hand to the metal, and all the markings and lines of the door faded into a flat wall of metal that once again sealed the room.

The men were silent, tense, as they walked back towards the stairs, but the other sounds persisted—a cry from up ahead, a deathly groan from just behind. Eldred was unnerved. He had received such treasures, but he felt on the very edge of his sanity. As he gripped the hilt of Capito, the urge to strike off Kunz's head bubbled up in him.

When they reached the five-sided room with its detestable attendant, Burgold went directly to the stairs. Eldred went to follow, but the voice came back, as if the speaker was right at Eldred's side. "Don't leave me. By the Mother, do not go."

Eldred stopped so abruptly that the guard behind him bumped against his back. Everyone was staring at Eldred. Every guard had their hand on their sword.

"What is troubling you, Eldred?" asked Burgold. His voice was clear and calm.

Eldred blew out his breath. "I heard the voice again."

"There was no one speaking," said Kunz.

The pale-eyed attendant got off the bench and started walking towards Eldred. "What is the meaning of this, Adept Burgold? Whatever Lady Yslana was intending, this Mercian must be exiting the sanctuary immediately."

Burgold bowed. "Yes, High Adept Nymandus. I am most apologetic, but something is troubling this man."

"There's something wrong," said Eldred. "Somebody is injured. Can you check the area, Burgold? I need someone to check."

Nymandus narrowed his eyes to slits. "You will be leaving this moment, or we will put an end to you."

"Hold, now," said Gundlach. "This man has saved the life of Lady Yslana. His work in her service may well be saving us all. We are only here because I was bringing him to get his well-earned reward, to be closing a difficult contract. If he says there is something wrong, we should be trusting him. Let us be taking a moment and investigate his warning. Adept Burgold, can you search? You have the blessing of the Goddess."

Nymandus paused and turned his unblinking gaze from Eldred to Gundlach.

Burgold nodded. "What harm would we be doing? Let us be taking a moment, High Adept. I can be making a quick investigation of the chamber behind you to put this valued man's worries to rest."

Nymandus's eyes slid over to Burgold, who forced a weak smile. "Very well. To appease Lady Yslana, you may be investigating for three minutes,

Adept Burgold. But then, all of you, including this troublesome Mercian, must be climbing the stairs with haste."

Burgold bowed. "Thank you, High Adept Nymandus. I will be hurrying as fast as my old legs allow me."

As Burgold skittered past Nymandus, Gundlach moved to stand next to Eldred. "Just relax, Eldred. I am not knowing what is troubling you, but we will soon be up on top again. You will be feeling so much better in the open air."

"I hope so," said Eldred wearily.

They had been standing there for a minute, looking after Burgold, who had disappeared down the corridor, when the voice came again. This time the voice was clearer, stronger. "Come down. By the Mother, come to me."

Eldred raised his hands to his temples. He knew the voice. "I have to go down there."

High Adept Nymandus shot him a look of disbelief. Gundlach grabbed at Eldred's shoulder, but Eldred brushed his hand away.

Eldred strode calmly forward, his hands raised in front of him, palms out. All around, the guards drew their weapons. Some men were shouting.

Gundlach was yelling. "Be staying your swords—this man is under contract to Lady Yslana!"

Eldred stepped around Nymandus, fighting the urge to grab his neck, and started down the corridor which descended to a wide double door crafted of wood and iron, set forty feet down the hallway.

To Eldred's surprise, the men did not follow him. Some of them shouted insults, a few were laughing, but all stayed by the entrance to the hallway save for Gundlach, who came running partway down after him.

"What are you doing?" shouted Gundlach.

Eldred paused and looked back. "I need to go down there."

"You cannot be going down there. You will be killed," said Gundlach.

"We'll see," said Eldred.

Gundlach shook his head slowly as Eldred continued on down the hall.

THE GODDESS

Eldred shoved the doors open and stepped through into a wide circular chamber several hundred feet across. The ceiling rose in a dome over the room, rising up thirty feet. The floor sloped down, flattening out into a large depression about fifteen feet below the level of the door. Four other doors exited the room at even intervals around the perimeter.

On a dais set in the center of the depression, surrounded by five towering red stones, sat a woman with long red hair and hazel eyes, lounging on a throne set with graceful lines. Burgold kneeled before the woman and two featureless guardians stood by her side, each a good bit larger than the one Eldred had fought. He studied her face, a tight mask of skin that glowed like the light of the setting sun. Though he had never seen her, he knew her in the same manner he had recognized the guards.

Eldred paused just inside the door. "I know you, Goddess. You bring the pain."

She gave an amused smile and motioned with her hand. Behind Eldred, the door swung shut. "To some, I am bringing pain. To others, I am bringing joy. To my enemies, I bring an end."

"I heard my father's voice," said Eldred.

"Your father?" she said, blinking. "Oh, yes, I am seeing it now. You are his." She laughed. "I was not even considering that. Everyone was calling you the Mercian. I am blaming the Second for this oversight." She frowned. "But you are more than that. I am seeing something else about you."

"You will hand over my father immediately," demanded Eldred.

"No," she said in a dismissive tone. "I am finding him too useful." She fixed her eyes on Eldred. "No one was even mentioning that you wear

Maldavian eyes." She sighed. "Such a thing is so obvious, yet no one was saying this to me. All they were saying is that you were a Mercian. It always is coming to me to set things right."

She clapped her hands lightly. The doors to the left of Eldred opened, and a squad of featureless guardians lumbered out, waking down into the depression to form a line next to some stone benches, standing between the woman and Eldred. These looked the same size as the one Eldred had battled. When they stopped and settled, ten guardians stood lined up in front of her. The two larger guardians remained by her side.

"Are you having any final thoughts?" she inquired.

Eldred took a shallow breath of the corrupted air, eyeing the guardians. There were twelve of them. He didn't doubt that they might be able to do it. "Lady Yslana has a good plan. Withdraw from here and return to Corporia. Withdraw and return my father and whoever else you have captive. As Gundlach, her guard put it, we could all benefit. We don't have to battle to the death."

The Goddess pursed her lips. "But you were fooling them, were you not? You were coming here to kill us, and you have. Six are lying dead unless the Second is wrong on that count as well."

"I came for revenge; that's true. But I've truly come to believe in Lady Yslana's plan." Eldred blew out his breath. "Those five men, your champions, they shouldn't have been wearing those rings—especially the ring of my father. The first man, the other man—that was an accident."

"My doltish subjects have been forming their plan based on your deception. You have been confusing those fools so much that they are believing a simple Mercian can defeat one of my guardians—a lie. You are no simple Mercian. You are wearing the shard of Regula's stone. You are the poor, weak reflection of her so-called son." The Goddess gestured at Eldred. "You have not been holding it long, have you? You are showing no sense in bringing it here, to my sanctuary."

"We should stick to Lady Yslana's plan. There is nothing to be gained from us fighting each other," said Eldred.

A thin smile spread across her face. "Oh, but there is. Once my guardians crush you, stamping the life out of you, I will be taking the shard. One of my acolytes will be wearing it; I know just the one. Once we are holding the power of Regula, your petty armies will be swept away, be they Deiran or Mercian."

Eldred straightened his shoulders, outwardly calm even as his heart beat faster. "You may be overconfident. The Son killed Korinna in the halls of Megara. Even you must admit she was mightier than you."

The Goddess nodded. "Yes, I was once knowing her. She and Regula both were always standing above me. Those two were ruling the world, and even that was not enough for Regula. As for the Son, even that headstrong fool was thoughtful enough to bring an army to Megara. I am seeing only a single witless boy before me. Goodbye." The Goddess waved her hand.

"I—" started Eldred, but the ten guardians facing him were jogging forward. He drew Capito, taking heart in its purple glow. He sliced through the head of the first guardian to reach him, but the others did not hesitate.

The mob bore him down at the foot of the wooden doors. Eldred's right hand, which gripped Capito, was pinned under one of the brutes. Another guardian lay on Eldred's chest and started ripping at his face with its sharded hands. Others were grabbing at his legs. Each sought to pin Eldred and rip at any of his flesh they could find. Eldred yelled out in horrified pain.

Eldred tried to free his sword hand, but the guardian that pinned his arm was stuck to the floor in the same way the guardian from the duel had locked its feet. Screaming, thrashing, for all he was worth, he snaked his left hand down to the dagger on his belt. He had to fight to bring his hand back to his shoulder, where he stabbed the guardian sitting on his chest through the forehead.

The guardian slumped down, its weight pressing into Eldred's chest.

Eldred blinked the blood from his eyes and stabbed the guardian pinning his right arm through the back of its head. It lost its strange attachment to the floor, and Eldred pulled his right arm free. Rolling away the inert guardian on his chest, Eldred struck out with Capito and sliced through the blank faces of two guardians that were mauling his legs.

A guardian standing nearby launched itself at Eldred's head. Eldred got Capito up in time to catch it in the chest, but the sword was yanked from his hands. Eldred scrambled up to a crouching position, dagger in his right hand. He slashed at a nearby guardian, but another launched itself at Eldred, slamming him back into a sitting position against the wooden doors.

Eldred kept his grip on the knife and finished the one that pinned him down. Before he could roll it off, another guardian had jumped on top of that one and reached around to strike a powerful blow on the left side of Eldred's head. Eldred could feel the blood seeping through his hair. He yelled and got his left hand up to ward off the next blow, grabbing at its arm. Two other guardians were stomping on his legs. Eldred screamed and wormed his right hand up to stab the guardian that was attacking his head. It stopped moving.

He shoved off the two lifeless guardians and pulled his legs away from the three remaining attackers. They came at him as he rose to his feet, but Eldred stabbed one through the eye. One of the remaining two struck Eldred a savage blow in the shoulder, pounding him back into the wall. Eldred bounced off and drove the dagger into its forehead.

Then there was only one. Eldred was battered, bloody and wracked with pain, but he was still faster than the guardian. He stabbed it between the eyes.

Eldred stood there for a moment, crouched over as he willed his bloody wounds to close.

The Goddess's eyes brimmed with anger. She rose to her feet and produced a dagger that glowed with a fierce red corruption. "Finish him!"

The two oversized guardians by her side started jogging towards Eldred. Eldred rolled over one of the dead guardians and pulled Capito from its chest. He surveyed the two charging guardians, Capito in his right hand and the dagger in his left. He took a halting step to the right on his battered legs and started to run along the sloping floor that led down to the depression. The guardians gave pursuit slowly, seemingly hampered by the uneven surface.

Eldred led them halfway across the wide room, before turning and sprinting back towards the Goddess, who stood by her throne in the middle of the five standing stones. She stepped close to one of the stones, apparently looking to stay on the other side of it from Eldred. Her guardians began to circle back to her defense.

When Eldred reached the stone, she tried to slide away, but Eldred dropped his dagger and caught her by the arm. As she struck at him with her blade, Eldred brought Capito around in a powerful swing and took her head off. Eldred stood, holding her arm, as her head and body fell separately to the ground.

He had just released her hand, watching her head roll across the floor, when one of the guardians slammed into his side, knocking him down. He slid to a stop on his chest with the guardian on his back. As the guardian wrestled, trying to lock its arms around Eldred, the other came around the front and aimed a kick at Eldred's face. Eldred was able to get Capito up to block the kick, cutting into the guardian's leg.

As the guardian reset to try another kick, Eldred struck out with Capito and cleaved its foot out from under it. The guardian fell with a crash. It lay still for a second before using its arms to lift its chest off the ground. It turned its fiery eyes on Eldred and scrabbled toward him, only to stop as Eldred stabbed it through the head.

The last remaining guardian succeeded in getting its arms around Eldred, squeezing him, trying to crush the life out of him. Eldred fought to keep his breath and brought Capito to bear on its left shoulder, weakly stabbing at it around the side of his head.

As the two fought, Burgold wandered up with tears streaming down his face. He put his hands together and bowed once to the Goddess's body and once to her head, which lay a few feet to the side, balanced on its cheek. Burgold paused there for a moment, seemingly oblivious to Eldred's struggle just a few feet away. Then he reached down and gingerly picked up the Goddess's head and ran slowly towards the wooden doors, cradling it in his hands.

"No, no," grunted Eldred, still locked in battle. "No." He chiseled away at the guardian's left shoulder with even greater urgency.

Burgold reached the doors and—after careful rearrangement of the Goddess's head—laid one hand on them. After a long pause, there was a soft clicking sound, and he pushed it open.

Eldred yelled, "Stop!"

Burgold paid no mind and trudged up the slanting corridor.

Desperately, Eldred glanced around and spotted the dagger a few feet to his side. He let go of Capito and dragged himself and the guardian that rode him close enough that he could snatch up the blade. Three quick thrusts loosened the grip of the vindictive guardian, putting it to rest. Eldred grabbed Capito and took off in pursuit.

As Eldred ran into the corridor, he looked ahead to see the gasping Burgold handing off his burden to Nymandus three quarters up the hallway. Nymandus glanced down at Eldred with a look of shock, his pale green eyes filled with terror. The Corporians were shouting. Eldred charged up the incline, forcing his battered body onward.

Burgold fell to his knees, and Nymandus disappeared behind the Corporian warriors, who were advancing towards Eldred with their swords drawn. Gundlach and Kunz strode side by side at their front. The other men were shouting, but Gundlach paced forward silently. He looked uncertain, but he was still pointing the tip of his blade towards Eldred.

Eldred didn't slow; there was no time for niceties. He deflected Kunz's attack and slashed his throat. He ducked under Gundlach's swing and tossed him back against the wall. Gundlach fell to the floor and his blade clattered out of reach. Eldred mowed through the other warriors, leaving some dead, others dazed. They did not injure Eldred seriously, but they slowed him. Even the winded Burgold grabbed at Eldred's leg.

Past the men, Eldred flew up the stairs, leaping up three steps at a time. He caught Nymandus halfway up, slamming him into the wall and pinned him there, one hand around the adept's throat. He put Capito in its sheath and snatched the head of the Goddess from Nymandus's hands, holding it out of Nymandus's reach by the soft tresses of her hair.

For a moment, Eldred just stood and breathed in the air, corrupt as it was. He was more tired and breathless and beaten up than he had ever been since taking the shard. Nymandus was a torrent of threats and curses, but Eldred paid no heed. Then Eldred heard noises from above. Someone was shouting orders. The men were getting ready for something. They must have known something about the events below. There had been three adepts below with High Adept Nymandus earlier, but Eldred had not seen them as he had cut his way through the soldiers.

Eldred took a deep breath and studied Nymandus's face. The adept was silent, having run out of curses, but his eyes were still full of contempt. For a moment, Eldred was on the verge of crushing the man's throat. He knew this man; he knew the man had done terrible things. He just couldn't recall what terrible things these had been.

"Where's my father?" asked Eldred.

Nymandus didn't say anything. He looked back with hollow eyes, a sneer plastered on his sweaty face.

"I'll ask once more, then I'll kill you. Where's my father?" shouted Eldred.

The sneer veered into a smirk. "It is too late. Only her will was keeping those vile men alive."

Eldred shook the adept and tightened his grip. "Where are they?"

Nymandus sputtered and choked, pulling at Eldred's fingers. As Eldred relaxed his grip, Nymandus gave a short tinny-sounding laugh. "I can show you. Just down these stairs, Mercian. I can be showing you all of your dead friends." He patted Eldred's hand. "Just let me go. I am assuring you that I will be leading you there directly."

Eldred released the man and drew Capito, motioning down the stairs with his blade while the Goddess's head dangled from his other hand.

Nymandus straightened his vestments, smoothing them out. He glanced at the dead face of the Goddess, whose hazel eyes started out sightlessly, and started down the steps.

THE RESCUE

Eldred watched for pursuit from above or below as they made their descent, but none came. The red plates in the walls continued to glow, lighting the way for Nymandus, who made his way down with Capito hovering a few inches from the back of his neck.

They came out on the bottom level and entered the corridor to the Goddess's chamber to find Burgold tending to an injured man, while Gundlach stood close by with his blade drawn. Down the corridor was a gathering of acolytes, a mix of men and women. A few had started up the incline, but they all stopped when Eldred and Nymandus came into view. A few gasped when they saw what Eldred held in his hand.

"What're they doing?" asked Eldred.

"They are those who have been serving the Goddess. They would be leaving now that you have murdered her. Or are you desiring to spill their blood as well?" asked Nymandus in a sour tone.

Eldred peered down the hallway at the acolytes; he could see them clearly enough. As had been the case before, he felt he recognized a few of them.

Closer at hand, Gundlach shifted, moving a half step out from the wall into the passageway. He held his blade firmly in his hand. The point was lowered, but he looked ready.

Eldred sighed and motioned with his blade. "They may pass. But if any seek to interfere with me or to take back that which I hold, there will be consequences for all of you."

The acolytes stayed where they were. High Adept Nymandus beckoned them to no effect.

"Be moving, now!" shouted Nymandus. "If you are standing between this man and his friends, he will be killing you. Do not be doubting that!"

A few of the acolytes started up the incline, though most hung back. As they passed Eldred, they stared in horror at the face of the Goddess. One woman stopped, unable to break her gaze from the sight, until the others behind urged her onward.

Once the first passed safely by, the rest found their courage and came up the incline.

Several of the warriors who had faced Eldred in the corridor were alive but injured. Burgold tasked a group of passing acolytes to help the men to the surface.

As the wounded men were borne away, Burgold swiveled around, still sitting on the floor near Gundlach's feet, and looked up at Eldred. "Why? Why have you been doing this?"

"Me?" asked Eldred, looking through the line of passing acolytes. "You were there. She set her guardians on me." Eldred glanced down at her dangling head. "I urged her to follow Lady Yslana's plan, and I warned her. She thought she could take my gift."

"No. All of the deceiving, all of your lying. Your deceit has been destroying everything," said Burgold.

Nymandus eyed the nearby acolytes and waved his hand. "Enough, Adept Burgold. I will be asking you when I am wanting to hear your voice."

Burgold frowned and slid back to lean against the wall.

After the last acolyte passed by, it was only Eldred, Nymandus, Gundlach and Burgold alive in the passage.

"We will continue," said Eldred. He turned to Gundlach and Burgold. "You may come, but don't get in my way or try to take this back." He shook the Goddess's head. "I don't want to hurt you."

Burgold raised his hand to Gundlach, who helped him to his feet. "We will be coming, Eldred. But we will be stopping you from any further crimes."

"On that subject, I must ask you to sheath your blade, Gundlach," said Eldred.

Gundlach surveyed Eldred with a grim stare. "You are having your blade free."

"Yes, but not for you." Eldred gave a small shake of Capito towards Nymandus. "Now, put it away. I promise you that you'll gain nothing from wielding it against me, but you might force me to injure you."

"Huh," said Gundlach. After a slight pause he returned his sword to his belt. "I am putting it aside for now. If you turn to killing more people, Eldred, be counting on killing me as well."

Eldred nodded glumly and urged the Corporians to go ahead.

Gundlach, who was in front, stopped and cried out when he came to the doors and saw the body of the Goddess sprawled on the dais. Nymandus also stopped, his neck and shoulders tight. Burgold's tears, which had come before, resumed.

"Keep going. I need to get to my father," said Eldred. He felt a rising urgency. He hadn't heard any cries or voices since the battle with the Goddess.

Nymandus gave Eldred a wary look as he started down the slope into the depression. As they walked through the line of stone benches set before the dais, Eldred noticed the red dagger of the Goddess continued to glow on the floor with its evil red light, no less dim than when she had held it in her hand.

Nymandus led the group to one of the doors in the back of the chamber. He set his hand on the door and, as with the barrier to the storeroom earlier, the lines of an inner door took shape. When they fully formed, he pushed the door open and stepped through.

Gundlach paused at the entrance, suddenly looking befuddled.

Burgold patted him on the arm. "The old rules are dropping away, my friend. If you can be in here, in her throne room, you are within your rights to be going anywhere."

Gundlach looked back at the throne, set in the five towering stones that pulsed with energy. Then with a shudder, he stepped through and followed Nymandus.

Eldred was the last through the door. He stepped out into a wide corridor and stopped. Down below was a smaller version of the throne room above, but instead of a throne, the dais held an instrument of torture.

He recoiled at the sight of his father, starved down to his bones, strapped to a tilted stone disk, his feet tied near the center and his head lolling near the outer edge. All four members of his pod shared the same fate: Pounder, Stace, Bate and Mack, each caught in their own body-shaped indentation in the disk's surface as they rotated slowly around. Four other disks, each with their own complement of prisoners, completed the unnerving sculpture, which formed a circle around a steaming vat of green liquid. The foul green substance dribbled down onto the upper edge of the disks, washing over the surface and pooling against the bodies of the naked men before dripping off the lower edge into half-filled troughs that ringed the abhorrent device.

Eldred dashed forward. "Stay back!"

He dropped the head of the Goddess and sheathed Capito. Drawing his dagger, he cut the leg and arm restraints and reached into the goo to pull out his father's emaciated body. He tried to lean Alfred against the disc in a sitting position, but the slowly spinning contraption pushed Alfred over on his side.

"Get some blankets!" shouted Eldred, cradling his father in the crook of his arm.

"I was telling you, they are all dead." said Nymandus. "They have barely stayed living these last few weeks. She was keeping these men alive by her will."

Eldred glanced over Alfred's skeletal body. He did seem dead, but he had heard his father's voice only minutes ago. "The blankets," he growled.

"We store no blankets in this room. Are you wishing us to go to the other chambers and fetch them? I wish to avoid any misunderstanding," said Nymandus.

"Not you, just him!" snapped Eldred, pointing at Gundlach. "You two adepts keep away from the door, or I'll cut you down." He paid no attention as Nymandus shared instructions with Gundlach, who left the room.

Father's body was cold to the touch. It seemed to be partly due to the congealed green goo, which clung to his skin and was getting all over Eldred as well. But the chill seemed to go deeper than that. Eldred wiped Alfred's eyes clear with his bloodied sleeve. There was still a layer of the goo, but it was thinner. Alfred's eyes remained closed.

As Eldred wiped his father's forehead, he uncovered five small red stones set in his skin. Eldred probed them with his fingers. They were set like the fatum lapis lodged behind his father's temple and did not come free when Eldred gave them a gentle tug. Concentrating, Eldred studied the stones. They didn't blaze with corruption like everything else down there, but they were corrupt—corrupt enough to suit the odious needs of the Goddess.

Checking his father's body further, he found five stones set across the outer palm of each hand, set at the base of the finger and thumb bones. Likewise, five stones were set in the toe bones of each foot, on the bottom side. Five and five and five and five and five, everything was fives—the favored number of the Mother and the Goddess alike. And Father was dead.

Eldred was still holding Alfred's lifeless body when Gundlach returned carrying a bundle of blankets.

"What are you needing us to do?" asked Gundlach.

"Lay them out on the floor," said Eldred quietly.

Eldred watched them laying out the blankets. Dead—he was certain of that. Not dead on the battlefield, which was a shame, for that was surely the way he would have wished to die. But he had heard Father's voice just before the fight, just before the confrontation. If he had outlived the Goddess, then that was something of a triumph, a victory. Had not Father called him down to complete the task? He had died with honor, and so must be buried with honor. Seven days, that's what Eldred had by Deiran custom. Seven days to return Father for burial at Boar's Tusk. It was possible, just on the edge of possibility.

He glanced over the men still trussed to the stone disk from which he had taken his father's corpse. It could not have been an accident; five men from the same pod had not been selected by chance. Somehow, this arrangement served the vile purpose of the Goddess.

Eldred got to his feet and lifted Alfred's body, which barely weighed anything at all, and set it on the nearest blanket. As he straightened out the corpse and rested the hands over its chest, he noticed the Corporians kept staring at the head of the Goddess. He couldn't fault them for that.

Eldred went back for Pounder's body next. He had always been Eldred's favorite among his father's pod, even though he had once tried to kill Eldred. It had been due to the curse, the curse that had turned every bonded warrior against Eldred, blessedly gone since Eldred had taken the shard. Any bonded warrior would have done the same. Eldred sighed as he lined up Pounder's skinny corpse up on his blanket.

Stace, the oldest of the pod members, had lost all of his hair. Proof, if any was needed, that they had been alive during their time on the disk. As for Bate, he had been a thin man, thin and tall for a Deiran. He had wasted away to practically nothing. Eldred moved him carefully, worried that his corpse would fall apart in his hands.

Last was Mack, who was slowly rotating down from his position at the topmost side of the disk, nearest the vat. He had not only tried to kill Eldred, but had actually killed Morris, Alfred's steward. He had always been heavy for a Deiran—heavy and rude—and now, though thin, he was nowhere as wasted away as Bate or the others. Eldred cut his bonds. As he went to lift out the corpse, the arm moved. Eldred jumped back and shouted, startling the Corporians, who yelled in turn.

Eldred stood, watching in disgust, as Mack pulled in his limbs and turned to his side, sucking at the green ooze. "What's he doing?"

"He is feeding. The jelly is for cleaning him as well as giving him sustenance," said Nymandus.

Eldred gave Nymandus a cold look. "Torture—that's what this is, plain and simple."

Nymandus said nothing. He merely returned Eldred's heated gaze.

Burgold cleared his throat. "These men were lying at our gates, wet with the blood of a thousand of our fellow citizens. If they had been coming inside, would they not have killed every single one of us?"

Eldred nodded. "Yes, they would've. They planned to do that very thing. But still, just kill them! And with bravery, not trickery, if you have the strength to do it. This"—Eldred gestured at the diabolical contraption—"is evil through and through."

"We were doing this in service of the Goddess, not for our amusement," said Nymandus.

As Eldred looked back to study Nymandus's neck, which he still wanted to snap, he heard Mack slurping down the foul slime. "Amusement? I am realizing now that I must have seen your stupid face with their eyes, for I recognized you, you and your miserable friends. It must have been during my attacks, my fits. The pain I felt, it was terrible; it was their pain. They hated you. You, Nymandus, they hated you, not for being a Corporian, but for what you did to them. When I saw your face today, when I look at you now, I can't forget that."

Nymandus frowned back defiantly.

Eldred threw up his hands. "Fetch some water, Gundlach. We have to wash them all clean, starting with Mack."

Gundlach brought water from a nearby chamber, and the Corporians set to washing down their victims while Eldred got the rest of the bodies down. Through his combination of toughness and heftiness, the murderous lout, Mack, had outlasted twenty-four bonded warriors. Eldred shook his head in disbelief. Did honor count for nothing?

Finally, Eldred reluctantly knelt next to Mack, taking in his unpleasant odor and listening to his strained breathing. Mack twitched and shook, despite being covered with three thick blankets.

"What do you have to feed him?" asked Eldred.

Nymandus stepped forward hesitantly. "Our foods would not be serving him well. Only the jelly will be keeping him alive."

Eldred knotted his forehead, feeling his rage building. "The slime? You think I should be feeding him that slime?"

"Yes," said Nymandus.

Eldred looked over at the ooze which was still dripping down the stone disks. Whatever else it was, it didn't appear contaminated, which had been the case for every other morsel of food he had seen in New Wismar, even the bread. He took a breath. "Very well. Get him some of your 'jelly'."

Burgold took a cup from a table near the dais and procured a sample of warm sludge.

Eldred made a face as Burgold pushed some of the ooze into Mack's mouth using his finger. It seemed to soothe the feeble man, but his breath was still rasping. Eldred motioned at the small red stones set across Mack's forehead. "How do I get these out?"

"You cannot," said Nymandus. "Even if he were still strong, cutting those from his flesh would certainly be killing him."

Eldred found himself believing the adept. Looking at Gundlach and Burgold, it seemed they did as well. "He's going to die," said Eldred slowly.

Nymandus nodded. "Yes. It will not be taking long."

Eldred rubbed his chin, glancing over at his father. "What're these stones doing? Why did the Goddess torture these men so?"

The Corporians made no reply and avoided meeting his gaze.

After a moment, Eldred drew his dagger and leaned over Mack.

"If you are digging those out, he will be dying sooner," said Nymandus.

"He may as well die free of this foul corruption," said Eldred.

Nymandus raised his eyebrows and looked away.

Eldred placed his finger on one of the stones. It felt as if its tendrils went deep, as deep as the tendrils of a fatum lapis if not deeper. If he dug it out, it would only leave a messier corpse.

He crinkled up his face and tested the stone again, taking it between his thumb and forefinger and tugging. The stone didn't feel connected to the skin; it felt tethered inside. He tested a stone on Mack's right hand. It felt the same.

"Hmm," said Eldred. He looked over the three Corporians. As he had come to notice, they all had the faint glow of corruption inside them, a reddish glow that was just a trace in Gundlach and much stronger in Burgold and Nymandus. Mack, weak and floppy as he was, didn't glow. He was a child of the Mother.

Eldred studied Mack's face, studying it with the same silent intensity that he had studied his dagger when he had found it in the storeroom. That had been the first time he had seen the purple glow, the flowing power that marked the knife as an artifact of the Mother. He stared at Mack for a minute, perhaps longer, before he caught a faint sense of the Mother's energy. It was muted as might be expected in a dying man sprawled in the depths of a stronghold of the Goddess, but there was something, a slight bluish tint to the center of Mack's face, between the eyes and just above the bridge of the nose.

Eldred set his right index finger on the spot and noticed the energy inside his own flesh. A purple flux streamed through his arm, flowing through flesh and blood and bone, sweeping out to his fingers before running back up his arm into his chest. He bore the Shard of the Mother; he was alive with her energy. No such trifling stones of corruption could ever exist in his flesh. He breathed in deep from the foul air that filled the chamber and cleansed it. The energy bubbled within him, and he willed it to pour into the broken vessel before him.

Breath by breath, he imagined filling up the depleted reserve of the man before him. Mack's breath began to fall and rise with his own, sounding stronger, no longer the rattling whisper of a man about to die. Mack moved his arm, lifting it from the floor to place it on his chest unassisted. His eyelids started to flutter. Eventually, his eyes opened.

Eldred stared Mack right in the eye. It was Mack, not some empty shell, looking at him. Eldred recognized the spirit of the man—the same chaotic thug that he always had been.

Mack lifted his hand again, shifting his eyes to examine it. As he did, the five red stones dropped away, landing on his chest and rolling to the ground, leaving five small indentations in his hand.

Eldred removed his finger from Mack's forehead and rested his hand on his knee. Mack rolled onto his side, facing away from him. The stones set in Mack's forehead slid free and Mack brushed weakly at them.

Eldred remained kneeling, staring at the blanket in front of him. He felt slightly light-headed and content, as if he had no need to move. He felt good. After a moment, he looked for the head of the Goddess. It was still present on the dais where he had left it.

The three Corporians stood looking at Mack, who had rolled over onto his stomach and pushed himself up to gaze at them.

Mack shuddered and looked back at Eldred, a glimmer of recognition in his eyes.

Eldred pressed his lips together. "Yes, it's me, Eldred."

Mack continued to stare at him.

"I came to rescue all of you, but it's just you." Eldred gestured at the corpses. "None of them survived."

Mack worked his mouth, which still bore traces of the green slime. "What of the king?"

Eldred grimaced. "My father's dead."

Mack took a few deep breaths and looked over Nymandus, Gundlach and Burgold. "My sword, my sword. I'll kill them. I'll cut their Motherless eyes out." His wavering voice undercut the threat of his words.

Gundlach's hand drifted over near the hilt of his sword.

Eldred sighed. "No, Mack. I already killed enough of them, at least, for now. Besides, we have work to do, and we could use their help."

Mack's eyes glazed over. "What damned work?"

Eldred was about to answer when a deafening clang roared through the chamber, shaking the floor. Burgold dropped to his knees and covered his ears. Mack curled up screaming on the blanket. The sound echoed through the chamber for several seconds.

"What was that?" asked Eldred when the air finally stilled.

"They are closing the portal," said Nymandus. "They are shutting us in."

CAPTIVES

They set out from the torture chamber with Gundlach out in front. Nymandus and Burgold followed side by side; Eldred and Mack brought up the rear. With his right arm, Eldred supported Mack— who was nearly naked, only wrapped in a loincloth, having refused to wear any offered Corporian clothing. Though Mack required help, he moved well for someone who had lain inert for such a long period.

When they reached the throne, Eldred stopped. "She's gone. Her dagger's missing too."

Gundlach turned. "They were taking her away when I was gathering the blankets. Surely, you are not begrudging us that?" His eyes drifted down to the Goddess's head, dangling by its hair from Eldred's left hand.

Eldred grimaced at her bloodless face, dead but somehow still full of reproach. No doubt it would be his own head being carted around some day after he faced his final foe. "No. I'm—pleased you honor her. But you mustn't be sneaking around. If you're up to something, tell me first."

"If you are so full of desire to honor her, why not be handing over your trophy?" asked Nymandus.

Eldred fixed him with a hard look. "I've no wish to carry her in this manner, but if she was going to take my shard, then I'm entitled to her stone. If you remove the Roter Kristall, I'll hand over her head without delay. I've removed one before, my shard." Eldred shook his head. "It wouldn't be— with my skill in that—it wouldn't be anything anyone wanted. You must have some means. Your Goddesses aren't immortal."

Neither adept responded.

"Well, let me know when one of you is ready to be useful. Now, let's get moving," said Eldred.

Mack was breathing hard as they trudged up the incline from the Goddess's chamber. Eldred was practically carrying him.

"Who's gone? Who were you talking about?" asked Mack.

"The Goddess," said Eldred.

"What Goddess?" asked Mack.

"Their stonebearer. Her body was down there before some of the Corporians came and took it," said Eldred.

Mack looked up at Eldred with a confused expression. "Something happened to their stonebearer?"

Eldred raised the Goddess's head into Mack's line of view. "I killed her. Why do you think I'm carrying this around?"

Mack gasped. "I've seen her before. She was there."

Eldred lowered the head. "Yes, I think she was."

Mack shuddered and motioned weakly at the trio in front of them. "You'll have to kill them too. You have to kill all of them. They'll want revenge."

"I'm certain they're giving it some thought. But for now, I've got the situation in hand," said Eldred.

"How can that be?" muttered Mack.

"Trust me," said Eldred.

The echoes of metallic banging reached down the stairs to greet them as they climbed up the stairway to the portal, growing louder the closer they came to the top. When they reached the final steps, the Corporians moved to the side, and Eldred looked up to see a corrupt metal barrier laying across the stairs, covering the twenty foot opening. A small locked hatch was set in the center. Five metal legs dangled down from the barrier, each set with a peg on the end that scratched against the walls. The holes for the pegs were evident, but they were not lined up. It was evidently a barrier meant to keep invaders out, not to trap people inside.

As he looked up, considering what to do, it seemed that he could trace the sound of people walking across the top side of the barrier. There was banging too, the sound of things being piled up on top. He lowered Mack down to sit on the stairs and turned to face the Corporians. "Is there some other way out?"

Nymandus moved a step closer. "No. This is the only entrance to the sanctuary. You can try digging your way out, but it will be taking you a hundred years. The walls, the stones, are imbued with her power. You killed her. In your treachery, you killed her. But even in death, she is defeating you."

Eldred frowned. "We'll see about that."

He continued up until his head was just below the barrier. He gently set down the Goddess's head on a stair, careful that it did not roll, then tested the barrier with his hands. It was heavy, very heavy, but it was not fixed.

Eldred took a breath and turned to face the side of the stairs. He put both hands on the barrier and pushed with all of his strength. As he strained, the barrier lifted slightly and slid a few inches to the side. An explosion of shouts came from above, as if from hundreds of voices. Almost immediately, Eldred felt an opposing force on the barrier, stopping it.

He reset his hands and pushed again, but now the barrier was sliding back despite his greatest effort. It sounded a tremendous clang as it dropped over the lip, fitting once more into the circular opening of the staircase. Eldred covered his ears. Mack started screaming and writhing; Burgold moved up to prevent him from tumbling down the stairs.

The sound was still reverberating through the stairway as Eldred pressed up on the barrier again, shoving for all he was worth. This time it felt heavier. He was barely able to edge it to the side before his efforts were blocked. Once again, a mighty clang sounded as the barrier dropped off the lip, shaking them as if they were in the center of a ringing bell.

"Stop it!" screamed Mack.

Eldred opened and closed his hands, flexing his fingers. "Now is the time. They'll only get more settled in up there."

Nymandus shook his head. "You will not be getting out. By now, they will be having a thousand men encircling the portal."

Eldred glared at him. "If I'm trapped down here, so are you."

A smirk crossed the adept's face, but he did not answer.

Eldred reached over to the hatch, eight inches on each side, and slid back the deadbolt holding it shut. The hatch dropped down, held by hinges on one side. Eldred looked up past a row of corrupted metal bars, each four inches thick, into the glowering face of Keeper Enolf.

"Murderer. You sneaking, conniving murderer," snarled Enolf.

Eldred stared back, momentarily at a loss for words.

"The acolytes said you were toting around her head. Is that true?" asked Enolf.

Eldred took a breath. "Yes. I have her stone."

"You are lying beneath any animal, lower even than the worms that are eating their way through shit," said Enolf.

Eldred rubbed behind his left temple, where his fatum lapides had formerly been set, those blessings of the Mother that had fallen out when he had taken her shard. "I'm certain you feel that way. I was also displeased when I found my father dead on the Goddess's torture rack." Eldred made a fist. "I'm angry still, but our circumstances call for more than exchanging insults."

Enolf flashed a manic grin. "We are burying you. You are standing in your tomb. You might be lasting a while eating the corpses of your dead friends, but within a week or two, you will be passing."

Eldred shook his head. "You're wrong about that. The others may starve or perish from thirst, your adepts and Gundlach, but I can live for years down here—not that I have to." Eldred reached down and lifted the Goddess's head up to where Enolf could see it. "I have her stone. You can't make the Deirans fall down anymore. How many days do you have, Keeper? How many days until the last of you is cut down by my avenging Deiran brothers?"

Enolf's eyes burned with fury. "You—"

"It doesn't have to be that way." Eldred carefully returned the head to its ledge. "I can see another path, one that leads to fewer deaths all around. Go fetch Lady Yslana. Fetch the Second as well. I need to speak with both of them."

"I will not be having them within a hundred yards of you, you filthy Mercian," said Enolf.

"They'll be safe. Just as Nymandus is safe. Just as Burgold and Gundlach are safe," said Eldred.

"Gundlach is a traitorous dog! As soon as I am getting my hands on him, I will be gutting him!" shouted Enolf.

Eldred glanced down the stairs at Gundlach, who had heard every word. His lips were pressed together, and he was staring at his feet. Eldred looked back up at Enolf. "You hold the gate. You've done well, Keeper. But now, I must speak with your true leaders. Bring them here, or you'll all surely perish."

Enolf shot Eldred one last look of unmitigated hatred and stomped away, his feet echoing as he clanged across the top of the barrier.

After a moment, Eldred settled down on the step next to the Goddess's head.

Burgold looked over from where he was hunched by Mack, who was sprawled across several steps and appeared to be asleep. "Can you truly be lasting for many years down here?"

Eldred nodded. "Yes, I believe so." He waved his hand at his forehead. "A previous shard bearer faced similar circumstances and survived. You needn't worry about me eating any of you. I won't."

"They will not be letting you out," said Nymandus, though he seemed less confident than before.

"Perhaps not, but then they'll die. I'm certain of it," said Eldred.

"Even if the Deirans come, they may not be finding you here. Enolf and his men could be burying the portal under ten feet of dirt and rock. How would your friends know to look for you?" asked Nymandus with increased bluster.

Eldred tilted his head to the side. "I have her stone. Your people, the Corporians, might be different, but my people would never lock away the Mother's stone in a tomb. What sort of people would knowingly condemn themselves to be barbarians? There's no worse fate."

"What will you be saying to the Second?" asked Gundlach.

Eldred sat silently for a moment, considering. "I don't know. I'll have to see. But your people will be leaving this city; I'll tell you that."

"You will not be deciding such matters!" snapped Nymandus. "As for you"—he turned to Gundlach—"stop assisting him. You are already well beyond the bounds of treason."

"Helping him?" sputtered Gundlach. "I was only repaying Lady Yslana's debt. We met both you and Captain Kunz; I heard no warnings that the guardians would fall. We all watched him walking down to her chambers; you never expressed that she was in danger. How should I be knowing what you did not, High Adept?"

Burgold waved Gundlach and Nymandus to silence. "There will be a time for discussing such matters, a later time. For now, hold the peace."

Gundlach and Nymandus exchanged grim stares.

"That's right. Be calm. I'll talk to them. I'm not necessarily here to destroy you," said Eldred.

"How comforting," said Nymandus.

Eldred studied the man's face and realized he no longer felt the urge to kill him—at least not the powerful urge he had fought before. "Yes, be comforted, adept. I intend to spare you. And if that should change, you'll pass quickly—as did your Goddess. Unlike you, I'll not torture anyone."

PARLEY

They sat, listening to Corporians stomping across the barrier. Clangs and crashes, probably rocks or other debris being piled up top, sounded constantly. Somehow Mack slept, his whooshing snores occasionally rising above the background din. Burgold continued his watch, sitting next to the precariously balanced Deiran. Nymandus and Gundlach stood a few stairs down, a current of tension passing between them. Eldred sat above on a step with the Goddess's head at hand, looking through the hatch, watching the narrow view that it provided.

After an hour, the activity above stopped and a silence fell, only broken by Mack's fitful gasps. Then Eldred heard the unmistakable sound of people marching in step out onto the barrier. He rose from his seat to get a better look. The Second and Lady Yslana had arrived, standing on the edge of the barrier with a wall of shields between them and the grate from which Eldred peered. Keeper Enolf, Keeper Renz and Baron Wortwin were also present with the Baron—as usual—tucked in at Lady Yslana's side.

"You came," said Eldred.

The Second nodded. "We are here to listen to your words, your final words, before we seal your tomb."

Eldred paused. "If this is my tomb, then the city will be yours. You can't hold this place without the Roter Kristall, and Lady Yslana has seen what happens when we catch you outside the walls."

He looked over their faces, waiting for one of them to answer, but they were all silent. Even Keeper Enolf glumly held his tongue.

"Well, do any of you see it differently?" asked Eldred.

Baron Wortwin glanced at Lady Yslana before turning to Eldred. "We are seeing the challenges you mentioned. We are understanding the danger and cunning of our enemies more clearly now than ever before, informed as we are by your deceit. But allow me to be gaining insight into how you are viewing the current situation for yourself. Keeper Enolf has been telling us that you are not fearing entombment, that you are confident in your ability to survive a thousand quiet days in isolation. Is that truly what you are saying?"

Eldred smiled. "I could last a thousand days or a thousand years. Nymandus says it'll take a hundred years to tunnel out of this corrupt pit. I could do that. If I did, I would come out to find the remains of your dead city, the bleached corpse of New Wismar. I wouldn't see your skeletons though. I'm certain by then they would've turned to dust."

"Is that so?" asked the Baron with a hint of anger.

"Yes, I think it is," said Eldred. "But I wouldn't enjoy those hundred years. I also doubt any of you would take pleasure in the sacking of your city. Perhaps there's another way."

The Baron gestured grandly. "We are listening."

Eldred turned his gaze to Lady Yslana. "Lady Yslana is wise. Her plan, her strategy, remains sound. Now, there was some confusion. I never said I was a poor simple Mercian; you came up with that on your own. Does it make me a liar that you all tricked yourselves? Even the Goddess complained to me before she died that you all called me 'the Mercian'. She noticed my Maldavian eyes right away. But take away the confusion, and you'll see that now everything is exactly as Lady Yslana warned. The Deirans will no longer fall down. Whether it's the Deirans or the Mercians who menace you, this city cannot stand. It's time you returned home to Corporia, to your true capital, Wismar."

"And passage on that perilous route? How will we be managing that safely?" asked the Baron.

"Before you were counting on the Goddess. She was going to protect you. Now, I'll be providing you with my protection," said Eldred.

"Your protection?" scoffed the Baron. "After all you have been doing?"

Eldred nodded. "My protection. You'll gain the goodwill of my people by returning their dead, such as you have. You'll provide wagons and oxen ready to move them immediately. And the weapons and armor down below in the storage room, they're dear to the Deiran lords and nobles. You'll also return them, earning even more goodwill."

"Will we also be baring our necks? Kneeling down and letting those bastards chop off our heads?" shouted Keeper Enolf.

Baron Wortwin gave Enolf a sideways glance. "The Keeper is making a good point. Have you not been proving the danger of these weapons, Eldred?"

"It's true that they'll be more dangerous with these weapons back in their hands. But it will change nothing if they come for you. The Bond—that's what'll spell your doom if you fight them, not a few swords," said Eldred.

"Huh," said the Baron. "So we are to be left with nothing after returning everything. We will only be having your 'promises' for our protection."

"I'll return the head of the Goddess to you for proper burial or to take with you, whichever you prefer. But I'll keep her stone for now. When the last of you have crossed back into Corporia, I'll hand over the Roter Kristall to the Second. Balance will be restored. I don't see that my fellow Deirans will have any interest in continuing the matter. I know I won't."

"What will be stopping you from keeping it?" asked Keeper Enolf, his mouth twisted in a sneer.

"I don't want it," said Eldred. "As I told the Second, its force, its essence, wears on me. I don't want it here, in the land of the Mother, but I have no care about it residing in Corporia."

"Fine words, Eldred," said Lady Yslana. "Your words are almost making sense. But when we were meeting, you and I, you were busy with revenge. And now, we have been learning that your father died here, in our sanctuary. Revenge, Eldred—when will you be taking your revenge?"

Eldred's face grew tight. "I'm not happy about what happened, about what was done, but she's dead. That's enough. I can leave it at that. The rest of you had no say. She was your Goddess. I know you weren't all happy with her and neither was I."

There was a pause, and in the silence all heads turned toward the Second. She stood with poise, adorned as always with silver and gold, though her eyes were sad, lacking their usual mischievous glint. "You were speaking correctly earlier regarding the wisdom of Lady Yslana, Eldred. She is wise. So, when she is mentioning your appetite for revenge, it is creating great concern in me. Even if you were saying the right words and offered to return everything now, the head of our beloved Goddess as well as the stone, how could we safely be making an exchange with you? How could we be stopping you, the slayer of the Goddess and her guardians, from taking it back if we set you free?"

"I wouldn't," said Eldred.

The crowd stirred uneasily.

Eldred wagged his finger at the men below. "I didn't kill them. I didn't kill Nymandus, or Burgold, or Gundlach. I even spared the acolytes. There must have been fifty of them."

Keeper Enolf sniffed. "Sometimes the cat will be playing with the mice."

Eldred shook his head. "You'll have to trust me, or you'll all die."

The Second frowned and looked up towards the red dome above. After a moment, she shook her head. "Keeper Enolf, I agree that you should be continuing with your works."

Enolf nodded and started to bark out orders. The Second, Lady Yslana, the Baron and the others turned to leave.

"Did you hear me?" shouted Eldred. "You have to trust me, or you'll all die!"

DEBATE

Eldred slammed the hatch shut and ran the deadbolt through. He looked down at the three Corporians. "Are they all fools? Do they think they can keep the Deirans at bay without the stone?"

Burgold sighed. "They are not being foolish, Eldred." His face appeared older and more creased than it had earlier that morning. "They are facing impossible choices."

High Adept Nymandus's smirk resurfaced. "Were you truly thinking they would let you go free? That you could be taking the Roter Kristall and all your evil weapons in exchange for your empty promises of safety?"

Eldred pointed at Gundlach. "You agreed with Lady Yslana's plan before. How is it not the same now? If anything, the danger for this city has grown dramatically worse. The Deirans are right outside. They're not stupid. They'll figure it out. And once they do, they'll unleash a river of blood as they cut through your defenses."

"Everything has been changing." Gundlach looked mournfully at the head of the Goddess. "This morning we were having courage; we were having some measure of hope. Now the Goddess is dead, and Keeper Enolf is burying our own sanctuary."

"What should I do then?" asked Eldred.

"You should sit down and die," said Nymandus.

Eldred narrowed his eyes. "Not bloody likely." He paused for a breath. "Very well, let's get moving. I want everyone down below."

Nymandus shrugged and headed down. After a brief hesitation, Gundlach and Burgold followed. Eldred came after, shaking Mack awake and helping him down the stairs.

When they reached the bottom, Eldred cast his gaze over the five passages leading out of the room. "What do we have down here? We'll have to make do until they come to their senses."

None of the Corporians said a word.

Eldred frowned. "Let's start with the water. Gundlach, you brought water down to wash the corpses. Where did you get it from?"

Gundlach pointed towards the passage that led to the throne room. "There was a room down there, but they shut the door when they claimed the body of the Goddess."

"Then we need to open that door," said Eldred.

Nymandus and Burgold exchanged a look, but neither said anything.

"Well?" demanded Eldred.

"You can be having the jelly," said Nymandus. "The door is standing open down to the lower chamber. But we will not be opening any more doors for you, and all other doors are shut."

"What?" exclaimed Eldred. "Are you forgetting your own needs? You eat food. You drink water. You truly plan to die of thirst when a drink can be had only a few paces away?"

"If need be, Eldred," said Burgold softly. "As High Adept Nymandus said, we cannot be opening any more passageways."

"Then you'll die," said Eldred.

"Yes," said Burgold. "We are understanding the consequences. We are prepared."

Mack shifted in Eldred's right arm. "Ahh, there you go. Even they know they have to die. Just kill the bastards already."

Eldred rolled his eyes. "They're going to change their minds up there. The Second is reasonable. How can they defend this city without the help of a Goddess, without the stone? I just need for all of you to cooperate for a few days, maybe just for one day. As for your brave stand, it means nothing. If they seal the portal and keep it shut, a few morsels of food won't be making any difference to me. You're just hurting yourselves."

Gundlach shook his head. "We cannot be helping you, Eldred." He glanced at Nymandus. "Already some are saying that we have been working with you, which I have not. I was merely repaying Lady Yslana's debt."

"You should never have been bringing him here!" snapped Nymandus. "Your reckless behavior has been destroying us, destroying all of our peoples."

"Who knew what he could do?" asked Gundlach.

"Enough!" shouted Eldred.

Nymandus laughed. "Or what? Are you going to be breaking my neck or stabbing me through the chest? Cease your idle threats. As things are standing now, I would prefer death to hearing your screeching voice. We are done here, Mercian. Our time is done."

"I'll do it," said Mack, but he remained hanging on Eldred's arm.

Eldred looked down at the Goddess's head, dangling from his hand. "Fine. If we're trapped here, I'll kill anyone who wants to die. But first, for those who wish to live or those who care about the people above, let's take a moment to think. The key to your people's survival, the only way they can avoid becoming barbarians even, lies right here." He gave the head a small shake. "Now, how about we find a table, get some food, get some water and discuss our options."

Burgold looked to High Adept Nymandus, but Nymandus just smirked and gave a small shake of his head.

"In my experience," said Nymands, "I am finding that Deirans—and I should be supposing all of the degenerate children of Regula—prefer slop for their meals. Can I be interesting you in a cup of jelly—delicious, tasty jelly?"

"What's he talking about?" muttered Mack.

Eldred sighed. "It was part of your captivity. I guess you're not remembering it, which is probably for the best." Eldred motioned the Corporians. "I don't know where the rest of your supplies are, but I know where you keep your looted weapons."

"My sword?" asked Mack eagerly.

"I expect so," said Eldred.

<h1 align="center">THE DOOR</h1>

The featureless barrier blocked the entrance to the storeroom just as it had when they had left it. Eldred tested the barrier with his hands while Mack reclined against the opposite wall. The Corporians watched from a few paces away, occasionally frowning at the head of the Goddess, which rested by Eldred's feet.

"You are already having weapons," observed Burgold.

Mack scratched at his thin beard. "I don't have one."

Eldred pressed both his hands on the barrier, trying to push it over. When that failed, he tried to push it to the side, straining first left, then right. The barrier didn't budge. He tried again, then again. Nothing shifted the barrier. Finally, he tried shoving the barrier upward, but this also proved fruitless. As he leaned against the barrier, he looked over at Nymandus, who wore a broad smile.

"Are you understanding now, Mercian?" asked Nymandus. "It is sealed forever. I hope you were picking the right sword and dagger, fine gifts from your friend, Gundlach, since you will never be getting in there again."

"Come over here, Nymandus," said Eldred.

"No," said Nymandus.

"I can drag you over if I want," said Eldred.

Nymandus crossed his arms.

Eldred stalked over to grab Nymandus by the arm. Nymandus made a weak show of resistance as Eldred pulled him in front of the door.

"Now, put your hand in the center," said Eldred.

"Are you thinking her creations are so simple? You are thinking I just need place my hand there and the door will form and open before you?" Nymandus laughed and pressed his palm to the center of the barrier. "There, are you seeing now?"

Eldred stepped closer. The corruption appeared slightly stronger on the barrier around Nymandus's hand, but otherwise, the barrier remained the same. No lines formed on its surface.

"Next, I am thinking you will be threatening me. Perhaps you will be twisting my arm or stabbing my foot. It will not be mattering. It will only be opening if I freely lay my hand upon it and imagine the door," said Nymandus.

Eldred glanced at Burgold. "Could you not do it for another?"

Nymandus gave a sly smile. "So, you would be torturing an old man."

"Just as you did," said Eldred.

Burgold tensed up and stepped behind Gundlach.

"I want my sword," said Mack, pushing himself up a bit straighter.

Eldred motioned Nymandus out of the way. He drew his dagger and held it up near the entrance. The purple glow of the Mother danced on the blade. It would be the pure energy of the Mother against the corrupted energy of the Goddess.

As he pressed the blade against the barrier, the hilt pushed back, as if trying to avoid touching the foul surface. But Eldred forced it down with all of his strength. The edge cut into the metal, emitting a terrible shrieking sound that filled the passageway and releasing a burst of heat that washed across his face. He continued the cut, slicing into the barrier as the Corporians covered their ears and ran down the hallway. Mack also dragged himself up and made his escape, half crawling away as he cursed at the top of his lungs.

Eldred kept pushing the knife through the barrier. There was a visible slit through the door: one inch long, two inches long. As he pushed the blade through to three inches, the sound grew in intensity; his hair started to catch fire; and the blade blew apart into dozens of tiny fragments, three of which struck him. One dug into his thigh. Another, with burning heat, lodged in his shoulder. The final one, the most painful of the three, tore into his side.

Eldred's scream echoed through the passageway. He reflexively pinched the molten metal bits from his body and flung them away. He fell back against the far wall, where Mack had slouched a minute before, still bathed in the heat that radiated from the angry barrier.

He was still lying against the wall, breathing through his pain, when the Corporians came creeping back. Gundlach, who was in front, came to a halt a dozen paces away, looking back and forth between Eldred and the head of the Goddess.

"Kill him," hissed Nymandus, stepping past Burgold to stand directly behind Gundlach.

Gundlach bit his lip and placed his hand on the hilt of his sword.

Eldred gave a half smile and slowed his breathing. The pain was fading—not so terrible as what he had suffered from the guardians, but respectable.

Nymandus pushed Gundlach in the small of his back, his eyes fixed on the head lying by the foot of the barrier. "At least be grabbing it."

"No. Don't," grunted Eldred.

"If not now, then when?" asked Nymandus.

"Never," said Eldred softly.

They stayed, locked in silence, for a moment longer, then Eldred pushed himself up to his feet. He looked through the slit into the chamber. He could make out the faint glow of the other named sword past the boxes of daggers and under a table—so close. He cast a pained expression at the melted remains of his beautiful dagger on the floor. Thank the Mother he hadn't tried that with Capito.

"Did you kill Mack?" asked Eldred as he picked up the head. It was undamaged.

"No," said Gundlach.

"Good," said Eldred. "Let's get something to eat."

JELLY

Mack glowered with disgust at the cup Eldred held out to him. "What's this Motherless shit?"

"It's what they've been feeding you these last eight months. It seems to have kept you reasonably alive," said Eldred. He glanced at the corpses laid out on their blankets with their ribs showing. "Though not everyone."

Mack pushed the cup away. "You can have mine."

Eldred straightened up and stepped back. Mack was leaning against one of the stone disks next to the head of the Goddess. The disks were stationary now, a change since they had last been there. The three Corporians were lined up behind the corpses away from the door. Adept Burgold stood between Gundlach and High Adept Nymandus, who continued to glare at one another.

Eldred studied the greenish brew. It ran like a liquid if heated and poured. But when cooled and collected in a cup, it seems almost solid. It could hold its shape and wobble when shaken. They had about twelve gallons in the vat, which had stopped heating. Things appeared to be shutting down now that the Goddess was dead.

"Well, at least it's not contaminated," said Eldred. He reached in and pulled out a small globule that shook on his palm. After examining it, he let it roll down to his fingers and pushed it to his lips. He was braced for something terrible, but it was almost pleasant—mostly tasteless, with perhaps a faint hint of lime. The globule slid around inside his mouth as it dissolved back into a liquid and disappeared down his throat.

"Hmm, interesting," said Eldred. He dug out a larger chunk with his fingers and ate it. "I recommend it to anyone who's hungry."

"I knew you would be liking it. Slop for the pigs," commented Nymandus airily.

Eldred turned and looked around the room. The light panels were set every thirty feet along the walls. Most still shone bright, but there were two that were noticeably dimmer than the others. "I see changes. The disks stopped spinning. The vat went cold. And it seems a few of the lights are failing."

"Yes, some effects require the active will of the Goddess," remarked Nymandus. "Now that you have been murdering her, a number of her creations will fail. I expect it will go dark in the next few days unless someone takes up the Roter Kristall. Will you be enjoying that, Mercian? Locked forever in the depths without a trace of light?"

Eldred laughed. "Mercian? I'm not Mercian. I said as much up above. I'm Deiran, Maldivian and Mercian. In particular, my eyes are Maldavian. I can see in the dark. It's you that'll be blind; that is, if I haven't agreed to break your neck by then."

"Your friend will be suffering," said Nymandus.

Eldred glanced at Mack. His sour face didn't look too different from when he had tried to kill Eldred back in Boar's Tusk. "That's true." Eldred dug out another lump of jelly. "Doesn't anyone else want some?"

Burgold swallowed. The old man looked tired. "I may be needing something."

Eldred made a sweeping gesture towards the vat. "Please help yourself."

Burgold tottered down the incline to the lower level of the chamber, slowly walking through the dead warriors laid out on the blankets.

High Adept Nymandus took a half step towards Gundlach and whispered, "Gutless."

Gundlach pointed at the head, set next to Mack. "Go and be grabbing it yourself, High Adept, if your courage shines so."

"He is standing now," said Nymandus, glowering at Eldred.

"Can you be thinking that makes a difference?" commented Gundlach.

Burgold took a cup from a table near the disks and filled it from the vat. After a moment's hesitation, he sampled the green concoction. He started with a dour face, but his expression warmed as he swallowed the jelly. "I am finding it better than I was expecting."

Eldred raised his cup. "Exactly."

Mack made a face.

Eldred waggled his finger. "You were slurping it down when we found you. I'm certain you'll like it."

Mack pointed at Nymandus. "I'd rather eat him."

The Corporians eyed Mack uneasily.

"I doubt they'd let you," said Eldred.

Mack raised his eyebrow. "He just told the other one to kill you."

Eldred shrugged. "I heard, but nothing happened."

"Wait till you sleep. They'll find new reserves of courage once you shut your eyes," said Mack.

"I may not sleep for a while," said Eldred.

For a few moments, there was only the sound of Eldred and Burgold snacking on the jelly.

Mack grabbed his head. "By the Mother, stop smacking your lips. You'll drive me insane."

Nymandus gave a thin smile. "Just wait till you are passing the hours in total darkness."

"Ahhh, why won't you kill him?" moaned Mack.

Eldred shrugged. "I don't see the need as yet."

"You will," said Mack.

"No. You will be needing him to open doors," said Gundlach quietly.

"Hmmph, he said he wouldn't," said Eldred.

"One of them will have to be doing it." Gundlach gestured at the corpses. "Once these bodies are festering, it will be unbearable. It may not be taking long. There must be some empty storage room we can be using."

Mack sniffed. "I already smell something ripe."

Burgold and Nymandus exchanged another look; Nymandus shook his head.

Gundlach grimaced. "This is not a matter of helping him. There must be some space without weapons or food, some neutral spot. The odor of two dozen men rotting is not something we can be ignoring."

"Once the odor is bothering you, you can ask him to end your discomfort," said Nymandus.

"Burgold?" asked Gundlach.

Burgold looked over the bodies without comment.

Eldred walked over to his father's body and knelt down. Seven days—if only the stupid Corporians were not so unreasonable, it might be possible.

But unless they came to their senses soon, there would be no honors for Father in Boar's Tusk.

"Perhaps I will give them her head," mused Eldred.

"What?" asked Gundlach, taking a step closer.

Eldred glanced around the room. The others, including Mack, were watching him intently.

"I said perhaps I'll return her head. I wasn't lying when I said I don't want it. I was planning to return it anyway, only after the last one of you crossed back into Corporia."

"I am not seeing how you can," said Burgold.

"Why is that?" asked Eldred.

"You cannot be passing the head of the Goddess through the bars of the hatch, and they will not ever be unblocking the portal to release you. They are fearing you, as well they should," said Burgold.

"I should've gone straight up and killed them," muttered Eldred.

Burgold gestured at Mack. "You were saving your friend."

Eldred nodded slowly. "Yes, I suppose."

"There could be another means," said Gundlach.

"What's that?" asked Eldred.

"The stone," said Gundlach. "If you were removing the stone from the Goddess, you could be handing it up through the bars. You could be getting that to the Second at least."

Eldred gave a short laugh. "Oh, that would do it. If she had the stone, she could keep me down here forever. She could probably hold the city too, if she is as strong as you were saying. At least now, I can probably dig my way out. It may take a hundred years, but I'll get free. Hand over the stone, not likely."

"She might be giving you her word. She would be keeping it if she did," said Gundlach.

"She might be keeping her word, but she wouldn't be keeping her head," protested Nymandus. "Think about all he has been doing."

Mack jabbed his finger at the bodies spread out across the room. "You Motherless bastard! What about us? You starved us to death."

"We were not starving anyone," snarled Nymandus. "If she had been wanting to torture you worthless barbarians, you would not be looking at such fine corpses as these. She was having a purpose, a need. She was using these men to track you fools, but they were too weak. They were withering under the bright light of her glorious power despite her mercy."

"I'll give you a taste of my mercy!" shouted Mack, but he stayed sitting by the disks.

The shouting continued on, mostly Mack and Nymandus, though sometimes the others chimed in. Eldred ignored them and sat staring at his father, resting his hand on his father's shoulder.

King Alfred—perhaps not a good man, but a great king, at least until the doomed assault on New Wismar. Of course, that had been the Goddess's trap and would have destroyed all the Deiran forces except for Father's insistence on leading with his golden pod. It had been a feat, a considerable feat, for Eldred to slay the Goddess and free him—if only to death. There was only one question left: would he be buried with honor alongside the revered dead in Boar's Tusk, or lie neglected and forgotten in the depths of the Goddess's lair?

If Father were returned to the world of sunlight and breezes and stars and clouds, they'd see the withered husk he'd become. They'd know that he'd been held as her captive slave for almost a year and passed away in the first moments of his freedom. Mack, being Mack, would tell it all. They'd know that Father had lain naked, strapped to those cold stone disks, licking up green slime to stay alive.

He had done it, though. It had been Father's voice that had reached out and brought Eldred down to face the Goddess. That was a shared victory. The head of the Goddess belonged to both of them. Didn't that outweigh the rest? There would be scornful comments—Lord Ferris, for certain—but the alternative was this corrupt room of fading light, an uneasy rest in the cold depths of the Goddess's sanctuary. Eldred blinked—they were still arguing.

"It won't be ninety days till they hunt down the last of your worthless kind," declared Mack with a smug smile. "And I don't just mean here, in your wretched city. I mean in the whole of Corporia. You won't be barbarians; you'll be extinct!"

Gundlach glowered back. "Your warriors will be finding tall walls here and taller walls still in Wismar. If they are not growing wings and flying, they may be stymied."

"Enough!" said Eldred. "I've made my decision. I'll give the Second the stone."

ENOLF

Eldred unbolted the hatch and banged on the barrier. "Who's up there? I need to talk."

It appeared to be night, though the red dome above still glowed with an eerie shimmer through the bars. A wall of rocks and dirt several feet high had grown up around the hatch entrance. Fortunately, they had not covered it up. Eldred could not see anyone, but he heard sounds of movement.

He glanced back down the darkening stairway; a third of the lights had gone out. He had come up alone, not wanting to risk unhelpful comments from the others, a concern that included Mack as much as the Corporians. He trusted that they wouldn't kill Mack down below, though it was a possibility. All he had with him was the stone and Capito.

Eldred had eventually succeeded in getting Burgold to bring water for cleaning up. None of the Corporians had wanted to look at the mess. The stone gleamed in his hand—a pulsing red ruby, free now of the debris that such things collected inside someone's skull. The head was less pleasant to view, but he had done his best. In the end, it had to be him. It was doubtful that the Corporians would have spared Burgold if he had done the job. Eldred sighed. In any case, it was done. With luck, it would be the last time he dug a stone out of someone's forehead.

Keeper Enolf appeared, looking down through the hatch. His hair was rumpled, but he wore a smile. His good humor had returned to him. "What is it, Mercian? Are you wanting a story to put you to sleep? Or are you having some other reason for bothering me in the middle of the night?"

"I need to see the Second," said Eldred.

"Do you? Are you needing to get in one more victim before the sun rises?" asked Enolf.

Eldred held up the stone. "No. I wish to give her the stone. I have it here in my hand."

Enolf knelt down, staring intently at the hatch. After a moment, he called for a torch and lowered it down to just above the bars. He must have seen it flash, for his face brightened with a greedy smile. "Huh, just a few hours and you are breaking already. I was predicting as much."

"Fine. Get the Second."

Enolf glanced around, surveying the layers of rock and dirt with pride. "This portal is mine. I was directing its blockage. I am managing the forces that guard it. If you are wishing to pass something up from below, it is fitting that you pass it to me."

"No. I'll only put it in the hand of the Second."

"So you are saying tonight. Perhaps tomorrow night, or next week, or even next month you will be feeling differently. We are having all sorts of time, you and I. We could be having years. Well, if you are staying alive, that is," finished Enolf.

Eldred grimaced. "You're quite right about that, Keeper. I'll feel different tomorrow for certain. Because tonight is the last night it could work. I'm not even sure it can. My father lies below, dead."

"How sad," said Enolf, though his eyes said something different.

"By our customs, I have seven days in which to transport him to Boar's Tusk and bury him with honors. Seven days, which already includes today, the day he died. So, if there's some deal to be made, it must be made right away, and I won't make it with you. Bring the Second."

"Huh. It could be as you are saying, though if you were down there crying about it, I do not see why you were waiting until the middle of the night to raise the issue. Or perhaps you are having trouble sleeping down there, trapped. Perhaps the realization that you will be dying down there is sinking in," said Enolf.

Eldred laughed. "No, Enolf. As you said, we have all the time in the world. I'm content if you wish to ignore my offer—your wanton act will relieve me of the obligation. We could just stay here chatting, you and I. I think you'll have an interesting tale to share. I'll certainly be fascinated to hear how your city falls and your people are put to the sword. Is that what you want—to entertain me over the next few months—or will you bring the Second?"

Enolf glowered at Eldred through the bars, still holding the torch low. The mirth had drained from his face. "We will be seeing who shares which tales with whom." He pulled up the torch and departed.

Eldred sat down on the steps, setting the stone beside him. He took a deep breath. The air was fresher at the top of the stairs, looking up through the bars. He took pleasure in studying the dome above, focusing on something far away; it was so confining below. He still felt the hot glow of the Goddess's stone—not a real heat, just the glare of its power. It was less hateful since it had been removed from the Goddess's head. It might not hate him again until the Second took it for herself.

The Second

It was an hour before the Second appeared, kneeling down and peering into the hatch. Morning was not far off; a few of the alien birds were already starting their eerie morning calls.

"You were asking for me, Eldred?" she said.

She was a vision in the darkness. Her corruption glowed as bright as ever, overshadowing her jewelry and accentuating her features. Her lips looked more full. Her eyes seemed larger and glimmered in the flickering torchlight.

"Yes, I did," said Eldred. "I wish to discuss an exchange, one I'm sure you'll agree is to our mutual advantage."

She frowned. "Has the offer been changing from what you mentioned previously?"

"Oh, yes. I considered what you said and also remembered obligations of my own. I'm sure Enolf informed you."

"He said you are needing to bury your father. I sympathize. I should note that we were not meaning to harm him or the other men. I can understand how you might be misconstruing the apparatus below. Its visage, its appearance, is one that was always troubling to me. But it had a utility; it was giving the Goddess an understanding of where your people were gathering."

Eldred's face crinkled up. "Yes, I understand. Nymandus was mentioning something of that sort. It was"—he forced out the words—"necessary for your protection."

She smiled sadly. "So many actions we are taking now that nobody is truly wanting. We are being pressed now, you and I. The future grows dark, and no answers are coming."

"Do you really feel that way?" asked Eldred.

"I do."

"What if we find a way forward together?"

She leaned forward slightly. Her red glowing form appeared beautiful, not corrupt, against the faint glow of sunrise. "I would be happy if we were discovering such a thing."

Eldred picked up the stone and raised it to the grate. "You can see this. I know you can."

She pressed her lips together. "I do."

"I'll give you the stone. I'll pass it to you right now."

She blinked. "And what will you be taking in return?"

"Nothing but your word. Your word that you'll clear this portal and let me out. Your word that you'll supply me with oxen and wagons to transport my father and the other dead men back home."

She raised her eyebrow. "Is that all you are requesting?"

Eldred nodded. "Yes. I'll try to convince them to grant you a truce, say for six months. It would help if you let me take the weapons, but—in truth— I don't know what I can get from the Deirans on this point. You can go back to your lands if you wish, or stay here, though I'm certain staying here will be very dangerous."

"And what will you be doing? Will you be returning to kill me, to kill all of us?" she asked softly.

"No. Not during the truce," said Eldred, shaking his head. "Friends don't kill friends. I didn't realize it until now, but I think we could be friends. I don't like all of you—some Corporians are horrible; you must see that yourself. Others are trustworthy, good, honorable. I think you must be honorable. Can I hand you this stone? Will you give your word to let me go forth and bury my father?"

She sighed. "I would be agreeing. I should like to be friends, and I would forever be keeping my word. But you are not understanding us and how we work. I am the Second, presumed to succeed the Goddess and to be bearing the stone. But first, we will be having our examinations, and only then will a Goddess be named. For the moment, I am not commanding anyone."

Eldred lowered the stone slightly and considered. "I've seen your people, both those down here below the portal and those above. Of all the Corporians I've seen, aside from the Goddess herself, you shine brightest with the power of your people. You'll be the Goddess. I know it. Here, take it." He pinched the stone between two of his fingers and reached it up between the bars. "Convince them to let me out today if you can. Or, if it must be so, become the Goddess first."

She lay flat and stretched down her hand to take the stone. As she did, the power surged through her, and her eyes grew wide.

Eldred smiled. "It suits you."

"I was not expecting this," she said. "I will be doing what I can for you, Eldred. You can be trusting in that."

"I do," said Eldred.

After she left, Eldred remained sitting under the grate, watching the sun climb higher behind the dome. The fresh air and the absence of his bickering companions down below made for a pleasant change. He leaned back against the wall, almost falling asleep. Everytime he was about to drop off, doubt stirred in his gut and brought him awake. He had given everything away in return for her promises. It had all seemed right, very comfortable, in the moment. She seemed honest, extremely honorable. But as she had admitted, she commanded no one. They might be up there laughing at him, laughing at the dull-witted Mercian who had handed over the most valuable artifact of their civilization in return for nothing.

He wrestled with his fears for hours—the sun was well up—before the sound of vigorous activity suddenly filled the air. Shovels scraped on stones; grunting men sounded their efforts; and Keeper Enolf's angry face appeared above, looking down on Eldred through the grate.

"It has been decided, we are letting you out," said Enolf.

"Am I getting oxen and carts?" asked Eldred.

Enolf raised his index finger. "One wagon. You will be finding it near the entrance to the dome."

"And our weapons?" asked Eldred.

"Some few. I am to be picking them out. Mind you, it is all foolishness; I am certain we will be seeing them again in the hands of our enemies. But the Second was successful in persuading the others."

Eldred smiled. "She is an honorable woman."

"Huh. Well, whatever you are finding the case, I am to be helping you leave the city as quickly as possible."

"Good. I'll need a number of your men to carry the bodies up to the top. If you can convince one of the adepts below to open the storeroom, I can help sort the weapons while you are clearing the barrier," said Eldred.

"Do not be bothering with that. As I was saying, I will do the picking."

Eldred rose to his feet. "Very well. I'll bring the bodies here. Time is ticking away."

RELEASE

While the Corporians worked at clearing off the portal, Eldred carried the bodies of the fallen warriors up the stairs, each carefully wrapped in its blanket and tucked against the wall in a descending line that started with his father's corpse. When he was done, he sat underneath the open hatch and waited, dusted by occasional showers of dirt.

Burgold sat a few steps below, mournfully watching over the ruined head of the Goddess, emptied now of its precious stone. He had wrapped it in a decorative table covering from her throne room. Mack and Gundlach waited further down the stairs in the growing darkness as more lights dimmed.

Nymandus was gone, having left while Eldred had been above bargaining with the Second. He was hiding down in one of the rooms, probably drunk, or so Eldred imagined. He had been dead set against Eldred escaping the sanctuary, so by logic he should have been the most unhappy at the turn of events. If that were so, he must have been sad indeed. Gundlach was unresponsive and morose. Even Mack, the only survivor, seemed fearful at leaving the pit where he had been held captive for eight months.

Finally, there was a scraping noise as the Corporians began shifting the barrier. Eldred stood up and helped push. It slid easily now with Eldred working with them; its five dangling legs bounced up the side and disappeared over the edge as the portal covering was dragged away.

Eldred didn't hesitate. He snatched up his father's body and trotted up the steps, followed by Burgold and Mack, both of whom moved a bit unsteadily. Gundlach came up last, head down and shoulders stooped.

The five-sided portal building was light and airy; an open gap showed in the ceiling where the barrier had been fixed above the circular stairway. There was a flurry of motion as the men who had been clearing the portal vacated the room, running out to join the throngs of soldiers who encircled the building. If they were going to fight, it would be out there, out in the open where there would be no wall to guard Eldred's back.

After a brief pause to allow his companions to catch up, Eldred set his face and walked out the door they had entered the previous day. Thousands of soldiers crowded around, filling the lowest terraces to capacity—so many men! They carried swords and spears and shields and bows. A gasp filled the air when Burgold walked out behind him bearing his bundle; everyone knew what it was.

For a moment, Eldred felt so certain that they meant to attack that he considered dropping his father and drawing Capito. He stopped himself just short, glad that he did. The men surrounding him looked tense, on the edge of violence. The sight of him raising his sword might have been enough to push them over.

As Eldred came to a stop, Burgold tottered past him, hurrying over to the line of men fifty feet away. As he neared his compatriots, two figures walked out to greet him: Keeper Enolf and Baron Wortwin. They motioned Burgold forward. When he reached the line, he handed the head to the nearest soldier, who turned and handed it to the man behind him. A series of rapid exchanges quickly bore the head far away, climbing up the terraces off to Eldred's right.

Eldred shuddered with a sense of relief watching it disappear through the throng of soldiers. All the same problems remained, but her head was such a nasty reminder of what he'd been forced to do. He might go on to kill thousands, but he never wanted to dig a stone out of someone's head ever again.

Meanwhile, the Baron and the Keeper approached, stopping some fifteen feet in front of Eldred.

"Keep moving. The wagon is waiting at the top," commanded Keeper Enolf.

Eldred nodded and lifted his father slightly. "I've got him. Twenty-three more for your men to carry. I also need someone to help him"—he jerked his head at Mack—"make the climb."

Enolf gave a thin smile. "Why not Gundlach? He is always ready to be helping your kind."

Gundlach frowned. "No. I am done."

"Are you?" asked Enolf, turning to glance at the Baron.

The Baron rolled his eyes. "I need you to be coming with me for a moment, Gundlach. I have information I must be relaying to you."

"What?" demanded Gundlach.

"I am preferring to tell you over there," said Baron Wortwin, gesturing at Gundlach to follow them.

There was a pause as the Corporians stepped away and started arguing in low voices. Mack fidgeted at Eldred's side, darting his head in all directions as he took in the mass of foes that stood ready to destroy him. Weak and feeble as he was, he seemed ready to make a go of it.

Eldred looked Enolf in the eye. "And the arms, the more you bring up, the better I can negotiate on your behalf."

Enolf laughed. "Really? On my behalf?"

"Yes," said Eldred in a forceful tone. "I don't need a truce, but you do if you hope to escape back to Corporia with your people. I gave the Second my word I'd do my best to convince them. How strange that I'm working harder for your people than you are."

A dark look passed over Enolf's face. "Fortunately for you, I am having my orders. I will be getting you out of the city with the greatest possible speed. But do not for a moment consider lingering or turning back once you have left. Should you be doing that, I will not hesitate to order your death. As you can see, I am having the men to do it."

Eldred shrugged. "It's possible. The weapons?"

"I am having my orders," said Enolf, through gritted teeth. "I will be deciding which you get. Now, move your feet and start climbing the stairs."

Gundlach caught up to them as they were crossing the field; his face was filled with fury.

"What is it?" asked Eldred.

"I am coming with you," said Gundlach.

"Why?" asked Eldred.

"A dozen slippery reasons, none of which is making any sense!" snapped Gundlach.

"Oh," said Eldred.

Mack narrowed his eyes. "All the way to Boar's Tusk?"

Gundlach nodded.

Mack snorted. "I don't fancy your chances."

Gundlach swept his arm, gesturing at the masses of men. "If you two fools can be walking out of here, I am not seeing why I cannot be surviving Boar's Tusk."

Behind them, a line of men was already coming out of the portal building bearing the corpses. Other men were following Enolf down below. Eldred hoped he would be generous. The return of family heirlooms would put the Deirans in good spirits, and they would have to be in the best possible spirits to even consider sparing their enemies.

142

DEPARTURE

Halfway up the stairs, Eldred paced back and forth on a landing, holding his father's corpse and waiting for Mack to resume the climb. He was slow, dead slow, and Gundlach was too lost in his own thoughts to be much help. Meanwhile, time continued to slip away. It felt as if only Eldred had any sense of urgency. Even the Corporian soldiers who surrounded them in all directions, both up and down the stairs and across the terraces, seemed more sullen than actively threatening.

As Eldred crossed the landing for the fiftieth time, he spotted Keeper Enolf approaching from below followed by seven men bearing medium-sized boxes, too small to contain anything other than the daggers seized from the golden pod. Eldred groaned inwardly. Useful as those daggers would prove, it was the swords that would elicit the most cooperation from the Deiran lords. Why couldn't Keeper Enolf understand such a simple matter?

Mack was still taking his rest five minutes later when Enolf reached the landing.

Eldred shook his head. "No armor? Not a single sword?"

"No," said Enolf. He appeared winded by the ascent.

"I told you: I need something to bargain with," said Eldred.

Enolf waved the men onward and stopped, leaning against the railing at the edge of the stairs. "I was checking those knives; some are still bearing the blood of my friends, my relatives. If it were up to me, I would be giving you nothing. But the Baron was insisting on behalf of Lady Yslana."

Eldred frowned. There had been at least one other named sword down there.

Gundlach watched the boxes go on by, up the stairs. "The Baron was saying this was enough?"

"He did," said Enolf. "But I am certain that he was knowing what foolishness this all is."

"So, it was Lady Yslana who gave the order?" asked Eldred.

Enolf nodded. "At the urging of the Second. You tricked that foolish girl into believing you."

Eldred felt warm at the mention of Ennlin. "She's honorable. How could I not keep my word to someone so honorable?"

"I am thinking it would come easily to you. When you are returning with your friends, though, that will not be easy." Enolf pointed out at the mass of men who surrounded them. "One of them, I am not knowing who, will be killing you."

Eldred shrugged. "Just pack the wagon, and don't forget my things from the inn. We'll be leaving the very instant Mack makes it up."

Enolf glanced at Mack and then back at Eldred. "So much easier to just be dealing with you now. You are alone, or as close to being alone as someone can be if they were not. In any case, at least you are getting what you deserve, Gundlach." With that he turned and climbed on after his men.

"What did he mean?" asked Eldred as he watched Enolf topping the next flight of stairs.

Gundlach sighed. "They are exiling me. I am not to be returning until after I bear witness to your bargain with the Deirans. Until then, I cannot be coming here or pressing on to Wismar under penalty of death."

"Exile? For you?" asked Eldred. "Well, don't worry. I'm certain I can reach some understanding with my cousin. You'll get back to your family."

Gundlach said nothing. Mack stirred like he might rise but didn't.

Eldred ground his teeth. "Come on, Mack. You heard him. If we linger, we'll be tempting the Keeper to deal with us."

"Stop nagging me. You won't make it anyway. It's too far for seven days. Six is even worse," said Mack.

"Amazing insight, Mack. Now, get moving," said Eldred.

Mack frowned and struggled up to his feet.

It was a long while with more breaks for Mack before they reached the top. They found a sturdy looking wagon led by four horses. Off to the side, Enolf sat on horseback with a few hundred mounted men.

Inside the wagon, Eldred found a small sack with his belongings from the Iron Gate, including the rings he had won and his daggers. Other than that, the wagon was packed with supplies that must have been meant for Gundlach, including a store of corrupted bread and his large gold-colored shield. Next to the food supplies, much too close in Eldred's view, the corpses were stacked six across and four deep at the back of the wagon. Eldred placed the body of his father on top, as much a place of honor as was to be had. Gundlach retrieved his shield, dusting it clean, and went up front to take the reins. Eldred and Mack joined Gundlach on the driver's bench, and soon they jerked forward, moving swiftly down the street and exiting the dome.

Eldred kept an eye out for the Second as they traveled through the city. He expected to spot her somewhere, perhaps on one of the walls or up in some high tower. But if she was there, he missed her. The streets were empty except for soldiers and Enolf's horsemen, who followed closely behind. No sign of her, but the corruption gradually faded as they made the journey outwards.

When they exited the main gate, coming out on the grassy plateau, it was like a fever breaking. Eldred took a deep breath, sampling the first pure air in many days. Mack, who was seated on the bench to the other side of Gundlach, said nothing, but a small smile crossed his lips, the first one that Eldred had seen since he had rescued the man. It was good for both of them.

Gundlach peered back at the city with a strained face. The city gate was already swinging shut.

"You needn't be concerned. I'll make the deal. You'll be coming back with good news," said Eldred.

Mack snickered.

Eldred sighed. "Don't mind him. We'll get these men buried with honor. We'll return these knives. They're just knives, but probably some of them are quite valuable. I also have the rings I took. And by that time we're there, the Second will have taken the stone. Your people will be safe."

Both Gundlach and Mack looked back with skeptical expressions.

"Trust me," said Eldred, but he had the sense that neither of them did.

First Contact

The wagon rocked from side to side as they crossed the plateau. The land was empty except for them; the Corporians had pulled in their herds. Perhaps they had not been out since Eldred had killed the Goddess. Eldred nodded to himself, expecting that was the case. They would be locked up tight. The gates would remain shut until the Second, that is to say the new Goddess, was confident in her abilities.

Ennlin would be a great replacement for the former Goddess, who'd been a horrible woman. The former Goddess had invaded Gauraci, won a battle by trickery and tortured honorable men. She'd wanted to kill Eldred too. That glowing red dagger she'd been holding must have been their equivalent of Capito. If she'd driven that into his side before he'd taken her head, she'd have had her way.

The new Goddess: she was fair-minded, honorable—and pretty, too. She might be a bit vain, judging by the amount of jewelry she wore. That could've just been a Corporian practice, though she seemed to wear a good deal more of it than any of the other women in the city, certainly more than Lady Yslana.

Lady Yslana would also have to be pleased. Thanks to Eldred, a more gifted woman was stepping up as the Goddess, a Goddess who would be agreeable to returning to Corporia, or so Ennlin had said. The vile city, New Wismar, which scarred the Mother's land, would be abandoned. Perhaps the Deirans would raze it, though that would take quite a bit of sustained effort; hard to see them putting in the labor required. Still, they'd want some personal share in the revenge. They wouldn't be satisfied by Eldred killing the Goddess. There might even be a few raids on Corporia.

Eldred gripped the bench as they started descending the steep trail down to the river. His eyes went first to the spot where Hobbie had died, killed by a stupid minion of Lord Ferris. It had been eight months before, but the pain and anger felt fresh. His gaze drifted to several Deirans who were down in the trees alongside the riverbank. He pressed his lips together and glanced at Gundlach, who was focused on steering the wagon down that awful track. He wouldn't allow a repeat of that horrible day.

"They're down there, by the river," said Eldred with a recollection of having said something similar the previous time.

Gundlach's hands tightened on the reins, but he made no comment. Mack, too, was quiet.

"Well, aren't you glad, Mack?" prompted Eldred.

Mack turned his beady eyes on Eldred. "I'll be glad when they've killed the last stinking Corporian that stains our soil. They can start with this one." He glared at Gundlach.

Gundlach kept his eyes on the horses.

"No, Mack. I'll not have anyone killing Gundlach. It would be a poor showing for our diplomacy," said Eldred.

"Maybe for your weak diplomacy," said Mack.

"Leave it," said Eldred. "Let's bury my father first. If you want to stir things up after, that's fine. I wouldn't expect anything less from you. But in case you've forgotten, I'm the one who got you out of that place. You might think on that."

Mack scowled, but to Eldred's surprise, he kept his tongue.

The men below were in motion. A few forded the river, riding back through the woods. The others were forming up in a line, eight bonded warriors on horseback.

Eldred frowned. What would they do? If it came to a fight, they weren't half-blind in a cave and there wasn't any force of Corporians to distract them. Well, there was Gundlach. Eldred put his hand on Capito's hilt; he could see the purple energy swirling there. He was exceedingly well armed. That might even the odds.

Gundlach made slow progress down the hill, perhaps reluctant to see what would happen once they completed their descent. For their part, the horsemen held their line by the river and did not advance. Eldred suspected that would have changed if Gundlach had shown any indication of turning the wagon around.

They arrived at the bottom, just fifty yards from the Deirans, when

Eldred caught the motion of more riders coming back through the woods. Maybe thirty men or more in total, six pods. For a moment, his breath left him. That was too many, Capito or not. These were bonded warriors, not lame Corporians. He glanced over the woods; off the trail, it was quite a tangle. He might be faster than their horses there.

He had been leaning forward, tensing up, when suddenly he heaved a sigh of relief. There, in the middle of the reinforcements coming out from the trees was Dederick—not Lord Ferris, but Dederick.

Gundlach brought the wagon to a stop.

Eldred stood up on the wagon bench, suddenly conscious of his tattered tunic and blood stained breeches. "It's me, Dederick. It's Eldred, son of Alfred. I've returned."

The Deiran line thickened with the new arrivals and parted to let Dederick pass through. He rode slowly through the line, peering at the men in the wagon.

"Eldred?" he called. "I wasn't expecting to find you riding down this hill. I wasn't expecting you at all."

"No. I'm sure not. But nonetheless, here you find me. And not just me. I'm bringing Mack. And bodies, I'm bringing the corpses of my father and twenty-three men of great honor: Pounder, Bate, Stace and many others. They died yesterday."

Dederick stopped some twenty feet in front of them. "Yesterday?" He shook his head. "No, not yesterday. More like a year ago. And what about him?" He pointed at Gundlach.

"A Corporian diplomat. He's coming with me to Boar's Tusk," said Eldred.

Dederick squinted at Mack. "Is that really you, Mack? Where are your clothes? You look terrible."

"Screw you, Dederick!" spat Mack, who slid over and fell off the side of the wagon trying to get down. He landed flat on his back and was slow to rise.

Eldred hopped down from his side of the wagon to help, but Dederick was quicker. Dederick pulled Mack up to his feet and started dusting him off.

"You're looking worse now that I'm close. They've been holding you there for all this time?" Dederick's eyes slid up to Gundlach, who sat stiffly, staring straight ahead.

"Yes, I suppose. I—they tortured us, or at least they tortured me. They must have. I can't remember much," mumbled Mack as he glared at Eldred, who had walked up behind Dederick.

The rest of Dederick's forces dismounted and started leading their horses closer.

Dederick released his hold on Mack, who kept on his feet. "I don't know, Eldred. I can't say I was expecting this. You have the king's corpse in there?"

Eldred nodded. "Come back. I'll show you. And all of you, leave the Corporian alone. He's under my protection—I have the sword." He pulled Capito out of its scabbard and raised it over his head.

"By the Mother, that's Capito!" shouted someone.

"He's got bloody Capito," echoed one of the other men.

Dederick motioned downwards with his hands. "Alright, alright. We'll leave the Corporian fellow for now. Put your sword away, Eldred. Don't draw it unless you mean to use it."

Eldred stared back defiantly, but sheathed Capito. "I just wanted to make sure everyone knew before someone went and made a mistake. Come with me; they're all back here."

The men were jostling around as Eldred parted the cover at the back of the wagon. There was a trace of odor and some flies too. Eldred grimaced. He remembered that smell from a previous wagon ride. It was only going to get worse.

Eldred reached in and lifted Alfred's corpse out of the wagon. He turned and set the body down on the ground, shifting the blankets to reveal his father's thin, haggard face; he looked so forlorn.

Dederick sighed. "That's him. I don't know that he died yesterday, but that's him."

"He was tortured, like Mack," said Eldred. "When I killed the Goddess and freed them, they all died, except for Mack."

Dederick jerked up his head. "Are you saying you killed their stonebearer?"

"I did. Mack saw that much. He saw me carrying her head around anyway," said Eldred.

The men turned their eyes on Mack, who was standing off to the side.

"Yeah, well, he had some woman's head, and he cut something out of it. He was real torn up about it," said Mack in a dismissive tone.

A gleam shone in Dederick's eyes. "So, you have her stone?"

"Not anymore. I had to give it back or they would've kept us trapped in there, in her sanctuary," said Eldred.

Dederick laughed. "Well, of course. Cut off her head, but then give the stone right back. By the Mother, I'm not sure what to make of that. Let's go back to camp. We can get you some clothes and talk it over. We're set up in the glade on the other side of the river, where we made camp before."

"I'm not riding with them!" snapped Mack.

"Fine." Dederick motioned at one of his men. "You take him. Follow us over there, Eldred."

The men mounted up and headed back across the river, except for a few sentries who stayed put by the trees.

Eldred climbed back up on the seat at the front of the wagon. "See, you're still alive."

Gundlach grunted. "For now."

"We won't be staying long. There's still a few hours of daylight. We have to keep moving," said Eldred.

"Why not just be telling them?" asked Gundlach.

"Tell them what?" asked Eldred.

"Burgold was clear. You may no longer be holding the Goddess's stone, but you bear the shard of the Mother. She said as much before you were murdering her."

Eldred stiffened. "I didn't murder anyone. And if you want to live, you'll keep the information about the shard to yourself."

Gundlach scowled. "Or you will be killing me?"

"No. They'll do it. Believe me in this: it's not a thing that's safe to mention. The person who bore it before me hid away in a cellar." Eldred smiled. "Strange, yes. Why would a person with such power cower so?"

Gundlach kept silent, guiding the wagon into the water as he watched Eldred from the corner of his eye.

Eldred tapped his forehead. "Power such as this can be taken. I took it from the Goddess. She was planning to take it from me. One of these men, perhaps Dederick, might like to hold such a gift. Deirans love power. If you want my protection, you'll make no mention of the shard."

Gundlach shook his head. "You are all only a bunch of cutthroat bastards."

Eldred gave a short laugh. "Don't worry. If there's one thing I've learned, it's how to deal with bastards."

DEDERICK'S CAMP

ldred tore the meat off the chicken leg with his teeth and savored it, sucking in half the blackened greasy skin in one bite. It was the first clean food he'd eaten since before he had entered the city and, before that, the meals had been pretty paltry. As he chewed, he straightened the black cloak Dederick had loaned him and looked over the camp.

The glade was much as it had been before in terms of layout, though it was now more sparsely populated than it had been before the great battle, the great disaster. Only the men who had come out to greet Eldred were present aside from a single cook who labored in the center of the meadow where a squad of stewards had prepared food before.

Eldred and Dederick were seated on a log off by themselves. The rest of the men gathered around Mack, listening to his tales as he occasionally shouted threats at Gundlach, who remained seated by himself near the wagon.

Dederick scratched his chin and studied the horses. "You'll make it if you push through. Their horses don't have much speed, but they're steady. We were chasing some riders a few months ago and damned if their mounts didn't make it close. Still, we caught them before they got to the zone."

"The zone?" asked Eldred.

"If you get close enough to the city, they can lay you out. Or at least they could before; not sure after your business. That's how they won that battle, you know."

Eldred's face froze. "So you figured that out. You finally figured that out. People had been blaming me for the golden pod keeling over."

"Well, perhaps at first. People shared many opinions after the defeat at the gates. But we've seen these incidents a number of times now. Everyone up here on the front lines knows about the zone. It's nothing to do with you."

"That's right. It absolutely isn't!" exclaimed Eldred, waving the drumstick.

"Right, I know," said Dederick.

Eldred took a breath. "Alright then. The zone. How far out does it go?"

"Half the plateau by my measure. We actually had a bit of luck with your father's insistence on sending the golden pod in first. If we'd all been in close, they'd have killed us all or captured us."

"Killed. They only needed the five pods. They built a contraption the Goddess used to track all of you. Or at least that's what they said. Mack was strapped in it when I rescued him, not that he's shown an ounce of gratitude for my efforts."

Dederick smiled. "I noticed. You're likely to find more of the same with others, given what happened with your kinsman."

"My kinsman? You mean my cousin, Henreit?"

"Yes. I think that's him. They say you murdered him, that you murdered all of your companions at that country estate."

Eldred lowered the drumstick. "I didn't. I killed one man, only one man. It wasn't Henreit."

Dederick shrugged. "Maybe, but now you've killed their stonebearer. It kind of fits. I didn't know you had it in you, but it seems you are a very dangerous young man."

"I am."

"You had better hope you are if you're planning to take those corpses to Boar's Tusk. You may find the going much easier than the leaving."

"Why so? It seems you all finally know that I didn't make the golden pod fall down. If even stupid Harold has figured it out, nobody can hang treason around my neck. As for Henreit, even if you don't believe me, that's Maldavian business; no reason for any Deiran to raise a fuss."

Dederick paused and considered. "That's all true, but you're missing the main point: people don't like you. I mean, I like you. But other people, well, they don't."

Eldred gestured at the wagon. "I have gifts in there—seven boxes of knives, all very fine blades. I'm going to return them when I bring the men back for burial."

"Seven boxes—how many knives is that? Is that all the knives that were there?" Dederick rubbed his chin. "I had a few cousins in the golden pod. By the Mother, what a loss. Bad enough to lose a hundred men, but we couldn't recover anything, not arms nor armor. It was a disgrace. Can I see those blades?"

Eldred smiled and shook his head. "No. I'm certain some knives aren't there—a few were broken. As for going through them now, I trust you, but it's easier to hand them all out at once. Besides, I need to make an impression. I'm hoping to convince everyone to extend a truce to the Corporians."

"Why would you do that?"

"So they can leave and return to Corporia."

Dederick made a face. "I don't think they're leaving."

"I think they will. They have problems of their own at home. They won't talk about it, but some of them already wanted to leave even before I killed their Goddess. Now, with that change, the ones in power are ready to go."

"It's a huge city. I can't believe they're willing to just walk away."

"If I can get Harold's guarantee, they'll go."

"Your trip keeps getting more and more interesting," said Dederick.

"Why don't you come with me?" asked Eldred.

"I'm up here guarding things, or didn't you notice?"

"I can guarantee you that nothing will be happening for some time. They're picking a new Goddess, and, even after that, they'll be sitting there with the gates shut while she gets used to the stone."

"Sounds plausible. Except for their mangy herds, they don't come out much anyway," said Dederick.

"It's the truth. Will you come?" asked Eldred.

Dederick rubbed his hands together. "I suppose I could make you an escort. But first, I need to know if you're up to any more funny business."

Eldred raised his eyebrows. "Funny business?"

"You know, funny business. Say, with Harold. You aren't planning on killing another cousin are you?"

"No. And I never did. Not with Henreit, anyway."

"Good. Two pods should do then, but don't bring me into it if you're murdering anyone."

HOMEWARD

They set out shortly after with Gundlach at the reins of the wagon and Mack back as his surly passenger, still too unsteady for riding long distances on horseback. Eldred kept close at hand, jogging or walking depending on the speed of the wagon, which was never that fast over the mountain track. Dederick and his men rode on ahead, often out of sight for minutes at a time as they wound through the trees.

It was getting dark when they reached the campsites the golden pod had used the night before their destruction. Eldred directed Gundlach to park the wagon in the same spot where his father had set his tent. Somehow, it seemed fitting.

The men built a fire and spread out around it, perched on stones and stumps. One of Dederick's men passed out strips of dried meat. They had been sitting a while when Dederick pointed at Gundlach, who was sitting apart by the Corporian horses, eating some of his stores.

"Can he come over here, Eldred?"

The men around the campfire went silent.

Eldred glanced around the circle uneasily. "Why?"

Dederick shrugged. "I'd be interested in what he has to say."

Eldred stood up, slightly apprehensive. "Gundlach, do you want to sit with us?"

Gundlach slowly rose to his feet and walked over to sit next to Eldred.

Dederick examined the Corporian. "You don't have the look of a diplomat to me. You seem more like a fighter."

"Or what passes for one among your kind," quipped one of Dederick's podmen, which elicited some laughter.

Gundlach stared back at the man, who was much smaller than the Corporian, before turning back to Dederick. "You are having the right of it."

"You ever killed anyone with that sword?" asked another of Dederick's men.

Gundlach rested his hand on the hilt. "I have."

Dederick motioned lightly at his men. "That's enough. He's a guest, a guest of the prince."

"That's right," said Eldred.

"I'm interested, though, in something Eldred said. He said you and your people might leave your city if he gets a truce for you. Is that so?" asked Dederick.

Gundlach nodded. "Yes. I am coming to bear witness to the agreement."

"You'd really leave, abandon that huge city you've built?" asked Dederick.

"I would be doing so," said Gundlach.

"Just because Eldred supposedly killed your stonebearer?" asked Dederick.

Gundlach glanced at Eldred and then back at Dederick. "No. It is having nothing to do with that. We must be returning home. We have matters we must be settling."

"What matters?" asked Dederick.

Grundlach stiffened. "I cannot be speaking of such things."

One of the men, a shorter man with an annoying smirk, spoke up. "Shame if it's the end of you lot."

Gundlach gave a slight shake of his head. "We will not be passing."

"What if you don't get a truce?" asked Dederick.

"We still have a Goddess," said Gundlach.

"It's true," said Eldred. "I've met the woman who will become their new Goddess. She's quite strong. Everyone says she's far stronger than the last Goddess. Dederick told me you all know about the zone. Well, that zone will now be wider and deadlier."

"Thanks to you," said Mack.

Eldred swung his head around toward Mack. "It's nothing I planned. I had to do it. Did you want to sit in Goddess's sanctuary for a hundred years, starving, dying in the dark?"

Mack glowered back. "I've suffered worse things. I was starved, but that's not the worst of it. If only you knew." He reached up and rubbed his forehead. "To be fair, I can see handing over the stone. Your father might've done that too. Nobody wants to die when they've got another option. But why, Eldred, why are you so keen on this stupid truce? As for me, all I want to do is to kill them."

"Yes. I know," said Eldred. "Killing people—it's what we Deirans do best. The problem is that with those high walls and the Goddess, they won't be easy to finish off. They could hold on for years, years of polluting the Mother's land with their energy, their corruption. If we don't want that— and I don't—then I say let's help them get back to their other business. Let's unblock the roads. Let's get them moving. Once they're back in their lands, if you want to raid, go do it."

Mack narrowed his eyes. "You were never a true Deiran; you're weak. Your father wouldn't just hope his enemies would go away."

"I'm weak? You're saying I'm weak?" Eldred frowned. "You sit here talking about how you want to kill every Corporian, but you can't even kill one." Eldred looked over the men. "I'm sure some of you agree with him. Well, fine. Then do as I did. Go into their city and kill their stonebearer. I'll sit here and wait. Who's going? Anyone?"

The men sat silently, staring into the fire.

Eldred sighed. "You're brave men. I'm not saying you aren't. But we have to face the truth: they're dug in. You haven't seen their defenses; I have. Their city is like an onion with a wall guarding each layer. They have thousands of soldiers and a stonebearer, their Goddess. Until someone has something better than empty boasts, I say truce. And if anyone thinks I'm weak, just ask me for a boxing lesson. You can gauge how feeble my arms are as I knock your teeth out."

Dederick laughed. Eldred raised a questioning eyebrow.

"Oh, no, Eldred. I'm on your side," said Dederick, raising his cup. "After all, men, who's stuck with this boring guard duty? We watch the herds come out. We watch the herds go in. Everyone was excited when the wagon came down the hill. It was something different. A truce is fine. I'm not going to pay my debts by capturing some fly-ridden cow."

A few men nodded.

"Just for now, just for six months," said Eldred. "Right, Gundlach? After that, you'll put up a good fight if we come to Corporia, to Wismar?"

Gundlach looked Eldred in the eye. "Yes, I would be fighting. Anyone who is coming to Wismar will be finding their last and most savage battle."

Eldred smiled. "I think that may be so."

TO BERT

Dederick and his men were off at first light the next morning, eager to get to Bert as early as possible. It seemed that a number of men, including Dederick, had formed romantic partnerships during breaks taken over their months of patrolling around the Corporian city. To Eldred's surprise and relief, Mack went with them. He didn't look comfortable seated on the horse as he set out, but he looked far stronger than the wretch Eldred had pulled from Goddess's device two days before.

Eldred jogged alongside as Gundlach started at the reins. They made great progress throughout the morning with Gundlach pressing the horses hard, but fell far behind the riders, whom they did not see after the first few minutes.

When noon came, Eldred jumped aboard to drive and Gundlach took his lunch, a few pieces of bread and a wedge of glowing Corporian cheese.

"They are not making much of an escort," said Gundlach between bites.

Eldred shrugged. "I suppose not. But are you missing them?"

"No."

"So all is good."

"I am not feeling so certain," said Gundlach. "Mack has been saying he would kill me more than a hundred times. I am sensing that others are thinking the same."

Eldred nodded as he steered the wagon around a turn. "Perhaps. For what it's worth, Dederick says nobody likes me either."

Gundlach swatted a fly on his forehead and wiped off its remains. "Because of your cousin. I have been hearing them talk."

Eldred sighed. "Yes. They all think I killed my cousin, Henreit."

"Did you?"

"No. I was there when it happened. It was—terrible. He begged for his life, but there was no mercy for him." Eldred winced. "It was the one who wore the shard before me. He killed Henreit, and I killed him, the Maledictus."

Gundlach's eyes narrowed. "How were you killing the shard bearer?"

Eldred smiled. "I won't be sharing that."

"I would not be using it against you."

"No, but it's just best not to say. I don't like to think about it anyway."

"Huh. So you cannot be explaining this to them."

"Not in any way that makes sense. Even if I tell the whole story, it isn't any more reasonable. I was a cripple, you see. I couldn't walk. I was trapped in a cell, too." Eldred shook his head. "I wouldn't believe it myself."

They rode in silence for a few minutes while Gundlach shooed away more flies.

Gundlach cleared his throat. "I am sorry you are being kept so distant from your people."

"It's not so bad. I only have a few friends. It's my mother that worries me. I'm certain this nonsense about Henreit is causing her some grief."

Gundlach raised his eyebrows. "Could you not at least be telling her?"

"I should. Now that your people know, she should as well. But still, it makes no sense. My people think the last Maledictus died a thousand years ago. What about your people? Do they know of any from more recent times?"

"No. For us, we say it was the First Goddess, along with Regula and Korinna, who was slaying the last of the Maledicti in ancient days. I am finding it hard to be thinking of you as one. You are not seeming like a Maledictus to me."

Eldred glanced over. "It could be anyone, you know. You don't even have to follow the rituals perfectly. I used the powder from the Sun People, the same powder I used on Lady Yslana. I think it may have made the shard more powerful in me. Of the others, Bonitus, the Son, he wore the shard first. Of course, he was extraordinary. But those who followed, they weren't as great. I killed the one who cowered in the cellar. The other one killed himself; he willed himself dead. I'd say he died better." Eldred shuddered. "You wouldn't believe what I had to do to kill Magner. I stabbed him so many times—stabbed him and poisoned him."

Gundlach's green eyes, lightly touched by the glow of corruption, grew concerned. "That is sounding to be a terrible ordeal."

"I expect I'll see the other side of it before I go."

"We are all dying in the end," said Gundlach.

Eldred blew out his breath. "Not like that. Only a Maledictus can die like that."

BERT

Eldred was driving the wagon when they topped a low ridge and Bert came into view below them some five miles further on. The city looked unchanged at that distance. Even the gate was open, as it had been before the great battle, removing any protection the citizens derived from the poorly maintained city wall.

"There's people out," said Eldred.

"Huh?" asked Gundlach.

"There's a crowd outside the gate."

Gundlach straightened up on the bench, straining his eyes. "Are they being friendly?"

"I can't tell from here. But they might not be. There's a lord out in these parts who wants me dead."

"We are having your friend, Dederick."

"Perhaps," said Eldred. "He says he's not in for killing anyone, which is a bit of a surprise. Anyway, even if Lord Ferris is present, we're delivering these bodies for burial. It's no law, but I think it would be poor manners if anyone interferes."

Gundlach set his face and said nothing.

"It should be fine. We don't all have poor manners," added Eldred.

Gundlach remained silent.

As they approached the city, having descended the ridge and passed through a wood, Eldred still had difficulty interpreting the emotion of the crowd. Though some of the people were armed, they looked more like a chance gathering of citizens than a war party. They appeared neither angry nor welcoming, except for Dederick, who waved them forward. Eldred spotted him by the gate with a group of elderly men. His podmen were nowhere to be seen. Mack was also absent.

Eldred drove past the outskirts of the crowd and pulled the wagon to a stop before Dederick.

An older man next to Dederick stepped forward and gave a slight bow. He had thinning white hair, but his eyes looked alert. "Welcome to Bert, Prince Eldred."

"Thank you," said Eldred. "Who am I addressing?"

"I'm Lord Esbiorn. I've been set as the mayor of Bert by King Harold."

Eldred cast a quick glance over the gathering. They weren't drawing weapons. "I see. I'm on a mission of peace, carrying the bodies of my father and other champions. I aim to get them to Boar's Tusk in time for their rites."

Lord Esbiorn glanced at Gundlach. "We've spoken about this with Dederick. We're not here to hinder you, Prince. But we request that you let us see King Alfred. We should also like to honor the other men."

Eldred grimaced. "These men are three day's dead."

"I understand, Prince," said Lord Esbiorn.

"They're in bad shape—not properly clothed or tended to. I'm not going to lay them down here in the dirt just so people can gawk at them," said Eldred.

Lord Esbiorn gestured to the gathering. "These are your father's subjects. We merely seek to pay our respects."

"Then come with me to Boar's Tusk if you're all so eager."

Lord Esbiorn frowned. "We wish to see the remains of our king. We can forgo the others. Mack gave us their names. But I must insist that we see the king. We have the right to see with our own eyes."

Eldred looked over the gathering—the good people of Bert. They couldn't all ride to Boar's Tusk where most of them would never venture even once in their short lives. Of course, he'd have hated it—laid out for the commoners to see, ungroomed, unwashed. But he was dead and he had been their ruler.

"Very well," said Eldred. "I won't take them out here. This is—this is not the right spot. In the center of your town, on the commons, my father met with Dederick before the battle under the shade of some birch trees near the stream. There was a patch of grass. I can set them down there. But everyone should understand that these men were starved and tortured. Anyone of us would appear diminished by that experience. You shouldn't judge these men or feel pity for them."

Lord Esbiorn nodded. "It shall be as you request, Prince."

The procession moved through the gates and into the town with Lord Esbiorn at the front along with Dederick and the town elders. Eldred drove the wagon after them, and the citizens fell in line behind him.

As Eldred looked over the town and the people, they seemed both familiar and unfamiliar at the same time. He'd last passed through the town as an unpopular prince hoping to earn a named sword by empowering his father, the king. Now, he was a rebel, a kinslayer in most of their eyes, and Alfred was dead. He had the sword he'd wanted, better even than whatever blade his father was going to turn up for him. The biggest change, one they didn't know and he hoped they wouldn't learn: he was a Maledictus.

Eldred laid out his father first, lifting his body out of the wagon and setting it down in the thick, green grass. He parted the blankets to show his father's sad face, marred as it was by the five red stones the Goddess had set there. He then brought out Pounder, Stace and Bate—all of his father's pod, except for Mack. That undeserving survivor was likely off drinking and whoring.

Eldred bade Lord Esbiorn to get down the rest of the corpses as he liked, and sat down between his father and Pounder. After all the bodies were laid out in a line, the townspeople began to approach. At first, Eldred was quite tense, waiting to hear some untoward comment on the disheveled appearance of the men, but nobody said a word and Eldred waved away any flies that presumed to walk on his father's face.

It took some time as each person examined his father carefully, trying to match the ruin of what they saw against the grand king who had stormed through almost a year before. As they passed, Eldred studied the foul stones the Goddess had implanted in Alfred's forehead. They seemed weaker, more brittle, than they had deep in the Goddess's sanctuary under her red dome.

Finally, he reached out and laid his finger on the center stone. It still had strength, running lines of power through his father's corpse to its fingers and toes, but it was no longer on its native soil. All around, the strength of the Mother was humming, alive in the plants, in the stones, in the air. He brushed aside a short tuft of his father's gray hair to reveal his fatum lapis. He had only one, a proper blue Deiran stone. It still gleamed with the power of the Mother, but Eldred had the sense it was fading.

Idly, Eldred traced a line down from behind his father's left temple where the fatum lapis was set to his father's forehead, now sullied with those wretched stones. As he stared, he began to see where the Mother's power had pooled before, as if someone had taken the darkest blue ink and drawn a wide circle centered just above his father's eyes.

He turned his attention to Pounder's face. As he focused, he saw that Pounder too had a blue circle. But where Alfred's had been more than three inches across, Pounder's was a little more than an inch. The shade was lighter too. Still, a lustrous dark blue, but lighter than the mark his father bore. Both were creatures of the Mother. They had been born so, and lived so, and died so. Such beings should not, could not, wear the binding stones of the Goddess.

Oblivious to everyone, wholly absorbed in the task, Eldred reached out to the foul stones on his father's forehead and tapped them with his finger and his mind. After a moment, the tight strings between the stones snapped apart before his strength. Eldred took a breath and dusted the stones away. It was so much easier than it had been with Mack in the furnace of the Goddess's power.

Next, Eldred freed Pounder's corpse. It was simple now that he had the knack of it. He rousted himself and freed each of the remaining men, ignoring the questions and comments of the citizens as he did.

When he returned to sit next to his father, Lord Esbiorn and Dederick were there, standing over him.

"What was that you were doing?" asked Lord Esbiorn.

Eldred stared at the two of them and smiled at what was newly revealed to his sight. It showed more clearly on Dederick, but it was there on Lord Esbiorn as well. Dederick bore a dark blue circle set between his eyes that was every bit the match of the one Alfred had for size and depth of color. He was alive, though, and it showed in a glimmer that passed across the patch from moment to moment. Lord Esbiorn's mark was smaller and lighter than Pounder's, but that had been true for all the corpses in the line save for one.

"Well?" continued Lord Esbiorn when Eldred did not reply.

"Just removing some Corporian filth," said Eldred.

Lord Esbiorn frowned. "Yes, that's well done, but the people aren't happy to see our great men in this state. And they're asking about him." He pointed towards Gundlach, who was sitting on the wagon bench looking off into the distance.

Eldred shrugged. "He's a Corporian diplomat, He's coming with me to Boar's Tusk."

"Why don't you just kill him?" asked Lord Esbiorn through clenched teeth.

"Didn't Dederick tell you? I plan to make a truce with the Corporians," said Eldred.

"I told him," said Dederick.

"How can you want a truce with the enemies who tortured your father to death?" asked Lord Esbiorn.

"I killed the person responsible for torturing my father. As for Gundlach, he's a good man, more honorable than many Deirans I've dealt with. He had nothing to do with what befell these men. Like me, he first went to their city, New Wismar, just a short time ago. Even the people there were just doing what the Goddess told them."

"Well, I don't like it," said Lord Esbiorn.

"Fine. If you want to kill Corporians, you can do that once they are back in Corporia. My goal is to get them out of the Motherland. If we stop them from leaving, then we'll be battling them there in that city for a hundred years or more. They have walls and more walls. I believe the air inside that place is enough to make you and the others sick. And of course, the Goddess can just strike you down. A truce is best. It's better for everyone."

Lord Esbiorn ground his teeth. "If you truly killed their former Goddess, why can't you kill the new one?"

Eldred grinned. "I shouldn't wish to. I like the new Goddess. She is a noble person, honorable, like Gundlach. Besides, I caught the last Goddess off guard. You can be certain the new Goddess won't give me a similar opportunity, even though I think she trusts me to a fair extent."

"You seem to have lost your way, prince," said Lord Esbiorn.

"I liberated my father and killed his tormentor, since nobody else would rise to the occasion. If you don't care for it, that's not my concern."

"I see. Very well," said Lord Esbiorn, who paced away angrily.

Dederick clasped his hands. "What did I tell you, Eldred? Even if the facts are on your side, it won't make a lick of difference if you piss on everyone."

"He was calling me a coward for wanting a truce."

"Get used to it. I think most of us are going to feel the same. If it's just your personal truce, I think you're doing well. But if you want company, you need to convince someone."

"You've seen it, Dederick. You and your men are the ones sitting up there below the plateau. There's no starving them out. You've seen the herds and I've seen warehouses they said were full of grain." Eldred waved his hand. "I know, they could've been lying. I'm certain they weren't. They could stay there a dozen years, maybe more. If a truce is cowardly, then what is just sitting here and watching them? Isn't that just as craven? Why don't the brave men do what I did and go fight the Corporians? Once they're all dead, maybe the rest can be reasonable and offer a truce."

Dederick smiled. "Making out that we're all cowards won't gain you any friends. Keep trying."

"So I will," said Eldred.

It seemed as if everyone in the town had come by for a gander. But eventually, they had their fill of surveying the dead and departed. Eldred and Gundlach loaded the bodies back on the wagon and made camp.

As the sun was setting, a boy from the inn came out with a basket of food and a pitcher of ale. "Dederick sent this," said the boy, setting it down by Eldred.

"That's good of him," said Eldred as he rifled through the basket. There was boiled chicken, bread, turnips and greens.

"He wants to know if he should come out here," said the boy.

"No, that's fine. Gundlach and I can watch the wagon," said Eldred.

After the boy left, Eldred pulled out a hunk of bread and a turnip. "Once you finish your stores, you'll want to stick with fare like this."

Gundlach wet his lips. "Are you seeing something wrong with the chicken?"

"In a manner of speaking," said Eldred. "You face the same situation here that I faced in your city. Remember, I only ever ate toast. I expect anything from here will make you sick, but meat is likely the worst."

"No meat? This journey is getting worse and worse. I heard what the citizens were saying. Everyone was wanting to hang me or run me through."

Eldred picked up a chicken wing. "It was an ugly sight. Good men, strong men, laid low in a cowardly way. I told them you'd nothing to do with it. Nonetheless, you should stay close and be on your guard."

Gundlach took a bite of stale bread from his stores. "That lord was speaking quite loudly. I heard what he said about the truce."

"Yes, not a surprise."

"Then how are you planning to make it work?" asked Gundlach.

Eldred ripped the chicken wing apart. "The Deirans come down to one man, my weak-kneed cousin, Harold. He's the only one I need persuade."

"And what is making him accept your proposal?"

"I'm not sure he will. But I think I can get him to act. Sitting around out here, that's not doing anything. I think I can get him to either attack or to make a truce. I'll paint anything other than that as the craven act it is."

Gundlach's eyes grew large. "You are planning to provoke him into attacking?"

"Yes, it's one or the other. But don't worry. He can't really attack. New Wismar has high walls, and the new Goddess will have had time to make ready. So, it'll be a truce if Harold has any sense at all."

"If she has not had enough time to be preparing herself—"

"The walls, Gundlach. You have high walls on each of the outer rings. If your people put up a good fight, there should be more than enough time for the Goddess to figure that business out."

"You are gambling with my people's lives."

"Perhaps so. But if you get the truce, stamped and approved by Harold, then your people can safely open your gates and ride home to Corporia without delay. The Deirans aren't the Maldavians or the Torvid. He'll keep his word. Even Harold will have to show some honor."

"Deiran honor." Gundlach made a face. "It seems that the fate of my people is now depending on it."

"Don't worry. I'll make it work. We just can't be getting my father home late."

TO BOAR'S TUSK

Eldred and Gundlach started at dawn the next morning, only stopping by the inn for some supplies. Dederick was still in bed upstairs but sent down word that he and his men would soon follow. So, they set out, with Gundlach snapping the reins and Eldred jogging briskly beside the wagon. It was the fourth day since Alfred had died. They had three more left to deliver him to Boar's Tusk.

Dederick caught up in the afternoon when they stopped to water the horses at a stream. Eldred immediately looked over the men to find Mack, who was riding at the rear. Mack glowered back, but Eldred ignored his challenge, studying the mark between his eyes. It was blue, though not the darkest blue, and smaller in size than Pounder's. Looking across Dederick's men, it seemed to be a common size. If the extent and color of the mark truly reflected the strength of the Mother's blessing, it showed that Mack had survived due to his heft, not due to any strength he possessed in the Bond. The discovery brought a smile of relief to Eldred's face. He'd known this had to be the case. By no measure of honor did Mack stand higher than his father or Pounder.

A new man was present in Dederick's squad. Dederick dismounted and gestured up at him as the man remained seated on his horse. "This is Judkin. Lord Esbiorn is sending him ahead to announce our coming."

Eldred peered up at Judkin, who bore no mark. "What news precisely will you be sharing?"

"Just what the lord put to writing," said Judkin.

Eldred held out his hand. "Could you let me see what he wrote?"

Judkin glanced to Dederick and back to Eldred. "The letter I carry is addressed to your cousin, the king. I'll pass it only to him."

"I see," said Eldred. "Of course. I was just interested in what Lord Esbiorn had to say."

"Yes. Well, I'll be off," said Judkin. He made a quick salute and kicked his horse into action.

Eldred watched him ride away as Dederick drew close.

"Esbiorn sent out couriers in all directions. The news will spread wide before you reach Boar's Tusk," said Dederick.

"I take your meaning," said Eldred. Friends and foes alike might be waiting for them.

As they resumed their journey, Dederick appeared moved to make a more formal escort than he had previously. He rode some fifty feet ahead of the wagon with his direct podmen, four in number, and Mack. The second pod followed the wagon at a similar distance, doubtlessly picking up more of the odor generated by the decaying corpses. Eldred was on foot, having taken a turn driving the wagon earlier.

They had been traveling for about an hour when Eldred saw the first strand. He was back, even with the wagon, when he saw a gossamer thread appear for just an instant between Dederick and the podman to his right, a thin dark line that floated in the air. Then it was gone. After a moment of confusion, Eldred trotted forward and caught up to the men, inserting himself between their horses.

Dederick glanced down, the large blue mark evident on his forehead. "What is it, Eldred?"

Eldred looked back and forth between the men. "Did either of you feel anything just now?"

"No. What do you mean?" asked Dederick.

By his face, the podman was equally unaware.

"Nothing, I guess. I thought I saw something," said Eldred.

Dederick swept his eyes over their surroundings. "There's nothing out here. Just a long empty plain until we reach the hills around Boar's Tusk."

"Quite so," said Eldred. He nodded and slowed his pace, dropping back next to the wagon.

Gundlach looked down from the driver's bench. "I could be using a break."

"Of course," said Eldred, hopping up. Gundlach had been driving more than half the day.

As Eldred settled down on the seat, Gundlach slid to the side and curled up for a nap. Driving occupied Eldred to some extent, steering the horses around obstacles and keeping up speed, but his attention—his focus—was to see another strand. It was not an hour before he did; a strand formed between Dederick and the man on the far left of the pod. From there a few more strands twinkled in and out of existence. Some strands were truly ephemeral and left Eldred with only a vague impression that he'd seen them. Others stood out, like a bolt of lightning stretched across the sky, and left no doubt whatsoever.

An excitement welled up in Eldred. He was seeing the Bond. It was right there—the men bound together by the threads. He wondered who had ever seen this before. He'd never heard anyone mention anything like this. The Mother must have known, given her abilities. But the men, from his father to the headmaster, they'd squinted and strained just to see if someone had the Bond. They wouldn't have had to do that if they could see the marks or watch for the threads.

Later that day in camp, Eldred shared his observations with Gundlach when they were alone. The others made their beds further from the wagon.

Gundlach sat up, patiently watching the Deirans snoring in their blankets thirty feet away.

"There's another one," whispered Eldred.

Gundlach sighed. "Still, I am seeing nothing."

Thirty more minutes passed.

"That's a big one," said Eldred.

"I will be leaving you to it," said Gundlach, who pulled his blankets up and turned to his side.

"You don't understand. This is the most important thing. This is the greatest creation of the Mother, the greatest of the stone bearers. And I can see it. I can see it right there."

Gundlach opened his eyes. "I am understanding you, but I am not seeing the importance."

"What do you mean?"

Gundlach scratched his beard. "If a man is seeing a blade coming at him, but he cannot turn it, what is the use? Can you be changing it? Can you be stopping it?"

"Hmm, you mean can I make them fall down."

Gundlach grinned. "Yes. That would be something worth getting worked up about. But you might have to be bearing a stone, not a shard, for such adventures. Or are you feeling the power is within you?"

"I don't know. I don't see how you could take any action against such a thing. It's so quick. It's gone in the instant it forms."

Gundlach shrugged and rolled over. Within a few minutes his snores joined those of the others.

SPARRING

The next morning was pleasant; a warm sun shone down on the plain. The clear skies afforded a wide view over the treeless expanse; you could look for fifty miles in any direction. Eldred ignored these pleasures, however, and quizzed Dederick about the Bond over a bowl of steaming oatmeal.

Dederick chewed slowly while he looked at Eldred with a skeptical eye. "The Bond is the Bond. It's there when it's needed. It's not when it's not."

"But surely you can rouse it when you have cause. I know you don't have to be in battle. I've seen my father summon it up for mock trials," said Eldred.

"Then it was needed; he needed it at the time," said Dederick.

"Alright. Let's say you need it now, you and your pod," said Eldred.

Dederick looked over his men who were sitting around the campfire. "We don't."

"But say you did," insisted Eldred.

Dederick groaned and put his hand to his forehead. "What's this about?"

"I need to study the Bond," said Eldred.

"The last time you tried to get the Bond, it was a disaster. You drove everyone mad. Best to leave it alone," said Dederick.

"I'm not trying to get it. I just need to watch you while you have it. What if you sparred with your other pod? That worked when my father had a contest with Harold," said Eldred.

"That was a serious business," said Mack, who was lying nearby, still in his blankets.

"It doesn't have to be. Not for this," said Eldred.

Dederick gave a small smile. "It wouldn't work, Eldred. In that case, they were two different pods with two different leaders. All of my men here are in my pods. It's like saying you're going to let your arms fight each other. You can't do that. Can you?"

Eldred frowned and tapped his fingers together.

"Let them have your precious Corporian," offered Mack, propping himself up on his elbow. "If they fight him, you could study the Bond for all of five seconds."

Dederick and his men laughed while Gundlach glared at Mack from his perch on the wagon's bench.

"No. Enough with the threats, Mack," said Eldred. "But there might be something to that."

Dederick spread his hands. "Do you want us to fight him?"

"Perhaps you could fight me," said Eldred. "Not with swords; we would all put down our weapons. What if we had trial combat with fists?"

Dederick tilted his head to the side. "We could. I suppose we could load you in the wagon once we beat you unconscious. But let me ask, what is it you want—to get your father to Boar's Tusk in time or to brawl in the dirt?"

"I want both," said Eldred.

Dederick chuckled. "So much for decorum."

There was a patch free of bushes and thistles close to camp. Dederick and four of his podmen went to one side; Eldred stood across from them. Dederick's other men huddled nearby, chortling with amusement. Gundlach and Mack looked on with more reserve, but no less interest.

Dederick gestured towards Eldred. "So, this ends once we knock you down?"

Eldred nodded. "Around then."

"Then we will, as gently as we can," said Dederick.

Eldred looked for threads, but there were none. The last he'd seen had flashed for an instant several minutes before. Even with him towering over the men, it seemed they didn't take him for much of a threat. Eldred took a breath, put his head down and charged at Dederick, running faster than any other man could.

They changed before his eyes. Their smiles fell away, replaced with watchful, blank expressions. Threads shot into existence, linking Dederick to each of his podmen. They hung in the air; they didn't blink away.

The men moved with amazing quickness. Dederick, who had been in the center, stretched out his hand to the man on his left. The man grabbed Dederick and swung him wide of Eldred's charge, even as the man further left of him was grabbing the first man's hips to make the swing more powerful. The men on the right were diving down, reaching for Eldred's feet with darting hands.

Eldred thought that they were merely grabbing his legs and ignored them, confident they couldn't contain him, but instead they bent down his toes, and he found himself tumbling across the dirt. As he leapt up, they were charging at him. The threads between Dederick and his men seemed to squirm with power. Other threads were there too, flashing in and out of existence between some of the men.

Eldred darted towards the man closing on his right and swiped at him. His hand was faster than theirs, and he caught the man on the arm, sending him flying. The man was still lifting into the air as two podman dived down at Eldred's feet, deftly pulling his legs from behind the knee. Dederick kicked Eldred in the chest as another podman kicked him in the hip. Eldred tumbled backwards to the ground but flared out his legs, catching one of the podmen on the side.

As Eldred sprang to his feet, Dederick and two of his men were charging him, but they paused as he put out his hands, warding them off. None of them wanted to get in range of another swipe. Eldred spared a quick glance at the other two who were hanging back. They were injured. The one he'd hit was holding his arm at an odd angle. The other was cradling his ribs.

For a moment, everyone just held their ground. Dederick and his two remaining men tested the distance between themselves and Eldred, legs bent, ready to spring. Eldred kept his hands in motion, using his long reach to keep them back. He was in no hurry to end the fight. He wanted more time to study the threads.

After a few moments, one of the threads pulsed, catching Eldred's attention. As he turned his gaze, the men on either side of Dederick ducked under Eldred's arms while Dederick grabbed his wrists. Eldred yanked his arms free, but each of the men landed a powerful kick on Eldred's shin before rolling out of reach.

Eldred stumbled back, suppressing a howl of pain, and raised his hands again. The men were back in a line, pressing forward, looking to repeat their trick. Eldred swiped at the man on the left, but he danced back out of reach. As the man returned to the line, Eldred reached for the man on the right, but he too ducked away.

This routine repeated a few times before Dederick and his men moved to encircle Eldred. Dederick stayed where he was, eyeing Eldred coldly as his companions stepped out and around Eldred, keeping their distance. As they did, the threads between them and Dederick drifted within Eldred's reach. Eldred shot out his hand towards the nearest thread, seeking to touch the Bond, to feel it on his palm. But there was nothing; instead, the thread faded away under his touch. Disappointed, Eldred stretched for the other thread, which also disappeared.

At that moment, the fight ended. It was just Eldred surrounded by three sweaty men breathing hard. Dederick was still connected to the injured podmen, but the two nearby warriors looked surprised, like someone who had woken up to a slap. They weren't hurt—they kept their feet and their senses—but they didn't even seem to consider fighting without the Bond. Eldred understood the sense of that.

What he didn't understand, as he stood there looking at his hands, was why his touch would make the threads disappear. If anything, he had expected the opposite effect, making the Bond stronger. Even before, with his curse, he'd boosted the power of his father. Now he carried the Mother's Shard. Why wouldn't the shard be a friend to the Bond?

"We're done!" called Dederick. His connection to the injured men faded away.

Eldred watched as Dederick's other pod rushed over to help the two injured men. "I'm sorry. I didn't mean…"

Nobody paid attention to his words as they helped the injured men over to the campfire. Mack shot Eldred a baleful glance. Gundlach looked nervous.

Dederick studied Eldred as he drank from a waterskin one of his men had tossed him. "No apologies needed, Prince."

"His arm doesn't look good," said Eldred.

Dederick sniffed. "A broken arm, some crunched ribs—these are all things we've had before. The Mother will set us right soon enough. On the other hand, you did something different at the end. What was that? Some new curse?"

Eldred shook his head. "It's no curse. Like I told you, I just wanted to study you while you used the Bond."

"You took the Bond away from us just like they did that day of the battle," continued Dederick.

"I don't think so. That was something else that made everyone with the Bond ill. You all seem fine to me," said Eldred.

Dederick rinsed his mouth with water and spat it in the dirt. Then he advanced on Eldred, grabbing his tunic and staring up in his face. "Whatever that trick was, it's nothing a man can do."

Eldred frowned and said nothing.

Dederick cleared his throat and spoke softly. "Are you Eldred?"

"What do you mean?" asked Eldred.

"That stuff before—killing everyone in the country house, killing their Goddess. I didn't give it much thought. I mean, of course, it's all ludicrous, but I wasn't there so I don't know. Perhaps it could happen. But now, with this, I know the old Eldred. I know he could throw bricks better than just about anyone. This business today though—nobody can do that, certainly not him."

Eldred placed his hand on Dederick's shoulder. "It's me."

Dederick took a half step closer. "I don't know how much you heard back there in Bert. Everyone noticed the dead patches are gone from your face. Maybe you got better. The curse is gone too, some more good fortune for you. But your fatum lapides are missing, and those usually stick around. And now, you're such a friend to the Corporians. Almost seemed like you were ready to marry their Goddess, you were so full of praise for her. Seems an odd circumstance given your dead father over in the wagon."

"Ask me something, then. It's me, Dederick. I remember you snickering after I hit my father with a brick. I remember you taking my bacon when we first met as you plopped down on the seat next to mine in the Great Hall."

Dederick stared Eldred in the eye. "You have those right."

"I have them all right. It's me."

"This changes things." Dederick sighed.

Eldred tightened his grip on Dederick's shoulder. "We can still ride together to Boar's Tusk. Can't we?"

Dederick nodded slowly. "Yes. We can do that. No more sparring though. Let's keep things simple."

"I agree," said Eldred.

Eldred and Gundlach started off in the wagon as the others tended to the injured men, Gundlach at the reins and Eldred trotting beside the wagon.

"You must never be doing that again," declared Gundlach once they had covered some distance.

Eldred looked over. "You mean fighting Dederick?"

"I am meaning that you should not be fighting any of them, not in their pods."

"Perhaps," said Eldred. "I did learn something. You saw how it stopped."

"I saw them giving up. Should I have been noticing something more?"

"I took away their threads." Eldred pantomimed pawing at the air. "When I touched them, they disappeared. I can break the Bond."

Gundlach pursed his lips. "For all of them?"

"No," said Eldred. "Just for those who are within my reach."

They traveled in silence for a moment while Gundlach considered. "If they are standing in your reach, then you are standing in theirs."

Eldred nodded. "That's true."

"I am going back to my first point; you must not be fighting them."

Fair enough," said Eldred. "We'll bury my father and get the truce. That's all I aim to do."

WELCOME COMMITTEE

In the afternoon the following day, Eldred noticed a cloud of dust in the distance as he walked. He jumped up on the wagon next to Gundlach for a better look. "Riders!" he called out.

Dederick looked back from his pod where he was riding ahead of the wagon. "How many?"

"Twenty or more," answered Eldred.

Everyone was peering off into the distance, though Eldred doubted that most of them could even see the disturbance, let alone make out the horsemen.

"A silver pod. Must be Harold, don't you think?" asked Dederick.

"I don't know who else," said Eldred, studying Dederick's face. The man had made it clear he wouldn't be killing anyone at Eldred's request before they set out. What would he do if Eldred were attacked?

"Is it trouble that is coming?" asked Gundlach.

"I've no reason to think so," said Eldred. "Well, perhaps, some reason. Still, let's keep on."

"Should we not be doing something?" asked Gundlach, lowering his voice.

Eldred rubbed his chin. His father had mastered Harold and his pod in their scrimmage. The mark on Dederick's forehead suggested he could do the same. That could help offset the difference in numbers. It didn't help that Dederick's pod had two injured men thanks to the earlier tussle. Still, there was Eldred himself. He could steal the Bond away from Harold if he got close enough; that would disrupt things. And he had Capito. Nothing could stop him from killing the first man he faced.

"Well?" persisted Gundlach.

Eldred adjusted the cloak Dederick had loaned him. He still wore the patchwork leggings. "We need to see what happens."

"I can be telling you what will happen. Here, take the reins. I must be getting my shield."

Eldred was still driving the wagon when they met Harold and his silver pod. Dederick was lined up off to the right of the wagon with both his pods in tight formation. Mack sat on his horse off to the other side of them; he didn't look particularly happy to be meeting up with the new king. Harold's men spread out in a line with him at the center—five pods, the same number as were laid out dead in the wagon.

Eldred studied Harold's face. His blue mark was only a smidge larger than the one on Pounder's forehead, even fed as it was by his fatum lapis. That was no surprise. Eldred had been certain it couldn't match the size or depth of color possessed by either his father or Dederick. Harold had only passed the trial at one arch removed.

What did surprise Eldred was the absence of malice shown on Harold's countenance. He looked friendly, as if he was glad to see Eldred.

Harold raised his hand and smiled. "Greetings, cousin. Well met, Dederick. Welcome home, Mack. I was so intrigued when I received the news of this party coming that I couldn't wait. I just had to come see myself."

"You know we have my father here?" asked Eldred.

Harold nodded. "Yes. And in time for his honors, if you keep a good pace."

"That's right," said Eldred. "We have until the end of day tomorrow."

"Then let's get your wagon moving. I've no mind to delay you. We can converse while we go," said Harold. His men parted, and he moved his horse to the side.

Eldred glanced over his forces: Gundlach clutching his shield, Dederick grinning from atop his horse, and Mack, still frowning. He gave the reins a slap and started the wagon forward. Harold came up on the left, even with Eldred. Dederick rode to the right.

Harold eyed Gundlach. "So you're the Corporian emissary?"

"I am," said Gundlach, keeping hold of his shield.

"You're the first Corporian I've spoken to. All the others I've met were dead," said Harold.

Gundlach looked back without comment.

"The city is full of them, thousands of warriors and their Goddess," said Eldred.

"One less Goddess. The word, or the claim anyway, is that you killed one. Is that right, cousin?" asked Harold.

"I did," said Eldred.

"And now you want a truce?" asked Harold.

"I think it would be best for everyone, even those who wish to kill Corporians," said Eldred.

The corners of Harold's lips curved up. "Well, that would be me. But let's leave such matters until after Uncle Alfred gets his due honors. We have Wilky cooking up a feast. I also sent word to my father. I think he'll be there tomorrow. I know he'd want to be. Unfortunately, I doubt Aunt Ghyslaine can make it in time."

"Yes, it's a hasty business." Eldred jerked his head back towards the wagon. "I don't know about how they'll present. The smell gets worse each day."

"I'm sure something can be worked out. He's not the first king to return home for burial. Though, I suppose, it might be the farthest anyone has come. Tomorrow is the last possible day," said Harold.

"It was far," said Eldred glumly.

Harold leaned forward, meeting eyes with Dederick. "Who's up there guarding the plateau?"

"Don't worry. I've good men there. It's all in hand," said Dederick.

"We can always kill their emissary if they make trouble," said Harold breezily.

Gundlach shifted slightly on the bench.

Dederick chuckled. "I doubt they will. They weren't even putting their cattle out when we left."

"I'm glad to hear it. Seems everything is as the messenger reported," said Harold. "I'll be heading back now to oversee preparations. Just get him there by noon, Eldred. That should be doable. We'll feast and then bury these dead heroes."

"You don't want to see him?" asked Eldred.

"No. Tomorrow will do," said Harold.

"What about me?" called Mack abruptly.

Harold peered over at Mack's red face. "Save your voice tonight, worthy podman. Everyone will be chasing after you tomorrow to hear your tale."

Mack glanced at Gundlach. "Not everyone."

"So be it. Tomorrow, in Boar's Tusk." He saluted Mack and rode away.

Eldred watched the silver pod disappear into the distance as he drove the wagon.

"Is everything going as it should?" asked Gundlach.

"I think so, perhaps even better than I'd have expected. Still, I remember Dederick's words: it might be easier to enter Boar's Tusk than to leave."

THE FEAST

After a pre-dawn start the next morning, they were easily on schedule for their arrival. It was well before noon when Eldred spotted the city walls of Boar's Tusk only a few miles away. Beyond them, on the far side of the city, rose the castle that until recently had been his father's.

An excitement ran through Eldred, excitement at returning home—as much as he had a home—and curiosity at how everyone would celebrate the day. When they'd started the journey, he'd imagined arguing to get his father his due honors, shouting at Harold and shaming him into action. The previous day hadn't gone that way.

Dederick's men were also stirred by anticipation. Even the two injured men had washed themselves thoroughly, hoping—per the chatter in the camp—for some excitement with the ladies in the town, cracked ribs be damned. Eldred smiled at that. They were the perfect escort for his father.

Only Mack and Gundlach seemed unenthusiastic about the day's impending events. It made sense for Gundlach, surrounded as he would be by sworn enemies. Mack was harder to understand. While it was true that Alfred was dead, along with all Mack's podmates, there would be some glory for Mack. As the sole remaining member of the golden pod, he would be able to finagle a plum position. It wouldn't matter that he was a thuggish brute who only survived due to his extra girth. With that, and his escape from confinement, he ought to have been happy. His face said otherwise.

They could have ridden around the city; it wasn't that much farther. But Eldred drove the wagon straight for the main gate. Boar's Tusk was much smaller than New Wismar. Longinus, Eldred's former minder from among the Sun People, had once mentioned that it was only a small farming village back in the days of Regula, before she became the Mother. But small as it was, the city possessed a power, an essence that no other place could match. It was the home of the greatest warriors the Mother had ever fashioned. And despite the recent defeat, it was still true. Absent trickery, the bonded warriors were invincible.

As they passed through the gate with Dederick's forces in escort formation, Eldred looked all around. Hardly anyone was out. The city seemed empty.

"Have the people been deserting your town?" asked Gundlach.

"I don't know. I've never seen it like this," answered Eldred. It wasn't right.

The few people present were not disrespectful. They paused in their activities, some bowed their heads. But once the wagon passed by, they scampered off, seemingly hurrying about their chores.

"Are they giving the honors here?" asked Gundlach.

"No, of course not," said Eldred sharply. "That'll be at the castle. I don't know what all the citizens are doing. Perhaps they don't care that their king has returned."

Gundlach kept his tongue the rest of the way through the town. Even Dederick's men looked a bit bewildered. They'd all expected a bit more interest in the wagon bearing the dead king of Deira.

As they came out the far gate, the one closest to the castle, Eldred felt his guts tighten. He set his face and felt a trace of wetness in the corner of his eyes. There, before the castle, were all the missing people. Everyone in the city was there, some sitting at tables they had carried over from their homes. A hundred fires roasted a hundred sides of beef. The people were rising to their feet and shouting, "Hail King Alfred! The king has returned!" They lifted their cups, saluting the wagon and its escort.

"This is where they were hiding," said Gundlach.

"Yes," said Eldred softly. "They did not forget him." He glanced at Mack; tough as he was, the man was leaking tears.

It took some care to drive the horses through the shouting throng. Inside the castle gate stood the nobles, lined up ten deep on both sides of the courtyard between the Great Hall and the main tower. Men of valor and their ladies wore their finest clothes of dark gray and black.

At the head of the gathering, on a wide raised platform, stood Harold and Uncle Benedict. The old codger had made it. He bore a small gray dot between his eyes—so that was what a decayed Bond looked like. A sense of relief welled up in Eldred. Benedict would know what to do. It was done. It was all done. Eldred drove the wagon past Dederick and his men, who had stopped just inside the gate. Only Mack came forward with the wagon as Eldred brought the wagon slowly past the line of nobles, each of whom bowed or curtsied as he passed. Suddenly, he was there, at the front. He stopped and sat next to Gundlach, unsure what to do.

Benedict beckoned him. "Bring him up. They'll get the others. You just have to bring him."

Eldred nodded and finally noticed the layout of the platform—a wooden walkway with twenty-three tables each large enough for a man to lay on, and one larger table as might befit a king.

It was terrible to reach into the back of the wagon. They had not shifted the corpses for some days. The smell was almost enough to knock Eldred over. Flies buzzed everywhere, seeking gaps in the coverings. He slid his hands under his father's blanket and lifted the remains, which were no longer stiff. It took care to avoid having the blanket slither out of his grasp.

Eldred held it tight, like something valuable, and climbed the steps up the platform, laying the remains down on the center table. Men were coming up with the other corpses. Gingerly, not really wanting to see what lay inside, Eldred uncovered his father's face. It wasn't pretty, but it wasn't as bad as he had feared. After a moment of staring, he only saw the sadness. Eldred took a breath. Why did he have to be sad? He had his honors. He was avenged.

Benedict was beside him, hand on his shoulder. "You've brought him home, Eldred. By the Mother, I can't say I ever expected to see either of you again."

"I got him," murmured Eldred.

To the right, a man uncovered Pounder's resolute face; he didn't look off except for his pale skin. On the left, they set Stace; an older man; he looked long dead, his skin peeling away like thin parchment.

Benedict twisted around, looking out over the crowd. "There's food. After we eat, and after everyone's had a viewing who wants one, we should say some words. I thought we four should speak, you, Mack, Harold and myself."

Eldred crinkled up his face. "I don't know what to say."

"You have time to work it out. I expect it will take a few hours before the last commoner files past. In the meantime, we have a sumptuous feast laid out in the Great Hall," said Benedict.

"Very well." Eldred turned around. Harold was down off the platform, halfway to the hall with Mack beside him. As for Gundlach—Eldred scanned the wagon and the surroundings—Gundlach was gone. Eldred did a double take and took a wider look. There—Gundlach was entering the tower in the company of five men, some pod.

Eldred tapped Benedict on the arm and pointed at Gundlach, who was just disappearing through the archway. "What business is this? Where is he going and for what cause?"

Benedict glanced over. "The Corporian? Well, we don't want him here for this, do we? It's his people who killed these men."

"But he didn't."

Benedict waved his hand at the line of corpses. Flies still buzzed about, but they weren't so thick now, spread as they were over all the tables. "Even so, it's best for him. Many of these men have kinfolk here. If they get worked up, they won't think twice about splitting his skull."

Eldred frowned. They were starting to line up on the left, nobles first, ready to start the viewing, the men armed with daggers and swords. "You'll make certain he's safe?"

Benedict smiled. "As safe as he has any right to be in Boar's Tusk. Come on. Let's get some food. Wilky made quite an effort, cooking all night. We mustn't let it go to waste."

People were already shuffling up the walkway to view the corpses, but they made room for Benedict and Eldred to pass.

"They're quite eager," observed Eldred.

"Very much so. Everyone thought these men died almost a year ago. Now, like magic, you turn up with them. It's all anyone's been talking about since I arrived last night. Fortunately, we had their names, or everyone would have gone mad with speculation. If only we had known they were alive, we could have done something," said Benedict.

"I didn't know either. It was only by chance that I came across them. They were already in desperate condition. When I killed the Goddess, they all perished, except for Mack. Still, Father was avenged. He must have outlived her by at least a minute or two."

Benedict nodded. "Always good to outlive your enemies."

The inside of the Great Hall was humming with activity. Many nobles were putting off their inspection of the corpses to eat first, which made sense; Alfred and his men weren't going anywhere. Platters of boiled beef, stacks of boiled eggs and heaps of fresh bread were on hand. Young children and squires skipped proper food, opting for sweet cakes and plum pie instead—so many squires; it seemed like almost everyone from the Academy.

Eldred paused and scanned the room. He spotted them, the headmaster and Preceptor Garaint, in their seats halfway up the hall. There was no sign of Preceptor Grimes. Neither instructor looked pleased to see him, but Eldred was interested to see them or at least their foreheads. Garaint, Eldred's least favorite preceptor from the Academy, was average, something Eldred was tempted to share with him. His mark was about the same as Mack's, definitely smaller than Pounder's.

The headmaster, though, was as formidable as Eldred had always imagined he must be. He bore a large mark, not the size of Father's or Dederick's, but nearly the same. Interestingly, his mark was a deeper shade of blue. Eldred didn't know what to make of that.

The headmaster stared back with a disapproving expression, his cup raised halfway to his lips.

Benedict took Eldred's arm. "Let's keep moving. You will not find a friendly conversation with them."

"Why is that?" asked Eldred, stepping along with Benedict.

"I have heard they made some comments about your time with the Maldavians, with your cousin," said Benedict.

"What could they know about that?"

Benedict shrugged. "They said that it was to be expected, some comment on your low character—as they saw it."

"Hmmph," said Eldred. "What're your thoughts on the matter, Uncle?"

"I don't know. I wouldn't judge. When people ask, and they do, I just say I expect you did what the situation required. You were never one to be needlessly cruel."

Eldred nodded vigorously. "That's right. I didn't kill Henreit. I only killed one man, one who deserved it."

Benedict offered a small smile. "Exactly as I thought."

Harold and Mack sat at the head table, with Harold sitting in the middle seat where Alfred used to take his meals. Mack sat on his right, drinking more than eating as Eldred and Benedict made their approach.

Harold glanced up, his face not quite as welcoming when seeing Eldred unexpectedly. But then he grinned and held up his cup. "Father, cousin, join us. You can have your old seat, Eldred."

"Thanks, cousin," said Eldred, but he remained standing.

"I was thinking we would all give speeches," said Benedict after a pause.

"Of course," said Harold as he eyed Capito hanging on Eldred's belt.

"Do you want to speak first, Eldred? You're the son," said Benedict.

Eldred nodded. "I can."

Harold wagged his finger. "Nothing about this truce business. That's not for today. We can settle that after."

"Fine," said Eldred.

"What else do you have?" Harold gestured at Capito. "What else were you able to recover?"

Eldred set his hand on the hilt. "I have several boxes of daggers. I also have some signet rings, including Father's."

"What do you plan to do with them?" asked Benedict.

"I'll give back the daggers to the families of their owners; the rings as well," said Eldred.

"Today? When you are speaking?" asked Benedict.

"I was thinking so, but it's also about the truce. The Corporians handed over the daggers to help build support for that cause," said Eldred.

Harold nudged Mack. "Is that so?"

Mack shrugged. "It seemed to be. It was his idea though." He pointed at Eldred. "He seemed to want the truce as much as they did."

"Well, I do. I want them gone, out of the Motherland. We could be rid of them in six months with a proper truce," said Eldred.

"Or, we could raise an army and be rid of them sooner," said Harold.

"I don't think so," said Eldred. "Their walls aren't getting any shorter. I've seen their provisions; they could fill this hall ten times over. And their new Goddess is powerful. She'll be much stronger than the old one."

Harold made a face. "In time, perhaps, but what about at this moment? It takes time, doesn't it, to really take on a stone. If we strike now, it may not go as it went before. Besides, we can bring the Mercians and the Maldavaians. They're not great, but they might work against Corporians."

Eldred clasped his hands. "They've walls within walls and a horde of archers for each layer. You'd pay an awful cost."

"I'm certain we'll take casualties either way. But with my approach, we wouldn't give them another six months to dig in. In any case, bravery has its consequences," said Harold.

"I'll try to remember that," said Eldred, raising an eyebrow.

"Well, as we said, it's a matter for after," said Benedict. "Let us not mix these concerns. For your part, Eldred, I would hold off returning any of your loot until tomorrow. Multiple claimants are likely to be at hand, and everyone's drinking. It would mar the occasion if we ended up having to dig more graves."

Eldred rubbed his neck. "There's that."

"Why do you wear his sword, but not his ring?" asked Harold.

"You know the answer to that," said Eldred. When Harold said nothing, Eldred reached in his pocket and dug it out, displaying it on his palm. "It's too small. I've Mercian fingers. I'm shocked that I have to be reminding you of the same."

Harold put down his cup. "May I hold it?"

"I suppose," said Eldred.

Harold plucked it out of Eldred's hand, holding up to inspect it. As he did, his fatum lapis stirred, and a few gossamer threads briefly appeared, directing Eldred's eyes to Harold's nearby podmen. "This was my father's before it went to Uncle Alfred."

Eldred stiffened.

Harold glanced down at Capito. "Like everything my father had, it was taken away."

Benedict rolled his eyes. "It was his right, son. The sword, the ring, they always go to the king."

Harold smiled slyly. "What about now?"

Eldred narrowed his eyes.

"Oh, don't mind him, Eldred. He's just having some sport with you," said Benedict.

Harold looked Eldred in the eye, his smirk growing wider.

Eldred put out his hand and Harold returned the ring.

"He can't even wear the damned thing," muttered Mack.

Eldred made his excuses and pressed into the kitchen in search of Wilky. He spotted the steward kneading a ball of dough at a table between the ovens. He was so busy with the bread and barking orders at his cooks that he didn't notice Eldred at first. When he finally noticed Eldred by the door, his face split into a manic grin. He waved Eldred over. "We're truly honored today."

Eldred approached, studying all the cooks at work. "Why is everyone baking bread?"

"We're boiling the beef for all the nobles in the hall, but we're also turning out bread for everyone, all the commoners outside the gates—your father's last gift to his people." Wilky lowered his voice and shot a glance towards the door. "Of course, it's really from him, and he makes certain everyone knows."

"I suppose. Father's dead," said Eldred.

"You're not though, thank the Mother," said Wilky.

Eldred nodded. "Not yet."

"They say you killed that Goddess of theirs," said Wilky.

"I did," said Eldred.

Wilky punched down the dough. "How could you do that?"

"It wasn't easy," said Eldred.

"I didn't think it would be. I don't see how it would be possible at all. And even if somehow you did, why would they let you leave? This is what everyone's asking. You'll hear it soon enough once you start talking to people."

Eldred rubbed his hands together. "Well, it's a long story, but the main point is that some folks there, some Corporians, have the same thoughts I do. They want to leave. That's part of why I'm here. I'm here to bury my father, but also to forge a truce."

"Oh, my. You'd have more luck raising Alfred from the dead than getting Harold to agree to that. He's planning to raise a great army: all the Deirans, all the Mercians, and all the Maldavians. They say he's even going to take Deirans without the Bond."

Eldred's eyes went wide. "You mean the unblessed?"

"Yes, even them. It just makes for bigger armies. I hate feeding troops. I'd rather feed the commoners," said Wilky.

"You could just have someone else manage the cooking," said Eldred.

"What do you mean?" asked Wilky.

"You're the head steward. I'm sure you can find someone else to run the kitchen if you've grown tired of it."

Wilky made a face. "Oh, not anymore, not since Lady Ghyslaine left. I'm back to head cook." He glanced out through the door, which had momentarily opened. "He brought his own head steward from someplace, a worm of a man named Gosbert."

Eldred grimaced. "I'm sorry to hear that."

Wilky gave a small shake of his head. "It's nothing to worry yourself about. But what am I doing? Do you want something to eat?"

"No, don't bother about that. There's piles of food out in the hall. I'll grab something there."

Wilky motioned Eldred in close. "Are you going to be king?" he whispered.

"No. Harold's king," said Eldred.

Wilky smiled. "I thought maybe with you back—"

"I know," said Eldred. "But I'm just here to bury Father."

SPEECHES

Eldred stood on the platform near Alfred's corpse facing a sea of people. He felt more comfortable in the soft, gray linen tunic and black breeches, old clothes of his that Wilky had kept tucked away somewhere, but the crowd made him uneasy. Hundreds of nobles were pressed in close, the nearest stood only six feet away. Beyond them, a mass of commoners extended out of the gate—the subjects he would never have. He turned for one last look at Benedict's encouraging face and started.

"My father was a great man." Eldred paused and stared into the distance. "He did things that no one else could. He often spoke of his first blood match against the Maldavians. You've all heard it. That day he wiped out four hundred men with only two silver pods, fifty men."

The audience stirred slightly; a few murmured agreement.

"But even that day pales in comparison to the battle against the Corporians. It was incredible. One hundred men, the finest golden pod ever constructed, fought thousands. They weren't riff-raff; the Corporians put forth a decent army, men with strong armor, men bearing well-crafted arms. And so many archers—you couldn't walk across the field without stepping on their missiles, a death trap that no other troop could've hoped to survive."

"Well, I was there watching, fearing for those who didn't fear for themselves. They walked through a hail of arrows; not a man fell. Then they engaged a force of over three thousand men—brave, capable men. A hundred against three thousand, only one man could win that, my father, your king. Some will say different. Some will tell lies. The truth is they cut through the Corporians like a hot steel blade. They would have killed them all—except for the Goddess."

Eldred sighed. "The Goddess would be no match for the Mother, not even a match for treacherous Korrina. However, that day she showed her might. She knocked down the golden pod and sent brave warriors to flight, their Bond shattered. Because of my father's courage, only a hundred men were lost. It could have been all of us, the entire Deiran army, but it wasn't thanks to his bravery."

"Now, I don't know exactly what the Goddess would have done if her trap had worked, but I can tell you she was a hard woman. With her strength and her armies, she might have killed everyone here at this gathering, everyone present who you see here. I expect she would have wanted that. Instead, she had to make due with torturing my father and these men lying on these tables. She was a terror.

"I don't say this to make you hate her. I expect you already do. I expect that you hate the Corporians. I did. They took everything from me. I couldn't even walk after the battle. I sank as low as a man can go. I saw my own death coming for me. By luck, by amazing fortune, I escaped. By more fortune, more than I ever deserved, I avenged these men and freed them. I killed the Goddess."

Eldred gazed out over the crowd. "And so we are here to bury a great king and his champions. Some will say that we should raise an army and kill all the Corporians, that we should sack their high-walled city. I would say that if King Alfred cannot take their city, who can? If the greatest golden pod to ever walk the land cannot win a battle at their gates, who is so foolish as to make the attempt? Let's have a truce. Next time there might not be any of us to do the burying."

Utter silence filled the castle for a long moment. Then behind Eldred, someone started to clap. Eldred turned to see Harold clapping slowly, forcefully smacking his hands together. The clap spread to Benedict, then to Mack. Soon, the whole crowd was repeating Harold's insolent clapping.

Harold walked forward and raised his arms to silence the audience. "Thank you, Eldred."

"He's a whimpering dog!" shouted a man from nearby.

Harold turned and waved him to silence. "Eldred's a brave man. I thank him for returning these men, especially King Alfred. For such deeds, we all owe him our respect. I still puzzle at how he brought these good men to freedom, but there's no doubting he did it. He also brought a bevy of daggers freed from those awful Corporians and some signet rings, another fine deed. We'll distribute those tomorrow per Eldred's request."

The crowd warmed to that news. A few shouted questions, but Harold shook his head and went on. "I asked Eldred to leave out this business about a truce, but since the matter's been raised, let's ask the one man who survived. Mack, come forward!"

Mack stepped slowly across the platform, looking over the crowd distrustfully.

Harold rested his hand on Mack's shoulder. "What do you say, Mack? Should we have peace with the Corporians?"

"Never!" shouted Mack. "Those Motherless bastards tortured us for months. They starved me! They beat me! They killed my friends! But I'm not soft. I'd go back today and fight! And whatever he says"—he pointed at Eldred—"King Alfred would be the first to mount up!"

"He would!" shouted Harold and the crowd yelled their approval.

Eldred turned to Benedict, who raised his eyebrows and shook his head.

"Nobody likes peace," said Benedict, barely audible above the screaming crowd.

✦

GUNDLACH

Not long after workers bore away the bodies of the dead men for their internment, Eldred went to the tower, carrying a fresh loaf of Wilky's bread, still warm. He was directed to the third floor of the tower, to the same quarters where he had once survived an attack by Pounder. Pounder, Mack and the others had beaten down the door, driven to mindless violence. Mack had even killed Morris, the former head steward, in his rage. The thought played in his mind as he looked over the five men lounging on chairs outside the door of the room, but they showed no sign of being stirred by the curse, silenced as it had been by the Mother's shard. One of the men—the leader of the pod, judging by the slightly larger mark between his eyes—even wished Eldred a good day.

He found Gundlach perched on the edge of the bed, his shield and sword laid out beside him. Eldred nodded; there had been no need to take those. Tough as Gundlach was, the diminutive Deirans in the hall would have finished him off before he completed his first swing.

"Greetings, Gundlach. You look well. I trust they didn't mistreat you."

Gundlach looked up with hollow eyes. "No. They are treating me well enough, for now."

"I brought you this," said Eldred, holding out the bread.

Gundlach took it without comment, clutching it in his lap.

Eldred clasped his hands. "The people received my father well, rather better than they received my suggestion of a truce."

Gundlach looked off to the left, glancing down at the floor. "I was thinking it might prove unpopular."

"We'll give out the daggers tomorrow and the signet rights. That could warm people to my suggestions."

"I am hoping," said Gundlach quietly.

"You should take heart," said Eldred. "They've given you good quarters. This was my favorite room back when I was at the Academy." He waved his arm, gesturing at the threadbare carpet and the beaten up drawers, the same furnishings that had been present the night Eldred had almost died. Now, he preferred other lodgings.

Gundlach didn't look up. "They were saying that I would be put to death, the men outside. They were joking about it. They were not saying when, but they were seeming quite certain it would happen."

"Well, you're a diplomat of the Corporians, of the new Goddess. You can't expect Deirans to be pleasant, but I can assure you, they won't be killing you just like that. It would be dishonorable—you're an emissary."

Gundlach gave a weak laugh. "It is good I am having that to count on."

"You should eat. You'll find this bread tasty, even soured as it is for you by the power of the Mother."

Gundlach set the loaf on the bed, next to his sword. "I will be eating later. For the moment, I can only be sitting here."

Eldred frowned. "I can stay in here with you if you like, if that puts you more at ease."

"No, it is better that you are keeping at work, finding a truce. That is why we were coming here"—he peered out the window—"to this place."

"It will take a little time, and you'll see more bluster from them before I can make this happen," said Eldred.

Gundlach shifted and laid his hand on his sword. "You are their champion. If you were sharing that information, would they not be impressed?"

Eldred pressed his lips together and whispered. "Such words will not do, Gundlach. If these men knew of my treasure, they'd not respect it; they'd take it. We're not like your people."

Gundlach rocked forward, crouching over. "Even with your escort?"

Eldred shook his head. "You should not be considering Dederick a friend to me. He's a good man. I like him. But if the word got out, he might be the first to cut me open."

"You are having some friends here though, do you not?" queried Gundlach.

"I do. And besides, nobody wants to camp outside the walls of New Wismar for five years. Even Harold wouldn't want to pay all the costs for that."

"I am hoping you are right. Five years would be taking much too long. Even if we were having that time in New Wismar, I am certain we lack it in Wismar."

Eldred frowned. "What is this trouble? You never tell me."

"I cannot," said Gundlach stiffly. "I would be trusting you if I had not given my oath. All I can say is that an evil is growing there, one which nobody is understanding."

Eldred glanced out the window. "That's nothing special. Evil is everywhere, everywhere there's people. Still, keep your heart. I'll get you home."

GIFTS

Early the next morning, they began the disbursement of the recovered items in the Great Hall. Sixty-seven blades and thirty-six rings were laid out on tables, carefully watched over by the new head steward, Gosbert, and his phalanx of servants. Gosbert was a surprisingly young man for the job, only a few years older than Eldred. He looked earnest and fit, though he walked with a slight limp. Eldred observed Gosbert going about his work, watching for the behavior that had so upset Wilky, but the man seemed cordial and efficient. The process reflected this.

The potential claimants, of which there were many, perhaps two hundred, were brought past the tables to examine the items, only handling them under the tightest scrutiny. During the first pass, no items were handed over, not even those for which the claim was widely agreed. Instead, the stewards in charge of the specific treasures kept note of who made which claim.

After everyone had a chance to inspect the goods, the men lined up, standing before the king's table in rows stretching back nearly the full length of the hall. Harold, Mack and Benedict sat at the table along with Gosbert. Eldred hovered behind them.

One by one, the items which had a single claimant were brought to the front and placed in Gosbert's hands. He held up each one, giving a brief description and naming the supposed claimant. Through this orderly process, he quickly passed out most of the treasures and soon only a dozen blades and a few rings were left.

A hush fell as Gosbert took the first contested item in hand. It was a well-crafted blade that had the slightest purple shimmer about it to Eldred's eyes, nothing like the amazing dagger Eldred had briefly wielded in the Goddess's lair, but fine nonetheless.

Eldred eyed the knife with interest. If only one of Father's blades had been in the boxes, he could've taken it. He had looked through the boxes a few times on the trip, but none of the knives looked familiar, nor that powerful. Now, if he'd taken one himself from the storage room deep in the Goddess's hideaway, that would be one thing. It hadn't seemed right, though, to pilfer someone else's dagger from the boxes.

"By the Mother, it's mine," proclaimed a burly man in the front row. "It was my Uncle Froger's knife, the brother of my father. We were on good terms, and I can make proper use of it; I have the Bond."

Eldred looked the man over; he bore the mark, vibrant and blue, not faded and gray as for the unfortunate Benedict.

"For my mother, the widow of my father, Froger, I make the claim!" called a poorly dressed young woman standing off to the side. She had a thin, pensive face and an uncertain voice.

Eldred checked, but of course she didn't have the Bond. No woman had ever been granted that good fortune.

The crowd stirred as men shifted to try and catch a look at the woman.

"So this is Froger's blade?" called out Gosbert, checking over the hall. "To be clear, nobody is disputing that?"

When no one replied, Gosbert continued. "So we have established this was the property of Froger, an armsman of Lord Hargraves who was known to have been in King Alfred's golden pod. As to the claimants, does anyone have cause to question the relationships they have proffered?"

The hall was silent. Gosbert nodded. "So that's agreed. We still have a dispute, of a sort." He turned to Harold. "My liege, do you have more questions, or are you ready to make a ruling on the matter?"

Everyone turned to look at Harold, who swirled the contents of his cup and seemed to give the matter brief consideration. "I am afraid you're mistaken, Gosbert, a rare error on your part. These goods, this loot, was procured by my cousin, not by me. It is his judgment we'll depend upon today." He glanced over his shoulder. "Well, Eldred, your recommendation? Of course, you can keep it for yourself if you don't see merit on either side."

Eldred took a steep breath. "My decision?"

Harold gave a small smile. "Yes, if you have an opinion."

Eldred took another quick look at the two of them. On second look, the man had a disagreeable air to him: his eyes seemed too close together, his smile vaguely disingenuous. But he was a bonded warrior; that was clear. The young woman appeared anxious and properly so as she stood, holding her arms tightly across her chest. No one in the room was giving her a moment's thought.

Eldred rubbed his neck. "Is there any law or custom that would apply here?"

The man, Froger's nephew, pointed to the woman. "Fluri's not going to use that dagger properly. It's not meant for cutting up chicken."

Men throughout the hall yelled their agreement. Benedict turned to give Eldred a significant look.

"I expect that's true; it's a good blade," said Eldred. "Still, we are talking about Froger's widow, not Fluri. Perhaps she'd look to sell the knife. She might have some need."

Froger's nephew laughed. "Aunt Blitha's taken care of her needs already. She cast Froger aside and married a farmer just last month. He wasn't even gone a year before you brought him back yesterday. Now we know he wasn't even dead when she lay with her new husband!"

Mack jerked upright at the table, spilling his drink. "Yeah, he wasn't dead. I wasn't dead either. People like to forget."

Fluri cringed. People around the hall were shouting their opinions, almost all in opposition to Froger's widow and Fluri.

Benedict motioned Eldred close. "If you aim to grow goodwill, you need to settle this quickly. You can see what they want."

Eldred sighed. "I can see."

He looked again at Froger's nephew, who wore an unbearable grin.

"Any verdict, Eldred?" asked Gosbert.

The hall quieted down. Harold scooted his chair to join the others in studying Eldred, his old smirk was back. Perhaps it had always been there to see if Eldred had looked carefully enough.

A growing discomfort stirred in Eldred as he studied the burly man's smug face, so confident that he would receive the dagger, just like all the other bonded warriors who always got everything. Yet, if the goal was to influence those who mattered, how could it be otherwise? The needs of the widow—she should have come herself instead of sending her daughter—couldn't be put above the need for a truce.

"We have more to go through after this, Eldred," said Gosbert.

Eldred nodded. "It's fine. I've reached my decision. As the person who actually went to the Corporian city, I declare this dagger for Fluri and her mother, Blitha."

Benedict's eyebrows rose in surprise. The nephew's face exploded with anger. The crowd around him seemed hardly less incensed. Near at hand, Harold laughed quietly.

"By the blood of the Mother, you cannot be serious!" screamed the man, taking a step towards Eldred.

"I am," said Eldred, resting his hand lightly on Capito's hilt, feeling the pulsing power of the blade. "I aim to split the difference. The dagger for the widow, the sword for you. Wouldn't a sword be a better instrument for a bonded warrior than a knife?"

The man paused, scanning the tables. "I don't see any swords."

"Not here," said Eldred, lifting Capito out of its scabbard and raising it into the air; its purple edge bright with the Mother's energy to Eldred's eyes. "But in the room where I claimed Capito there were many swords, dozens, perhaps a hundred, scattered across the floor and piled on tables. Froger's sword is likely there. Wouldn't you prefer that to his knife?"

"Of course, but it's not here," said the man.

Eldred looked out over the men. "No, it's not. But you, the kinsmen to the golden pod gathered here, I have seen your heirlooms, your wealth. It's all piled up in that room: armor, swords and knives. If we make a truce, you'll have it, not in five years, but in a few months. And once your arms are restored, if your blood runs hot for vengeance, you can seek it. The Corporians will be back in their lands where they belong, but we can fight them there. The truce wouldn't last forever, just six months. I'd say you could fight them better with proper steel in hand."

The man paused, apparently thinking over the proposition.

Eldred motioned to Gosbert. "Give Fluri the dagger. This man needs to wait for his sword."

As Fluri came up to claim her prize, the air in the room changed. The daggers and rings still drew their interest, but the precious items which remained stored deep in the lair of the Goddess weighed on the minds of the men. They could have it all for the cost of a truce. Judging by their faces, many would make that choice. But not Harold; his face was set like stone.

The other cases were more straightforward, claims of brother against brother, or nephew against nephew—they all were men with the Bond. Though Eldred's decisions left winners and losers, he kept emphasizing that more prizes remained to be claimed once a truce was declared, and most of the men were moderately appeased at this suggestion.

When Gosbert handed over the last signet ring and the crowd started filing out, Benedict stood up and clapped Eldred on the shoulder. "Well done. After a shaky start, you handled that quite smoothly."

"Thank you," said Eldred.

Harold shook his head. "You were wrong though to suggest they're getting back their heirlooms via this supposed truce. If they get them—and I don't know that they all deserve them—it will be through battle. I'm not looking for handouts from your Corporian friends."

"They're not my friends. I killed their soldiers. I killed their Goddess. I expect they hate me more than anyone else who was born of the Mother," said Eldred.

"Perhaps, but if so, why did they just let you walk out of their city? Mack told me all about it. I promise you that if your friend, their emissary, cut off my head, he wouldn't get to saunter off back to his people. He wouldn't take two steps before someone cut him down," said Harold.

Mack nodded vigorously behind him.

"If he told you everything, then he told you about the trade. I gave them back the head of their Goddess and her stone in return for our passage. The Corporians kept their word. I hope in a similar situation that your bonded warriors would likewise show honor. I know those who served my father would have."

"Honor, yes, honor," said Harold with a fleeting smile. "Very good. I tell you what, cousin, why don't you join me for lunch in an hour. I'd like to discuss this truce of yours with an advisor of mine. Are you free?"

Eldred shrugged. "Certainly."

"Should I join as well?" asked Benedict.

"Not this time, Father. For this meeting, I just need Eldred," said Harold.

LUNCH

When Eldred entered the private dining room in the tower, passing through Harold's podmen outside, he found Harold with his head steward, Gosbert, along with another man whom Eldred didn't recognize. He paused just inside the door; the room looked the same with a warm fire throwing shadows on the familiar wood panels, but it felt oddly different with Harold seated at the table in place of Mother and Father.

Harold rose from his seat. "Come in, dear cousin. Have a seat. I was just telling Gosbert to get Wilky's best boiled beef. That's your favorite, is it not?"

"I'm sure that'd be good," said Eldred, though he'd lost most of his ardor for that dish after sampling the more flavorful cuisine of the Sun People.

"Excellent. Go on, Gosbert," said Harold.

Gosbert gave a half bow and left, leaving the door ajar behind him.

Eldred sat at the table across from Harold and the man, who was short and unkempt with a modest blue mark between his eyes. The man appeared nervous and wouldn't meet his eye. "Who's this? Is this your chief diplomat?"

Harold flashed a supercilious smile. "Aistan is my expert on Corporians and their treachery."

"More so than Mack?" asked Eldred.

"Well, that's a good point, cousin. I would say that Mack suffered to a greater degree at the hands of the Corporians than Aistan, but Aistan's suffering shouldn't be discounted."

It was on the third time that Harold said the man's name that recognition set in for Eldred. It was him. The anxious man was none other than the leader of the pod that Eldred had defeated in the cave while in flight with Gundlach and Lady Yslana. Eldred turned to check the door, still open with Harold's pod just behind it.

"Do you think you two might have met before?" asked Harold.

Eldred paused. "It might be. I've been to many of my father's functions. Are you from around here, Aistan?"

Aistan nodded. "I'm from Boar's Tusk. I've seen you. You stand out."

"Yes, my Mercian appearance," said Eldred. "So, do you have thoughts regarding a truce, Aistan? Do you see how a truce might be necessary—for survival?"

Aistan gave a slight shudder. "I don't know."

"Do you have any questions for me?" demanded Eldred.

"I, uhh—" began Aistan, then he paused, groping for words.

Eldred put his hand on Capito under the table and glanced over at Harold. There were no threads from Harold floating over to the door. If it was a trap, it had yet to be sprung.

Harold let Aistan fumble for his words for a moment before cutting in. "He's a bit addled today."

He beckoned Aistan closer, and the two whispered back and forth under Eldred's gaze.

Harold leaned back in his chair. "That's fine, Aistan. You may go. Remember my instructions on this matter."

Aistan cast a last sideways glance at Eldred and hurried from the room, stopping at the door and making a motion to shut it.

"Leave it open!" called Harold. "Just a crack. Gosbert will be back shortly with the food."

Harold and Eldred sat and viewed each other in silence.

After a few moments, Harold rested his hands on the table, a seemingly peaceful movement. But Eldred could see threads blinking in and out of existence between Harold and his podmen outside the door.

"You know what this was about, don't you," asked Harold. "You worried him, but he confirmed it."

Eldred nodded. "Yes."

Harold arched his eyebrows. "You can see why I find this concerning."

"I do," said Eldred.

"And there's far more than just this. You don't look the same; your face patches are gone. Even your fatum lapides are missing, and you had three, cousin—two more than anyone else. Add to that you went lame per reports, but now you can walk. Taken altogether, it gets suspicious. Especially as all you seem to want, all you talk about, is this blessed truce of yours. The answer to everyone's problems: it will make those claimants this morning rich; it will get the Corporians out of my lands; and it's even the answer for those of us who want to kill them."

"That's because it is the answer," said Eldred evenly.

Harold gave a small laugh. "At best, it's only one answer. But first, before we discuss further, answer me this: are you on our side?"

Eldred sat up. "Yes, of course. Are you serious? I warned Aistan repeatedly what would happen if he entered the cave, but he didn't listen. I spared as many of his pod as I could."

"You had help, didn't you?" asked Harold. "There were Corporians with you in the cave who fought with you against Aistan's pod?"

"Yes," said Eldred slowly.

"Well, that explains it. When he tells the story, he gets confused. He makes it sound as if his pod was fighting a single man. But no man could defeat a pod, not even in the dark with the advantage of dark vision."

Eldred shrugged. "For the other issues—my face, my legs and my fatum lapides—I had some healing powder from the Wretcheds. It worked after a fashion but at the cost of my stones." He traced where they had been behind his left temple with his finger.

Harold nodded slowly. "I did hear something about that perversion. Your cousin mentioned it in his letter to your uncle. You must have been desperate."

"I was," answered Eldred.

"Still, better if you hadn't killed him."

"I didn't!" snapped Eldred. "I killed only one man, the man who killed Henreit."

Harold smiled, seemingly relaxed; the floating threads were fading away. "Well, that stands as a matter of dispute between you and your Maldavian relatives. Once it's settled, perhaps we can start meeting behind closed doors."

"So, have I put your concerns to rest?" asked Eldred.

"Some of them. A few of them. However, we are still in disagreement. So, let me be clear. There'll be no truce. I've already sent word to the Mercians and the Maldavians. They'll be raising armies to support our efforts. I'm also looking to put some of our lesser Deirans to use, those without the Bond. That's where I think we might be able to work together."

"How so?" asked Eldred.

"This force of Deirans, the unblessed, has to be led by someone. My father is very insistent that I should offer you the position. If you're actually loyal, I can see some merit to the proposition."

"That's good of you," mumbled Eldred. "But why not have a truce?"

"I think you made it perfectly clear in your speech to the gathering yesterday. You said, I'm recalling this, you said if your father couldn't take that Motherless city, then who could? I give you your answer: I can. Oh, I give your father great credit. I told you that day that he was a fool to attack with only his golden pod, that the numbers were against him. But he was correct. He was a better judge of their strength, or rather their weakness, than I was. It was the Goddess who laid him low. If we can account for her, we can kill them all."

Eldred put out his hand. "The city is like an onion, each of the outer layers has its own wall manned with hordes of archers. Father could ignore them as could any strong force of bonded warriors, but Mercians, Maldavians and unblessed Deirans will fall in droves." Eldred shook his head. "And the Goddess will be at the very heart of the city under her dome, deep in her lair. If she should shut the portal, and she would if threatened, you would never reach her—never."

"You have useful information, cousin. That's why I'm inclined to grant my father's request. And—if your word is true, something Mack can't verify—you've accomplished impressive feats: you killed the old Goddess. Unfortunately, you empowered the new one. This new one, the one that so beguiles you, is a novice. You give her too much credit. If you could vanquish the old one, the one who held the stone for many years, I'm certain we'll find a way to put an end to the new one. Perhaps you'll be the one to cut her head off as well."

"I see," said Eldred with a sinking feeling. "If you're set in this view, we should send their emissary back to share the news."

"No," said Harold. "I don't intend to send him back, not alive anyway. When I cut off his head, that will get the point across to everyone that we're committed to battle. I don't see us getting strong Maldavian or Mercian support without such a display. I expect their representatives in the next few days. I believe your uncle, Julian, is sending your cousin, Oudin. However, he demanded guarantees for his safety." Harold laughed. "You have them worried, cousin."

"Did Julian really ask for that?" asked Eldred. "I'd never harm Oudin. Why, the man helped save my life."

Harold smirked.

Eldred sighed. "Well, then, regarding the Corporian emissary, is a beheading necessary? What if we just sent him back with a firm message about there being no truce?"

Harold shook his head. "No. It's all settled, Eldred. No truce and an end to their surly diplomat. It's my edict, my rule. We're not talking about the trinkets you brought back—that's where your opinion mattered. Still, there's an offer for you to lead. If you're interested, ride down to the Academy. That's where I have the first unblessed forces gathered for training. I would be depending on you to get them ready for battle against the Corporian dregs."

At that moment, Gosbert entered, carrying two large platters of boiled beef and fresh rolls. "Lunch is ready, my liege. Steward Wilky was even more efficient than usual once he learned it was for Eldred."

Harold nodded. "It's good to have Eldred back. He's considering the offer."

Gosbert set a plate before Eldred. "You should accept, Lord Eldred. The unblessed brigade will be a real force, representing all of Deira, leading the way to striking down the Goddess."

"That's right," agreed Harold. "And if it's you—if you manage to kill this Goddess as well—I expect that would be something of a record. You could make your place in history, Eldred."

Eldred eyed the watery beef with no appetite, squeezed by the news he had just heard. "History is calling," he said softly, but he had no thought of harming either Ennlin or Gundlach.

BENEDICT

After lunch, Eldred hurried over to Benedict's rooms; he was staying in Ghyslaine's former apartment. The main sitting room was still adorned with her furnishing, and Eldred perched on her former couch, soft and white. But there were no ladies in waiting, or scones, or tea. Instead, there was just Benedict slouching in Ghyslaine's chair.

Benedict took a moment, pouring a glass of ale. "Do you want a drink, Eldred?"

Eldred shook his head.

"You are still the same in that way—never much of a drinker. I expect you would be a fearful one if you put your mind to it. Why, with your Mercian lineage, I expect you could drink any Deiran to their knees."

"Perhaps," said Eldred. "But there are more pressing matters to discuss."

Benedict nodded. "We will get to those. But first, let me say you are looking quite well. Your face is restored; that splotch is gone. We had reports you had gone lame. And look at you, you're walking and looking quite fit. It's good to see, Eldred. I have been worried about you."

"Thank you, Uncle. On the matter of the Corporian emissary, I have some concerns," said Eldred.

Benedict smiled. "Oh, don't worry about him. It's all settled. Harold is going to carry out the execution himself. So, it will be handled well; you can trust my son there."

Eldred rubbed his chin. "Umm, I'm certain I can. But still, I wonder what message it sends if we kill their emissary. He's come here under the flag of diplomacy. Does it not dishonor all of us if he is put to death for no discernible reason?"

"Well, I don't expect the Corporians to be pleased by the action. However, the message should be clear to everyone, to all of us. We are going to drive the Corporian filth from the land. My Harold will see it done."

"If that's the message, shouldn't he be the one to take it back to them? That's what diplomats, emissaries, do."

"I believe Harold intends to have someone throw his head over the wall. Just how high is it? In any case, it's quite honorable. We are not sneaking up on them in the middle of the night. They will know our intent."

"It's still not how it's done," protested Eldred.

"By whom? If you mean my brother, your father, I think he would do exactly the same. He didn't start the war with an exchange of diplomats or sending them some treaty to sign. He gathered an army and was hacking his way through them when he had a setback. Forget this emissary. He is of no consequence. I say this having met the man myself this morning. He's the most tongue-tied diplomat I have ever met. What were they thinking?"

Eldred pressed his lips together. "He seems to have a reputation with his people for honesty and integrity."

Benedict laughed. "Well, that's wasted on a diplomat. Let's move on. Now, at this lunch of yours, your special lunch which I did not attend, did my son offer you a position of leadership over our unblessed forces?"

"Yes, he did."

"Excellent! Did you accept?"

"Not yet. I'm still thinking it over."

"Well, stop that. Stop that right now. Go over there and tell him you want it. I've been working him on this, Eldred. Harold doesn't usually take my advice, but I have him going on this one. Many of the unblessed are interested in the position, as you should well understand. It's a chance to fight, a chance to shine. You wouldn't be hanging back as you did in that last disastrous battle. You would be right in the front. And if it goes well, I see them as a permanent force for Deira. We could use their numbers."

"Yes, it could be good," said Eldred haltingly. "However, the Corporians don't have a weak position. They are, of course, much weaker than our bonded warriors. If we can apply them, we would win easily. My father proved it. However, while the Goddess is alive—and you should count on her being alive—bonded warriors can't go near the city. Our other forces—be they Maldavians, Mercians or unblessed Deirans—will be in a very tough position under the bare walls of the city. Enemy archers will decimate our ranks. And should we get through, Corporian warriors are not weak. Perhaps Mercians are tougher, but with their walls and their numbers, the Corporians will likely win."

"It is early to declare that, Eldred. Did you not just kill their Goddess on your own?"

"They underestimated me, a mistake. Don't count on them making the same mistake again."

"Well, perhaps you should not underestimate us, nephew. We have plans. What about a force of bonded warriors with unblessed support? They do their trick; they bring us down. The unblessed forces help the weakened bonded forces withdraw. Then two days later, maybe three, we're right back. The question is: can this novice stone bearer for the Corporians do this spell every three days? Can she even do it at all? Harold saw all of this. It's not my plan; it's all his."

Eldred spread his hands. "None of us know what she can do."

Benedict smiled and jabbed his finger towards Eldred. "My brother was naturally stronger. As everyone knows, he passed the trial at four arches removed. We all grant that his golden pod was the greatest ever, even if it met an unfortunate end. But Harold can be an even greater leader than Alfred because he thinks. It was too easy for my brother; he could just destroy his enemies. Harold has to reason it out. And Mother bless him, he did. We will fight united, Eldred. For the first time ever, Maldavians, Mercians and unblessed Deirans striving in support of our champions."

Eldred blew out his breath. "A mixed army, bonded and unblessed."

"Yes. A great deal to consider. You should go down to the Academy and meet the men. I expect you know a good many of them."

"I just might," said Eldred.

GUNDLACH

When Eldred entered the room in the early afternoon, Gundlach was standing by the window looking out.

"Enjoying the view?" asked Eldred.

Gundlach turned; his face was lined with worry. "You have been staying away for a long time."

Eldred shut the door. "I was busy this morning. We passed out the daggers and rings. Then I met with my cousin and uncle."

"Your uncle, he came to see me," said Gundlach, resting his hand on the window sill. "He said my keepers were speaking truthfully; I will be facing execution."

Eldred froze up, surprised Benedict had been so forthright, before stammering a response. "I'm sorry. He said the same to me. It doesn't mean that it's going to happen."

Gundlach's green eyes glimmered with a hint of moisture. "I am thinking that this execution may take place. Your uncle was explaining that this is the wish of your cousin, the king. Our customs may be differing, but still, are not the wishes of your monarch paramount?"

"Sometimes," said Eldred hurriedly. "Though certainly plans can change. We are just having this news, so we've had no time to make our own plans in response."

"Yes," said Gundlach in a grave tone. "I am also fretting over the truce. Your uncle was suggesting that it would not come to pass. Were you successful in explaining its necessity to your relatives?"

"I tried to," said Eldred. "They have different ideas."

Gundlach rubbed his lips. "But what would they be doing? They cannot be taking the city. We are having the walls; we are having the supplies; we are having the Goddess—stronger than ever."

"Yes, I explained. However, they have a new tactic, one they feel can overcome all of that."

"How is this tactic working?" asked Gundlach.

"I can't go into it, just like you can't fully explain what's happening in Wismar. And I'm not even certain it makes a difference. But what it does do is give them confidence. I don't see them passing on it until they give it a try."

Gundlach's eyes narrowed. "Why can you not be sharing this plan? Am I not already dying?"

"No, not yet. They won't harm you until the Maldavian and Mercian delegates arrive. They're not expected for a few days."

"A few days," said Gundlach, leaning more heavily on the window sill. "Have they said how I will die?"

"They say, not that it makes it so, that Harold will be the one, that he will behead you."

Gundlach looked down at the floor. "Beheading ..."

Eldred's face crinkled up. "It wouldn't be a slight, anyway. It's how they would kill me if it came to it."

"Honorable, then," said Gundlach slowly.

"We've plenty of time before then. They want me to lead a force of the unblessed Deiran warriors. Perhaps that could give me some leverage over our situation."

Gundlach frowned. "You would be fighting with them against my people? That could be shifting the balance. Would you be doing that?"

"I don't think so. But for now, it's best they think I will. I plan to go tonight—to meet with them at the Academy. It's only a few hours away. I'll look to return tomorrow, the day after at the very latest."

"Huh, I may not be seeing you in two days."

Eldred shook his head. "News always gets there quickly. If I hear the delegates have arrived, I'll come at once."

"Or do not be coming. If it is not in your power to be changing things, perhaps you might stay away."

"I won't. I'll come back. I'm not giving up on anything. You shouldn't either," said Eldred.

Gundlach smiled and rubbed his temples. "More than once I have been thinking I was dead, and you changed things. You are a powerful man. I should be having faith. I am sorry I do not."

"There's a way. I don't know what it is, but we'll find it."

THE ACADEMY REVISITED

Eldred could have borrowed a mount from the stables; he was not limited to using the Corporian draft horses that had pulled the wagon. However, rather than use any horse, he set out on foot, taking only Capito and his father's signet ring. He jogged along the roads next to the Clyde River making good time, likely traveling faster than he would on any mount save dearest Hobbie, greatest of all the horses while he lived.

As he ran, Eldred thought over the situation. On the one hand, Harold really did seem to be doing a good job as king. He was weaker than Father as Benedict noted, but he was trying new approaches. If Father had taken the Mercians and Maldavians as allies, it might all be different. A strong force of Mercian spearmen backed by Maldavian archers could have kept the Corporian counter charge at bay, giving the golden pod time to recover and withdraw. Father could have fought another day, killing everyone in the city.

On the other hand, killing everyone in the city had never sounded that grand to Eldred. Even that day, before he ever met her, he had hoped the Second would escape. The feeling was stronger now; Ennlin was a good person, full of life, full of energy. She'd kept her word and let him leave the sanctuary where he could have sat for decades, even centuries. She'd be sensible and leave the city if only Harold didn't get in the way.

And there were others too who didn't deserve to die. Lady Yslana, Adept Burgold and Gundlach, to name a few. Gundlach—it was so wrong, so despicable. You should never kill an emissary! To do so betrayed all honor, all decency. Yet as he ran, the thought nagged at him that Benedict was right: Father would do the same.

He was still deep in thought as the Academy came into view, with the black arches laid out before its scattered buildings in the dying light of the day. It was the first time that Eldred had seen the trial arches since he had taken the shard. He moved forward and paused in the center arch, the one where he had so briefly ascended, and ran his hand over the cool stone. He had expected he would see something, some magic of the Mother's that made the place special. He saw only cold, dark stone without the barest glimmer of her energy. If there were any answers there, they eluded him.

He turned his attention to the Academy, that collection of poorly made shacks surrounding Bordin Hall that had once formed his entire world. It looked the same, but he knew that most of the occupants of the huts were members of the newly formed unblessed brigade. Who they were and where they were housed, he didn't know, but he knew the man who did.

$$\sim\!\!\mathbf{M}\!\!\sim$$

THE HEADMASTER

It was dark by the time Eldred knocked on the door of the headmaster's study. At first he heard no response, though he could see the fire was lit behind the curtain in the window, so he rapped his fist again. This time he heard a faint stirring and a softly muttered curse. There was the sound of a few footsteps, and then the corner of the curtain was drawn back to reveal the surprised face of Headmaster Tibbot.

The headmaster opened the door. "Lord Eldred, I was not expecting you. Please come in." The headmaster waved Eldred over to the two chairs nearest the fire. "Have you had supper?"

Eldred was slightly hungry after his journey, but found the idea of eating with his old headmaster too odd to consider. The man had ruled his life for thirteen years. "No, thank you. I'll find something later. I just wanted to get some information regarding the new brigade, where they are staying and who they have for officers."

The headmaster returned to his chair, where he had a book balanced on the arm and a steaming cup of milk set on a table to the side. "I can tell you that. Tenny is here, which I expect is of interest to you. But first, have a seat. I would like to examine you."

A smile slipped onto Eldred's face at the mention of Tenny's name. He was also curious what the headmaster's examination would reveal. The man's opinions and thoughts had once been so crucial to Eldred. Now they were mere curiosities.

"Very well," said Eldred, taking a seat.

The headmaster sat motionless, studying Eldred's forehead intensely. Unlike before, Eldred was also studying the headmaster, watching the vibrant blue mark between his eyes. It was larger than anyone's save for the marks on Father and Dederick, though, of course, Father was dead. Small floating threads issued from the headmaster, disappearing almost as soon as Eldred glimpsed them. The headmaster gave his full attention to his examination, and then he was done.

"Thank you," said the headmaster with a slight shudder.

Eldred grinned slyly. "I gather you didn't see the Bond."

The headmaster made a face and reached for his milk. He took a sip and looked into the fire.

"Well?" prodded Eldred.

"No, I did not see the Bond, but you are different," answered the headmaster.

"Different how?" asked Eldred.

The headmaster turned slowly to meet Eldred's eye. "I would say you have taken on a new curse if I were to hazard a guess."

Eldred blinked. "Cursed? I'm the very opposite of cursed."

The headmaster looked back into the fire. "Perhaps so. I am just telling you what I saw. You seem strange to me, like some stranger who is wearing your skin in disguise."

"Hmmph. I've been hearing people worrying about changes, concerned that the patches on my face healed and the like. I'm surprised to hear the most outrageous claims from you though, headmaster. I always thought you were reasonable, if indifferent."

A small smile came to the headmaster's lips. "I find it quite impossible to be indifferent about you, Eldred, if you are still him. You have in every way been the most challenging squire to manage here at the Academy. How fitting that you have returned for the end."

"What do you mean?"

"The reason for your visit—the common men who are here to train as warriors. It is coming to seem that training such men has become our function. But beyond that, our last two trials have not advanced any squires."

Eldred arched an eyebrow. "I remember that happened once before. Not on two consecutive trials, but for two out of three with only one successful pair of candidates for the middle trial. I think it was Batkin and Parkin."

The headmaster nodded. "The difference this time is that I do not see any squires showing strong potential with the Bond. There are a few weaker boys, similar to your old friend Dreven, but no one with true strength, such as Traden and Noll."

Eldred set his face. "I wouldn't call Dreven weak. You didn't see what he did that day of the battle."

"Oh, I did not mean like that. I only meant with the Bond. I heard about his misfortune. I grieved for him as I do for any of our former students who pass on."

"A hard death," said Eldred, frowning. "I get angry every time I think about it. He was trying to help me, you know, when Lord Ferris caught him. They celebrated Ferris's podman, Wulsan. They went on and on about his lucky throw. But they forgot—luck and misfortune, they circle around each other, intertwined."

"That is one view," offered the headmaster distractedly.

"You should let me see them," said Eldred.

"Who?"

"Your weak ones. With all my changes, I can see things now. I can see who has the Bond. Perhaps I can pick out some squires for you to keep an eye on."

The headmaster narrowed his eyes. "What?"

"I can see things. My Maldavian vision has expanded perhaps. Take you, for example. I can see that your marking with the Bond, right there between your eyes, is bigger than for anyone else I have seen save for my father and Dederick."

"A mark, you say?"

Eldred wagged his finger. "Though yours is smaller than theirs, it's still a good size bigger than anyone else's; it also has deeper color than anyone's. Does that make any sense to you? Is there something about you that could account for that?"

"None of that makes any sense at all," said the headmaster. "How can you be sensing a mark when you do not have the Bond yourself?"

"The mysteries, headmaster, I only find the world getting more puzzling the longer I live. Just take my word for it, or attribute it to whatever you thought you saw when you studied me. Nonetheless, I would like to see these squires tomorrow before I go. It'll bring no harm to any of them—I can promise you that."

"Very well. I suppose I can arrange that. So, you will be leaving tomorrow?"

"I'm just here to visit the new troops, to get a sense of their capabilities."

"It is more their lack of capability that you will find," commented the headmaster. "We have eight hundred of them doubled and tripled up in the dorms. Two solid pods of real warriors would kill all of them as did not run away."

"Well, they have the likes of Tenny. Unless he's gone soft, he's a formidable fighter."

The headmaster shook his head. "His arm is strong, as you would expect from a blacksmith. But despite his strength and his training from his time with us, he is nothing compared to a bonded warrior."

"He'd still be the best of them. Where did you put him?"

"In your old quarters. Where else?"

TENNY

A sense of excitement filled Eldred as he navigated through the barracks to his former lodgings. Tenny was there, at the Academy training for war. It felt so much like old times. Things had been simpler back then. Life had consisted of endless practice sessions, reading books and spending time with friends—not just Tenny, but Dreven, Mance and Yeowars, all of the old timers. They'd had such hopes. They were all gone now, this way and that, except for Tenny.

Eldred knocked and waited expectantly. After some shuffling from within, someone Eldred didn't know opened the door to reveal a room packed with men. Three men were sleeping on the floor with another set of blankets for the one who had gotten up. Each of the two beds held two men sleeping head to foot. Eldred took a step back, unsettled to find such a crowd, when Tenny poked his head up from his old bed.

"Eldred?" asked Tenny, shaking himself awake. "By the Mother, it's Eldred, everyone, the prince who just brought back King Alfred's corpse. This is him!"

Eldred smiled. "It's good to see you, Tenny."

The men grudgingly stirred themselves to glance at Eldred with sleepy eyes while Tenny scrambled up and pulled on his clothes and boots. After Tenny gave Eldred a hard but affectionate punch in the shoulder, they went out for a walk.

They started off in silence, happy for their reunion, but not finding the right words to start with.

As they neared the arches, Tenny gestured at them. "You've done it all.

You killed the dragon. You ascended. You fought in the great battle. And you, well, I guess there was some trouble with your Maldavian relatives. But now you've brought your father home, and they say you killed the Corporian Goddess. Is that true? Half the men here say you didn't kill her. I keep saying you did."

Eldred nodded. "I did."

Tenny laughed. "One man, not some pod. You give us all hope. They laugh at us, you know. But we're only here since we're necessary. King Harold and his bonded warriors can't go where we can go, can't kill who we can kill."

"That's true enough, up to a point. I'm actually here to meet up with all of you. Harold has offered me command of the brigade."

"That's fantastic!" exclaimed Tenny. "That awful Garaint has been taking us through our drills. With you at the lead, why, we could do anything. We could capture the Corporian city tomorrow and paint the ground red with their blood."

Eldred gave a fixed smile. "Well, it wouldn't be as easy as that. I've been telling Harold and Benedict that the city, New Wismar, will be no easy undertaking, not even for this brigade. It has walls within walls within walls. And at each layer, a mass of archers set to rain down missiles."

"That's why we've shields," said Tenny.

"Those will help, but it's quite a risky undertaking. I'm actually proposing another approach, a truce."

"I heard something about that, but I didn't know what to make of it. A messenger who came yesterday was saying that you were making out that a truce is the best way to kill the Corporians. How would that work? Is it a trick? A false truce? I didn't think you'd do something like that."

"No. I wouldn't," said Eldred. "The truce would be true enough. It would get them out of the Motherland and back in Corporia, where it would be easier to fight them. I know it sounds odd, but if they're in their own lands, we can decide what victory means. We could sack some small city or— if we've good fortune—fight a large battle on some open plain. When we've had enough and done enough, we can return home. But if they stay in New Wismar, then victory means only one thing—taking the city. And that, my friend, we cannot do."

"Walls can be breached," said Tenny. "Anything made by men can be broken by men. As a blacksmith, I've seen it often enough."

Eldred smiled and sat down on a stone facing the arches. "I'm sure you have."

Tenny frowned and sat across from him. "Are you going to lead the brigade?"

"I'd like to."

"But you won't?" asked Tenny.

"I'm not certain. I only had the offer today."

"This is bigger than this matter of the Corporians. Of course, it's good to kill them, but this brigade—it's the first time the king and the nobles have really said they need unblessed men, that we matter."

"Everyone has always mattered," said Eldred.

Tenny scoffed. "You know that's not true."

"You're the one who told me. You reminded me when I was losing all hope. You said that most people never even thought of this place, the Academy."

"Well, that's true. I'm not saying unblessed people don't matter to me. I prefer common men to overbearing bonded warriors, with all their endless demands. But everyone knows that when people think about Deira, they're thinking about the Bond. They're not thinking about who's crafting armor down in Hog's End."

"Well, that's the way of things, Tenny. The world is a hard place. Let down your guard for a minute and you'll be crippled or dead."

"I've no intention of letting down my guard," said Tenny.

Eldred groaned and rubbed his forehead. "They, the Corporians, came out for my father because it was a trap. And they could do it because we didn't know her power, what the Goddess could do. Now we know and they know we know. They won't come out. When Harold and Julian and King Capuan get tired of paying for their armies to sit, they'll send in this brigade. Maybe not alone, but it won't matter. When will you run? When the man on your left dies? What about when the men on both sides of you are dead? You won't even swing at them. They'll be up on their wall."

Tenny grimaced. "We're going to mix in the bonded warriors; they can deflect any missile. And your Maldavian relatives are better archers than those stupid Corporians. We'll keep them back as we throw up ladders and take their gates. You could be the first one up the wall, Eldred. That's a ton better than Harold milling around in the back."

"You've always looked out for me. I'm just trying to look out for you. I've seen so many people die." Eldred took a steep breath. "I was only an inch from it myself more than once. You'd think it would be noble, but it isn't. You're just eaten by a dragon, or die on a torture rack, or get hung by coward, or stabbed by a nobody, or hunted by a madman. Death doesn't know honor."

"I'm already here. You can't talk me out of joining," said Tenny.

"I know. It also seems I can't talk anyone into supporting a truce. I'm just saying that we could attack a small town or fight in an open field if battle must be done. As for killing Corporians, I'm not seeing the need if they leave. There's good ones and bad ones, the same as us."

Tenny chuckled. "So that's it. Those are the other rumors. People say you love their Goddess. Is that what this is about?"

Eldred laughed. "No. I barely know her. Still, she's as honorable a person as I've met. She's strong, vibrant—mischievous."

"How is her appearance?" asked Tenny.

"Strange, at least by how we see things. She has blond hair and green eyes. She stands almost as tall as a Mercian. And she's covered in silver and golden ornaments. I gather she cannot pass a piece of jewelry without hanging it from her person."

Tenny smiled. "She sounds strange enough, but I've met stranger."

Eldred rolled his eyes. "Very well. I'll inspect the troops tomorrow, but don't count on me leading them."

"I won't," said Tenny. "But you should."

MORNING AT THE ACADEMY

Eldred woke up before first light and lay there, lying in his old bed, watching the men sleeping on the floor. He hadn't needed to kick anyone out of the bed. When he and Tenny had returned around midnight, they found both beds empty. Perhaps they'd known it was Eldred's former bed, or perhaps they'd just figured he was important. In any case, it was a pleasant homecoming.

When dawn came, Eldred dressed quietly and picked his way through the men piled on the floor and stepped outside. As he surveyed the arches in the distance, he was tempted to run back to Boar's Tusk. There was nothing to be done about the truce; Harold seemed quite set on killing Corporians. But Gundlach might be saved. There had to be some other way for Harold to show he was serious about rushing to war that didn't involve killing an accidental diplomat.

With a sigh, Eldred turned and walked towards the dining hall. He'd inspect the brigade first. That's what Benedict and Harold expected. Perhaps, leading the troops would give him some standing to change Harold's thinking, though he suspected that was not the case.

The cook greeted Eldred warmly and without surprise, which Eldred took to mean that the headmaster had spread the word of his return. She placed triple rations on two plates for him, including a pile of fried bacon. He took his seat at the old timers' table, the place for older boys who had not passed the trial, trying to remember who would be there now. Neither he nor Tenny had ever paid much attention to the younger ones. In any case, nobody joined him and he spent his breakfast munching bacon and studying the squires, who seemed to number around two hundred.

There were a few squires who had something like a gray mark between their eyes, some harbinger of the Bond, it seemed. Unless the marks expanded terrifically in size, though, they did seem to be of the type that the headmaster had made mention of—weak. If they were all that was left, the headmaster's bleak assessment appeared to be true.

Eldred was contemplating that fact and considering what it would mean in twenty years if there were no more bonded warriors when Preceptor Grimes sat down abruptly across from him. "Mind if I join you, Eldred?"

"Not at all," said Eldred, staring at his forehead. A nice blue mark sat there, about the size of Pounder's, a good size.

The preceptor set down his plate and scooped up a forkful of egg. "The headmaster let me know you were here."

"Just for the day, I expect," said Eldred. "I'm here to inspect the brigade of unblessed warriors. I might be taking command of them."

"Wouldn't you be staying on longer if you did?" asked Grimes.

"Well, yes, in the future. At the moment though, I've important business in Boar's Tusk."

"I see," said Grimes, picking up a piece of toast.

"How are things here with this new force? I heard Preceptor Garaint is managing their training."

"Yes, he's taken that on. He's doing what he can. As you know, all our work here is for squires, our students, to get the Bond. Once they have that, they're warriors, the greatest warriors in the world. Working with men who are just men is very different. It's like trying to train Mercians, but they're not huge and strong and stupid. They're just men."

"Ah," said Eldred.

"Oh, of course, present company excepted," said Grimes apologetically. "You're not Mercian, Eldred. I don't think anybody quite knows what you are, but you certainly aren't just some Mercian."

"No, I'm not," agreed Eldred.

They ate in silence for a few moments after that until Grimes looked Eldred in the eye.

"You know, you ought to consider carefully before you take this position," said Grimes. "You passed the trial, sort of, so you should probably try to find something else."

Eldred wiped some of the bacon grease on his hands off onto his pants.

"I met the headmaster last night. He said that he doesn't see the Bond in me."

"Well, he never did. So, that doesn't change things."

"I guess not," agreed Eldred.

"I just mean the brigade—they're not much. Preceptor Garaint is doing everything he can think of, but they'd be wiped out by anyone: Mercians, Maldavians, and—I expect—Corporians. They're just men; men who—I gather—want to fight. Now you've never really had the Bond in my view, but you've always had something. You were tough. If they were like you, well, that'd be something else. As it is, best you stay clear of them."

"Tenny's not bad," said Eldred.

"He's a bit of a fighter, but do you see him beating a Mercian warrior? Do you see him dodging a slew of Maldavian arrows? You know more than I about the Corporians, but by all accounts, they're big."

"Yes, Corporians can fight," allowed Eldred.

"There's a lot of good people mixed up in this, many of our former students. I wouldn't want to see them get massacred."

Eldred nodded. "Nor would I." He gestured at the students eating at the nearby tables. "How are you finding the current crop of squires?"

"We've got some good ones," said Grimes with a note of uncertainty.

Eldred leaned closer. "The headmaster doesn't seem to think so."

Grimes looked away. "There are always dry spells. I expect someone will come up big next trial. I don't know who, though. I guess if nobody does, it'll be time for another run at transference." He finished with a weak smile.

Eldred smiled sadly. "Thanks again for your efforts there. And I'm sorry—sorry about that business at my trial. I didn't know that my father was going to threaten you. That's nothing I ever wanted."

"I know," said Grimes. "Your father was a bloody-minded bastard. He did what he did to get his way. I expect you must know more about that than I do."

"I do. He always got his way, but for the once—a record I'll never match."

An hour before lunch, Preceptor Garaint lined up the entire brigade in the main training square. With their numbers, on the order of eight hundred, they filled the square with their irregular lines. Eldred sat next to the headmaster on a bench looking over the troops. The displaced squires were visible in the distance, training in small groups in the grassy fields around the Academy. Eldred kept turning to watch the squires studying with Preceptor Grimes; advanced sword techniques had been his favorite.

What Garaint had on display was dull. He took the men through simple exercises that they performed without precision or snap. Spears were raised around the same time, but not together. Formation movements were sloppy—just a mass of men shuffling around. Throughout the entire exercise, the headmaster kept tensing up, as if he were trying to correct the mistakes of the men through twisting his stomach or clenching his fist. Of course, it didn't help.

At the end of the sorry display, Garaint came up before Eldred and the headmaster with twelve men behind him, the brigade officers with Tenny among them.

"That is them through their paces, Lord Eldred," said Garaint. His voice suggested his dissatisfaction.

Eldred stood up. "Thank you, Preceptor. I can see there are some challenges still needing to be worked out."

Garaint nodded. "That is certainly the case."

"I can see they don't march smartly," said Eldred, noticing a sour expression spreading across the faces of the nearby men. "But what I can't tell is how they would actually fight. There's two things I expect will come for this brigade. I expect them to come under heavy missile fire. And I expect they will be called upon to take enemy fortifications. Do you have any idea how they would fare on these points?"

"I do. They would fare poorly," said Preceptor Garaint.

"Has this been tested?" asked Eldred.

"It is self-evident," said Garaint.

"Self-evident, my ass!" called out a heavyset man with a thinning gray beard standing next to Tenny. Eldred didn't know him.

Garaint raised an eyebrow but did not turn to face the man. "Would you like me to have him lashed for insubordination, Lord Eldred?"

Eldred froze, realizing that he probably should have the man flogged, but not wanting to give the order.

"It would not be the first time for Pascall," observed the headmaster.

"Yes, or rather, let's have the flogging if the man, Pascall, can't back up his words," said Eldred.

A murmur passed among the men along with a brief flash of excitement on their faces.

"I propose two exercises to test your strength," said Eldred. "First, let us see how you handle missiles. I want a group of twenty-five men—you officers can pick them out. We'll do the same test my father gave his golden pod. It's time to dance, men. Twenty-five soldiers with shields and swords. Once we do this we can move on to the fortifications test."

"Do we have to face your arm?" asked Tenny.

Eldred smiled. "No. Not this time. Preceptor Garaint, can you get twenty-five of your older squires? Have them gather up a mess of dirt clods, at least ten apiece, and report here."

"Very well, Lord Eldred," said Garaint, who headed off towards the group that Preceptor Grimes was leading.

The twelve brigade officers started arguing about who to put forward. Pascall was the loudest, but the others, including Tenny, were quite vocal as well.

"What do you hope to accomplish?" asked the headmaster.

"I'm just giving them a chance to prove themselves," said Eldred. "I'm interested to see what the men can do."

"Garaint already told you what they can do."

Eldred gave a slight shrug. "Perhaps. By the way, I saw your students this morning at breakfast. You were right. There's not much there. That means"—he waved his hand at the brigade behind him—"that this might be all we have soon. So, it's worth checking them out."

"It will be years before we have to depend on them," said the headmaster dismissively.

Eldred paced behind the headmaster's bench as the squires and brigade members got ready. He kept glancing off past the black arches towards Boar's Tusk, where Gundlach sat waiting for his execution. That must not happen.

After fifteen minutes or so, the exercise was laid out. A boisterous group of squires stood next to their piles of dirt clods. Eldred could see their eagerness to pelt the unblessed warriors standing twenty feet across from them. For their part, the brigade members, who included Tenny and Pascall, also looked ready for action, sporting shields and swords. Eldred had directed that they form one long line rather than the five by five formation of a silver pod.

Eldred faced the line of men and pointed at the squires. "They're going to throw their dirt clods trying to hit you in the leg, or arm, or face—any part of your skin. If they do, you're dead—not really dead, but dead for the purpose of this exercise. Now, if we go to New Wismar, that's the Corporian city, you'll face many more archers, and they'll have many more arrows. And a hit really could mean death. Ready? Let them fly!"

The scrimmage took less than two minutes from start to finish. The squires were smart and immediately switched up from throwing at the men straight across from them. They looked down the lines, picking out men who were turned in the other direction, focused on some other threat. Though most of the dirt clods exploded on men's legs, some hit arms and a few struck men on the side of the head. The last man standing was hit by a dozen missiles hurled by the squad of hooting boys.

"Every man was struck, Lord Eldred," reported Preceptor Garaint without prompting.

"I saw. Good job, squires. Please hold for a minute before returning to your lessons," said Eldred. Then he walked down the line, inspecting each man, noting where the missiles had left their mark.

When he reached Pascall, who had been struck three times on the leg, the man reached out and tapped Eldred on the shoulder with his sword. "I'd like to see you do better."

Eldred stopped and smiled incredulously at the man. "You would, would you?"

"Shut up, Pascall," muttered Tenny, who was standing next to him.

Pascall ignored Tenny. "Yes, I would!"

Eldred clapped his hands. "Very well. I'll join the squires on the next exercise. We'll have the same squires opposing the same men. This time, the objective is for the men to capture the dining hall. It's only twelve feet high, much shorter than the fortifications of New Wismar. The goal will be accomplished when the twenty-five squires are pulled down from the roof and at least one man from the brigade remains on top."

The headmaster rose from the bench. "I cannot have my students getting injured."

Eldred glanced at the squires, who appeared ready to do battle. "We'll lay down some hay bales from the stables. And you"—Eldred motioned at Pascall and Tenny—"have your men show some care. Bruises are acceptable, broken bones are not. And for both sides, if you get dropped down onto the hay, you're out."

The headmaster took a moment studying his pleading charges before slowly nodding his head. "I do not see any point to this exercise, but I will humor you, Lord Eldred. Preceptor Garaint, please see to procuring the hay."

"So, you're up on the roof too?" asked Pascall.

"Yes, that's right," said Eldred.

"The rumor is that you're to be our commander. Will we face any penalties when we toss you down on your ass?" asked Pascall.

Eldred smiled. "None at all. As far as I'm concerned, the man who throws me over will be due a promotion."

"Sounds good to me," said Tenny with a grin.

"No going easy on your friend!" snapped Pascall.

"That was never how it worked," said Eldred.

Preceptor Garaint took a squad of two hundred men to get the hay. The other men in the brigade started hunting through the Academy for ladders and boxes they could use in their siege attempt. The squires started climbing up onto the dining hall, forming a ragged line along the edge of the sloping roof. Other groups of squires started coming in to watch the proceedings, calling encouragement to the boys on the roof.

The headmaster approached Eldred. "What will it prove if these men take a low hanging roof from these youths?"

"Well, it won't mean they can take on the Corporians, but it'll give me a chance to see if they can work together. The marching, the exercises earlier with Preceptor Garaint—I couldn't tell anything from that."

"I could," said the headmaster. "I saw men who lacked discipline, who could barely walk in step. Now, with this"—the headmaster waved his hand at the dining hall—"you will be giving them encouragement. But I tell you, a decent pod could hold even this meager fortification from the entire brigade."

"Perhaps. However, against the Corporians, your pod would fall to the ground by the will of the Goddess. These men, this out of step brigade, is what we have for the job."

In half an hour, the preparations were complete. The men found six ladders with varying degrees of sturdiness. Under Preceptor Garaint's exacting eye, the brigade had carpeted the area next to the dining hall with bales of hay.

Eldred stood on the roof in the middle of the squires, looking out over the assembly below. Everyone associated with the Academy was there: squires, preceptors, cooks and stewards. Their shouts made their allegiances clear. The men of the brigade also looked on, their confidence in their team showing on their faces. Nobody looked more confident than Tenny, who was paired up with three other men holding a ladder on the left. Nobody looked more serious than Pascall, who gripped a ladder with two other men on the right.

"No broken bones! Let the scrimmage begin!" shouted Eldred.

The men from the brigade charged forward and slapped their ladders against the edge of the roof. As the first men clambered up, groups of squires gathered at the top of the ladders, trying to tip them to the side. Only one ladder gave, dropping one of the men to the ground.

Eldred stood apart and clapped. "That's one down."

Meanwhile, as the errant ladder was reset, the first men came even with the roof. One man in the middle tried to force his way past the boys, batting them away, but two squires jumped on him and bore him down to the hay, though they fell themselves. Another man clung to the roof while the squires around him pelted him with blows and kicks. After a decent beating, he retreated out of reach down the ladder but didn't fall.

It was Tenny who found the winning method. He came up to just below the roof and grabbed the squires who reached for him, carefully pulling them down one after another and dropping them to the ground until his way was clear. Once he was up, he set on the squires on the next ladder over, pushing and tossing them down while more men followed up behind him.

As the men followed Tenny's example, the battle turned into a rout. The squires dropped two more men; however, the roof was quickly cleared, and soon only Eldred stood for the defense, watching as twenty-one men climbed up to join him.

"I take it you yield?" asked Pascall once the full complement of men faced Eldred.

"No, I do not," said Eldred.

"Then I take you!" shouted Pascall, charging at Eldred and leaping to embrace him.

Eldred snatched him from the air by his shoulder and sent him tumbling over the edge.

Five other men charged in as the others, including Tenny, started to circle around him.

Eldred sent two of the men down to the ground with reasonable gentleness, but the others dove on his legs, trying to bear him over. Once the men were on him, other emboldened men charged forward and Eldred felt his feet starting to slip down the smooth wooden planks towards the edge.

At that moment, Eldred remembered the Guardian who could not be shoved from the circle. The corrupt energy of the Goddess had stuck its feet fast to the ground. The roof and everything around, including Eldred, was fashioned with the energy of the Mother. Not so deep and burning an energy as had been present there by the dome of the Goddess, but enough—it was energy enough. So, with a thought, with a brief exertion of will, Eldred bound his feet to the sturdy planks, which held him fast.

The men struggled furiously, pushing Eldred with all of their might, as he plucked them up one by one and rolled them off the roof. A few men tried boxing with Eldred, but he grabbed them and sent them over, uninjured by their hardest blows.

The last man standing was Tenny, who stood eight feet up from Eldred, staring at him in amazement.

"How are you doing this?" called Tenny.

Eldred smiled and unstuck his feet, pleased at having learned the trick. "Doing what?"

Tenny shook his head and grinned. "You bastard."

"I'm right here, Tenny," said Eldred.

"Down you go!" shouted Tenny, putting his head down and charging Eldred.

Eldred caught him and then took the squirming Tenny to the edge and dropped him down. The scrimmage was over.

Below, the squires were leaping up and down in victory, basking in the cheers from the other assembled youths. Tenny, Pascall and the other men from the brigade looked shocked, victory having seemed so close to them.

"The fortification is held!" shouted Eldred. "The squires did well, sending a number of men to the ground. The men of the brigade also did well. They made good use of their numbers and strength. In other circumstances, they may well have earned a victory."

"What does it mean? Two tests and we fail both?" demanded Pascall.

"You tried your best. There'll be no lashes for you, if that's what you're asking. However, if we tried this exercise with the Corporians on the walls of New Wismar, you'd all be dead. Tough as unarmed squires are, Corporian soldiers with spears and arrows are more dangerous. I would urge more time, more training. I would suggest a truce."

Pascall crossed his arms. "That sounds weak."

"You're not alone in saying that," said Eldred. "It's possible we'll soon go and try this against the enemy—higher walls, no hay. If we do, I'll do my best to get you all through it alive. In the meantime, it's more training with Garaint."

"Are you going to lead us?" asked Tenny.

Eldred clasped his hands. "I'm going to Boar's Tusk to find out. If that's what comes from it, it'll be an honor for me. Now, best we get this cleared up. Men of the brigade, if you brought a bale, please take it back."

Eldred jumped down onto a bare patch of dirt.

Tenny walked over to meet him. "Did you mean that?"

"I did," affirmed Eldred.

Pascall came up behind Tenny. "If you want us battle ready, you can't have us training with that Motherless preceptor."

"That's how it is for now. But I agree this is no place for you men. The Academy is for the old way, for squires and the Bond. We'd be better off out in a field somewhere with tents," said Eldred.

"That's right. Every day here is just an earful of how weak we are. The preceptors have no respect at all," said Pascall.

"Do you really think you can get a truce?" asked Tenny.

Eldred frowned. "I don't know. I see sound reasons for one. We'll soon find out."

Tenny leaned in and clasped Eldred's shoulder. "What'd you do up there on the roof? There's no way you could stand up to all of us."

Eldred raised his eyebrows. "Who said I did anything?"

"At least you haven't changed," said Tenny, shaking his head.

Eldred found the headmaster along with Preceptor Grimes and Preceptor Garaint near the bench where the headmaster had been sitting earlier. The three men were standing close to each other, speaking quietly.

"I'm off to Boar's Tusk to give my assessment of the brigade," said Eldred.

"I see," said the headmaster. "You mentioned that they required more training. Is that truly necessary? From your entertaining exercises and Preceptor Garaint's display of their skills, it seems quite clear that these men have no military utility. Fine men, some of them, but they will not prove decisive in the war with the Corporians."

"Well, I'm not certain I would go as far as that, but I'll look to move them to another location for training," said Eldred.

"That would be most welcome," said the headmaster.

"In the meantime, and it may just be a day or two, please keep them at their drills, Preceptor Garaint," said Eldred.

Garaint tilted his head. "Do you wish me to add your drills to their instruction—dodging dirt clods and climbing up ladders?"

"No need for those, but perhaps Preceptor Grimes could add in some of his sword instruction. They'll need to be in top form if they meet the Corporians with blades in hand," said Eldred.

Grimes shrugged. "I can help."

"Thanks," said Eldred.

"Do you require the loan of a mount? I understand that you arrived on foot," said the headmaster.

"No. I'm fine on my feet," said Eldred.

"It would be no trouble," persisted the headmaster.

Eldred shook his head. "No. I just don't ride horses anymore, not since I lost my horse in battle. I—I had the finest horse that ever lived."

"Then enjoy your walk, Lord Eldred. We will wait for your return," said the headmaster.

DEBATE

Eldred did not walk, but ran the distance back to Boar's Tusk. As he ran, it weighed on him how little time might be left for Gundlach, and he increased his speed, running even faster than he had on the journey out to the Academy. He arrived in the midafternoon at the main gate to the castle covered in a thin sheen of sweat.

A guardsman waved him down. "Hold, Lord Eldred."

"Yes? What is it?" asked Eldred, catching his breath.

"Your cousin, Prince Oudin has arrived. He asks that you visit him in his chambers," said the man.

Eldred blew out his breath. "And what of the Mercian delegate? Has he also arrived?"

"Not yet. He is expected either this evening or early tomorrow," answered the man.

Eldred pressed his hands together and raised them to his lips, thinking. Once the Mercian delegate arrived, Gundlach's execution would take place.

"Should I tell Prince Oudin that you are coming to see him?" asked the guard.

Eldred nodded distractedly. "Yes. I'll see him. I just need to see Harold first, King Harold."

The man gave a short bow. "Very well. I'll inform Prince Oudin."

After a hurried search, Eldred tracked Harold to the private dining room in the tower. In the anteroom to the dining room, he came across Gosbert, the head steward, and the podmen of both Harold and Dederick.

"I need to see Harold immediately," said Eldred.

"Oh, I was just stepping out to get some ale. I'm sure they will be happy to see you. Go on in," said Gosbert, gesturing at the half open door behind him.

As Gosbert stepped away, Eldred knocked on the door, then pushed it open to find Harold and Dederick sitting together at the table.

Harold glanced up with a look of surprise. "Eldred? I wasn't expecting you back for a few days. Did you go to the Academy?"

"Yes, I'm there and back," said Eldred.

Harold gestured at a chair across from him. "Leave the door a crack and have a seat. So, you saw the brigade. What did you think?"

Eldred nodded at Dederick, who seemed in good spirits, and sat down. "I think they need more training."

Dederick laughed. "That's an understatement."

"The headmaster and Preceptor Garaint agree with my assessment," continued Eldred.

Harold shrugged. "They've never been very happy with their guests. Their concerns will have more weight once they resume producing bonded warriors."

"Right, well, my concern is that we might have to postpone any attack on the Corporians until the brigade is brought up to form. It'll take me some time, at least a few months, perhaps longer," said Eldred.

"Ah, some ale," said Harold, eyeing Gosbert coming through the door. "You're a true hero, Gosbert, the best man in my realm."

Gosbert set down a tray with a flagon of ale and three tall cups. "You do me too much honor, my liege."

"Not at all," said Harold, pouring a cup. "Some ale, cousin?"

"No, thank you. I don't drink," said Eldred.

Harold crinkled up his face. "Really? The word I had from Maldavia was that you had come to appreciate your wine before all that business with your cousin."

Eldred held up his palm. "I did. But I don't drink now."

Harold poured out another cup. "This isn't more silly business about Academy oaths, is it?"

"No, it's a personal matter," said Eldred.

"That's for you, then, Dederick," said Harold, sliding the cup over to Dederick's waiting hand.

"He didn't drink on the way out here, either," said Dederick.

"Hmm," said Harold. "What do you know?"

"Do you require anything else, my liege?" asked Gosbert.

"No, this is golden. I'll meet you in a few moments up in my chambers," said Harold.

As Gosbert made his exit, Eldred set his hand lightly on the table. "I was saying that the men aren't ready."

"Right. Well, nobody's disagreeing, cousin," said Harold. "Though, given they lack the Bond, you might say they're neither ready nor not ready."

"They do eat and take up space," said Dederick.

"That they do," said Harold, taking a hearty drink.

"Well, I'm given to understand that we depend on them—that you're counting on them to push back the Corporians at least until the Goddess is dealt with," said Eldred.

"They're part of it, but mostly we're counting on the Mercians. If you manage things properly, I expect you can have the Mercians take the brunt of the casualties. That would probably be for the best," said Harold.

"King Capuan himself will be up front leading the charge," said Dederick.

"What charge? The Corporians will just stay behind their walls," said Eldred.

"Or not," said Harold with a wink.

Eldred narrowed his eyes. "What do you mean?"

Harold smirked. "Nothing. Just, what if they didn't have any walls?"

"But they do," said Eldred.

"For now. Forget about it, cousin. I'm just speculating," said Harold.

"I see," said Eldred with a bemused expression.

Harold took a drink and rolled the cup back and forth between his palms. "Don't feel bad, cousin. You're included. They may be riff-raff, but you'll lead a brigade roughly equal in size to what I'll take. You go first, with the Mercians and Maldavians. Then Dederick with his golden pod. Then me, with my forces. It's all set."

Dederick nodded in agreement.

"So, you lead the golden pod this time," said Eldred.

"The honor falls to me," said Dederick with a pleased expression.

Eldred gestured at Harold with his right hand. "With all this lined up, do you really need to kill the Corporian?"

"It's expected. It's agreed to," said Harold.

"He's an honorable man," said Eldred.

"He's just one man. We're going to kill everyone in their city. Is he more deserving than everyone there?" asked Harold.

"Perhaps not, but he's a diplomat. The proper thing is to let him return and let them know that there's no truce," said Eldred.

Harold grinned. "I think they'll know. They should always have known."

Eldred sighed. "What if I traded you something for him?"

"Like what?" asked Harold.

Eldred dug into his pocket and pulled out his father's signet ring. "You seemed to take an interest in this."

Harold's eyes locked on the black onyx ring.

"Well, is it a trade? He's just one Corporian. You have plans to kill thousands," said Eldred.

Harold pressed his lips tight, contemplating for a moment, then shook his head. "No. It's already settled. It's expected that I'll take his head tomorrow."

"It's a fine ring. It belongs with the king. You said so yourself," said Eldred.

"I know, but it's settled," said Harold.

Eldred set the ring down on the table between them. "I don't know why you don't take it. You could just cut the head off a hog, or something. Who else but me cares if you kill the man or not?"

"Someone does," said Harold softly.

"Nonsense!" snapped Eldred.

Harold clapped his cup on the table. "Careful, cousin. I'm your king,"

Eldred shrugged.

Harold glared. "Look, if you're so set on this, put up something of real value. Everything is fixed. Everything is planned. Still, I can change it all if you want. Capito—the price for that wretched Corporian is Capito."

Eldred's eyes went wide. "Are you insane? A named sword—the greatest named sword—for one man's life? You can't expect me to do that."

"Perhaps I don't," admitted Harold. "But such is the price. The Mercians should arrive tonight. The execution will be tomorrow at noon. As is obvious, you need to decide before then."

"I can decide right now. I'll never give up Capito."

"Nobody would expect anything different," said Harold. "Now, you'll have a few weeks to tune up your men, to get them ready. You'll see. We'll all kill so many Corporians that this one won't matter at all."

OUDIN

Eldred stormed off from the dining room in a foul mood. He was not inclined to see Oudin, but couldn't face Gundlach. So he climbed the stairs, passing the floor where Gundlach was held captive, and made his way to the fifth floor where Oudin had been given chambers. A dozen Maldavian warriors lined the corridor leading to Oudin's room. They eyed him suspiciously and gripped their swords as he passed. They didn't say it, but he could sense them thinking it—kinslayer.

A warrior opened the door, and Eldred stepped in. Oudin sat by the window looking out. As he turned, his eyes—formerly so merry and bright—held the same trepidation as his men. A weak smile immediately faded to a frown.

"Cousin, I am honored to see you," said Oudin stiffly.

"And I, you," said Eldred.

Oudin looked Eldred up and down. "It is as they said—you are healed in all ways: walking, your face, your hand. How did this come to pass?"

Eldred watched with concern as Oudin pushed himself to his feet with difficulty. "I had my powder from the Wretcheds. Eventually, it came to heal me."

Oudin mustered a quick grin as he leaned heavily on a table at his side. "Have you any left? Perhaps I will partake of your miracle, even though it comes from so foul a source."

"I don't," said Eldred. "Are you well?"

"No, not since that night. I do not complain. I have had much the greater fortune than dear Domard, as you know."

"Yes. That was—horrible. How is Mateline? Is she well?"

"In some ways she is quite well, blessed as she is with the strength she shares with you, though she pays a bitter price."

"What do you mean?" asked Eldred.

"She took injury. The savage assassin was unsparing with his dagger. She is not unsteady like me, but—"

"But what?"

"Well, you were once her fiancé. I would say you can share this knowledge. She is—she will not be having her children."

"Oh," said Eldred.

"Physician Genevote did everything possible, but there is no way for such damage to be undone. At least for all of us but you."

Eldred stood, feeling empty. "I'm so sorry."

"I know. Let us sit. I am much more comfortable on my tush. Here, sit on the bed." Oudin lowered himself back to his chair.

Eldred took a seat on the edge of the bed and wet his lips. "Let me explain about Henreit."

Oudin rubbed his temple. "I know."

"You know?" asked Eldred in surprise.

"I know you would not kill him. It is a puzzle though, a very winding, deceitful puzzle. Henreit could be most annoying, endless in his words. But though you may have struck him—I could envision that—you would never have stabbed him a hundred times, such as was his sorry fate."

"Do the others think as you do?" asked Eldred.

"Hmmph, only a few perceive this truth: Roscille, dearest Mateline and—of course—your own sweet mother. The two survivors were most convincing in spreading your guilt. I believe they spoke in earnest."

"Thank you. Your belief in me means a great deal."

"But of course."

"It was the man whose body was nearest my cell. He killed everyone. Afterwards, he came for me. I—had healed by then. I was able to put up a fight and won, though I was still trapped in the cell. When Weltrude came— the First Born healer—she turned everyone against me. I felt I had no choice but to flee."

"Yes, it must be so," said Oudin with a trace of hesitation.

"After that, I sought revenge. Not against her—against my enemies. I didn't think that anyone would believe me."

"Of course, the circumstances were very dark. But still, you should have sought me out. It would have been so much easier to make everything clear back then. Now the stories about you have been told so many times, it will be a most difficult challenge to change anyone's mind," said Oudin with a sigh. "My father—his mind is set like stone. You should persist in your distance for now. He is most distrustful towards you."

"I understand."

Oudin smiled. "Not forever, you know. You are back to doing good deeds. They say you killed their Goddess, that you chopped off her head."

"I did. I had to."

"And you rescued this warrior, this Mack."

Eldred frowned. "Right."

"So, that is very good. Deeds such as this can set everything to the better."

"I hope so."

"Your cousin, King Harold, tells me you have a position, you are in command of a brigade."

"I may be," said Eldred.

"Well, are you in command or are you not?"

"Yes, I'm in command of the brigade, the brigade of unblessed warriors. Harold says that we're to fight alongside the Maldavians and Mercians. What of you? Do you command a detachment?" asked Eldred.

"I am afraid not. My injuries are too hampering. I may travel out with our army, but only to observe. Frankly, I may not even do that. I am only here because of you. Otherwise, I should be taking my rest in Emon."

"I'm glad you came."

"Your mother, dearest Ghyslaine, she is very concerned on your behalf," said Oudin.

"She needn't be," said Eldred. "I'm well."

Oudin nodded. "I will let her know. That is why I am here."

Eldred sighed. "On other matters, do you know about the Corporian diplomat?"

"Yes, he is to meet his end tomorrow at noon, providing our Mercian friends arrive in timely fashion."

"My cousin seems set on this. Do you know why? I mean, not even my father would just kill a diplomat for no reason," said Eldred, spreading his hands.

Oudin took a breath. "Well, I do not know about that. All of this seems quite consistent with what I know regarding Deiran customs. But yes, this event was shared in the missive that came to my father. We—the Maldavians—are content with the proffered plan.”

“What if you objected?” asked Eldred.

“We do not,” said Oudin.

“But what if you did?”

Oudin shrugged. “I would object and then I would watch your cousin cut off his head.”

Eldred glanced down. “Yes. I suppose so.”

“Is this important to you? Are we not going to go on to sack the city? I would say the death toll will be very high.”

“For both sides,” said Eldred softly.

“That remains to be seen,” said Oudin.

THE PRISONER

In the evening, Eldred stood in the dark corridor observing the pod guarding Gundlach's door. They were a different set of guards than from the previous day. Like the earlier group, they didn't take their charge very seriously. Two of the men were napping on a couch that someone had dragged over near the door. Another two of the men were playing dice against the wall. The last man, an older man, and this surprised Eldred, was reading a book of children's tales. Reading of any sort was rare.

Most importantly, none of the men bore a mark of any real distinction. The man with the book had the largest mark, and it was half the size of Mack's. It made sense, an unimportant task for a weak pod. Eldred felt his hand drifting to Capito's hilt. He could do it—it was very clear he could do it. Perhaps, he wouldn't even have to kill them. He could just knock them unconscious. But to what end? It would be much too far to New Wismar if Harold ordered a pursuit.

"It's not my fault," muttered Eldred.

As he spoke, the man with the book looked up and spotted Eldred down the hall. He didn't say anything. He just shut his book and sat, staring at Eldred.

After a moment, Eldred stepped forward and approached the man. "I'm here to visit the prisoner."

The man smiled. "Yes, Lord Eldred. Do you remember me? I'm Robelot. I was there your first year at the Academy."

"My first year? I was only five."

"I know. I always said you were my good luck charm. I didn't ascend until you showed up. I had been two years sitting at the old timers' table," said Robelot.

The men paused their dice game to look over, watching with bored faces.

"I hated that table," said Eldred.

"Everyone did," agreed Robelot. "Are you here to interrogate the prisoner?"

"Well, to talk with him," said Eldred.

"Just call us if he gives any trouble. He has his arms," said Robelot.

"I'm aware," said Eldred.

Eldred entered the room and found Gundlach curled up asleep on the bed despite the early hour, his shield and sword laid out next to him. On the table beside the bed sat a plate with two pork chops, untouched except for one small bite. It was the worst food for him, practically poison. He'd shown good sense in leaving it.

Eldred stood, watching Gundlach snore his rasping snores, a sound he had become familiar with on their recent journey. He slept peacefully. Was there any need to wake him? There was no good news, not of the truce or anything else. Still, there were words to say.

Eldred stepped forward, reaching out to tap Gundlach's shoulder, but Gundlach jolted awake before he was touched and snatched his sword. He was halfway off the bed when he recognized Eldred and settled back down.

"Ack, you were giving me the frights, Eldred. You cannot be creeping in here. You have to be calling from outside the door," said Gundlach, breathing hard.

"I will in future," said Eldred, moving back from the bed.

Gundlach repositioned himself, leaning his back against the headboard. "Good. I am appreciating that. What news have you been finding?"

"Not much. I visited the unblessed troops at the Academy. They're not strong, but it seems that my cousin doesn't truly depend upon them. So their state, such as it is, does not change his decision. There'll be no truce."

"Then I am meeting my end in any case. If I am returning to Wismar— old or new—without a truce, they will be putting me to death. Perhaps it is better here at the hands of a barbarian. I will not be staining the hands of my countrymen." Gundlach smiled sadly. "I was just sleeping, you know. Before I took my nap, the guards were telling their news. The Mercians have arrived. I will be dying tomorrow at noon."

Eldred leaned against the wall. "I'm sorry. I didn't know they'd arrived. I knew they were expected."

"Well, we had been saying back in New Wismar that the Mercians would be the death of us. I am seeing now that such is my fate."

"I'm sorry about those lies," said Eldred.

Gundlach shook his head. "I think we were fooling ourselves. You were just being clever."

"I still regret it," said Eldred.

Gundlach looked Eldred in the eye. "You will be marching with them against New Wismar?"

Eldred walked to the window and looked out without answering.

"Well?" persisted Gundlach.

Eldred glanced down at the guards posted directly below the window—there were always a few pods stationed in that spot. There would be no jump to freedom for Gundlach. After a moment, he turned back to Gundlach. "It seems I might be. I don't want to, but that seems to be my role."

Gundlach set his hand lightly on his sword. "I understand. I would be guarding the walls myself, if I were free."

Eldred chewed his lip. "I know."

They were silent for a moment, then Gundlach looked down at his shield. "Do you know how this execution works? I am still holding my sword, my shield. Will your cousin be coming against me on his own in this room? I could be fighting him. I could be killing him."

Eldred shook his head. "I don't think it'll be like that. They'll bind your arms and take you out into the square where we arrived. He'll make you kneel and then take his swing."

"Huh, I am not thinking so. I will be dying in this room with my blade in motion. They will not be catching me asleep."

"Good," said Eldred.

They paused in silence for a moment.

"I did everything I could, everything that was reasonable," said Eldred.

Gundlach nodded. "I am certain. Will you be standing out there with the others?"

"I will."

Gundlach smiled. "Well, you will not be seeing me. I will be fighting them in here. This is a good place to be doing battle."

Eldred glanced at the closed door, remembering how Pounder and the others had smashed it down when they'd attacked him. "Yes, this is a room that knows fighting."

"What are you saying?" asked Gundlach.

"Uhh, nothing," said Eldred absently. He was staring out the window at a man in a white cloak who was riding out the main gate in the company of his pod. It was just a quick glance at a good distance, but there was no mistaking who it was. Lord Ferris, the lowest and most base person Eldred had ever met, was in Boar's Tusk.

FINAL DAY

Eldred didn't sleep. Since taking the shard, it was no longer a necessity. He could sleep if he wished to, and sometimes he did. That night he sat up with Capito laid on the bed beside him in its scabbard. From time to time, he would draw the blade and watch the power of the Mother course through the steel. It was the most beautiful thing he had ever seen, and it had saved his life. The Goddess and her guardians would have beaten him down and cut the shard out of his head if he hadn't wielded the sword. He needed it. Without it, he knew he'd die sooner. He didn't know how much sooner, but he suspected it could be at any time.

Gundlach was doomed in any case. Eldred could sneak down the stairs and slaughter the unremarkable pod guarding him, but it wouldn't do anything for Gundlach. He had nowhere to go, not without the truce. The man had no future; he didn't even have a day.

The first rays of morning light found Eldred sitting on the bed with the sword back in its sheath. He felt nothing. None of it was his fault. If he felt anything at all, it was a trace of hunger, a pale residue of the feeling he had once experienced so often. He needn't have humored it; he could have put food out of his mind with half a thought. Still, he rose, dressed, and made his way down to the Great Hall.

Wilky and his crew were hard at work. He was rolling out loaves of bread with three of his cooks. Four other assistants were assembling pies, while two burly chefs were preparing a boar for the spit.

"Prince Eldred!" called Wilky, clapping his hands free of flour. "Did you find the plate I left for you in your room last night?"

"I did. Thank you, Wilky," said Eldred.

"I was expecting you to dine with your cousins. Where were you? Did you go into town?"

"No. I was visiting with the Corporian," said Eldred.

"Ah, well, that was nice of you. If you take your seat in the hall, I can bring you eggs and bacon. It'll be an hour for the loaves."

Eldred nodded. "Thanks."

He took his old seat at the head table. It was the first time he'd sat there since his return despite Harold's urging that he make himself at home. It was his home—no need to pretend. Eldred smiled as he looked over the Great Hall, quiet in the morning light except for the friendly chatter coming from the kitchen.

Presently, Wilky appeared bearing a huge plate laden with scrambled eggs, long greasy strips of bacon and two thick slices of buttered toast.

"The bread's from yesterday, but it's still good enough toasted," said Wilky, standing across from Eldred.

Eldred pulled the plate close. "It smells good. Tell me, Wilky, have you seen Lord Ferris? I believe I saw him leaving the castle last evening."

"Oh, yes," said Wilky. "He was there at dinner with the rest of them: both your cousins, your uncle and the Mercians. By the Mother, they could eat. Those four Mercians could eat more than twenty Deirans. Everything I sent out disappeared at once. Their leader, Galasso, was the biggest man I ever saw. You'd look like one of us if you were standing next to him."

"Did Lord Ferris say anything, or did anyone mention why he was here?"

"I was only out for a minute when I brought out the boiled pork, the same pork I put on your plate. Lord Ferris didn't say anything; he hardly ate anything either. When I was there, it was just the king poking fun at your uncle."

"Oh," said Eldred, frowning.

"He was saying that Lord Benedict was too cautious, that he was afraid of his own shadow. The Mercians, especially this Galasso, loved it. Glasso kept repeating it. I've never seen Lord Benedict get really angry, but I'd say he was at least halfway there."

Eldred gripped the table. "Did they say in what regard Benedict was being too cautious? Was there talk of the Corporian defenses? Anything like that?"

"There might have been, but like I said, I was just out for a moment."

"Hmm," said Eldred. "Can you make up another plate like this one? I'm thinking I'll take up Benedict's breakfast and sound him out on this matter."

Wilky leaned on the table. "Well, if he's keeping his usual schedule, he won't be up for some hours. He's not one who seems to enjoy the dawn."

Eldred picked up a piece of toast. "I've a feeling today will be an unusual day. Oh, and can you send a loaf up to the Corporian once they're baked?"

"I can. But don't you want to take it up?"

Eldred frowned. "No. If he's like me, he'll want me to stay away."

Benedict

It was still dark in Ghyslaine's former chambers when Eldred let himself in, carrying a plate heaped high with eggs and potatoes. The first thing Eldred noticed was Benedict's armor piled up on Ghyslaine's sewing table; that was not the place for such things. He sighed and continued through the sitting room until he came to a dead stop in front of his mother's chair, the place she had always sat and spoken with him.

The cushions of the chair were covered in the finest wool, pure white fabric. Or they had been. Now, in the center of the cushion where his mother had once sat so elegantly, was a stain, a greasy looking stain; it had the appearance of old gravy, though with that color and texture, other things came to mind.

Eldred took a breath and set his face, reaching up to rub the spot behind his left temple where his fatum lapides had once been attached. Staining a cushion may have been a minor transgression, at least in the view of some, but it was also one which was easily avoided by the most basic application of courtesy.

Eldred shook his head and continued to the bedroom door, rapping on it until he heard a groan from within.

"It's too damn early," said Benedict. "Come back in an hour."

"It's me," said Eldred.

"Eldred? What do you want?" asked Benedict.

"I need to talk."

"Can it wait?"

"No," said Eldred.

After a pause, Eldred heard some muttering and the sounds of someone stirring in the room. Presently, a disheveled-looking Benedict opened the door wearing Ghyslaine's white woolen robe—it fit him comfortably.

"By the Mother, Eldred. What is so damned important?"

"That's"—Eldred pointed at Benedict—"that's Mother's robe."

Benedict glanced down at the robe, bleary eyed. "This? Yes, well, she did not take it. She took everything she wanted. What is it you need?"

Eldred held out the plate. "I've got your breakfast."

"Well, that's something," muttered Benedict, taking the plate and shuffling over to her chair, where he sat down and started to eat with the plate balanced on his lap.

Eldred watched transfixed as Benedict chased a piece of egg around the plate with his fork.

"Why don't you open the curtains? What is this all about?" asked Benedict.

Eldred went to the window and parted the curtains, casting a dim light over the room. "I heard that you had some disagreements last night."

"Disagreements?" asked Benedict, frowning.

"I heard that you were mocked by the Mercians for being too cautious."

"Oh, that was Galasso. He is not the brightest Mercian, and that is saying something."

"What was your concern?" asked Eldred.

"It was a stupid argument about mixing wine with ale. Nothing that matters. Is that what you wanted to talk about?"

"No," said Eldred.

Benedict leaned down and set the plate on the floor. "What is it then?"

"I'm concerned about the diplomat."

Benedict looked up. "Oh, this again?"

"Yes," said Eldred. "I spoke to Harold, but he wanted too much, far too much, for sparing the man."

"That is interesting. What did he want?"

"He wanted Capito."

Benedict laughed. "Well, that is as you said. That sword is worth more than the lives of a thousand Corporians, let alone the grumpy one we are holding."

"Could you speak to Harold? I offered him Father's ring. That seems to me to be a fair enough trade. What does it matter whether we kill Gundlach or spare him?"

Benedict rubbed his neck. "I could speak to him, but my son keeps his own council. If he is set on this execution, it will take more than my opinion to change his mind."

"Could you try?"

"Well, I can. But I tell you it is pointless. You might just have to consider his offer."

"Give up Capito? Are you serious?"

"Perhaps I am," said Benedict excitedly. "You see, you were never supposed to have Capito."

Eldred narrowed his eyes. "What do you mean?"

"Before the unfortunate battle, Alfred arranged that I would give you my sword. At the time, even though you had passed the trial, everything my brother had was to pass to Harold, his heir."

Eldred shook his head. "I had the sense of that, but what is this business about your sword? My father promised me a named blade."

"Right, Pimis, my sword. Wait here. I will be right back." Benedict hurried into the bedroom and returned a moment later carrying a large sword tucked in its sheath, which he handed to Eldred.

Eldred pulled Primis from its sheath and examined the blade. It was similar in shape and weight to Capito; it was also well-crafted with a fine honed edge, but there was no trace of the Mother's power in the sword. It was lifeless.

Benedict settled back on Ghyslaine's chair, a wide smile across his face. "You know, that was the first one, hence the name, the very first named blade created by the Mother. I received Primis when our father presented Capito to Alfred, matching gifts."

Eldred examined Primis once more, but there was still nothing. "Are you certain it's a named blade?"

"Yes, I'm certain."

"I just mean, it doesn't feel the same."

"What do you mean by that?" asked Benedict, his smile fading. "It is a very valuable blade. As I said, it was the first. Well, in any case, it is for you to decide. If you wish to save this man you keep on about, here is the means. You can pass Capito to Harold and still have a named blade yourself, or you can choose to keep things as they are."

"Why didn't you mention Primis before?" demanded Eldred.

"Before? When I arrived, everyone already knew you had Capito, recovered by your own effort from those Corporian dogs. I did not see that you had any need."

Eldred drew Capito from its sheath and stood, holding Primis in his left hand and Capito in his right—one sword dead and lifeless, the other washed in a purple glow and filled with the power and might of the Mother.

Benedict sat, watching Eldred contemplating the swords for a long pause before clearing his throat. "Well, should I go back to bed?"

Eldred groaned. It was as if Capito was a part of him, his claws, his fangs. Without it, there would be no killing stone guardians. But if he kept it, a man would die in just a few hours, an honorable man, the man who got him Capito in the first place. He chewed his lip and gripped Capito's hilt more tightly. Then he sighed, feeling sick to his stomach. "No, Uncle. Get dressed. We have to see Harold."

DEALINGS

They found Harold in the study, meeting with the Mercian delegation as well as Prince Oudin. They all looked up as Gosbert led Benedict and Eldred into the room.

"Your father and cousin require a word, my liege," said Gosbert.

"On what matter?" asked Harold impatiently.

"Regarding the Corporian diplomat," answered Gosbert.

Harold shot a glare at Eldred. "I told you the price."

Eldred stiffened. "And I'm here. I agree."

"What?" exclaimed Harold, rising from his chair behind the desk. "You're willing to make the exchange?

Galasso, recognizable as the largest of the Mercians, twisted in his chair, looking back and forth between Eldred and Harold. "What's this business?"

"It's a personal matter, just between me and my cousin," said Harold. "We can resume our discussion later, say in an hour."

Galasso made a pained face. "I rode all day yesterday. I rode from dawn to dusk. I barely stopped to eat."

"So eat something now!" snapped Harold. "I need to attend to this matter."

"I rode here all the way from Tyrus. Now you don't even want to meet," said Galasso.

"We'll meet. By the Mother, we'll get this worked out today," said Harold.

"Yes, we must," interjected Oudin. "My father will not be providing any troops until these matters are settled. We cannot be sharing the spoils equally when one partner is hanging back, whatever the reason."

Harold held up his palm. "Nobody should doubt the strength of Deiran arms. We even have new recruits under Eldred, a formidable force of eight hundred."

"Formidable?" queried Oudin in a sarcastic tone.

"Yes, formidable," said Harold. "Now, please, we need some time."

"Very well," said Oudin, rising slowly from his seat.

Galasso hopped up, followed by the other Mercians. "If we're up front, we'll take more."

"That remains to be seen," said Harold, waving them to the door.

As Oudin and the Mercian delegates filed out, it occurred to Eldred that Harold's podmen weren't present, not even outside the study. He was about to be behind a closed door with just Harold, Benedict and Gosbert. Harold was slipping up.

Once they were alone, Harold leaned forward on the desk with both hands, his eyes looked hungry. "So, you're handing over Capito for this wretched Corporian?"

Eldred pulled Capito from its sheath and laid the mighty blade on the desk in front of Harold. "The sword and"—he dug in his pocket—"the ring."

Harold raised an eyebrow at seeing the ring on the desk next to Capito. "Very well, I'll spare him."

"It's not just him," said Eldred.

"What do you mean?" asked Harold.

"It's Gundlach and the truce. It's the both of them for this sword and this ring," said Eldred.

Harold groaned and raised his fingers to his forehead. "You're insufferable."

Benedict put his hand on Eldred's arm. "You did not mention this."

Eldred gazed stoically over the alarmed faces of Harold, Benedict and Gosbert. "It's a fair offer, more than fair. Capito alone is worth far more than I'm asking."

Harold hung his head down, leaning out over his arms as he examined the sword.

Eldred held his face tight as he looked at the brilliant purple fire that flowed across the blade. He doubted anyone could see the full spectacle of the Mother's design, but he suspected that Harold might sense it. "Pick it up, cousin. Hold the sword in your hands. Capito is the greatest blade ever forged, ever blessed."

Harold didn't look up.

"You're the Deiran king," continued Eldred. "If you command everyone to wait six months before smiting the Corporians, then wait they shall. And you'll have the better blade for butchering your enemies. Don't doubt that."

Gosbert shifted his feet. "There are obligations to consider."

Harold sat down abruptly without touching the sword. "You think I don't know that?"

"What obligations?" asked Eldred.

Nobody answered. Benedict joined Harold in taking a seat.

"I am the king," muttered Harold.

Gosbert nodded. "Yes, but—"

"Of course you are," said Eldred.

Harold shot a piercing gaze at Gosbert. "I can do this. I will do this."

Gosbert raised his eyebrows and gave a worried expression.

Harold motioned at Gosbert, moving his hand in a circular motion. "If I do this, how would I do it best? I wish to avoid upsetting certain people."

"If I may suggest, you should distance yourself from the decision as much as you can. Perhaps you have the Corporian at your feet and you spontaneously offer to spare him. You are moved to mercy," said Gosbert.

Harold shrugged. "I could do that, but what about the truce? That's the bigger issue, right? Why am I suddenly going back on that?"

"Ah, good point. Hmm, perhaps, you can make it about the troops. Everyone who has laid their eyes on the unblessed contingent has been of the same opinion: they are unfit," said Gosbert.

"I was telling everyone that yesterday," said Eldred indignantly.

Harold glowered. "Do you want this trade or not, cousin? This business with the troops has never been a good reason to put off the war, but it may serve as an excuse."

Gosbert pointed excitedly at Eldred. "One best delivered by him. Let him explain the truce."

Harold slapped the table. "Yes. I'll say it's his request. And it is. It is his request. This is all Eldred's fault."

"So, you want me to tell everyone that we'll have a truce?" asked Eldred.

"Yes," said Harold. "We'll have your friend up before the crowd on his knees. Then I'll spare him, mentioning your request. And then, you come up and lay it out. It's your idea, after all."

Eldred nodded. "Very well."

Benedict cleared his throat. "I fear the crowd may not take the news well."

Harold slid his hand across the table and picked up the ring, setting it on the ring finger of his left hand. "That's Eldred's problem. In any case, they can be dealt with." He stood up and took Capito, waving the blade twice through the air before smiling at Benedict.

Eldred sighed. "So, we've an agreement?"

"Just make sure your friend is cooperative," demanded Harold, pointing the blade at Eldred. "If he makes some stupid speech or shows me any disrespect, I'll take his head anyway."

"He won't," said Eldred.

Fair Tidings

Gundlach slouched on a chair by the window, wrapped in blankets, wearing a puzzled expression. His shield was propped up against the chair. On the table beside him was his sword, ready for action, and the remains of half a loaf of WIlky's bread.

"You are certain of this?" he asked gruffly. "The guards were just saying this morning that I was living my final hours."

"Yes. I'm certain. I settled the matter. But the key point is that you must not raise a fuss. If you resist them either here or down below in the square, the deal is off. That includes the truce," said Eldred.

"Why are they leading me down there if this is all settled?" asked Gundlach, blinking his red eyes.

"I guess it's for show. And they want to make it clear that it's my idea, not Harold's."

"So, I am just kneeling down, baring my neck to this barbarian?"

"That's right. And no speeches," said Eldred.

Gundlach grabbed the sides of his head. "I am not knowing what to think. What if they are tricking us? That savage could just be killing me."

Eldred stepped forward and gripped Gundlach on the shoulder. "It's paid for at great cost. Look"—Eldred drew Primis partially from its sheath—"I traded my sword and my ring. Just Capito itself is worth more than a hundred times its weight in gold."

Gundlach stared at Primis in confusion. "You traded your sword? Why?"

Eldred stepped back and took a breath. "I can get another with your help. There was another named sword in the Goddess's storage room. When we get back, you can convince them to deliver it to me. I want to search for another dagger as well."

Gundlach swallowed. "Of course. I am certain to be helping with that. I can see the sacrifice you are making. I cannot be finding the words. If we are bringing back the forces from New Wismar in time, it could be making all the difference."

Eldred frowned. "It's no great matter. I traded a ring I cannot use and a sword we'll soon replace. Just go with my plan. If they shove you or hit you, make no defense. When they force you to the ground and my cousin approaches, look away and ignore his words. At that dark moment, we'll be just a minute away from your freedom and my announcement of the truce. We'll leave this afternoon, you and I. You need to take back word of the truce, and I need that sword."

EXECUTION

A team of carpenters had reassembled a portion of the wooden platform that had been present when Eldred had first arrived with his father and the other honored dead. It stood at one end of the square between the tower and the Great Hall and boasted room enough for Harold to cut off Gundlach's head if Gundlach didn't move around too much.

A sparse line of guardsmen stood across the center of the square. The nearer half of the square was reserved for more elevated citizens: nobles, bonded warriors and wealthy peasants. The more distant half of the square was open to everyone, and a large contingent from the town had filled it up, apparently entranced by the novelty of seeing a Corporian put to death.

Eldred stood off to the side of the platform nearest the Great Hall, watching the gathering crowd with narrowed eyes and occasionally glancing up at the window of the room where Gundlach was held. No need to fear the upcoming speech, not like the eulogy for Father. He'd made the case for a truce a dozen times.

It was getting near the noon hour when Oudin appeared at the door to the tower, accompanied by his escort of Maldavian warriors. He walked slowly through the crowd, making his way to Eldred.

"I heard what is happening. Somehow, you have prevailed," said Oudin with a faint smile.

"Harold told you?" asked Eldred.

"No, the head steward. He informed both myself and the Mercian delegates. We are not to show our concern, he warns, or the terms of the war will be much worse for us," said Oudin.

"I'm sorry if it costs you anything," said Eldred.

"It is no worry, cousin. However we go, my father will make certain we are well paid. If we Maldavians do the work, we will claim the rewards."

"That's good," said Eldred, gesturing at the crowd. "If only they would be so understanding."

Oudin chuckled. "You must prepare yourself, cousin. You are ruining their fun. They came to see a man lose his head—instead they will only be hearing you lose your voice."

Eldred shook his head. "I'll be keeping it short. I already have the wagon supplied and the horses ready outside the gate. Harold says he'll give us an escort through the crowd."

Oudin settled back, leaning against the wall of the Great Hall. "Perhaps that will provide the missing entertainment. Try not to hurt them too badly, cousin."

"I won't," said Eldred, rubbing his neck. "Uhh, I didn't find time to write to Mother. I didn't know until this morning that I was leaving."

"Ah, it is no matter. I will let her know you are well and still making your mischief. And you will soon be back. Is that not so?"

"I will. I'll oversee some of their evacuation. But once they are streaming out of their foul city, there'll be no reason for me to stick around. Would it make sense for me to return to Emon then?" asked Eldred.

"Perhaps you should be waiting a trifle longer before your return to my father's court. He, uh, will be most saddened at the gold and silver making its way back to Corporia. It may make more sense in six months, at the end of your heralded truce, once we have found someplace worthy to plunder."

Eldred gave a small nod. "Very well."

"Oh, here is your man," said Oudin, pointing back to the tower.

Gundlach emerged into the view of those gathered in the square, stripped down to a loincloth with his hands bound behind his back. The crowd greeted him with a chorus of insults. Eldred silently thanked the Mother for the guards that surrounded him. Nobody was likely to be too difficult while Harold had a silver pod at hand.

They took him over to the platform. Robelot, who had been reading the book the previous day, and another guard took turns shoving Gundlach in the back, putting him off his balance. Eldred felt his shoulders tense—still, it was all the crowd would get, just a man getting pushed around.

Once they had him up before the audience, Robelot knocked Gundlach's to his knees. It looked painful on the hard wood. Gundlach looked exhausted and bewildered. He kept turning his head, peering into the crowd; he didn't see Eldred off to the side.

Eldred pressed his hands together. It wouldn't be much longer. And indeed, at that moment, Harold emerged from the Great Hall with his retinue: Benedict, Gosbert, Dederick, the Mercians and Mack, who looked drunk. The fat black onyx ring sat on Harold's finger. The sword—the great sword, the greatest sword—Capito rested on his hip. For a moment, Eldred felt as if Capito was calling to him. With a grimace, he considered reversing the deal. It was his sword, his birthright. But he said nothing; he just looked away.

A chant started in the crowd. "Justice, justice!" they cried.

Eldred raised his eyebrows at Oudin. "Justice?"

Oudin shrugged. "Of a sort."

Harold waved to the crowd and ascended the stairs to the platform, leaving his entourage standing next to Eldred and Oudin. Mack grinned gleefully at Eldred, showing all of his rotten teeth.

Eldred nodded back curtly, taken aback by Mack's enthusiasm. Either Mack didn't know what was about to happen, or Gundlach was right and Eldred had been deceived.

Up on the platform, Harold drew Capito and held it up over his head as the crowd continued their shout.

Eldred clasped his hands. At that moment, it seemed to him that Harold truly did want to kill Gundlach. Why else would he stir everyone up?

"I am the king!" shouted Harold.

Looking up at him, seeing him holding the glowing purple sword over his head, it seemed to Eldred for the first time that Harold was a king.

"A king metes out justice!" yelled Harold. "It is my sacred obligation under the Mother to kill our foes, to slay our enemies. Such is my right and privilege."

The crowd roared its approval. Gunlach huddled before Harold, looking forlorn.

Harold pointed down at Gundlach. "This man is our enemy. We will kill him, but—not today!"

Eldred sighed with relief, but the crowd seemed not to have heard Harold, though Mack did, to judge by his startled expression.

Harold quieted the crowd. "I said I'll not kill him today. This scum, this gutless worm, will die another day. And that day comes soon."

"What do you mean?" shouted someone in the mob.

Harold spun around in the man's direction. "My cousin, Eldred, begged a favor—mercy for this scoundrel, that I spare his life. And more, my cousin asks for more. Come up, Eldred. Come up and let them know what you've asked of me."

There was a discontented murmur from the crowd as Eldred ascended the stairs and turned to face them. "We'll have a truce!" called Eldred in a commanding voice. "We'll have a truce for six months, giving time for the invaders to flee our lands and return to their home."

"Why?" yelled someone.

"Coward!" called another.

Eldred continued. "Once they have returned to their homes, giving up that city they hold on the Mother's own good land, we can strike them; we can battle them. This is to our advantage. How do I know? I'm the only one who's had the courage to go and see their forces, see their defenses. I've fought them in their city. I've killed their champions. I've killed their Goddess! If there is anyone braver than me, let me hear your voice. If there is anyone braver than me, let me hear your deeds. All I know is that I was in New Wismar freeing our people and I didn't see any of you!"

The crowd quieted under Eldred's rebuke, but then came a voice.

"I was there!" called someone.

Eldred scanned the crowd. "Who said that?"

And then, through a small gap at the most distant edge of the gathering, he saw the thin, smirking wretch of a man, Lord Ferris, wearing his gaudy white cloak with his pod lined up behind him. It was Eldred's first good view of the man, and he took the measure of the mark on his forehead. It was smaller and paler than Mack's. The man was weak.

"I was there in the north with you," announced Lord Ferris.

"Yes, but what of it? That has nothing to do with this. By my request, the Corporian diplomat is spared, and we have a truce. Both favors granted and guaranteed by the wise edict of King Harold," said Eldred.

"Is this true, my liege?" asked Lord Ferris.

Harold hung back, standing behind Eldred. "It is so. I have granted my cousin this boon."

"Would you grant this favor if you knew Eldred to be a traitor?" asked Lord Ferris.

"I would not," answered Harold.

"What is your proof?" demanded Benedict, coming halfway up the stairs.

Eldred scanned the faces of the men near Lord Ferris, looking for Aistan or one of the other survivors from the battle in the caves. None were there.

"I saw it with my own two eyes!" shouted Lord Ferris, coming forward through the crowd with his pod in tow. "We were in that accursed city of the Wretcheds, the one they call Turicum. It was there that Eldred committed treason to the Mother and all that is good in the world."

"By what deed?" challenged Benedict, straining his thin voice.

Lord Ferris raised his hands high as he neared the platform. "Eldred left the expedition to take up residence with those degenerates, forsaking his comrades and his vows, lowering himself to the most base level. Lord Vance, that true hero, sent Lord Osbert and myself into that den of evil to retrieve this wayward youth. When we came to where he lived, we found him in a tent set out on the street with open sides so that anyone could see what was taking place inside."

Lord Ferris tilted his head and paused.

"What was he doing?" shouted someone.

"What did you see?" called another.

"I saw Eldred copulating with the Wretcheds. He serviced not just one of those vile women, but three bony hags. Lord Osbert and I were aghast. I could never speak of this while good King Alfred lived. But now that he is gone and bears none of the disgrace of his disgusting son, I can share the truth. And I am not the only witness. Lord Osbert saw it too."

"Liar!" shouted Eldred.

"Are you saying you didn't desire them, Eldred? Speak the truth!" demanded Lord Ferris.

"You never saw that. I didn't live in a tent. I had a house!" answered Eldred.

Lord Ferris made a rude gesture, thrusting up his arm. "He is a Mercian. He is of Mercian blood. They'll rut with any woman that they can find!" He turned, pointing at the Mercian delegates. "Isn't that the truth?"

Galasso laughed and repeated Lord Ferris's gesture. "It's always been true for me!"

The crowd cheered him.

Eldred waved them to silence. "It doesn't matter, Ferris. You can wear your stupid clothes and speak your stupid words—it doesn't change anything. You're just describing your own twisted desires, not my actions."

Lord Ferris gripped his white cloak and held it out in a fan behind him. "You do not care for my cloak?"

Eldred crossed his arms. "No. Not for your cloak, not for you."

"It is properly your cloak," said Lord Ferris.

Eldred made a face. "What do you mean?"

"How can you not recognize it? I cut the leather from your precious horse. What was his name, Hobbie? I paid so much to the tanners and clothiers of Bert, but gold well spent. A fine cloak, I wear it every day."

Eldred stared at Lord Ferris in horror.

Lord Ferris smiled. "Well, what do you say, Eldred? Does that change your opinion?"

"You—you…" Eldred rubbed his temples. "You hurt everyone. You destroy everything. I'll kill you!"

"We are not in your native Mercia!" barked Lord Ferris. "We fight in pods, not just as one brute against another. Where is your pod, Eldred?"

Eldred shuddered with rage and looked down the stairs at Dederick, but Dederick just turned away. Then he touched the hilt of the Primis, the dead sword at his side. After a moment of hesitation, he made a fist. "I need no pod, not against one as weak as you. I'll fight you and your craven friends right now on this very spot. Your final day has come!"

"You heard him! You heard him!" shouted Lord Ferris. "Clear the square! Clear the square, and you will get to witness the shortest pod duel ever fought."

Under the direction of Lord Ferris and his men, a small clearing started forming in the center of the square and continued to grow as everyone pressed back against the walls.

Benedict rushed forward and grabbed Eldred's arm. "What are you doing? Have you lost your senses?"

"No," snarled Eldred. "I'm ridding the land of the most disgusting and craven creature that ever lived."

Benedict lowered his voice. "You are getting yourself killed. You cannot defeat a pod."

"He's weak. They're weak," said Eldred.

"I can be helping," said Gundlach softly, still on his knees.

"What?" asked Eldred. "No, this is nothing to do with you."

Gundlach turned slowly to face Eldred better. "Please, be undoing my bonds."

Eldred jerked his hand at Robelot, who was standing nearby. "Get him up. Get those ropes off of him."

As Robelot freed Gundlach, Harold pressed up to Eldred with Gosbert beside him. "In the name of the Mother, what's this nonsense?"

"This man dishonors me. This man is a disgrace. I'll kill him," said Eldred.

"He'll kill you, cousin," said Harold.

Gundlach got to his feet, rubbing his wrists, looking every bit a disheveled mess. "I am needing my armor and arms, my shield and sword. They are all sitting up in that room."

"No," said Eldred, waving him off. "I've given up too much for you. I'll not have you getting yourself killed."

Harold rolled his eyes. "He's lost his mind."

Gundlach pointed down at Lord Ferris, standing in the widening clearing. "You think they will be letting me go? You think they will be waving to me as I ride from the town? If you are fighting, I am fighting. I took it all, as you were saying. I will not be taking any more."

"Fine, fine." Eldred sighed. "Robelot, go get his equipment. Go on, be quick. And take one of your podmen."

As Robelot and his companion ran off, Oudin slowly climbed the steps. "Eldred, this is most rash. What of your mother? Please, you must not make me bring this news to her. She will hate me for all of her days."

Eldred glanced over. "I'll win."

Oudin shook his head. "Be reasonable, cousin. The man was never born who could defeat a pod of bonded warriors."

"I know," said Eldred.

Suddenly, Harold was back at Eldred's side, pointing down at his waist. "Is that Primis?"

Eldred nodded. "Yes."

Harold turned to Benedict. "How does he have Primis? Did you give it to him?"

"I did, though I had hoped he would keep it longer," said Benedict.

Harold glowered. "Why did you do that? It was to go to me."

"You have the king's sword, son. You have no need for Primis," said Benedict.

"That's for me to decide," declared Harold.

Eldred hopped down onto the dirt below the platform.

"Wait! I am still needing my arms," protested Gundlach.

"I'll wait," said Eldred, studying Lord Ferris and his men as they prepared for the battle, stripping off their cloaks and donning light armor. They were all the same, or about the same, their marks of the same meager size and faded color. If he hadn't known it to be the case, he wouldn't have been able to pick out Lord Ferris as their leader. A few threads flitted around between them, appearing just as often between the men as between Ferris and the others. Still, they followed him. They would be disoriented when he fell.

"Justice," said a man behind him.

Eldred turned to see Mack, his gleeful smile shining once more. "What makes it justice, Mack?"

"Justice," repeated Mack.

Eldred sighed and noticed Dederick, who was standing beside Mack. "Is that what you think too?"

"I told you before we left: don't look for trouble," said Dederick.

"I suppose you did," agreed Eldred.

Lord Ferris's men had just finished donning their armor when a loud thud announced that Gundlach had joined Eldred in the square. His eyes were still red, but his face looked more composed. He was more dignified, having switched his loincloth for leather armor. His shield—his heavy, overly large shield—gleamed in the sun, and he carried his sword in his hand. He looked somewhat formidable.

"Stay back," warned Eldred. "I didn't trade Capito so you could spill your guts in the dirt."

Gundlach raised his shield without comment.

"Are you finally ready, Eldred?" called Lord Ferris.

"Hold up!" shouted Harold from up on the platform.

Lord Ferris frowned. "What is it?"

"Primis. Eldred is holding Primis. If he falls, Primis will not go to the victors. I reserve it. The sword belongs in my family; Eldred should never have had it," announced Harold.

Lord Ferris scoffed. "Am I to get nothing for killing this traitor?"

"It seems you'll get what you want most," said Harold.

Lord Ferris considered. "You are right. I agree. I'll cede the sword, but then I want his body."

Eldred growled.

Benedict's eyes went wide. "What?"

Harold nodded. "Very well. I claim the sword, but you may have his corpse."

"You cannot mean this, son," protested Benedict.

"Silence, Father. Eldred has brought this about. He can't let go of a meaningless slight."

"When I win, I'll take their bodies," proclaimed Eldred.

"What?" asked Harold.

Eldred drew Primis. "If he'll take mine, then I'll take theirs."

"Ugh, very well," said Harold as Lord Ferris and his pod chuckled incredulously. "Let the duel begin."

The pod drew swords and formed a line of four in front of Lord Ferris, who crouched behind them. Now that the threads were coming regularly, Eldred could see that they did mostly flow from Ferris to his men.

"Keep back!" shouted Eldred, taking a quick look over his shoulder.

Gundlach stood with shield raised and sword in hand ten feet behind, just in front of the platform.

Eldred turned his attention back to the pod, lined up in tight formation with swords out, like a vicious porcupine. They were waiting for him forty feet away, which surprised him, given Ferris's boast of a quick fight. Eldred was faster, he was stronger, he had a longer reach, but they would think more quickly, or they would have if they weren't so weak. He just had to get one loose or get close enough to break their Bond as he had in the scrimmage with Dederick's men.

Eldred stepped slowly towards them. If he angled for the one to the right, they slid over to aim him again at their center. If he angled for the one on the left, they did the same. If they had their way, he would have to step into the heart of their trap. Eldred stopped. He couldn't risk that.

After a moment, he called out, "Hold your position, Gundlach!" He took a quick look to confirm the same. Then Eldred began to circle around the pod to the left. They kept adjusting, keeping their line facing him.

Eldred frowned. They couldn't fear him that much. Lord Ferris must just have wanted the spectacle of him charging in and dying on their swords. Eldred tightened his grip and kept to his plan.

Finally, after backing up and circling around, he stood forty feet away from them, facing their line, with Gundlach positioned even with their line, forty feet straight over from their closest man. Eldred lowered his sword and laughed. "Is this your idea of a quick pod duel, Ferris? You're not laying siege—I have no walls."

Some in the audience smiled at that. Lord Ferris did not.

"I can see you fearing me, a Mercian, by your account!" called Eldred, raising his voice. "But how pathetic you are to cower before a Corporian!"

And then, the man went. The man closest to Gundlach took off sprinting for him. It made perfect sense. He would duck around Gundlach's heavy shield and cut his neck. It would only take an instant.

Eldred paused, standing flat on his feet, letting the man take his strides, while he faced the waiting line of Ferris's defenders. The moment the man was well clear of the line, Eldred exploded in his direction. Running as fast as a diving hawk, he closed on the man with dizzying speed. The threads alerted the man; he knew without turning that Eldred was upon him, and he veered away; the line abandoned its still pose and took after Eldred as fast as they could, but the pod was split; one podman was on his own and that was all Eldred needed.

The man was turning as Eldred approached, raising his sword to deflect Eldred's attack, but Eldred's swing could not be stopped. He hewed the man through the neck, not the delicate thrust that the man would have delivered to Gundlach, but no less effective. The man fell dead in a spray of blood.

The other four were charging for all they were worth. Eldred could have easily outrun them, but he wanted them in motion. They were less crafty when running, as one step must follow another, even for them. Eldred slammed his right foot to the ground and stopped immediately, shooting out a cloud of dirt. He charged their staggered line as they charged him.

Primis, though a dead sword, was a sharp sword. Eldred slashed the leading man down through the chest, cutting through his armor and killing the man in satisfying fashion. But as Eldred pulled back on Primis, ready to duck away from the three remaining podmen, the blade caught in a way that Capito never would. Instead of breaking clean away, Eldred found himself knocked by the corpse of his enemy, which was still stuck on his sword.

It was just an instant, but the others were there. The first warrior used the corpse of his brother as a shield and artfully thrust his sword deep into Eldred's chest. Even as Eldred choked on his own blood, he got his left hand up and thumped the man on the side of his head. The warrior fell away, pulling his blade free. Stunned, Eldred released his grip on Primis, letting the corpse of his foe drop.

Before the corpse hit the ground, Lord Ferris and the other man attacked. Both men easily evaded Eldred's flailing left arm. Lord Ferris's podman buried his steel in Eldred's left ribs. Lord Ferris's thrust pierced Eldred's chest, and he felt his heart burst.

As Eldred toppled slowly forward, his vision fading to black, he reached out for Lord Ferris, but he only lightly brushed Ferris's forehead before he smashed into the ground. He lay there, his heart convulsing violently in his chest, feeling the warmth drain from his body.

Eldred was dazed for a moment; he couldn't see, but then he heard something—a ring, a clang. He tried to drag himself up and failed. The sound kept coming, clang, clang, clang like it was right next to him. He lay still for a moment, exhausted, and then it seemed that his burst heart beat more steadily. His mouth and throat were still packed with blood, but it felt like he tasted a tiny breath of air. He made a weak sound. "Aaahhh."

Clang, clang, clang, the sound continued. Eldred's heart began to slow. It felt cloven in two, like two rough edges beating up against each other, but as his heart beat slower, it seemed the edge began to fade away. He made a louder sound. "Eewwahh!" He took a deeper breath. The taste of blood was thick in his mouth, but he could feel his lips and move his jaw.

He relaxed for a moment, shutting out the furious clanging sound that filled the air, and then he blinked. He could see, very dimly, but he could see. The attacker, the one who had first stabbed him, was lying on the ground right in front of him with his eyes shut.

Though the man looked unconscious, little threads were floating away up out of his forehead. Eldred groaned. The bastard still had the Bond even after he'd been knocked out. Then Eldred understood. The clanging was Gundlach's stupid shield. Eldred couldn't turn his head to see the fighting, but he could see the wretch right in front of him helping what was left of his pod. That's when Eldred noticed his own arm, his left arm. It was stretched out near the man in front of him. He couldn't feel his fingers, but he could see them. It was all he had; his right arm was trapped senseless under his body.

The clanging continued, and there was grunting too now that Eldred gained awareness, but he ignored both. He put all his effort, all of his will, into dragging himself forward, closer to the podman in front of him. He couldn't feel his arm, but he watched his fingers curl and catch the ground. Then his arm tightened, pushing the elbow outwards, and he moved forward just an inch. So much effort to move an inch, and he had at least a foot to go.

As he slid his hand out for another dragging attempt, he heard Gundlach cry out. Terror filled him then. If they struck down Gundlach, they would be back in an instant for him. They'd try to kill him, they'd try and try. How long would it take? How much suffering would he face before the shard gave up on keeping him alive?

Desperately, he pulled himself forward another few inches, watching the gossamer threads freely floating away from the unconscious podman. Moments before, he had flown across the ground, and now he could only crawl an inch at a time.

Another loud shriek from Gundlach; what had they cut? What had they sliced? Was Gundlach even on his feet? Eldred could see nothing of the fighting behind him. His weak breath caught in his throat as he listened. Then it came, the clanging resumed. Gundlach fought still.

Eldred crawled on. He began to feel the dirt sliding over his right hand, trapped down by his waist. His left arm, his pulling arm, began to move just a bit more forcefully. The clanging, the grunting, continued, though Eldred feared it could end at any moment.

Finally, he stretched out his hand and rested it on the podman's forehead. As had happened with Dederick's men, the threads stopped. He felt his lips twist into an odd smile. Perhaps Gundlach would strike down Lord Ferris before he fell. Please, Mother, let him at least kill that vile man.

Eldred was smiling at the thought when the podman opened his eyes and peered at Eldred from a foot away. Immediately, the man began to scramble back, mobile in a way that Eldred was not. By reflex as much as anything else, Eldred gripped the man's skull and was tugged forward a few inches in the man's bid to escape. Eldred held on and the man stopped, choosing instead to start twisting his neck and bringing his hands up to pry Eldred's fingers loose.

Eldred groaned. It wouldn't do. He couldn't let the man escape. He pressed his fingers in, squeezing them through the thin layer of flesh against the hard skull underneath. He tightened his grip, and there was a sharp crack. The man's eyes went wide, and he stopped struggling. There was no blood— the skin on his forehead remained unbroken—but the man was dead.

Eldred studied the man's face and took his first regular breath. He was starting to feel a bit warmer. Behind him, somewhere, it seemed further away than before, the clanging continued. Eldred began to shift, pressing his toes into the ground and straining to pull his right arm out from under his body.

Suddenly, the crowd let out a yell, and Eldred froze, trying to puzzle out what it meant. He could almost feel his ears twisting around on his head, straining to hear what was happening in the distant duel. There was no sound for a moment, then the clanging resumed, but the sound had changed. The rhythm was slower, as if only one sword beat the shield now instead of two. Lord Ferris? Eldred gave a bloody grin. Somehow, Gundlach had disabled one of his foes.

Eldred so wanted to see. He pulled again on his right arm and tried to shift his legs. Everything hurt, and nothing was working as it should. He was just easing his right hand free when the crowd yelled again. It seemed to be the same sound—did that mean Gundlach was victorious? Eldred listened and lay still. The clanging was done.

He heard footsteps. The victor—perhaps Gundlach, perhaps Lord Ferris—was striding in his direction. Ferris would happily stab him in the back, but if he rolled Eldred over, Eldred might grab something—a leg, and arm. He could shatter it as he had cracked the man's skull. It would be his only chance. He might not kill Ferris, but he could at least deliver a wound that would never heal.

Eldred flexed the fingers on his left hand, his working hand, and waited. The footsteps stopped, the man was kneeling down—his head might be in reach. Eldred tensed, ready to act, and then he saw Gundlach's blood-drenched face.

Gundlach smiled and set down his shield and sword. "I am seeing that you are still breathing, Eldred. This is making me very happy."

Eldred gave a ghost of a smile. "Yes," he whispered.

Gundlach pointed at the dead podmen across from him. "You were killing this one too."

Eldred licked his dry lips. "I did. Get water."

Gundlach nodded. He had a cut above his eye, which seemed to have spilled the blood on his face. "Yes. I will be getting water. Should I be moving you?"

"Not yet," whispered Eldred.

Then Gundlach was gone. Eldred focused on breathing; that seemed to be the best thing, that and moving his fingers and toes.

A moment later, a small cluster of men descended on Eldred. Kneeling across from him was Benedict and Oudin, examining him with appalled expressions. Crouched behind them, also looking concerned, was the Mercian delegation.

"Can you hear me?" asked Benedict.

"Yes," whispered Eldred.

"Are you—will you be surviving?" asked Oudin incredulously.

"Yes. Still more mischief," said Eldred slowly.

Gundlach returned with a waterskin. "Should I be turning you over?"

"No. A minute."

Gundlach sat down next to Benedict and wet a cloth, which he used to clean his face.

"You did it," whispered Eldred.

Gundlach grinned. "Let us never be doing that again."

Two of the Mercians stood up and started to drag away the bodies of the dead men.

"Hold up," said Benedict, rising and dusting off his knees. "That is Eldred's sword stuck in that one."

"Very well," said the Mercian holding the corpse. He laid the body of the man down and grabbed Primis by the hilt. It didn't come easily. He had to set his foot on the man's chest to work the blade free, accompanied by the screeching sound of metal against metal.

Benedict took the blade and wiped it clean before laying it next to Eldred's with a flourish. "Your blade is not lost, nephew."

Eldred eyed the sword doubtfully. Capito would never have betrayed him like that. "Roll me now. I need water."

Gundlach took the help of Galasso and got Eldred sitting up in as gentle a fashion as they could manage, leaning back against the two men. The world was bigger with his face out of the dirt. He could see the two corpses. Lord Ferris had gone down first, the closer of the two. The Mercians hadn't gotten to them, just leaving them there like a pile of rags. The crowd remained, standing silently in place. They looked shocked; some were angry.

Eldred smiled. No matter what they wished, he wouldn't die.

From somewhere, Gundlach procured a tin cup. The first sip of water felt good in Eldred's mouth. He spat it out, red with blood. Then another sip, also blood red. After many rinses, the water was light pink and Eldred cautiously took a drink.

"What of bandages, Eldred? We must remove your tunic and see you are carefully wrapped," said Oudin.

Eldred moved his left hand up, laying it over the spot where Ferris had stabbed him. "No, it's just a minor wound."

"Minor?" asked Oudin. "It was looking very deep. I thought Lord Ferris stabbed you through the heart."

"No. He never did," said Eldred, shakily taking a drink of water with his right hand.

Presently, Harold came out to stand before Eldred, with Dederick and Mack behind him. Mack glowered at Eldred with obvious hatred. Dederick contemplated Eldred with a solemn expression.

"So, what do you want done with their bodies?" asked Harold.

"Just send them home and bury them," said Eldred.

"I thought you wanted them," said Harold.

"If I did then, I don't now," said Eldred.

Harold shrugged. "I imagine you'll be staying here for your recovery."

Eldred turned his head to Gundlach. "Are you able to travel?"

Gundlach nodded. "I am sitting ready. But what of you?"

"Yes. Just another few minutes and I'll be up. We should be going," said Eldred.

"No, you have to stay," protested Benedict. "You are in no shape for anything."

Eldred smiled. "Thank you for your concern, Uncle. I'm well and getting ever better."

Harold and Mack wandered off, but Dederick stayed where he was. Benedict squatted down next to Eldred and started to clean him with a wet cloth.

After a few minutes, Wilky arrived, carrying a large flagon and a loaf of bread. His face told Eldred that despite Benedict's work, he was still a mess. "Would you be wanting any milk, Eldred? I also brought bread. Is there anything I can get, anything at all?"

"A touch of milk. Save the bread," said Eldred in his rasping voice. He set down his cup of water and took the flagon. The milk tasted rich and cold. He could feel his body craving more, and he drained the flagon. "More milk," he said softly.

A few minutes later, after another flagon of milk delivered by Wilky, Eldred reached up his hand. "It's time."

The crowd stirred. They had been waiting to see if Eldred would walk away or die on the spot.

Gundlach took Eldred's hand and gently pulled him to his feet. Eldred was unsteady, but with one arm around Gundlach's neck and the other reaching up over Galasso's shoulder, he could walk.

He went first to Ferris' body, which lay on its side. Ferris's eyes were open but unseeing. His mouth hung open above his spit soaked goatee. Gundlach had pierced his throat. A thin trickle of blood was still oozing out, painting the ground red. The villain had finally answered for his crimes.

"That's justice," rasped Eldred.

"I was just killing the two you left me," said Gundlach.

Galasso laughed boisterously. "This is a great victory. A Mercian has defeated a pod of warriors. I have a mind to cut some down myself." He looked over the dour faces of the crowd, pulling slightly away from Eldred. "Don't forget this victory, boys. This is what happens when you get a Mercian angry. Don't piss in my beer."

As Eldred shifted his feet and turned to the gate, Galasso started to chant, and the other Mercians behind him joined in. "Cut the dog and leave him dead. Chop his arms and stomp his head. I am strong, it's he that bled. The Mother's brood is winning. We are always, always winning."

Wilky, Oudin and Benedict filled out the rest of Eldred's escort. Wilky brought a container of milk. Benedict mindfully carried Primis. Oudin paced slowly behind, carrying the white cloak.

ON THE ROAD

Filled with water and milk, Eldred pressed his hands over his wounds and dozed in the sunlight as Gundlach drove the wagon down the road. When he woke in the late afternoon, they were climbing the ridge to the west of the city without anyone in sight.

"How are you feeling?" asked Gundlach.

"Better," said Eldred. He shifted his hands and inspected his injuries. They were difficult to assess, since he hadn't let Benedict wash them, but they appeared to have scabbed over.

"Do you think they are knowing what you are now?" asked Gundlach.

Eldred crinkled up his face. "How could they? It's not something that would come to mind."

"They were all seeing what happened," insisted Gundlach.

"They'll just think it's some curse, some Wretched magic," said Eldred. He reached over and picked up a loaf of Wilky's bread. The thick seeded crust contained soft, delicious bread. Eldred devoured the entire thing, his appetite just getting started.

After eating another loaf, Eldred took up a damp cloth that someone had left in the wagon and wiped away the dried blood from his chest and ribs.

"You know, I can never thank you enough," said Eldred as the sun dropped lower in the sky in front of them. "Ferris was the last one, my last enemy—at least, the last one I would bother to find."

Gundlach nodded. "I am congratulating you then. What is it you will be doing now?"

"I'm free. I could do anything. I guess I'll start by getting that sword from the Goddess. Once you're all on your way back to Corporia, it seems I can be with my people. Even the Maldavians are forgiving me, or they might. I could go to Emon. I could even return to the Academy and lead the forces there, my unblessed compatriots."

"To be making war on us?"

"No, I wouldn't," said Eldred. "I owe you that at least. You saved me from the worst death, full of pain and delivered by the person I hated most."

"Good. We are having enough troubles without fighting you."

Eldred made a circling motion with his hand. "You'll have to be prepared for them to come, though. I'm certain some will visit your lands. Even the most peaceable of them wants some measure of revenge or hopes for some treasure."

"I showed them what they can be expecting."

Eldred laughed. "Yes, you did. But be ready."

They camped near a stream and heated up a pot of stew that Wilky had packed. Gundlach picked out the vegetables for his portion while Eldred favored chunks of meat. Afterwards, Eldred pulled off his bloody garments and waded into the water for a thorough wash. The cuts in his chest looked fresh, but they had stopped leaking blood.

After drying himself, he donned fresh clothes: a soft gray woolen tunic and brown leggings that Wilky said he had gotten from the Maldavians. Taking a shovel and the white cloak, Eldred ventured away from the road up through a thicket, following animal trails to eventually arrive at a small glade enclosed by a ring of willow trees. He set the cloak down on a stone and began to dig in the rocky soil. It was a lengthy process. He paused his efforts whenever his heart throbbed too hard; it still felt fragile, like it could come apart at any moment.

Once the hole was deep enough, he set down the shovel and picked up the cloak, hugging it tight to his chest. As he stood there, watching a family of wood grouse pick their way through the bushes, he thought about Hobbie, Dreven, Henreit and the others he had seen fall. Tears welled in his eyes, and he became unsteady on his feet for a moment. He carefully took a seat and then lay on his back, still clutching the folded cloak. They had been so good; they had been so dear. They all had, all of them.

VISITORS

T he next afternoon, as the road turned around a hillock, Eldred saw a cloud of dust in the distance. "Someone's coming."

Gundlach squinted in the direction Eldred indicated. "Has the truce been ending so quickly?"

"No, it shouldn't. It could be that Lord Ferris brought another pod with him to Boar's Tusk. But then, they surely would have been standing next to him in the crowd."

"Was Lord Ferris having many friends?" asked Gundlach.

Eldred frowned. "I can't see how that could be the case." He rose and stepped carefully into the bed of the Corporian wagon, which was empty now except for the supplies packed by Wilky. He found Primis nestled between two sacks of apples.

The sword looked handsome enough when Eldred pulled it free of its sheath; Benedict had cleaned the blade well. Nonetheless, Eldred gave Primis a doubtful look. Whoever had stowed it had chosen the right place: the blade was best suited for slicing fruit.

Eldred was resheathing the sword when he paused and examined the hilt. There was a hint of purple around the grip he hadn't noticed before. It was so slight, he could have missed it earlier though he felt it must be new. However, the blade remained unchanged: dead and lifeless. "Interesting," he muttered.

He returned to the front of the wagon and tested his wounds with his fingers as he watched the cloud grow nearer.

"Are you able to be fighting?" asked Gundlach after a pause. He still looked beaten up himself, particularly the cut above his eye which was certain to leave a scar.

"If necessary," said Eldred. "I'm much better today. If they're friends of Ferris, they'd best be stronger than he was. I can do things out here that I couldn't do yesterday."

"What things?"

"I can throw the wheels of the wagon if it comes to that. They'd have a hard time dodging those even if they were the best bonded warriors, which—since they're Ferris's friends—they won't be."

"Let us be keeping the wheels if we can," said Gundlach.

A few minutes later, Eldred looked again and smiled. "Ah, it's Dederick, Dederick with both his pods."

"Their greatest warrior? How are you seeing this as a good thing?" asked Gundlach.

"Well, he didn't stand with me when I needed him, but I don't believe he'd be the one they'd send to kill me."

Gundlach raised his eyebrows. "Why not? From what you have been saying of his prowess, he would be the very one I would be picking."

Eldred shrugged. "Even after yesterday, they don't fear us that much. We wouldn't rate being killed by him."

"Very comforting," said Gudlach.

Dederick's troops caught up an hour later. At Eldred's insistence, Gundlach didn't stop the wagon. So the meeting began with Dederick riding up alongside Eldred.

"You look well, Eldred. Better than your friend," commented Dederick as he surveyed them.

"Thank you, Dederick. What's the occasion?" asked Eldred.

"I'm back off to my watch. We've got another six months of waiting, thanks to your truce," said Dederick.

"I'm sorry in that regard," said Eldred.

Dederick shrugged. "It's the price of war."

"Well, we'll be along after you," said Eldred.

Dederick nodded. After a pause, he pointed to Gundlach. "I can see why he's going back. He has to. But why are you going to their Motherless city, Eldred?"

Eldred raised his eyebrows. "Well, you must have noticed that Harold has Capito, whereas I bear Primis."

"I noticed," said Dederick.

"Well, I thank Benedict for Primis—a good sword by many a measure. But I saw a better sword in the storeroom where I claimed Capito, a storeroom deep under New Wismar. I'm hoping the Goddess will let me take it," said Eldred.

"You're such friends, are you?" asked Dederick.

"No. I wouldn't say that. But I helped get the truce. She might pay me some reward in return," said Eldred.

"So, you were working for them," said Dederick.

Eldred frowned. "No. I told everyone why I wanted the truce. My reasoning stands. It's the only way to get them out of the city unless you want to stand outside their walls for a hundred years. If they don't go, I'll be the first to take up arms against them."

Gundlach turned his head at that.

Eldred raised his hands. "Not that it'll happen. The Goddess is a reasonable person, just like Gundlach here. They have some business back in Corporia, some reason why they all have to get back. Isn't that right, Gundlach?"

"Yes. We must be returning," said Gundlach.

"Why?" asked Dederick.

"I cannot be saying," replied Gundlach.

"Sounds fishy to me," said Dederick.

"I trust him," said Eldred.

"As you like," said Dederick. "If they do grant you access to their storeroom, ask for me and my men. Don't forget, we gave you an escort to Boar's Tusk."

Eldred nodded. "I'll ask. I don't know what she'll decide. In any case, we'll stop by your camp on the way."

Dederick raised his hand in salute. "Till then, Eldred."

BERT

They traveled on a few days without encountering anyone. Eldred spent more time walking each day as he recovered his strength. Gundlach drove the horses hard, making the best time he could in his eagerness to bring his exile to an end.

When Bert's earthen walls came into sight, Eldred clapped his hands. "We can have a proper dinner tonight."

Gundlach gave a sour look from his perch on the wagon. "Why be tempting fortune? We are so close now. Let us pass around the city and whatever trouble lies waiting for us there."

Eldred smiled as he kept pace alongside the wagon. "There's no danger. Dederick and his men surely stopped to visit their women as they passed through and shared all the news regarding us. If he didn't kill us, there's no reason the citizens of Bert will take up the idea. Besides, news of our triumph will deter any fool who might threaten us."

"Why should we be taking risks? We can reach New Wismar tomorrow. Another day of stale bread will not be killing us."

"It will not be killing us, but it certainly will be boring me. Besides, our circumstances are about to reverse. This is my last night with decent meals. Once we get to New Wismar, it is I who will have to make do with bread and turnips while you feast on pork and drink your beer. Don't begrudge me."

Gundlach rolled his eyes. "Can you not see? Something will surely be happening. Some drunken warrior will be starting a row, or some woman will be taking offense at my manner, whatever manner I am showing."

Eldred laughed. "You worry too much, Gundlach. We have already faced our greatest challenge and won. Now it's time to enjoy ourselves: tonight for me, tomorrow for you. Once we get to New Wismar, don't worry about staying out in the Eighth Circle with me. I'll find other company. You should go on to the Third Circle and have a proper feast: all the great beer they imported from Wismar along with whatever else is to your taste."

Gundlach rubbed his chin. "Perhaps I will be doing that. Who are you thinking will keep you company though, the Baron?"

"I was thinking Ennlin might favor me with another visit. After all, I gave her the Roter Kristall and practically made her the Goddess. I also delivered a truce. And you've seen what a difficult and costly task that was."

"Yes," said Gundlach doubtfully. "Still, I would not be expecting her to visit anyone in the Eighth. And you should not be forgetting that grand as you are, you cut off the head of our last Goddess."

"I'll never forget that," said Eldred. "By the way, do your Goddesses ever take lovers?"

Gundlach made a face. "Pfui. No, Eldred. I do not wish to be discussing such things."

"Come on, Gundlach. It's not an unreasonable thing to ask. The Mother took lovers from among the Sun People back when she was Regula. I saw a statue of one of them in Turicum. He was quite a handsome fellow if the sculptor carved him true."

"And there you are, making the difference clear."

"Ha," said Eldred. "In all honesty, would it not be best if the Goddess and the bearer of the Mother's shard were friends? Wouldn't that be best for our peoples?"

"Yes, but please be keeping your focus on friendship and leave it at that."

"We'll see. Just keep an open mind. And for the moment, let's go to Bert. Those that dropped Lord Ferris and his pod in the dirt should not be fearing some tipsy podmen and discontented ladies."

Gundlach groaned. "If we must."

Eldred's confidence proved true. They made a quick and profitable visit to the town without any trouble. Lord Esbiorn exchanged pleasantries in a reserved fashion, and his citizens turned out in great numbers to observe the two travelers. But outside of Lord Esbiorn, everyone kept their distance, wary of the two men as they had not been on their previous visit.

As they drove away, Gundlach chewing on a bran muffin and Eldred eating a roasted chicken, Gundlach gestured back towards Bert.

"Are you still thinking they do not know what you are?" asked Gundlach.

Eldred wiped a drop of grease from his chin and considered. "They might just think it's strange we defeated a pod."

"It was much more than that. Their faces were brimming with fear."

"Well, if they know, I'll have to keep a close watch on Dederick. If there is anyone with the confidence to take the shard, it would be him."

Gundlach nodded. "You must be doing that."

THE GATE

When they reached Dederick's camp in the late afternoon of the next day, they found Dederick sitting on a log in the meadow. Eldred, who was walking ahead of the wagon, counted men from five pods, some idling by their tents, others attending to their horses, a few sitting with Dederick, to whom he waved.

"Greetings!"

Dederick rose and walked towards Eldred with an agreeable expression. "Well met, Eldred. Will you be staying the night?"

"No. We're headed directly up to the city. Just wanted to stop by," said Eldred.

"I'll come with you," said Dederick.

"To the river?" asked Eldred.

"All the way to the gate. I wish to observe how they take your news," said Dederick.

Eldred made a face, taking note of the deep blue mark on Dederick's forehead. "Should you place yourself at such risk?"

"Should you?" answered Dederick.

Dederick mounted up and rode out beside Eldred in short order. The other pod was where Eldred expected, lounging by the river. They barely stirred as the strange assembly passed by: to all appearances, a Mercian on foot, a Deiran on horseback and a Corporian driving a wagon.

They were halfway up the steep dirt trail to the plateau when Dederick motioned back to the wagon. "Don't you need your sword?"

Eldred rubbed his hands together. "I suppose. Are you certain you want to be here? We just entered the zone."

"Not until the top, halfway across the plateau," said Dederick.

"That was with the old Goddess. I feel it here, all around us. Her power—she is strong. Don't you feel anything?" asked Eldred.

"I'm not certain," said Dederick as he glanced from side to side.

Eldred went back to the wagon, which Gundlach did not pause in its slow climb up the hill, and hopped aboard for a moment to fetch Primis. As he jumped down, he pointed to the sword on his belt. "It's a better blade now. I think it likes my company. If she lets me take the other one, I could pass Primis to you. Harold won't like it, but I expect that Benedict would see the sense in you having it."

"Better how?" asked Dederick.

Eldred eyed the hilt which shone with a light blue hue to his eyes. The energy didn't flow out along the blade as yet, though Eldred suspected it might soon. "I don't know. It just seems more alive to me."

Dederick spared a suspicious glance for Gundlach, who sat smiling absently as he gripped the reins. "We'll see. I'd still like to go through what's in that storeroom."

Once they reached the plateau, the horses pulling the wagon strained forward towards the city walls seemingly in recognition of their home. Eldred and Dederick followed on behind.

"They see us now," said Eldred watching the activity on the city walls.

"I'll take your word for it," said Dederick.

"You've never been this close, have you?" asked Eldred.

Dederick gave a small shake of his head. "No, you saw me that day. I kept my men back."

Eldred pointed to a spot up to the left. "That's where I fell and came up lame."

"You're lucky to be alive," said Dederick.

"I agree, and not just for that day," said Eldred.

Walking closer to the walls, Eldred gestured at the ground ahead. "This was all covered with arrows. They must have shot thousands from their bows."

"Not that it did them any good," commented Dederick.

Eldred nodded. "Not that day."

As they drew nearer to the city, though still a few hundred yards away, Eldred spotted a crowd of soldiers and acolytes gathering on the wall above the gate. He recognized Baron Wortwin and Keeper Enolf in the front, gazing down on the wagon with sour expressions. He paid them no mind; he only had eyes for Ennlin. She glowed as bright as ever, flush with the power of the

Goddess. It was hard to make out her face behind her blond tresses, stirred as they were by the breeze.

Eldred turned and looked up to Dederick on his horse. "There she is, Ennlin, the new Goddess. She's up above the gate."

"They're keeping it shut," said Dederick.

Eldred grinned. "You must have made them nervous. They'll be more friendly once they learn of the truce."

Presently, Gundlach brought the wagon to a halt before the gate and stepped down from the wagon. He gave a deep bow. "Greetings, honored ones. We are returning with grand tidings." He gestured to Eldred, who was coming up behind him. "Eldred successfully concluded a truce with the Deirans. We will be getting six months to evacuate the city. He did this at great personal cost, as I can be attesting."

Up on the wall, the Baron and Keeper Enolf whispered furiously back and forth.

Eldred looked over the unfriendly faces staring down. "The truce wouldn't have happened without Gundlach's bravery. He joined me in battle. We had to defeat a pod of Deirans to get you this moratorium. He killed two of them. I don't know if any other Corporain could've done the same."

Baron Wortwin leaned out over the wall. "We will be accepting the truce with the hope that no deceit lies waiting to be uncovered. If we find it to be standing true, the exile placed on Gundlach will be lifted. We will hold him here within the city while we are making our assessment. During this period, which may be taking some time, we require that all Deiran forces—including you, Eldred—stay on the other side of the stream below the plateau. If you are venturing across, coming into our territory, you will have broken the truce and proved yourselves to be honorless cowards."

Eldred exchanged a quick glance with Gundlach before looking up to Ennlin. "If this is what you wish, I agree. However, I had hoped to stay and witness the evacuation of the city, or at least the start of it. I also have another request. I gave up my sword, the sword that had been my father's, in order to secure this truce that benefits us all. Gundlach can confirm the same. I am hoping that you'll allow me to take its replacement from the storeroom in your sanctuary. I can promise you no harm will come to anyone."

"Denied on both requests!" barked the Baron.

Eldred pointed at Ennlin. "I'm asking her, the Goddess."

"Then why are you speaking to the Second?" asked Keeper Enolf in a mocking tone.

"What?" asked Eldred, looking across the people gathered on the wall. They were not smiling at any joke.

"I remain the Second," confirmed Ennlin, her voice soft, but clear.

Eldred raised his hands. "How is this possible? Who here has more power than you?" He paused for a moment, then continued when no answer came. "You outshone everyone in New Wismar when I was here before. You still outshine everyone on this wall by a great measure. If you are not the Goddess, then who is?"

"It is not your concern, you murderous dog!" snapped Keeper Enolf.

Baron Wortwin shot Enolf a reproachful look. "The Keeper is speaking correctly, though not diplomatically. It is time you were going, Eldred. You should seek to be preserving this truce that you have worked so hard to establish."

"You speak for the Goddess?" asked Eldred. "If you're speaking for her, then it must be Lady Yslana. How can that be? I saw her those final days. She had no more strength, no more power, than Keeper Enolf."

"We are not caring what you think," said Keeper Enolf. "Leave now, or I will be leading my men out to kill you, truce be damned."

Eldred raised his eyebrows. "And how do you think you'll evacuate New Wismar once you break the truce? Lady Yslana, your new Goddess, knows how that will go if my people catch yours on the road. You yourself saw how few survived that engagement. Don't flatter yourself that you can make it any different, Enolf. You'll die as quickly as anyone."

"We are not leaving, you idiot!" spat Enolf.

Eldred narrowed his eyes. "Is that true, Baron?"

The Baron glared first at Keeper Enolf and then at Eldred. "No final determination has been made. We are still considering the options before us."

Eldred raised his arms. "What do you mean? How can you be saying this? Leaving was her plan. She came to New Wismar with nothing but that plan! I need to speak to her. I need to hear this directly from her if you want me to believe it."

The Baron placed a firm hand on Keeper Enolf's shoulder. "No, Eldred. The Goddess will never be speaking to you in person. You have shown that you cannot restrain your murderous tendencies. For the present time, we will be keeping the truce. I am hoping you will do the same. Farewell. Once you and the Deiran have taken your leave, the guards will be letting Gundlach through the gate."

Baron Wortwin turned and disappeared behind the wall, taking Keeper

Enolf with him. Ennlin, the Second, paused for just a moment to glance down at Eldred before leaving, followed by the acolytes, leaving only guards.

"Fine, that's just fine!" shouted Eldred after the departed Baron. "If you play this game, then do not be surprised by the outcome. If you truly consider your options, you'll see you only have one. If you're here, if a single one of you is here in six months, I'll be leading the force that takes these walls. Don't think it won't happen! Don't forget what you've seen me do. And I'll be coming with everyone, all the forces of the Mother: Deirans, Maldavians, Mercians, perhaps even the bloodthirsty Torvid! Gundlach will tell you. Ignore him at your peril!"

Fifty guards glowered down at Eldred without comment.

Eldred took a breath and turned to Gundlach. Dederick sat to the side on his horse, wearing a thoughtful expression.

"You'll make them see. Won't you?" asked Eldred, lowering his voice.

"I cannot say. I will be trying," said Gundlach.

"I understand it may be difficult," said Eldred. "But you must see that If they stay, then—it's war. You have to get them to leave."

Gundlach nodded. "I agree."

"How can this be?" asked Eldred, gesturing at the gate. "You know Lady Yslana, and I saw her those last days before we left. I grant there was something odd about her, but she had nowhere near the strength of the Ennlin. Nobody did. Did Lady Yslana bribe someone? Did she threaten Ennlin? How did she end up with the Roter Kristall?"

"I do not know, but I can be promising you that it was through no unjust means. Lady Yslana can be fierce, but honor beats as strongly in her heart as in yours," said Gundlach, his voice strong. "My brother wears the vestments in Wismar, so I am not without some understanding of these matters. Some examinations bring surprises. And you should not forget my lady's bloodline, ancient and potent. Perhaps the dangers we face stirred it to life."

"Stirred?" asked Eldred, setting his hands on his hips. "It was days before, but I gave her the powder, the powder of Balaur. I gave it to her." He took a breath. "I suppose it doesn't matter. I suppose none of it matters."

"It is too soon to be declaring such things. I am still holding my shield. You are still bearing your sword. I will be returning to Wismar, and I know you will be finding your path as well."

Eldred looked up at the walls. "I hope you're right. But I must tell you this—whatever else, don't be up there when I come. I won't kill you; however, those with me won't hesitate."

Gundlach gave a small smile. "It is not the same weight of promise, but I will also not be killing you if we meet in battle."

"No, that's a good contract, as good as anyone's," said Eldred.

Eldred extended his hand and they shook. Then Eldred turned and walked away while Dederick followed after him.

Once they were a ways from the gate, Dederick came up even with Eldred. "That was interesting."

"I'm glad you were entertained," said Eldred, staring down at the dirt.

"Do we have a truce then?" asked Dederick.

"Until Harold returns my sword and ring, I say we do. Unless, of course, they come charging out of the city with their spears in hand. I don't think they will."

"They'll just dig in, exactly as Harold predicted," said Dederick.

Eldred blew out his breath. "Yes. I expect they will."

Dederick pointed back towards the gate, which was opening for Gundlach. "Will you truly lead the charge? Even with your friends in there?"

Eldred paused and watched the wagon pass into the city. "If any Corporians still hold the city, I will; I must. It would be my duty. But by the Mother, I hope they're gone."

"They aren't leaving," said Dederick.

"I know," said Eldred wearily, walking onwards.

As they crossed the plateau, the wind kicked up, blowing dust in Eldred's eyes. He wiped them clear, feeling the weight of the Goddess's power on his shoulders. He pictured Lady Yslana sitting on her throne between the five standing stones, deep in her sanctuary, her face set hard. She was untouchable. She could stay for as long as she wished, whether or not Eldred sacked the city.

"I'd say this proves you're not a Corporian spy," said Dederick.

Eldred gave a weak smile. "Of course, I'm not."

"I'm still not certain what to make of you, though. You're very odd."

"Hmmph?" asked Eldred, glancing down. A smattering of thin red stalks hid in the grass, resembling the alien plants that lined the pit under the Goddess's dome. He hadn't noticed them on the walk up.

"I mean, what're you after? What do you aim to do?" Dederick persisted.

Eldred shielded his eyes from a gust of wind. "We're all magical—you more so than almost anyone, Dederick. What are your plans—the plans of the most powerful bonded warrior left to this world? Will you remain a vassal to a king you can crush whenever you have the whim to do so?"

Dederick laughed. "I was asking you."
Eldred smiled and gave a nod.
The two continued across the plateau and down the hill in silence.

ACKNOWLEDGMENTS

I thank my family for their interest and support during the development of this book: R. Bracher, A. Bracher, and J. Etow.

This book benefitted from great professional contributions, including the cover art, illustrations, editing, book design and beta reading. My thanks and appreciation to each of these individuals.

Cover by Jeff Brown, jeffbrowngraphics.com

Map Illustration by FictiveDesigns

Line Editing/Proofreading by Kit Duncan

Interior Book Design by Lorna Reid